Praise for Ellen Gilchrist's

Flights of Angels

"*Flights of Angels* soars. . . . Such is the operatic range of subjects in this wonderful, provocative collection."
— Marianne Gingher, *Raleigh News & Observer*

"The characters in Ellen Gilchrist's stories are like us but different, as though we were to awaken and find that our other selves had gotten out of the house fifteen minutes earlier and were doing things we might do if we were a little bolder, a bit more caffeinated, a tad more interested in raising hell. . . . It's hard not to think about Gilchrist's characters long after you've finished the book, to pity them, to love them a little, and to admire them."
— David Kirby, *Atlanta Journal-Constitution*

"*Flights of Angels* stirs up themes of love, power, pain, and loss with a decidedly Southern flavor. . . . Gilchrist's exultant voice fairly sings off the page."   — Betsy Kline, *Pittsburgh Post-Gazette*

"A collection of finely crafted short stories that ought to put Gilchrist in the hunt for Pulitzer consideration."
— Jeff Guinn, *Louisville Courier-Journal*

"A darkly funny collection. . . . Voice is surely one of the most impressive fortes of this writer. . . . Equally accomplished is Gilchrist's grasp of the tricky, often brutally comic politics of family relations and how they reflect on the larger world. . . . More often than not, Gilchrist's unfailing eye for character, with all its many-hued ironies, guides the stories into marvelously apt conclusions."   — Paula Friedman, *Miami Herald*

"A sparkling collection. . . . Gilchrist writes like a dream. And *Flights of Angels* is as dreamy as they come."
— Polly Paddock Gossett, *Norfolk Virginian-Pilot*

ALSO BY ELLEN GILCHRIST

In the Land of Dreamy Dreams
The Annunciation
Victory Over Japan
Drunk With Love
Falling Through Space
The Anna Papers
Light Can Be Both Wave and Particle
I Cannot Get You Close Enough
Net of Jewels
Starcarbon
Anabasis
The Age of Miracles
Rhoda
The Courts of Love
Sarah Conley

Flights of Angels

STORIES BY
ELLEN GILCHRIST

 LITTLE, BROWN AND COMPANY

BOSTON   NEW YORK   LONDON

Originally published in hardcover by Little, Brown and Company, 1998
First Back Bay paperback edition, 1999

Library of Congress Cataloging-in-Publication Data
Gilchrist, Ellen
    Flights of angels : stories / by Ellen Gilchrist. — 1st ed.
        p. cm.
    ISBN 0-316-31486-2 (hc) / 0-316-00230-5 (pb)
    I. Title.
    PS3557.I34258F58   1998
    813'.54 — dc21   98-21420

10 9 8 7 6 5 4 3 2 1

MV-NY

Book design: Barbara Werden Design

Printed in the United States of America

"Now cracks a noble heart. Good night, sweet prince,
And flights of angels sing thee to thy rest."
WILLIAM SHAKESPEARE

Contents

Part III Abstract and Brief Chronicles of the Times

PART I

A Prologue

SIX MONTHS before he died he told his daughter that he had not wanted to remarry her mother. He was brushing his teeth while he told her. She liked to watch him brush his teeth. He was so efficient, so dedicated, so determined.

"I did it to save the children," he said. "I came back to save the children."

"You gave up the mistress to save what children?" the daughter asked.

"To save Juliet. She was running around with the wrong crowd. She was going out with a black."

"So you tore up the life Mother was making for herself and made her marry you again to save Juliet?"

"Had to do it. Had to stop that." He was flossing now. He had been the first person she knew who used dental floss. It had been given to him by the pathological dentist who had ruined all their teeth in the sixties.

The old man was eighty-eight when this conversation took place. The year after he lost all the money. The year

3

before they took his car away and then his gun. He had had at one time almost twenty million dollars but he had lost it all. He had lost it by believing in his sons. Or else, he had lost it by being afraid to invest in the markets, by being afraid of the contemporary world, by being a racist and a misogynist and becoming an old man. His father had died a pauper and now he was about to die one too. Except for Social Security, a government program he would have ended if he could have. He had given at least one of his millions of dollars to the right wing of the Republican party. Now he was being taken care of by Social Security and Medicare. He saw the irony. What he could not see was how the weak destroy the strong within a family as well as in larger worlds. This happens in every family. It is as inevitable as the sun and rain. All the daughter wanted to know was how to keep it from happening to her.

A Tree to Be Desired

THE OLD MAN lay dying. His great-grandsons sat on either side of the bed. They had been there all night, barely moving or speaking. The only other person in the room was the black male nurse sent by Hospice. His name was Adam Harris. He was twenty-five years old. This was the fourteenth night he had sat by the bed feeding droppers of water to the dying man and wiping his mouth and tongue with the lemon-flavored glycerin swabs. He had sat by the bed on the two nights when the old man's sons had been there. He had sat by the bed when the youngest grandson had been there. He had sat by the bed when the old man's physician brother had come from Memphis and changed the medication. They had changed from Haldol to morphine. Now it would not be long. Now the long nights would soon be over.

The great-grandsons were the quietest men who had sat in the room all night. They were taller and sweeter and quieter than the redheaded sons and grandsons. Their sweet brown eyes met Adam's eyes with a deeper, stranger sadness than the sons and grandsons. The old man had never screamed at them or hit them with his belt. They were not conflicted in their sadness. All the old man had ever done to them was laugh at them and give them candy and tell them about baseball games. He had never made them cut off their hair or work all day at meaningless chores or laughed at them for playing musical instruments. They did not live in Mobile where the old man lay dying. They lived forty miles away in Pascagoula, Mississippi, and worked in their father's dry cleaning establishment and played in a band that had gone to Jazz Fest in New Orleans the year before.

The great-grandsons were the children of the old man's oldest granddaughter. Once she had been the prettiest girl in Mobile. She was still pretty. Tall and agile and full of the sort of restless energy that the sons and grandsons had. She had been in the house every one of the fourteen nights Adam had sat in the room feeding drops of water to the old man and bathing his lips and the inside of his mouth with the glycerin swabs. The old man was starving to death and dying of dehydration. He could not swallow and he refused to be taken to the hospital and put on a feeding tube. On the night that his physician brother had sat by the bed many people had wept many times. The brother had wept continually and the youngest grandson had wept and Adam had wept. The daughter had been there that night. She had kept thinking they should send the old man to the hospital whether he wanted to go or not. "It is too late," the brother said. "It would do no good now."

That was the night they all gave up. They were crying because they knew they had to give up.

The old man did not give up. When it was too late he called the oldest granddaughter into the room and rasped out five words. Take me to the hospital, he told her, but it was too late to go now. That was the night they changed the medication from Haldol to morphine.

The granddaughter came into the room now. She went to Adam's chair and put her hand on his shoulder. "How is he?" she asked. She was wearing the long pink-and-white chenille bathrobe she had worn every night since she had come to stay in the house. It belonged to the old man's wife, who had almost stopped coming into the room. In the beginning, when the old man was crying out for her all the time, she came into the room many times. Now he had stopped asking for anything but water and she did not come in very often. She was in the kitchen, directing the maids to cook things for all the people who had come to stay in the house.

"I don't know. He seemed better a while ago," Adam answered.

"Come outside and talk to me," the granddaughter said. "Willie and Sam can watch him." Adam stood up. One of the great-grandsons got up from his chair and went to Adam's place and put his hand in the old man's. The old man couldn't talk anymore but he could squeeze their hands to mean yes and no.

The granddaughter's name was Juliet. She and Adam walked out of the room and down a hall to the den and went out onto a patio and lit cigarettes. It was beginning to be light in the sky. The moon was still visible, a clean new moon. Around it were six or seven bright stars. The planet Venus sat in the sky, right above the moon just like the fraternity pin of the old man who lay dying. There was a redwood picnic table on the patio and six or seven wrought-iron chairs. Juliet sat on one of the chairs and blew the smoke from her cigarette in a long thin line. A waft of air carried it toward a backyard swing. The robe had fallen open and her legs stuck out from the bottom of her short white nightgown. She was wearing pink sandals she had found in a closet and her toenails were painted a bright pale pink. She had not washed her hair in three days and it hung down her back and was tied with a faded red ribbon. She had been so beautiful when she was young that she had learned not to bother about her hair or clothes. She had become disenchanted with her beauty. Her husband had a girlfriend and that made her hate her beauty since it had betrayed and failed her. She looked up at Adam and smiled. He was more beautiful than she was because he was not sad. He had been sad when he had broken his ankle and ended his hopes of being a professional basketball player but he was not sad now because he had this job making twenty dollars an hour for staying up all night and he had a new Jeep Cherokee and an apartment of his own and the fourteen nights he had been in the Manning house had been pleasant compared to some of the places he had been sent by the Hospice people.

"What do you think is going to happen?" Juliet asked. "How long do you think it's going to be?"

"He's mighty strong. He's the strongest man I've ever seen as old as he is. How old is he again?"

"He will be eighty-nine in May. Next month, if he lives that long. He won't live that long, will he?"

"He was talking to your sons a while ago."

"Did you change the morphine patch?"

"No. I wanted to wait until the nurse got here at eight.

His daughter told me not to give him the morphine unless the nurse was here."

"Don't pay any attention to her. She's going crazy. She can't take it. Neither can Grandmother. She's not doing very well."

Adam looked at the pink toenail polish. He was starting to desire her again. He had been suffering that on and off since the night the two of them had sat by the bed all night alone, or else, since the night she had fixed a sandwich for him and brought it to him on a tray. He raised his eyes and met her eyes. She took a long drag on her cigarette and then put it out in a black wrought-iron ashtray made in the shape of a doll's skillet.

Adam walked across the patio to the basketball goal and picked up an old half-inflated ball and tossed it through the hoop. Juliet stood up and walked to where he was and picked up the fallen ball and shot a perfect hook shot. The robe was completely open now. She stopped and tied it tightly around her waist. Adam retrieved the ball and passed it to her. She shot again. This time the ball went through the hoop without even touching the rim. Swoosh. "You're good," Adam said. "Where'd you learn a shot like that?"

"Basketball camp," she said. "I ran the cafeteria so the boys could go to camp. At Auburn in the summers. We used to play in the afternoons. The staff would play. Did you ever play?"

"I played for Delta State, up in Cleveland, Mississippi. Then I broke my ankle. I still can't run." He stood back about fifteen feet from the goal and shot the ball, but it bounced off the rim. "Damn. It's not inflated."

"I know. Mine were lucky shots." She picked up the ball and held it against her waist. It was growing light behind them. There was a fence across the back of the property and behind the fence a stand of pine and oak trees. Light was spreading through the trees and illuminating the soft cirrus clouds that hung in the late April sky. It was still cool in the mornings in Mobile, especially when the wind was blowing from the east. Juliet shivered. Adam walked to her and took off his windbreaker and put it around her shoulders. They stood there then, not talking, watching the moon fade into the growing blueness of the sky.

Juliet's grandmother came out onto the patio. She was still wearing her gown and robe. "Come in and get some breakfast," she said. "Allison and your uncle Freddy are on their way. I need someone to go and get them at the airport."

"I'll go," Adam said. "As soon as the nurse gets here."

"I'll go with him," Juliet said. "I need to get out of the house for a while."

"Good," the grandmother said. "Then eat breakfast and get dressed. The plane gets in at nine-fifteen. How is he, Adam?"

"He had a good night. He woke up about three and talked to the boys. The morphine's better than the Haldol. He's a lot more comfortable now."

"Thank you for taking such good care of him." She moved to him and put her hand on his arm. Juliet was still holding the basketball. She put it on one of the wrought-iron chairs. She went to her grandmother and put her arm around her waist.

"The moon is very nice," Juliet said. "It has Venus in its arms. Remember when you used to show us that and tell us it was Granddaddy's fraternity pin?"

They went into the kitchen where the grandmother had bacon cooking and toast warm on a tray. Adam took a seat at the table. Juliet stood by the stove. She picked up a piece of toast and began to nibble the hard edges of it. Her grandmother made delicious toast. It was made of white bread with four pats of butter on each slice. There were little pools of butter with the hard edges all around it. She had eaten this toast all her life when she visited them. It reminded her of the pond on her grandfather's farm. Hard on the edge and soft in the center. After her grandfather got sick her grandmother had started making the toast with margarine instead of butter but this morning she had gone back to butter. "Sit down," her grandmother said. "Let me feed you."

"No, this is all I want." Her grandmother shook her head and served Adam a plate of scrambled eggs and bacon. Juliet stood by the stove watching him eat. He had elegant manners. He was an elegant man, elegant and still.

"At least have some orange juice," her grandmother said. "You aren't eating enough."

"This is good. This is fine. I'm going to get dressed."

Her grandmother poured a glass of orange juice and gave it to Adam. Then she poured another one and handed it to Juliet. Juliet drank part of it. "Thank you," she said. Then she left the kitchen and went into the spare bedroom and took off the robe and gown and put on a pair of slacks and a blouse. She went into her grandmother's bathroom and washed her face and hands. She put some of her grandmother's moisturizer on her face. She found a lipstick in her purse and put some on her lips. She started to leave the bedroom. Then she went back to the dresser and picked up a bottle of Guerlain's Blue Hour and sprayed it on her hair. She brushed her hair very hard and pulled it back behind her ears. She shook her head at her reflection and turned and left the room and went out to the side yard to wait for Adam. A tree her grandmother had planted the day she was born grew in the side yard. It was a sturdy oak tree, now at least two feet in circumference. She stood looking at it, imagining her grandmother directing the yard man to set it in the hole, imagining the roots searching and seeking for water far down into the ground.

"Are you ready?" Adam had come out and was standing by his car waiting for her.

"Let's go," she said. He held the door open for her and she got in and put on the seat belt. They drove almost all the way to the airport in silence. "Meet me somewhere this afternoon," she said finally. "Somewhere where we can be alone."

"You're married."

"He has a girlfriend and the question isn't marriage. The question is you're black and I'm white. And, yes, I mean it. If you want it too."

He looked away, then back to her. "Go to the Ramada Inn on the highway. Get a room. At four o'clock. I'll be there. I have to go home first and get some sleep."

"At four. I'll be waiting there."

They picked up Juliet's uncle and aunt and drove them to the house. Then Adam left and Juliet went inside and took off her clothes and got into the shower and washed her hair and shaved her legs.

Then it was afternoon and she went to the motel and got a room and went up to it. Then he called and came up to the room and came inside and closed the door.

It was like silk. It was like water. It was without cruelty or ego. It confirmed everything she had believed all her life. It was a different thing, a completely different thing.

What was this difference? This vast unimaginable difference?

How flighty she seemed to him. How frightened. Like a bird imprisoned in a room, trying to find an open window or a door. He wanted music. "There should be music," he said.

"There is plenty of music," she answered. "I can hear it everywhere."

The old man died that night. Adam was in the room and one of the old man's sons and his oldest grandson. They sat with the body until the Hospice people came and took it away.

On the morning of the old man's funeral Adam woke up feeling lonely. His apartment was too quiet. There was no one there to talk to or eat breakfast with. It was a new apartment complex in a safe neighborhood and everyone had already gone to work. Adam's girlfriend had been there the night before but she had only stayed long enough to start an argument. She had gone there wanting to start an argument. She was sick of Adam. Sick of only seeing him in the afternoons. Sick of spending every night alone. She was twenty years old and ambitious. She had a job at a television studio and she got off work two hours before Adam had to go to work. Sometimes he even worked on the weekends. Sometimes he smelled like death. What he did reminded her of death and she was looking for life. She didn't care if he had a Jeep Cherokee and was the best-looking and most polite boyfriend she had ever had. She had young men waiting in the wings. She didn't have to sit around watching television all night by herself while he waited for someone to die. She went over to Adam's house to pick a fight and she picked one and then she left.

He woke up thinking he was glad she was gone. She was too bossy for him and too moody and unpredictable. Adam had gone to college for three years. He had a good job. He had a new Jeep Cherokee and an apartment with a new bed and a sofa and three good chairs. He had fifteen hundred dollars his father's insurance had sent him when his father died. He had a brother in law school and a mother who didn't bother him too often. He had a future in the health care provider world. He didn't have to sit around and wait for Janisa to decide to get in a good mood or have a dream come true of being a television anchorwoman. He had a life and he was going to live it. One thing about working for Hospice. You learned to appreciate your life.

I really liked that old man, Adam thought, as he eased his legs out of the bed and down onto the floor and walked naked into the bathroom and began to run the water in the shower. He was a strong old man and he held on. She's strong too, even if she is as scared as a bird. He stepped into the shower and felt the soft warm water caress his skin. Like her skin, so soft. She holds on like she is scared to death. There is danger in this. I won't even think about it.

He got out of the shower and thought about the old man's death instead. One of the old man's grandsons was a ship's captain on the Gulf of Mexico. He was the strongest of the men who had sat by the bed. He was as strong and quiet as the old man. The old man was quiet because his throat was paralyzed but the grandson was quiet because he had lived so long on the water and seen so much weather and such strange skies and many whales. The grandson took Adam's side of the bed and held the old man's hand. He did not ask questions and make the old man squeeze his hand to say yes or no. He just held his hand and was quiet and still.

About six in the afternoon the old man's second son came into the room and sat on the other side of the bed. He was the tallest of all the men. He was quiet too. He removed the bandages from the hand the old man had skinned the last time he stood up and tried to walk across the room. The son took the bandages off the hand and turned on the lights and examined the wound. "Goddamn it all to hell," he said. "This is getting infected. Get me some hydrogen peroxide, Jake. In there, in the bathroom." The grandson got up and brought the hydrogen peroxide. The old man's daughter came into the room and stood by the bed and watched. "What are you going to do?" she said.

"Treat this goddamn wound," the son said. He opened the hydrogen peroxide and poured it over the wound. The old man winced and shuddered. The daughter shook her head and moved back two paces. The grandson didn't move. The son opened a jar of aloe vera salve the oldest son had brought in from Texas the day before and began to spread it over the wound. "This will fix you up, Dad," the son said. "God-dammit, they're letting the goddamn thing fester."

Adam looked at the daughter. She returned his look and just kept shaking her head. Adam filled the syringe with water and put a few drops in the old man's mouth. Then he opened one of the glycerin swabs and began to gently swab the old man's lips. The son bandaged the hand with clean bandages. The grandson sat back down and took the old man's good hand. The daughter stood by the door.

"Turn the goddamn light off, Sister," the son said. "It's in his eyes."

She turned off the light. Adam pushed the button on the record player the oldest son had set up by the bed. They had been playing old Eddy Arnold albums and a three-record set of Christian hymns. "I come to the garden alone," Christy Lane started singing. "While the dew is still on the roses. And the voice I hear, falling on my ear, the son of God discloses. . . ."

When the old man could still talk a little and respond he had liked that song the most of anything Adam played for him.

The daughter came back into the room. She lay down on the bed beside her father and started saying something under her breath. It was the only thing she said when she was in the room the last three days. It was some sort of Tibetan chant. She had told Adam what it was but he had not understood what she was talking about.

Juliet had gone back to her house in Pascagoula to get ready for the funeral. She had washed her hair and rolled it up on heated rollers. She had put on makeup. Liquid foundation and powder and rouge and eyebrow pencil and eyelash thickener and blue eye shadow and lipstick liner and peach lipstick. She had put on her best dark blue suit and the pearls her grandmother had given her for her birthday. She put on black silk stockings and her highest black leather heels. She found a pair of black gloves to wear. She screwed small pearl earrings into her ears. Then she took them out and put in some amethyst earrings her husband had bought her once in New Orleans.

He came into the room. He wouldn't look at her. He hadn't looked at her since he started screwing his secretary. He had married Juliet when she was eighteen and he was nineteen. They had been allowed to get married because Juliet was pregnant with their oldest son. His father had been the mayor of

Pascagoula. He was embarrassed by what his son had done. He had always been embarrassed by his children. He had died thinking they were failures because none of them had grown up to be governor of the state of Mississippi. Juliet's husband was not a failure. He had made a lot of money running dry cleaning establishments all up and down the Gulf Coast. He was fucking his secretary because he was a workaholic and she was the only person who would listen to him talk about his business. Juliet had lost interest in the business. She made her own money running a catering business. He wanted to look at her. He wanted to get rid of his secretary who wasn't even very pretty and make a fresh start with Juliet but he couldn't figure out where to start. "You ready to go?" he said. "The boys are in the car."

"Just let me turn off the lights," she answered. She didn't look at him. She walked around the room turning off the lights. He went out of the room and down the stairs. He was waiting by the car to open the door for her but she wouldn't let him open it. She moved around him and opened it herself and got in and put on her seat belt. The boys were in the backseat in their suits. She was proud of them. They were going to be pallbearers. There were going to be eight pallbearers. The old man's three sons, his three grandsons, and her two boys. The other great-grandsons were too young to carry a coffin.

Her husband got into the driver's seat. They pulled out of the driveway and began to drive to the old man's funeral.

The old man was being buried in a country cemetery five miles outside of Mobile. He had moved his headstone three times trying to make sure he was buried in an all-white cemetery. Now it sat beneath two live oak trees on a rise of land that had been a farm only four years before. It was a brand-new cemetery.

There were scarcely twenty graves on the barren rise. The huge granite slab the old man had mined out of the Kentucky hills sat squarely in the center of a forty-plot area he had purchased for twelve thousand dollars.

To the right of the plot and down half a mile on the main road was the new funeral parlor where the old man had arranged to be pumped full of formaldehyde and laid out for viewing.

Juliet arrived after all the other cousins. Her husband had gotten lost trying to find the cemetery and funeral parlor. He was in a sweet mood, however, and did not seem irritated about having to miss a whole day's work in the middle of the week. He held her arm as they walked into the funeral parlor. He stood by her side as she embraced her cousins and her sisters and her brothers and her aunts and uncles. He was kind and sweet to her grandmother. He patted men on the back and embraced women. He was a part of the family. Secretary or no secretary there was not going to be a divorce in this family as long as he could help it. He loved his family. His family meant as much to him as his business. On this day, staring down into the coffin holding his powerful old grandfather-in-law, he thought that his family meant more to him than his business. He was proud of his sons as they took their places beside their great-uncles and cousins and closed the casket and picked it up to carry it to the waiting Cadillac. They were crying as they lifted it. He was proud of them for crying. He took Juliet's arm and led her to the car. This time she let him open the door for her. She let her skirt slide up her legs as she settled herself in the seat and she let him look and keep on looking. She opened her legs slightly instead of crossing them. She let him wonder.

The old man's brothers were there. One was a physician and the other was a general in the air force. The old man's first cousins were there. The one who had been a federal judge. The one who had been a naval commander. The one who was a newspaper editor. The cousin who had gone crazy and tried to kill his mother was dead. So was the one who had been the Speaker of the Mississippi House of Representatives. So was the girl cousin who had been a civil rights activist before there was a word for such a thing. All his first cousins who could walk were there and two who were in wheelchairs.

His second cousin who had given away his land and gone to a seminary when he was forty years old read the sparse, cold, Presbyterian burial service. The only music was a song played on a guitar by one of the old man's granddaughters' husbands.

Juliet stood behind her grandmother's chair. While the song was being played she looked around and behind herself. There was a sea of suits with some women among them. The old man had been a man's man. The men he had led and organized and lectured and set an example for were gathered on the hill as if in regiments. Juliet had not known so many people would come to the service. She had not known that many men could find their way to the obscure funeral parlor the old man had chosen for his laying out and burial. As she looked she saw Adam move to the side of one group of men. He stood alone on a small rise, wearing a beautiful dark blue suit with a white shirt and a tie. He looked like a movie star in the midst of a field of bankers. He looked right at her and nodded his head but he did not smile.

When the service was over and the people began to leave, Juliet left her family and walked over to Adam and took his arm. They walked off together toward a rise of land where a yellow Caterpillar tractor stood waiting to shovel the pile of waiting dirt upon the old man's grave. A young black man sat on the tractor seat reading a newspaper folded into an inconspicuous size. He had taken off his cap and sat with his face and head bathed in sunlight. He was the only other black person at the funeral.

"I didn't know you'd come," Juliet said, still holding on to Adam's arm. It was very strange to be with him like this, in sunlight, dressed up, after all the nights they had sat beside the bed. After the strange afternoon, which already seemed like a dream, bathed in unreality.

"I loved Mr. Manning," Adam said. "I thought a lot of that old man. I've never been so sad when someone died. Someone I'd taken care of."

"How many have you taken care of?" she asked. She kept on holding on to his arm. She had not expected to see him again.

"Too many," he said. "I don't know now much longer I can keep this up."

"Come over to Pascagoula and work for us," she said. "We have three businesses down there. I could find a lot of things for you to do." She felt in her pocket for a packet of business cards she had for her catering business. She knew it was there because the last time she had worn the suit was when she catered a party where she had to get dressed up. She extracted a card and handed it to him. He moved away from her and opened his billfold and found one of his own cards and handed it to her. They stood like that, holding each other's cards. The boy on the tractor started up the motor. He began to drive very slowly and respectfully toward the open grave. Not many people were left by the grave. The old man's daughter and her sons and her grandchild were there. The old man's sons were there and some of the grandsons. Juliet's sons had walked toward the car with their father. He stopped on the road and watched his wife and

Adam walk to the grave and join the ones who were going to stay until the dirt was shoveled on the grave. He felt a stirring, as of some terrible unease or something he could not understand. He took a deep breath and began to walk back toward the grave.

Juliet and Adam each took a handful of dirt and dropped it carefully on the coffin. They took in deep breaths of the clean country air. They waited for the tractor to finish the job.

"Oh, mani, padme hum, oh, mani, padme hum," the daughter was saying under her breath as the tractor pushed the dirt into the hole. Then she stopped saying it and followed her grandchild over to the huge granite stone. It said MANNING in large letters. On the lip of the slab were chiseled other names. They were the names of the old man's male ancestors in a line going back to 1750 when the first ancestors had left Scotland and come to the United States.

Juliet's husband came to her side and took her arm. "We better go," he said. "Someone's got to be at your uncle's to greet people when they come."

"There are plenty of people there," she answered. "Grandmother's there. They're coming to see her."

"Your wife was the mainstay," Adam said. "She was a champ. I guess she needs some rest now."

"Adam's coming over and see about applying to my business," Juliet said. "You know I've been needing an overseer for the out-of-town trips."

"Good," her husband said. "I'm sure that will be fine."

The old man had had a saying in the fifties and sixties when the civil rights battles were going on. "Turn the niggers loose and the women will be right behind them," he had said. He would laugh uproariously when he said it. Many people who had heard him say that remembered it when it happened.

21

II

It was several weeks before Adam drove over to Pascagoula to talk to Juliet about the job. First he was sent by Hospice to watch a man who was dying of skin cancer. It had started with an untreated patch over the man's ear, which his children had begged him to have treated. They kept saying that. "I told him to go to a doctor about it," the youngest daughter kept saying. "We told him a thousand times not to let that go."

Now it had spread everywhere. The man smelled terrible. It was all Adam could do to stay in the room with him. Everyone in the family hated to stay with him. They also seemed to hate each other.

After the third night Adam went to see his boss and told him he couldn't stay with the man another night. "It smells so bad," he said. "I think I'm going to faint."

"There's no one else to go," the boss said.

"I won't go back," Adam said. "I need some time off. I'm burned out. I can't do it anymore."

"Take a week." The boss had seen this before. There was no good in arguing with it. "How long do you think it will be before he dies?"

"A long time. He's not near to death."

"Maybe we shouldn't have gone in. I'll reevaluate it."

"I'm sorry."

"Take a week. Call me when you're ready."

That afternoon Adam went to his bank and found a young man his age and talked to him. He wore his suit and looked the man in the eye and kept insisting. Finally he got a promise that he liked. He stood up and shook the man's hand and went home and called Juliet.

"I want to buy part of a business," he said. "I don't want to work for anyone."

"Then come on over. We'll talk about it."

She told her husband about it that night. "The guy who nursed Granddaddy's coming to see about my business," she told him. "I might let him come in and help me run it. I need some help now that the boys won't do it. He may want to buy into it. Maybe I'll sell it to him."

"You don't need to go getting into any business with black guys."

"The girls who work for me are black. They'd like a black man for a boss. I might sell it to him if he wants it."

"You don't need to have a business, Juliet. We have plenty of money. Come back and help me with the stores."

"I want my own money. I don't want to work for you." She left the room and went out into the yard and lit a cigarette, thinking about having to work with his secretary-whore. Fuck you, she was thinking. Fuck your business and your money and your dick.

She was waiting on the porch of her house when Adam drove up in his Jeep Cherokee. She was sitting on the steps in a long flowered skirt. The azaleas were in full bloom all around the porch and the trees were green with splendor. So he came to her.

They went downtown to the building where she had her kitchen. Three young women prepared the food and a young man made the deliveries. Their main business was delivering lunches to businesses in the area. Also, they catered parties.

When there was a party, Juliet went with them to the house and directed things and sometimes worked as a waiter.

"So that's it," she said, when she had shown him the operation. "It's pretty simple really. Let's take some sandwiches and go look at the water. Do you like turkey? That turkey looked good, didn't it?"

"Turkey's fine." He waited at her desk while she packed a lunch in a cardboard box. Then they got back into his car and drove to a deserted pier outside of town and walked out on it and sat down and began to eat the lunch.

"So what would you want me to do?" he asked.

"Help me expand the business. I need a salesman. Someone to go around and tell people what we're doing. Help out at the parties. Dress up and be a waiter. I don't know. Come in. Be my partner. Help me make some money. My boys used to help me but now they're busy with their music."

"If it works out would you sell part of it to me? I want a business of my own. I can borrow ten thousand dollars any time I want it. People want to do business with black men. It gets them in good with the government."

"You believe that?"

"I have to believe in something."

"Let's try it for a few months and see how it works out. I'll pay you by the hour, whatever you were making. I'll be fair to you. I'm always fair. Ask anyone who knows me." She sat back on her arms. "Can you cook? Do you know anything about catering?"

"I can cook if I need to. I'll do whatever it takes to get a start."

"Then come to work in the morning. I'll meet you there at eight. At the kitchen."

24

"Whenever you want me." He was quiet then, looking out at the water, waiting for her to speak about the other thing. It was a long while coming.

"Do you ever think about that afternoon?" she asked.

"Yes."

"I don't really understand it. Why it was so different. Don't look away. Turn around and look at me. It made me think we are more different than I imagined. And you aren't even black. You're half white. So why was it so different? I can't stop thinking about it."

"You don't care what you say, do you?"

"I want to know the truth. That's all right, isn't it? To want to understand."

"Yes. I suppose it is."

"We have a house on the beach. In Pass Christian. We could go there sometime."

"Not at his house. We'll go to my place if you like. Or to a hotel. There are the casinos. Those hotels are nice."

"When?"

"What are you doing now?"

"Nothing. Then let's go." She stood up and he stood up beside her and took her hand. He decided she was right. It was different, the touch, the smell, the immediacy, the refusal of hesitation. He packed up the lunch things and deposited them in a trash can. Then he came back to her and took her hand again and they walked together toward the car. She was sorry no one was around. She wanted someone to see them. She wanted to be threatened and afraid. It was spring and she lived in a free country. Land of the free, home of the brave. Besides, her grandfather was dead and her father had gone back to his whores in Texas. There was no one to fear anymore. No one who could make her do a thing she didn't want to do. No one to beat or shame her. No one to threaten to lock her up in a loony bin for loving or being brave.

"Come on." She turned and took Adam's hand and they walked on to the car. The sun was pouring down upon them. It was noon on the Mississippi Gulf Coast and they were going to take the afternoon and make it one to remember.

While We Waited for You to Be Born

W. S. MERWIN was in town. He read his poetry for two hours in the Tulane Chapel, the one with the pretty stained-glass windows. He read at night. You couldn't see the sun coming in the leaded glass the way you can sometimes in the mornings. First he read for forty minutes, then talked and answered questions. Then he told us he would stay and read another hour for anyone who wanted to hear more poems. Twenty or thirty of us stayed. We moved nearer to the lectern. We made a circle around him. He read anything we asked to hear. He read "The Judgment of Paris" and "Come Back" and "Farewell" and "The Last One." All the poems that we adored.

In Southeast Asia children were being bombed and gassed. In Russia and China they were being jailed. In the French Quarter they were being sold to men from out of town. Young girls and young boys, too. I quit the ACLU because they defended a man in Little Rock, Arkansas, who sold his son. It was the first argument your father and I had where I stood up for something I believed. I believed it because you were in my womb and I knew you already. Within my womb as I listened to Merwin you were struggling and moving and getting ready to make your big move. Become an air breather, take that first long incredible gasp and the epiglottis would open to the oxygen that plants provide for us. Provide, provide, dear grass and shrubs and trees. And then they give us flowers.

Flower of my heart, flower of my soul, beautiful daughter of my heart. I love to think of when we sat in that chapel in the dim electric light and listened to Merwin read his poems. You were already six days late. Monday's child is fair of face. Tuesday's child is full of grace. Wednesday's child is full of woe. It was Wednesday when Merwin read. But I wasn't afraid. I didn't believe in superstitions or Gothic fears. I knew you already. I knew your bright red hair and wildness and power. I knew your will.

I was nineteen years old. I didn't have enough sense to be afraid of anything. Your father was afraid. He was thirty-three. A poet himself, a graduate of the Iowa writing program, a tall, funny, excited man. He kept me close to his side. He loved my pleasure in Merwin being there. He had taught me Merwin's poetry. He knew Merwin. They had marched together at Aldermaston in the late fifties when your father was still a boy. It was because of him that Merwin had come to Tulane.

Your father wanted us to be married before you came. I wanted to wait and have a white dress and a wedding in Brookhaven but finally, after the reading, I agreed to come back the next morning and be married in the chapel with Merwin as the best man.

But you were born at dawn, as you know, and so we had the wedding at the hospital instead, in a dingy little chapel there. It didn't seem dingy. It was Merwin who named you

Ariel. I'm sorry you hate your name. I'm sorry you are embarrassed by all of this. I'm sorry you hate me for it and I wish you would stop being so angry all the time. I cannot bring your father back to us. I don't know where he is.

> *"Oh come back we were watching all the time*
> *With the delight choking us and the piled*
> *Grief scrambling like guilt to leave us*
> *At the sight of you*
> *Looking well. . . ."*

I will write Merwin and see if he has heard from him. I know your father loves you. I know he wants to see you, to be with you. I think he will come back someday, if he is alive, if he can. He may be too far gone into sadness now. The sadness of being unsuccessful. The sadness of poems no one wants to read. It is the saddest thing I know for a man not to know how to make a living. He knew once. He was a good teacher at Tulane. They fired him when he married me and you were born. It wasn't your fault and we did not regret it. He said he didn't like teaching rich kids anyway. But he had liked the paycheck. After that we had to depend on my father. We went to Brookhaven and he worked for Daddy in the hardware store until Wal-Mart put us out of business. Then he left. He went to sea for a while. He wrote to us from ports around the world.

I don't know. I haven't heard in three years. You know all this. I cannot change the past, my love. I cannot lure it back to cancel half a line, nor all my tears wash out a word of it.

I thought you wanted to know. You told me to tell you and so I am telling you everything I know. Here it is. It is all I have to give. You are the age I was that night when Merwin read in the chapel. Exactly the age. It was nineteen years ago this week. You want all the rest? Here it is.

We lived in a small ground-floor apartment on Octavia Street. A doctor owned the house. He lived next door in a modern glass house with a swimming pool. He owned all the houses on the block and rented them to people that he liked. We were within walking distance of a grocery store and a Laundromat and a bar. Your father got up every morning and rode his bicycle to Tulane and taught until they fired him in the fall when they found out about me. The English Department knew about me. It was the administration that didn't know right away. The thought police. So for the first six months of your life he got up in the mornings and rode his bicycle to the school and taught English literature to the angry or sweet or spoiled or scared students who were mostly stoned or else in league with the thought police and listening to every word he said so they could tell their parents.

After he left I would feed you and change your diapers and put you in the bed with me and we would sleep away the soft, sultry summer mornings. Outside the bedroom window was a mock orange tree and a row of Cape jasmine bushes. If I opened the windows the scent of heaven came into the room and lulled us both into a paradise. You, soft against my skin with your fine golden skin. You in my arms as you slept and slept and slept. I adored you. He did too. But he did not get to hold you in his arms those long hot mornings as I did.

I was too lazy to even make coffee. After you woke I'd take you in the stroller around the corner and eat snowballs for breakfast and stroll you up and down Magazine Street in your borrowed, elegant, navy blue and white, canopied, shuttered stroller.

My family had cut me off those six months. My father was so angry he wouldn't let my mother write to me but my sister still called me up and came to visit and lent me things she had left over from the babies she had had five years before. She never stopped lecturing me but at least she lent me lots of things that came in handy as you grew.

Why did he leave? you ask and ask and ask. Because after we got back to Brookhaven I forgot the things I had learned at Tulane. I began to believe the things my parents believed again. I went to the Presbyterian church. I hated the black people and thought they were going to rape me. I hated the ACLU and not just because they represented that man in Little Rock. I went back into being afraid all the time. I thought everything would go wrong and it did.

Your father wanted me to go with him when he left for San Francisco but I would not go. I was pregnant again but I did not tell him. As soon as he was out of town Mother took me to New Orleans and I had an abortion. They got me a job as a receptionist in a dentist's office. It was three more years before they let me go back to Tulane. I took you with me part of the time. Part of the time I had to leave you in Brookhaven with your cousins. I had to get an education, Ariel. You must believe me when I say that. I did not abandon you. I was never gone more than a week at a time. I got my degree in social work. I got my duplex in Metairie. We have lived here ever since. Haven't we been happy? Why do you hate me so much? Why are you so angry?

Ariel says, "The results of the failed bond are guilt and shame. You refuse to believe that."

"How could there be a failed bond? I held you in my

31

arms morning, night, and noon. You slept in my arms. We lay in the bed in the mornings and smelled the jasmine and mock orange and I loved you as much as anyone could love a child."

"I remember maids."

"Only after we moved back to Brookhaven. Until then I took care of you all by myself. You never left my arms."

"I only remember Sally Lee. Every memory I have is of her big old body slowly bending over or giving me something to eat. No wonder I'm fat. All she did was feed me morning, night, and noon. I lived in a high chair. You weren't even there."

"You are not fat. You have to stop thinking you are fat."

"I need to lose fifteen pounds. I'm too fat. No one ever asks me out."

"If you were nice to people you'd be asked out. If you didn't always say such rude things to people. That's the part that's like your father. When you see him he will know who you are. He will be crazy about you when he finds out you turned out to be just like him. I'm going to cry, Ariel. Stop talking about this now. I need to rest. I can't talk about this forever. I'm sick. Can't you see it just upsets me and makes me worse."

"You aren't sick. You have psychosomatic migraine headaches from being horny. You need to get laid, Mother. Go get yourself a boyfriend."

Ariel left her mother's bedroom and walked out into the living room of the house they shared. It was very very neat. Not a magazine out of place. She went into the kitchen and got out some bread and cheese and made a cold sandwich and ate it as she went out and got into her car and drove over to Tulane to her English class. Write Merwin, she decided. Yes, he'll know where Daddy is and I will go and live with him. I'll get out of here. I'll find my father and a life a person with a brain can stand to live.

What was all that bullshit about her not wanting to marry him before I was born? Of course she wanted to marry him any way she could and any time. It's the oldest scam in the world. Fuck your professor or your boss and get pregnant and make them marry you. I bet he hated her guts. No one would want to be married to that boring, whiny bitch.

Ariel stopped off at P.J.'s coffeehouse and got an iced coffee to go and paid for it with the twenty-dollar bill her mother had given her the night before. Then she left the car where it was sure to get a parking ticket and walked onto the Tulane campus and over to the old stone building where a woman from Oregon was teaching eighteenth-century literature. She would write to W. S. Merwin and her father would come rescue her and she would no longer be a fatherless girl who was fifteen pounds overweight in a hot, boring city where nobody thought about a thing except how much money somebody's father had or if they were going to be the Queen of Mardi Gras.

What I have to remember, Ariel's mother consoled herself, is that I was happy once and she was part of it. I was happy when I loved Daniel and I was happy when I was pregnant with her. I was ecstatic all those months when we lived on Octavia Street. I loved to stroll her down the broken sidewalks underneath the live oak trees and breathe the soft, sweet air and eat coffee snowballs for breakfast and put her to my breast and let her suck. She could taste the sugar, maybe the coffee too. She tasted me seven times a day, or eight or nine or ten. I did not wean her until they made me do it. Until Mother went crazy when I got the lumps in my breast. They would have gone away. And she wouldn't have been sick all the time from drinking cow's milk. I made mistakes. How could I help it? I was a child with no real education. I had no money, no power, no knowledge of the world. Only my husband and my child and I lost him and now I'm losing her. I do not know how to keep her. I do not know what I am doing wrong.

She put on her old shoes and walked out into the yard to weed the flower garden. I'm too young to garden, she decided. I hate getting dirt in my fingernails. Where is my gardener? Where are my bells and shining whistles? Where are my maids?

At noon she went into the house and made some toast and ate it and then got into the tub and bathed herself and cleaned her hands and toes and fingernails. She got out of the tub and stood in the warm air thinking about the water evaporating. She went into her room and put on her best white skirt and a navy blue polo shirt. She put on sandals and makeup and a string of pearls and then she sprayed perfume on her hair. I'll get laid, she decided. Since that's what she wants me to do.

She went down to the Oak Street Bar and Grill where the poets had hung out in the seventies. There was no one there but the bartender, who knew her from the old days. "Hey, Sally," he said. "Come on in. You're looking great. What's going on?"

"My nineteen-year-old hates me," she said. "She told me to go get laid."

"Ariel? Ariel is nineteen years old? Don't tell me that. I must be a hundred. It's strange that you came in. I was talking to someone last night who saw Daniel. He's teaching at Hattiesburg now. Did you know that?"

"In Hattiesburg, Mississippi? My Daniel? Ariel's dad?"

"You didn't know that?"

"I haven't heard from him in three years. Since I sicced the cops on him for not paying my child support. He disappeared. He sends me money but he sends it through other people. My lawyer gave up looking for him. I don't care. I've been making plenty of money. I work for the city four days a week as a welfare checker. Did you know I was in the workforce?" She sat down at the end of the bar where the bartender was drying glasses with a cloth. "You think I ought to have a drink this early in the day?"

"No. Do you want one?"

"Not really. I was hoping someone would be here."

"Here I am." He looked her in the eyes. He was a sixty-year-old man who had taken one too many hits from life. Cancer three years before. Then losing half his teeth. It cheered him up to have Sally come walking in the bar at noon right after he heard that Daniel was in Hattiesburg.

"So he's teaching at the university there?"

"That's what Frank Hanley said. He's going up there to read next fall. He was really excited about it."

"Where can I find Frank?"

"Right here if you come back around four or five. He comes in as soon as he quits teaching."

"Don't tell him I was here. I want to surprise him."

She drove over to Tulane to look for Ariel. She went to the administration office and looked at the class schedule and then she went to the building where Ariel had a class at two.

She sat down on the stairs and let the young men admire her legs. The sun was warm on her arms and face. It was nice to be back on the campus with funny beautiful troubled young people all around her hustling each other as they walked by, young men ready to hustle her if she batted an eyelash at them. She almost forgot what she had come there for by the time Ariel showed up ten minutes late for the class. She looked up and Ariel was sprinting down the sidewalk for the building. "Stop," she said. "I know where your father is. Meet me here as soon as your class is over."

"What?" Ariel said. "What are you talking about?" They stood face-to-face, almost exactly the same height, their blue eyes saying many wonderful things while Sally babbled out her story.

"I won't go to class."

"No, don't do that. Meet me here at three. I'll be waiting."

"The class lasts two hours. It's a lab."

"Then meet me at four."

"I don't know."

"Go on. Don't miss a class. We might have to miss them all tomorrow. If you want to go and find him."

"Okay. I'll go. I like this lab. It's editing. I need it. I like the guy who teaches it."

"Go on. You're late."

At four Ariel emerged from the building and Sally took her arm and they walked to the car and got into it and drove down Saint Charles to Carrollton and turned and headed toward the Oak Street Bar and Grill. "What about my car?" Ariel asked. "I'll get tickets."

"We'll pay them." Sally looked straight ahead. It was the strangest thing, perhaps it was the campus, perhaps her short skirt, her clean fingernails, but she didn't feel that Ariel was her child. No longer her child but her accomplice, her ally in some forbidden adventure.

"If this guy knows where Dad is we are going this afternoon."

"I think it's certain. I think he's teaching at Hattiesburg. It's a two-hour drive. We could wait until tomorrow."

"I can't wait. It's all I think about. I haven't seen him in three years. I dream of him. I cry for him. I have to go, Mother. I have to face him and see if he hates me. If he does, then I hate him too. If he wants me to stay with him, I might do that for a while."

"Ariel."

"I'm his daughter. He's my father. I have to have this. I can't do without it anymore." She looked at her mother and Sally knew it was true and she took one hand from the wheel and put it on her daughter's hand and stroked her fine young smooth thick golden beloved skin.

Frank was at the bar when they arrived. In his accustomed seat at the far end near the Laundromat door and within hearing range of the pay phone. He was a poet and liked to eavesdrop on people's drunken telephone calls as that kept him from thinking he was alone in sadness and also helped him develop an ear for dialogue in case he ever gave up and started writing fiction.

"Frank," Sally said. "It's Sally Donohue. Do you remember me? This is Ariel. I think you were at her christening. If you remember."

"My God, Sally. I saw Daniel two days ago. He's in Hattiesburg, but I think you knew that."

"No. I didn't know. We stopped speaking. Ariel wants

to go and see him. Is there any reason why we shouldn't go there? Tell me the truth. For the sake of the old days. Don't lie to me."

"He's doing all right." Frank paused. "There isn't a woman with him, if that's what you mean. He's alone. He looks old, Sally. Real old. I don't know what's happened to him. He's very thin. Well, he was always thin. He quit drinking. Said he had to for some reason. I don't know what. Don't look like that. It isn't AIDS. Hattiesburg wouldn't have hired him. He wouldn't have applied. Anyway, there isn't any reason why she, why you shouldn't go. Was I supposed to keep it a secret, that he's there? There isn't some legal thing, is there?" Frank sighed, started to retreat, then marched on. "I don't get in the middle of things. How did you know of this?" He looked down the bar. "Oh, Redmond. He told you, didn't he? Well, no one told me to keep this a secret. He's got a good job. Visiting professor. He's been teaching in Hawaii and then in Washington State. I didn't mean he looked bad. He just looks old. I look old. We all look old, don't we? But not you, Sally. You look wonderful. Not a day older and it's a pleasure to see Ariel. Of course I remember her christening. Have a drink. How about a drink or a Coke for Ariel?"

"Not for me. You don't look old at all. You look like you always did. I hear good things about you. I hear the students love you. I hear that everywhere."

"Hope it's true. I try. I always keep on trying." He lifted his martini glass to them, then drained it. He set the glass down beside two empty ones. He had gotten away early that afternoon and had a head start.

Sally leaned over and kissed him on the cheek. He was an endearing man, a gifted man, a very special friend and man.

* * *

They walked back to the car and got in. "What do you want to do?" Sally asked. "It's your call. I'll do what you want."

"Drive up there now."

"Do you want to call and tell him we're coming?"

"No, I just want to go."

"Then we'll go. Can we stop at the Camellia Grill and get a sliced turkey sandwich to go? I haven't really eaten all day and I bet you haven't either."

"I don't need to eat. I'm too fat."

"You are not fat. You are not one bit fat."

"Okay, go by there and I'll go in and you can drive around the block if there's no parking."

"Get some money out of my purse."

"I have money. I have the money Grandmother sent me for my birthday. Let me pay."

Sally considered it. She came out with the best response. "Wonderful," she said. "Treat your old mother to a Camellia Grill sandwich and I'll split a chocolate freeze with you if you like."

"I'll let you drink it. I'm too fat."

Sally let her daughter off in front of the restaurant and eased her car into a parking space in front of the florist shop next door. She watched Ariel move in and through the door like the spirit she was named for and then come back out in a few minutes carrying the white Styrofoam boxes and the drink. "Let's go," Ariel said when she got into the car. "You don't know how this has bugged me. You don't know how sad I've been."

Sally continued down Carrollton to the I-10 exit, took the ramp, and drove up and out onto the four-lane highway going north across the lake. They went over the causeway and across the long bridge to Slidell, then headed up Highway 59 to Hattiesburg. Ariel played the radio. Sally drove.

Daniel thought he had already been saved. After two dead-end jobs with no tenure track he had been offered this job when the woman who had it was injured in a car accident. She was laid up in a New York loft with a broken back. It would be two years before she would even walk. So the big job fell open and the head of the English Department, who had been a colleague at Tulane, had called him and he said he'd come. That had happened fast. He had come in the middle of a semester. It had been tricky, but he had pulled it off. One thing about getting hepatitis. After they made you quit drinking you could get things done, what with all that time on your hands.

I can go and see Ariel soon, Daniel told himself. I can beg her to forgive me. Perhaps she will forgive me. Perhaps she never will. Perhaps I will only get to look at her and know that she is mine.

He was sitting at his desk in the half-furnished rented apartment with the boxes all around him and his clothes still lying on chairs in the bedroom and not a bite to eat in the refrigerator. He had been there for a week but all his time had been taken up with talking to the students and the woman whose job he was taking. She had been in New York visiting her lover when she was injured. She had to talk to Daniel on the phone using a headset, telling him where things were in her office, who the students were, what she had been doing with them. Daniel was half in love with the woman lying in the bed in New York. She was so brave, so forthright, so terribly compromised and scared and still so brave. He had begun to fantasize that he would fly up to New York and take her away from the man she was living with, a painter who couldn't possibly appreciate a poet of her skills and talents, one who could talk so rationally on the headset when she was on all those drugs and in so much pain.

"It's all right," she kept telling him. "This is it. This is what happened. It's what I have. It's mine. I'll deal with it."

"You'll walk again," he kept saying.

"Or I won't. Now tell me if you found the folder with the autobiographies they wrote in March. Some of them may have copies but I wouldn't count on it. We have to find it. I know I didn't bring it up here with me. It has to be in my house or in the office. . . ."

Sally stopped at a filling station in Lumberton and filled the car with gasoline and offered to let Ariel drive. "I'd be too nervous," Ariel said. "You better do it."

"It's your day, honey. I'm following your lead." Sally meant it. She kept having the strange awakening. That Ariel was a grown woman, that her ideas and plans were valuable and true. That she loved herself and knew what she needed and worked in her own best interests. Ariel could take care of herself. It was a revelation of the highest order.

Outside of Hattiesburg Sally stopped at a service station to use the telephone. "I'm going to call information and see if there's an address," she told Ariel. "Should I call if he has a listed number?"

"No. Let's just go to where he is." They went into the station and Sally called information and was given an address.

"Fifteen forty Hazelhurst Avenue," the operator told her. "You need anything else, honey?"

"No thank you. Tell me again."

"Fifteen forty Hazelhurst Avenue, apartment ten."

"We need a map of Hattiesburg," Sally told the girl behind the cash register. "Do you have one?"

"Right over there by the newspapers." Ariel pulled out the map and Sally paid for it and they spread it out on a table and found Hazelhurst and wrote down the streets leading to it.

"What if he isn't there?"

"Then we'll sit there until he comes home."

This is about our need, Sally was thinking. This is about how much we are divided, how much we need to find our missing parts. We could look inside ourselves, but only Tibetan monks know how to do that. I will help her find him. I almost said help her rope him in. Well, what he wants doesn't matter. He fucked me and we had her and now he has to deal with it. If he hurts her feelings I will kill him with my bare hands. I will tear him apart like a cat dismembering a captured bird.

She drove the car. She picked up speed.

Daniel started to go out to eat, then changed his mind and called and ordered a pepperoni pizza. It didn't matter. The main thing was to put all the books and clothes away and get some order in his life and then maybe go to the grocery store or else over to Dominica's house and look for the autobiographies again. He got into the shower and noticed that he hadn't had a hard-on for three or four days. That was strange. See what change and apprehension would do to a man. So thin, he thought as he dried himself. What has become of me?

He dressed very carefully in khaki pants with pleats and a blue-and-white-striped shirt he had bought years ago in Paris. He went out to sit on the stoop and wait for the pizza delivery man. He wanted to be able to call Dominica back before she went to sleep for the night and tell her he had found the folder. It didn't really matter. There wasn't a student in the class with real promise but it mattered to Dominica so he would get it done. Strange, funny how we become involved with people we have never met. All he had of this woman was a voice on the phone and an office full of books and posters and desk drawers stuffed with pieces of poems and disorganized folders. "Put everything in cardboard boxes and have it stored at my house," she had told him. "Just say which drawer it came from. I'll figure it out when I get home. You can live in my house, you know. You are welcome to my house. You don't have to rent an apartment."

"I'm seduced enough by your office," he had answered. "I don't think I'd dare live in your house."

"You'd be doing me a favor. It will fall apart with no one there. Will you think of it?"

"I will." She had started laughing then. He couldn't decide why and he was seduced again, as he had been every day he was in Hattiesburg. He sat on the stoop and wondered if he should move into her house. He wondered at the power of imagination. He wondered at his love of women, their breasts, their smiles, their lovely hands.

It was seven o'clock. Above the apartment buildings a flock of starlings were turning and turning against the clouds. "Ambiguous undulations as they sink, downward to darkness on extended wings . . ." The clouds are moisture from the Gulf of Mexico, from New Orleans where my child lives.

He watched the small white car pull up in front of the building and come to a stop. Sally got out of the driver's seat and waved to him. He stood up, then Ariel got out of the passenger's seat and walked around the car and began to run toward him. His Ariel, his lost meaning and purpose and dream. His child, that he had loved and resented and almost loved and stopped loving and feared and loved and had been afraid to write to or call.

She kept on coming, looking him squarely in the face and then she moved into his body and he began to weep and kept on weeping. The pizza van arrived. Sally paid the delivery boy and carried the pizza into the house and put it down on a kitchen counter where it stayed untouched for many hours. No one wanted to eat a pizza on such an evening. But they were hungry and began to say so.

"I'm starving," Sally said.

"I'm starving," Ariel echoed.

"I'm famished," Daniel added. "And I would not say metaphor for all the iambs in the English language."

Sally was stunned to remember a world where men said such things and knew that they were funny. She was living in a world where people asked each other questions and gave nothing away.

They went out to dinner in a restaurant near the campus. Waves of tenderness were all around them. They talked very softly to each other, almost in whispers. We are here, they wanted to say. Where have we been instead of this? What have we been thinking?

"How are you?" Daniel asked Sally, when Ariel left the table for a moment. It was the first time they had been alone.

"She says I need to get laid," Sally said. "She says I'm a nervous wreck."

"So am I," he answered. He was not laughing. "So do I."

"Well, she wants to stay here with you for a few days. Do you think she should miss two days of classes? I could bring her back on the weekend. Or she could drive. She has a car, not good enough to drive on the highway for any distance, but I could lend her my car. Or you could come to New Orleans. What do you think?"

"Let her stay. She can make it up. I'll bring her home. I can leave Friday morning after my eight o'clock class. So she could make her classes that day if they're in the afternoon."

"We better let her decide. I had an epiphany today. It was after she knew you were here. I touched her and I knew, suddenly, that she was an adult, able to make her own decisions. She's a powerful girl, Daniel. Able to take care of herself. She always has. She always will. If I can only hold that thought. I don't know if I can. Anyway, what were we saying? Oh, I'd like for her to stay here so I can think about all this."

"I owe you fifteen hundred dollars. I'll be able to pay it to you in a month. As soon as they pay me here."

"It's all right. I'm doing all right about money."

Ariel was returning to the table. She walked slowly toward them. I ruined their life, she decided. My psychology teacher says children invade a marriage and challenge it. Mother was too young to have me. I should leave her here with him and I'll go home. They look so good together. They look beautiful together. Oh, God, why do you treat us like you do? I hate you for your failed creation and your jokes and tricks.

She sat down at the table. She reached under the table and took her mother's hand. Then she turned to her father and took his hand and held it on the top of the table. Then she began to cry. "Don't anybody leave," she said. "I have to have you here. I don't care if it's crazy or not. I want our family. I want both of you. I want to stay here and take you with us to New Orleans. I want you both here."

"We'll stay," Sally said.

"I'll do anything you want if you'll forgive me." Daniel put his other hand on hers. "Whatever I can do. There's only one bed in my apartment but I can sleep on the floor. There's a sofa."

"What time is it?" Sally asked.

"Eight-thirty."

"Let's go to Wal-Mart and get some air mattresses. You're right, Ariel. We're spending this night under the same roof. All three of us. You and me and your father. You are our child. We are the ones who made you and we made you out of love, didn't we, Dan? Out of the greatest, sweetest love and sex in the world and we were glad I got pregnant and we adore you. Let's go and get those mattresses. They're cheap. I've been wanting some for Mother's summer house."

At the Wal-Mart Superstore they got silly. They bought two air mattresses and some blankets and a pillow. They bought a box of Sam's chocolate chip cookies and Häagen-Dazs ice cream and cereal and orange juice and milk. They bought napkins and paper towels and dehydrated soup and crackers and a hundred dollars' worth of other things they decided Daniel needed for his apartment. They went back over there and blew up the beds and made them up. They put Daniel's clothes away in the closets. They brushed their teeth with the new toothbrushes they had bought. Ariel and Sally put on Daniel's old T-shirts for pajamas. Sally borrowed his oldest summer jacket for a robe. They sat on the air mattresses and ate the cookies and ice cream and Daniel told about his life in Hawaii and Washington State and Ariel told about her classes at Tulane and Sally told about her welfare clients and the insanity of the Louisiana welfare system. They talked about the seventies and they told her about Merwin and Daniel searched through the boxes of books and found *The Lice* and *The Carrier of Ladders* that Merwin had signed the day before she was born. "We were waiting for you to be born," Daniel told her. "I was dreaming of you every night. I knew exactly what you would be, how you would look, it was as if I already knew you."

"We will never hate each other again," her mother vowed. "No matter what transpires between us we will not hate each other. I will not make your father hate me ever again. This is all my fault. I made him leave. I drove him to it."

"I want you both in my life forever," Daniel said. "I have always loved you both. I have suffered your loss like the loss of my limbs. Forgive me, it is all my fault. It won't happen again."

"It was my fault for being born," Ariel said. "You were all right until you had me. I got Dad in trouble at Tulane."

"No, no, no, no, no," both her parents said. "You are the reason. You are the good thing, the spirit. Merwin knew you would be special. He came and blessed us all."

"It's God's fault," Ariel said. "He made this mess and all of us just have to deal with it."

"There isn't any god," Daniel answered. "There is consciousness, and the central nervous system and our desire to be whole and well. And it isn't a mess, it's our lives. We are alive and well, thank goodness for this day." He went to his daughter and gathered her into his arms. "And forgiveness, for which I beg."

"Let's sleep on it," Ariel said. She was giggling and also trying to act wise. "Seize the day and all of that."

Daniel slept on an air mattress and the two women shared the bed. Late in the night, when she knew Ariel was asleep, Sally took her pillow and went into the living room and found Daniel and climbed down into his arms. He was awake. He had been waiting for her.

"What do you think?" Sally asked. "Does she seem all right to you?"

"She seems fine."

"She has problems. She never finishes anything she starts. This desire to find you is the first real passion I've seen her display in months. She's lost her enthusiasm. I don't know. Maybe I watch her too closely."

"We weren't good parents, Sally, because we didn't know how to be. I was the main villain because I gave up and left, but you weren't much better. We were both nuts. Driven nuts by our culture. Every time I read an article about early childhood development I get crazy thinking about how little we knew."

"We did the best we could. At least we had her. Most of my friends got abortions. I don't know anyone else who had a kid if they got pregnant without wanting to."

"She's supposed to be grateful for that?"

Sally pulled away from him. "I'd forgotten what it was like to talk to you, how unpleasant you are. The problem is how to help her now. She's got to finish college. If she has that she'll begin to believe in herself."

"That's simplistic. I counsel people her age. If they aren't doing well at something, often it's because they don't really like it. If they are truly interested in what they're studying, they will do well at it."

"Oh, God, don't go preaching that to her. That's the line that got half the people we knew into trouble. The ones who thought they would be poets." It was mean and she knew it but she couldn't seem to stop herself from saying it. She moved off the bed and sat cross-legged on the floor looking at him. "I'm sorry. I don't mean you. I don't know why I came in here. I guess I thought we'd make love and everything would be erased. I thought you'd kiss me and it would all fall into place. Sleeping Beauty, although it's more like Alice in Wonderland. I keep shrinking and expanding. She's all right most of the time, except for hating her body. She's okay. And I'm glad you're here so she can see you."

"Don't go getting down on poetry." He smiled and sat up and began to quote a poem of Merwin's that had been taped to the refrigerator in the house on Octavia Street.

> *"Long afterwards*
> *the intelligent could deduce what had been offered*
> *and not recognized*
> *and they suggest that bitterness should be confined*
> *to the fact that the gods chose for their arbiter*
> *a mind and character so ordinary*
> *albeit a prince. . . ."*

"You always did that when you wanted the last word. Well, I'm going back to bed. It's too late for this."

"If you want to get laid I'm available."

"Good night, Daniel." She stood up, then walked to him and kissed him and then went back to the bedroom and got in bed beside her child. She rolled over on her side and covered her arm with the old red wool blanket Daniel had owned as long as she had known him. It was one of the few things he had taken when he left. It touched her somehow that he had kept this same old blanket for so many years and kept it clean. He must have washed this thing a hundred times, she decided, and it's barely faded. She began to sink into sleep. She was thinking about the chapel at Tulane and Merwin reading and the hushed excitement of the night. I'm glad I had that, she decided. Or my whole life might have been as dull as the last few years. She began to tell herself the end of the poem Daniel had been quoting, a poem she had been so proud once of learning and understanding. A poem about human love, a force so powerful the Greeks had believed it was a goddess.

> *then a mason working above the gates of Troy*
> *in the sunlight thought he felt the stone*
> *shiver*
>
> *in the quiver on Paris's back the head*
> *of the arrow for Achilles' heel*
> *smiled in its sleep*
>
> *and Helen stepped from the palace to gather*
> *as she would do every day in that season*
> *from the grove the yellow ray flowers tall*
> *as herself*
>
> *whose roots are said to dispel pain*

The Carnival of the Stoned Children

ABBY AND I didn't have anything to do that day so we decided to go over to Mandeville and lie in the sun and try to starve ourselves. I have a house in Mandeville on a little river called the Bogue Chitta. It was once a small resort hotel and there is a pretty beach surrounded by Cape jasmine bushes and cypress trees and brilliant willows with capes of moss as thick as velvet. It is very romantic and morose. Abby needed to get away. She had just recovered from the first case of herpes simplex ever documented in New Orleans and she was in a strange and desperate mood. Her ex-husband had given it to her one night when he brought the children home and caught her in a lonely mood.

After it was diagnosed half the obstetricians and gynecologists on the Ochsner's staff were coming in and out of her hospital room taking notes for articles they were writing about the new epidemic. Her ex-husband stopped by and told her he had something similar a few weeks before but had recovered without going to a doctor. We didn't know it then but it turned out that his whole law firm and their wives and secretaries and the secretaries' husbands were infected.

This was not funny. This was very, very serious. Abby's father is an obstetrician at Ochsner's so he was forcing everyone to look at what had happened. The air was poisoned all over the downtown business district of New Orleans and in many houses in the upper and lower Garden Districts and down in the Irish Channel and in some apartments in the Quarter. It was the beginning of the end of the sexual revolution but we didn't know that yet.

While Abby was in the hospital with the terrible lesions on her body and the physicians coming and going I went down twice a day and sat by her bed. How could this have happened to us, I wondered. We were so pretty and well meaning and sweet. We overpaid our servants and never said mean things in public and marched against the war. We drove small energy-efficient automobiles and read books and went to poetry readings at Tulane and ran in the park and loved our children even if we hadn't wanted to have them. Why were we being picked out for a plague?

"If only there was someone to sue," she said many times. Abby had a degree in law from Tulane but she had never practiced because she had the children instead thanks to falling in love with a man who reminded her of her father. Plus she failed the bar and went into a depression.

"Someone to sue or someone to kill," I would answer. This was before it occurred to me that we could become biochemists and develop antiviral drugs. Something to kill was an idea I would develop later.

It was about a month after Abby recovered and before she realized the lesions were going to recur and recur and recur that we got so bored we decided to go spend the night in Mande-ville and starve ourselves. We believed in fasts at the time, quick fixes. At getting five pounds off in two days. We didn't give a damn what happened next. We had faith in the moment, the golden present, the day.

I parked my kids with my mother-in-law and Abby parked hers with her mother and we set off in my little Rambler station wagon with the windows down and the portable tape player on the seat beside us playing John Coltrane's "My Favorite Things." "Girls in white dresses with blue satin sashes. Snowflakes that stay on my nose and eyelashes. . . ."

"Has anybody else broken out with it?" I asked. I was driving. Abby was manning the tape player, rewinding it every time "My Favorite Things" was over. It was the only song we wanted to hear that week.

"Yeah. Frank Osler's wife is in bed and two of the secretaries at the firm. This is an epidemic, Rhoda. A sexually transmitted disease. It's like syphilis used to be only there aren't any drugs for it yet. Daddy said it's only beginning to be recognized. He's furious that there aren't any public health warnings about it."

"Oh, well, they'll find a cure. They always do."

"They might not. You don't know how much it hurt. I couldn't go to the bathroom for days. It hurt so much I would rather have died."

"Don't I know it. I was watching. If that dentist hadn't shown up with that topical anesthetic, you might have had your bladder burst."

"Who told you that?"

"Your mother did."

"Is this story all over town?"

53

"No." I was lying and she knew it.

"Yes, it is. Oh, God, why did this happen to me?"

"It's just bad luck. It's not like you did something wrong."

"Don't talk about it anymore. What are we going to do when we get to Mandeville?"

"We'll eat carrot sticks and drink water and maybe have a hard-boiled egg for lunch. Then for supper we'll have a salad and take a sleeping pill so we'll sleep. I have fourteen of them I saved from when I broke my leg."

"Are you sure they're still good?"

"I hope so. It's only been a year since I got them."

"What else will we do?"

"I don't know. Exercise, take a walk, go swimming. We could take out the canoe. I don't think the motorboat is working."

"We could go up to Red Falls and tube down to the house. Remember when we did that last summer? That would take up some time."

"That's the problem with starving. You have to keep finding things to do. Time passes so slowly when you're hungry."

We drove in silence for a while. I was glad to be away from my house. I was the mother of three bad teenage boys. Wild boys, the wildest boys in New Orleans, perhaps the world. Well, that's not true, but for fifteen years, since the first one was born, it had seemed that way. I didn't even want any children but here I was with a passel of wild boys, a career of boys, eating up about ninety percent of my brain on any given day, since the first one was born when I was nineteen years old and wilder than any of them would ever be. I knew wild. I was born wild and I was still wild so they couldn't fool me, except that they were fooling me and would keep on doing it.

While Abby was suffering the first documented case of herpes simplex in New Orleans, I had been breaking up a drug ring at Benjamin Franklin and Bob Taylor and Country Day. My fourteen-year-old had been mailing LSD to a Jewish friend up north in a school for the deaf. He was mailing something called White Rabbit. The friend had been mailing back something called blotter acid, which comes on blue paper that looks like the sheets Leonardo used for drawing. The mother of the deaf boy and I had intercepted the letters. Then we had searched their rooms and collected evidence and called the parents of the recipients of the drugs and had meetings with them in the living room. My husband is a lawyer and although he is not the children's natural father he is the best stepfather who ever lived and he was extremely good at calming down the panicked parents of what can only be called my son's clients.

"You aren't the only one who has troubles," I said to Abby. "You can't imagine what it was like when we got all those parents together to tell them their kids were taking LSD. You'd have thought Eric and I were selling the drugs. Some of them got mad at me."

"Kill the messenger. It's all straightened out now, isn't it?"

"Who knows. Jimmy swore he'd never take another drug. And his deaf friend is back at Bob Taylor. Jimmy cried, Abby. It almost broke my heart."

"He's such a darling child. He's the sweetest boy in the world."

We drove to the edge of town and out onto the Pontchartrain Causeway, a twenty-four-mile bridge that connects New Orleans with Mandeville. I have a great fondness for the causeway because of having run a marathon across it one February day. When I come to the span where I fell and cut my knee and got up and kept on running I always want to weep. It was my greatest moment, the apex of my physical courage.

"That's where I cut my knee," I said.

"I know," she answered. "And a great ball of dried blood formed and when you got finished with the race it fell off and the leg was well, proving we could heal if we let ourselves."

"It was a meaningful moment in my life."

"So you think the drug ring is busted?"

"We took away their money and their privileges. Danny is home from the deaf school. Jimmy is being tutored so he can catch up in his classes. We're just going to watch him like a hawk. We're not going to take our eyes off him."

"Is Eric at home? Will Jimmy be all right while we're gone?"

"He's going over to my mother-in-law's. Eric's gone to Chicago but he'll be back tomorrow. We're only going to spend the night, you know."

"I was only asking."

We drove along. I had been reading Hermann Hesse's *Glass Bead Game.* I was thinking about the marvelous passage where the hero, Joseph Knecht, the Magister Ludi, reminds his friend Plinio how to meditate. "Look," he said. "This landscape of clouds and sky. At first glance you might think the depths are there where it is darkest; but then you realize . . . that the depths of the universe begin only at the fringes and fjords of this mountain range of clouds. . . . The depths and mysteries of the universe lie not where the clouds and blackness are; the depths are to be found in the spaces of clarity and serenity. . . ."

Over at the Bob Taylor School, Jimmy was fighting his desire to go to sleep in algebra class. His deaf friend, Danny, was asleep beside him. They had smoked a joint on the way to school and now they were going to sleep. They had meant it when they swore off LSD. They were leaving LSD to their older brothers. But they were only planning on cutting down on marijuana. It was easy to cut down this week since neither of them had any money.

"I might be able to get some money from my grandmother this afternoon," Jimmy was saying. "I guess I could ask her for some."

"Didn't your mother tell her not to gib you any? My mother called everyone in the family and told them not to gib me money." Danny could talk extremely well for someone who was totally deaf but he still got some of the consonants wrong. His parents had spent almost eighty thousand dollars sending him to deaf schools and hiring elocution coaches. Of course, he hadn't become deaf until he got chicken pox in the second grade so he knew how to talk before he lost his hearing. Also, he had a very high IQ and he could learn fast. The best school he had gone to was the one in Rhode Island that had turned out to be the hotbed of drugs. It was a shame he had left it and come back to Bob Taylor, which was more a football camp than a school, but he and Jimmy didn't think so. They thought it was fabulous that they were back together. They were sworn friends and allies, who had smoked their first joint together in the vacant lot behind Trip Halley's house and known their first French Quarter whores that same night. Actually they had known the same whore, first Danny and then Jimmy.

Danny's head fell down on his desk. Jimmy's moved further down his arm. The algebra teacher, a man named Wedge, decided to ignore Danny and Jimmy. They were football players and couldn't be held to the standards of the other students.

❊   ❊   ❊

Down at his law office, my husband, Eric, was also having plenty of excitement. A water heater company he represented had just been presented with a petition for a union election. If there was one thing my husband hated it was a union trying to organize a company he represented when the management was already doing everything in their power to be fair and pay good wages and take care of their employees. It was Eric's job to make sure they did those things so he would never have to oversee and win a union election. He could do it. He had done it a hundred times successfully, which is why he is rich, but he hated doing it. His other job was to oversee his companies' hiring practices. He had been on his way to Chicago when the call came from the water heater company in Alabama. Now he would have to change his plans. The first thing he did was call me but I didn't answer the phone. If there was one thing Eric hated more than letting union organizers slip through his hiring nets it was having me not answer the phone when he wanted to talk to me.

Finally the maid answered the phone and told him I had gone to Mandeville for the day. "Tell her I'll be home for supper after all," he told the maid. "You all get something for me to eat. Cook me some of your fantastic fried chicken."

"I'll do it," she said. "And biscuits too. But Mrs. Pais isn't coming back. They went to spend the night and quit eating."

"Where are the boys going to be?"

"Over at your momma's."

"Okay. Go on home to your children as soon as you fry the chicken. How much is she paying you now, Charleen?"

"Twenty dollars a day."

"It's not enough. I'm giving you a raise. When do you get paid?"

"Friday."

"Expect a raise."

"Do you want me to call Mrs. Pais and tell her to send the boys home?"

"No, I'll do it when I get there. I don't know how late I'll be."

"Nothing ever happens anymore," I was telling Abby. "We need to have a party. There hasn't been a party in weeks."

"Let's go to your mother's house on the coast instead. We could take the children for Easter weekend like we did last year. Maybe your cousins will be there from North Carolina."

"We might." I rolled over on my back and felt the sun melt down into my skin. We were on beach blankets right at the edge of the water on the little private beach on the river. Sunlight and shadow, the cool smell of the small brown river. Luxury. It didn't matter if I was bored. At least Eric was gone to Chicago and I didn't have to stay home and get supper ready. I sank my head down into the sweet-smelling blanket. I started making up poems I might write down in a little while. Poems about Eric and me when we were madly in love and trying to figure out a way to get married. About holding hands with him and telling him there was nothing to fear, nothing we couldn't do together, no obstacles we couldn't overcome.

At the Bob Taylor School for Boys Jimmy and Danny were waking up from their algebra class. It was almost over. Five more minutes. They sat up straighter. They piled their books before them. They stretched and yawned. Wedge was moving around from behind the desk to sit on the edge of it. "You boys get that homework for tomorrow," he was saying. "If you goof off in here you're going to end up filling Coke machines for a living or get kicked off your teams. So do them problems, will you?" Jimmy smiled his most beautiful and trusting smile at Wedge. Wedge was really the assistant football coach. He was just filling in as an algebra teacher. Wedge liked Jimmy and had been the one to take him to the hospital when he broke his wrist in practice.

"That kid didn't even yell," he told the other coaches whenever Jimmy's name came up in an evaluation session. "He's a winner. He's got the stuff."

"But he won't study," Bob Taylor would say. "Goddammit, Wedge, this is a school."

"You come home with me when we get off the bus," Jimmy was saying to Danny, turned to face him so Danny could read his lips. "My grandmother loves your mother. She's glad we're friends. I'll bet she gives us some money if we're together. Then we can go to the park and find Little Mo and buy some grass. Let's call your mom and tell her you want to go home with me."

"She'll never let me go. I'm gwrrounded." Danny's speaking voice was very seductive to Jimmy. Every time Danny fucked up a consonant it reminded Jimmy of how brave he was to talk at all and what a fierce football player he was even though he couldn't hear behind him to know if he was going to be hit. Jimmy put his hand on Danny's arm. He was really glad Danny was home. He had only mailed the LSD to the school to make sure Danny was popular with the other kids. In Rhode Island they didn't know that Danny's father owned one of the largest steamship lines in the world and was the richest man in New Orleans.

"I'll talk to her," Jimmy said. "I'll tell her we aren't going to do anything bad. I'll tell her we're going to do our algebra homework so we won't get kicked off the team."

"Aw wite," Danny answered. "You do it then."

Jimmy called Danny's mother after the next class and begged her to let Danny come over to his grandmother's house. "You know my grandmother," he said. "We're just going to do homework, Mrs. Wainwright. I swear we aren't going to get in any trouble. Danny's really talking well since he went to that school. He's making every word something you can understand."

"If you're sure you aren't going to get in any trouble." Danny's mother, India Wainwright, was weakening. Mrs. Pais was on the symphony board with her. She was a lovely lady who certainly wouldn't let boys smoke dope or take LSD. Surely that was over, India Wainwright decided. Surely the nightmare of drugs entering the brain of her beautiful and gifted and deafened son was over. "Okay, Jimmy, he can go home with you. But he must be home by six o'clock. Remind him of the time."

"I'm going to turn over and do the other side," Rhoda was saying. "One hour on each side should do it. God, I love to lie in the sun. But I hate getting sand in the suntan lotion."

"Do you believe all this stuff about skin cancer?" Abby asked, sitting up to get her Bain de Soleil out of her bag. "I don't believe it. It's just another thing they're trying to stop everyone from doing."

Little Mo was waiting in the park when Jimmy and Danny got there with the ten dollars they had borrowed from Mrs. Pais. "I only got half a bag of grass," he said. "And it's not much good, but I got a sheet of acid I got from some hippies in a bus. I can let you have three hits for ten dollars. That's a final offer."

"Three. Hell, that's stealing." Jimmy hugged the small black boy and pretended to rub his head with his fist. "Come on, Mo. Make a better offer than that."

"That's it. That's final. I'll give you a reefer for lagniappe. Three hits and a reefer."

"We'll take it," Danny said. "Take it, Jimmy."

"Okay. Let's see you roll it. Make it big." They all sat down in the roots of the live oak tree and Little Mo got out his baggie of marijuana and a roll of papers and carefully separated a paper and sat it on his scrawny knee and filled it with grass.

He spit on his fingers and wet one side of the paper, then expertly rolled the joint. "Want to smoke with me?" he asked.

"No," Danny said, and stood up and looked around. "Let's go, Jimmy. I'm not supposed to be in the park. I'm gwrounded."

They took the stuff and left the park. "We'll go to my house," Jimmy said. "No one's there. My mom's in Mandeville and my stepfather's gone to Chicago."

They moved along Exposition Boulevard, underneath the live oak trees with their capes of moss, past the iron fences and the stone fences of the mansions and the smaller houses. It was a nice afternoon and there wasn't any football practice and they could look forward to getting high and having some crazy dreams.

Eric talked on the phone for an hour. Then he decided to go home and get to work on the election. He'd just sit down at the table and get this goddamn union election solved.

*　　*　　*

Jimmy and Danny let themselves in with the hidden key and ate a piece of fried chicken. "We going to take the acid now or what?" Danny asked.

"First let's smoke the joint. Three hits aren't going to last very long. Let's take our time and do the acid after we get high."

He got out peanut butter and crackers and cheese and pickles and spread the food out on the table. Then they sat down at the table and began to smoke. They started giggling as soon as they lit up. It was the best. A house to themselves and enough dope to last the afternoon.

Eric came up on the porch and put his briefcase down and began to search in his pants pockets for his key. Through the French doors of the living room he could see into the kitchen area. He saw Jimmy's head move in laughter. He pulled his briefcase back behind a stone pillar and drew in his breath. I have to do it, he decided. I have to spy and I have to be a snitch. Goddammit all to hell, will it never stop? What am I doing in this crazy marriage with these crazy kids? My mother warned me not to get in this but I am here and I will not let it come apart. I started this and I will finish it if it kills me.

"He's a good man," I was telling Abby. "And I love him. But he won't go anywhere. He works all the time. He never stops working. His father makes him work. We already have enough money to last the rest of our lives and still he keeps on working."

"You don't appreciate him," Abby answered. "You don't know what you have."

"Maybe I don't want to have anything," I said, knowing more than I knew I knew. "Maybe I just want to be alone."

* * *

Eric moved around the front porch until he had a clear view of the kitchen through the dining room doors. He squatted behind a fat concrete planter and watched as Jimmy and then Danny appeared in the kitchen door. They were eating something. Maybe they are just eating, Eric told himself. If there is a God, be merciful for once in your life and let them just be eating. But they aren't supposed to be over here and they aren't supposed to be together. I thought we had agreed to keep them apart for a while. He hung his head. He shrank back farther behind the planter.

It was at that point that my cousin Ingersol came driving down Webster Street and saw Eric perched on the side porch looking in the window. Ingersol came to a stop and blew the horn. "What are you doing, Eric?" he called out. He was in his Porsche with the top down. "Can I help you? Did you lose something?" Ingersol was probably just looking for someone to have a drink with but also Ingersol is really polite and helpful.

Eric put his fingers to his lips to shut Ingersol up and Ingersol got out of his car and came up onto the porch.

"The kids are inside," Eric whispered. "I want to see if they are smoking marijuana."

"Can I help?" Ingersol whispered back.

"Yes. Stay and be a witness."

Danny and Jimmy had gone to Jimmy's room to take the LSD. As soon as they took it they lay down upon the beds to listen to Bob Dylan. Lay, lady, lay. Lay across my big brass bed. I don't know how Danny listened when they played records. Maybe he just felt the vibrations in his head.

Eric and Ingersol came in the door and went into the kitchen. They smelled the marijuana and found the remains of the joint. They looked at each other. "Go around back and make sure they don't escape," Eric said. "I'm going to his room."

Ingersol was going out the back door when the phone rang. Jimmy answered it in his room. Ingersol picked up the extension to listen in.

"We got three hits of blotter acid," Jimmy was saying. "Me and Danny. We got the house to ourself for another hour. Come on over." Ingersol shook his head. He laid the phone down on the table and tiptoed back up the stairs to Eric.

I was writing. Propped up on a quilt with my legs in the warm sand and a glass of gin by my side and Abby asleep on a blanket. *The children sang in the trees,* I was writing. *The tallest ladder could not reach them. Rich ladies wept in the streets named for orators. Maids wept in the streets named for muses and anyone who slept kept one eye on the moving cloud of the starless nights. The schools melted, the catfish floated belly up, the river licked its levees, oil spread on the marshes. . . .*

The phone was ringing in the beach house. It continued to ring no matter how hard I tried to shut out the sound. Finally I got up and walked into the beach house and answered it.

"Where have you been?" Eric asked.

"Where are you?"

"At our house where your second oldest son and his friend Danny are now high on LSD and being kept in their room by your cousin Ingersol until a doctor can get here."

"Oh, my God. You didn't go to Chicago?"

"No. Come home now, Rhoda. We have to deal with this."

"Oh, God, don't tell my mother or your mother. Did you call India and tell her?"

"I called Hale and he called her. They're on their way. Come on as soon as you can."

"Don't let him out of the house. He might get to the Quarter like he did last time."

"Don't worry. Ingersol has them in tow."

I woke Abby and we put on our shorts and gathered up our stuff and got into the car and started driving. "You drive," I told her. "I have to finish my poem."

We were on the causeway before I began writing again. We had a pitcher of martinis on the seat between us and as soon as I took the first sip of mine it came to me, the next stanza of my poem. *The books were sewn shut, the librarians left in disgust, the fathers bled into the mirrors, the boy screamed, you are not my mother. The rains fell, the river rose, the ferry rammed the wharf, the batture dwellers stood on the roofs with wet feet, the tourists lit out for Houston, the police peered into the windows, the mayor wept on his tennis racket. . . .*

"God, that is so sad," Abby said when I read it to her. "Is it really that bad, do you think? Are we in that much trouble?"

"Well, poetic license. I'm never going to get published if I only write about good things. I have to delve into the darkness."

"Them taking LSD is plenty dark. Me getting herpes. God, I can't even bear to say the name."

"Don't think about it. Just drive the car. We'll stop them from taking drugs. We'll do it if it's the last thing we ever do. No goddamn teenage boy is going to get the best of me."

"What are they doing? What did Eric say?"

"He said Ingersol had them in tow. Ingersol was the tennis champion of New Orleans, Abby. He can handle it."

"I hope you're right."

Ingersol had them in tow, all right. He had Danny tied to the bed in Jimmy's room. He had Jimmy tied to a weight bar with two hundred pounds on each end. He was sitting in the hallway on a straight chair watching the stairs, the door to the backyard, and the bedroom where he had the boys tied up. He was waiting when Semmes Morgan and Morais Devaney came in looking for the party. Semmes was the boy Jimmy had been talking to on the phone. Ingersol knew them all and knew their parents.

"Come on in, boys," Ingersol said. "Come wait for the mothers to arrive. I guess soon they'll be calling your mommas too."

"We didn't do anything," Semmes said. "We just came by to see if Jimmy wanted to go ride bikes."

"He'll be riding bikes," Ingersol said. "Taking fucking LSD. Who in the hell are you kids trying to fool? What in the hell do you think you're doing? Tell me that. Tell me what in the hell do you think you're doing?"

"We're not doing anything." Semmes stuck to his story. "We just came by to see if anyone wanted to go ride bikes."

Danny's parents arrived. India and Hale Wainwright. India had been the best-behaved girl in New Orleans since the day she was born. She had married the richest man. How was she supposed to deal with having her son end up in a drug ring? There was no way she was prepared to deal with this but she was dealing with it and dealing with it well. She had on her

makeup and she was ready to go to war. There was not a snob-
bish bone in India Wainwright's body. She did not think for a
moment that wealth or beauty or power was supposed to be a
shield against disaster. India was ahead of everyone I knew in
this respect.

Abby and I got home half an hour after Hale and India
arrived. We all sat on the stairs in the downstairs hall and tried
to decide what to do. Ingersol had untied Jimmy and Danny
and they were sitting on the floor.

"Tell us what you took," my husband, Eric, asked.

"One hit of acid," Jimmy answered. "I'm not even sure
Danny took his. I just gave it to him when you came busting in."

"Did you take it, Danny?" India asked. She got up and
went to her son and touched his shoulder. "Look at me. Tell
me what you did. Look at me so you can hear me."

"Mother, Mother, Mother, Mother, Mother," Danny
said and grinned at Jimmy. "Mother, Mother, Mother,
Mother, Mother."

"He took it," Hale Wainwright said. "Or else, why is he
talking that way?"

Abby began to cry. Her little boys were only four and five years
old but she could see this happening to her in the future. The
world was full of darkness and nothing could save us from it.
Not money or knowing the governor or steamship lines or law
or medical degrees from Johns Hopkins or being on the staff
at Ochsner's Clinic. It was plague after plague after plague. No
one was safe.

"I have to go," she said. "I'm sorry. I really am. I wish I
could stay and help. I have to get home to my kids."

"Don't talk about this to anyone," Hale said. "I'm counting on you, Abby, to keep this to yourself."

"Who would I tell?" she asked. "Why would I want to talk about this to anyone?"

"Good," Hale said. "I'm glad you feel that way."

Abby was just going up the stairs to leave when Eric's uncle Sully came down the stairs carrying a black bag like the ones physicians have in old movies.

"What did they take?" he asked. "I need to know what they ingested."

"One hit of acid," Jimmy said. "One little hit and I'm not sure Danny even took his."

"Where did you get the acid?" Sully asked. His presence lent a sense of science and weight to the room. Eric got up and stood by his uncle. Sully was his mother's brother. A tall old-fashioned man who loved his work. He was a pediatrician. He took a stethoscope out of the bag and listened to Danny's and Jimmy's hearts. We all watched.

"I'm going to give them phenobarbital," he said at last. "Then we'd better let them sleep this off. I want them to go tomorrow and talk to Gunther Perdigao. We have to find out why they did it. Boys don't take drugs for no reason. They are looking for something they need. It's the wrong place to look, however." He took Jimmy's shoulder in his hand and looked him in the eye. "This is the wrong path to happiness and joy," he said. "This is the path to hell."

Jimmy began to cry. Then Danny began to babble again. "Mother, Mother, Mother," he said. "Going to go with Mother, Mother, Mother."

This was all a long long time ago. We gave them the phenobarbital and put them in the twin beds in the guest room and then we all went upstairs and sat in the living room and talked. "We must plot to save them," Eric said. "We have to get all the parents together and stay on top of this. There is a madness loose in the world and it will devour our children."

"We're with you." Danny's father sat on the edge of his chair. "I'll do anything. Nothing is too much."

I found a coffee cake in the kitchen and heated it and served it. I made coffee with chicory and boiled milk. The sun went down. We called Eric's mother and told her we were home. My oldest son came back from wherever he had been. My youngest son went into the den to watch some stupid television program. We called people on the phone. We went on talking.

"They are searching for ecstasy," Sully had said when he was leaving. He always talked like that. Straight to the point and oblivious of whatever small talk or niceties were going on. "All people and especially young people want joy and ecstasy. They do not count the cost when they find out where to get it. You must change your lives or you cannot win."

Then he left and we talked until nine o'clock and then we woke Danny and helped his parents put him in the car and then we went back to our house and decided to give up for the night.

Ingersol had not given up. He made himself a scotch and soda and was searching Jimmy's room for the rest of the LSD. "They said three hits," he kept saying. "There's another one somewhere."

The reason we had put the boys in the guest room was so we could search Jimmy's room, but I almost didn't have the heart to do it. Once I had found a syringe in Malcolm's drawer and was so horrified I threw it away and never mentioned it. The idea of anyone giving himself an injection was so terrible my mind would not let it in.

"Come on," Ingersol said. "Don't just stand there. Start looking." He was in the closet with the gerbil cages. Jimmy had about forty gerbils. Eric bonded with him by buying him pets, another item I tried to keep out of my conscious mind. Eric helped him clean up after them and feed them and I tried never to go in the room where they kept the cages.

Eric was behind me now. We moved into the room and began to search the dresser and the desk and the closet that held Jimmy's clothes. Ingersol had already searched the clothes he had been wearing but I searched them again. Way down inside a pocket of his pants I found it. A tiny pink square of paper with another paper folded over it. So small that it was stuck in a wrinkled corner of the pocket. I fished it out and laid it down upon Jimmy's bed, right in the middle of his University of Mississippi victory quilt that my brother had given him for Christmas. It was lying on top of the score of the Ole Miss–Alabama game of 1972. Ole Miss, fourteen, Alabama, thirteen.

We just stood there looking at it. "What should we do with it?" I asked.

"Take it to a laboratory," Eric answered. "They have a place at the police department where you can have things analyzed."

"I want a drink," I answered. "I can't even stand to look at the goddamn thing."

"Let's take him hunting," Ingersol suggested. "I have a friend who owns an island in the Mississippi. Let's get him off where we can reason with him."

"There should be someone to kill," I suggested. "I want to kill every drug dealer in the world."

I went upstairs and got the glass of vodka I'd been wanting for several hours and Eric and Ingersol and I sat in Jimmy's room and talked for a while. We put one of his phonograph records on the turntable and listened to the lyrics of the songs. One of them was a really good song, "Bye, bye, Miss American Pie. Drove my Chevy to the levee, but the levee was dry."

It wasn't all loss. The next morning I got up early and took some aspirins and a Dexedrine and finished writing my poem. *The drummers opened the spillway. They walked over the bridges, carrying the knives, the neckties, the uniforms, the candles, the matches, the children.*

Mississippi

SHE SAT in her cell awaiting her death. Death was imminent. They had done it, they had been caught, tried, and convicted, and unless the governor of Mississippi called in the next two hours they were going to be put to death. Larkin and Steven and Isaac too, although Isaac had not pulled a trigger. It would be the first triple execution in Mississippi in twenty years. If the governor didn't call. He won't call, Larkin decided, and I don't give a damn. I'm tired of all this. Tired as I can be but I wish they wouldn't kill Isaac. He didn't want to be there. He shouldn't have to die. He wouldn't have killed Jacob if he had been alone. He would have chickened out.

Larkin sat back on the bed. She was thinking about the night they danced at the Grace post office to raise money for the Red Cross. About the gray-and-white-striped nurses' dresses her grandmother had made for them to wear, Larkin and her sister, Charlotte, and her cousin Donna and her cousin Baby Sugar. She thought maybe she was still there, on a hot summer's night, in the Delta, with the mosquitoes and gnats and

sweet smell of cotton and earth and DDT and her grandfather driving her to the post office in his Buick and all the
ladies sitting around on chairs and her cousin Baby Sugar getting scared and her having to tell her all the words again. "Way
down yonder in New Orleans. In the land of the dreamy
dreams. There's a garden of Eden. That's what I mean."

The starch in their dresses was as fragrant as honeysuckle. Delicios had ironed all afternoon on them, making the
hats as stiff as cardboard and the sashes as crisp as toast. As
each dress was finished, Delicios had laid it carefully down on
the side of the big double bed. Larkin was propped up on the
bed watching her iron.

"Are you going to have a baby, Delio?" she asked. "Aunt
Estelle said you were going to get a baby even if you don't have
a husband. Is it true?"

"It might be. I don't want to talk now. I want to get these
dresses ironed and start on supper. Where are your cousins if
they're going to wear these dresses? When are they coming over?"

"I don't know. Some men were here from town and
Granddaddy and Uncle Flan went to talk to them. I guess
they'll get Baby Sugar and Donna when they get done with
that. Or their mother might bring them over. What time is it?"

"I don't know. Go out in the hall and look at the clock
and come tell me what it says."

"I will in a minute. It's too hot to get up. I want to go on
and put on my nurse's dress. Is that it you're ironing?"

"I don't know one from the other."

A little brown-skinned boy about five years old came
walking into the room. He was wearing an old washed-out
coverall and he was barefooted.

"There's Someral," Larkin said. "He woke up."

"I'm hungry," he said. He walked up to the dress that was being ironed and felt it with his hands. Then he buried his face in the smell of ironed starch.

"He's the cutest little boy who ever lived." Larkin was laughing now. "Look at what he's doing, Delio. He's eating the dress."

"Take him into the kitchen and give him a piece of cake if you want these dresses ready for tonight."

Larkin got up from the bed. She was a nine-year-old girl who ate too many mayonnaise sandwiches and fried potatoes. She didn't move as fast as her sister or her cousins. She got up from the bed and went to Someral and took him by the hand and started down the long dark hall to the kitchen. "Come on, sweet little old boy," she was saying. "Let's go round up some cake."

His hand was as warm and moist as a puppy. They walked down the hall together past the painting of Lake Washington made by Flan's old girlfriend from Aberdeen, past the faded reproductions of English hunt scenes, past the butter churns and the icebox dripping ice and on into the kitchen where Larkin's great-grandmother was making mayonnaise by the sink. Someral's grandfather was beside her dripping in the oil as she turned the beater. Neither of the old people seemed to notice as they went straight to the pantry and found the pinch cake and cut two pieces and put them on plates. They sat down at the table and began to eat the cake with their fingers. "Get a fork," Someral's grandfather said over his shoulder. "Don't be eating cake with your fingers."

When she thought of Someral it was of that summer day. His big eyes looking up at her, his hand in her hand, the newness of him before the world began to use him up. Before they found out how smart he was and all the things began that led to him being at Millsaps College in Jackson at the time of the troubles and standing out on Woodrow Wilson Avenue when a crazy man decided he wanted to kill a nigger. If she started to cry, Larkin thought about the long dark hall from her grandmother's room to the kitchen and the treasures that were there, the smells and the cypress floorboards that had come from the heart of trees that grew in the lake where they swam in lightning storms and dared the gods to strike them. In the end the gods won, didn't they, she would tell herself and then she'd go on and cry.

At the very end, when she was standing by the hospital bed watching him die, after the car had thrown him across the street and into the lamppost and the killer, Jacob Miley, had gone driving off down the street, after she rode to St. Vincent's Hospital in the ambulance, not knowing he was going to die, thinking he was going to live, not knowing she was going to have to drive to the Delta and tell Delicios that Someral was dead and the hope and promise and two years of college education were all dead now and all the hope everyone had had for everything, she remembered his small hand in hers, more than anything she remembered his hands.

Then she and Isaac told the police who it had been and months went by and nothing happened and Jacob Miley was not arrested and then she and Steven and Isaac went and killed him, only Isaac should not have gone with them, not even just to drive the car.

Her keepers walked by the cell again. The minister and the lawyers and her sister and the ones she was not going to talk to anymore no matter what the governor of the State of Mississippi didn't do or did. She was through with all of them and their courts and their law and she closed her eyes and tried not to think about the death room or Someral crumpled up against the lamppost or Isaac in his cell with his family and two rabbis or anyone crying anywhere in the world over anything at all and instead she thought about shooting Jacob and how much she had loved killing him and did not regret it any more than she regretted knocking a clay pigeon out of the sky on a Sunday afternoon down by Rosedale in her cousin's field. Not as much as a clay pigeon. Less. She had shot him in the face and Isaac watched and Steven shot him in the chest and stomach and then they tried to run away but the police caught them on the back road to Greenville, ran them to ground by the Wayside store.

It was the nineteen fifties when they danced at the post office to raise money for the Red Cross. It was to help American soldiers all over the world. Because Granddaddy's brother had been a general and cousin Dan Hotchkiss was still one and was in charge of helping the Red Cross in its drives. Cousin Dan Hotchkiss had killed twenty Japs in the Second World War and been decorated at the White House. He had sent Granddaddy a photograph of the ceremony and it sat on Granddaddy's dresser beside his photograph of his mother. We love the armed forces, Larkin thought. We are violent people and full of ire and venom. All of us, all the people of the earth, take revenge, we always take revenge. We do not wait on the vengeance of the Lord. I am sorry I killed him because now I am going to die, but I'm glad he's dead. Someral didn't even want to be there at the march. He wanted to go on a dig. All he really wanted to do was have a job and an education and go on a dig and not at our old mounds on Esperanza but far away in another country, where no one would even notice he was colored. So, what time is it now? Don't think of it. Think of us in our striped uniforms and our starched white hats and the red crosses made out of seam-binding tape that Miss Teddy sewed on our white aprons. Jimmy Turner was at the dance with his new bride. In his air force uniform, although he was home on leave, and his bride, Miss Courtney Isabel, in a light-colored dress with roses that melted into the folds when she walked. They danced the waltz alone on the floor in front of everyone. "Oh, how we danced on the night we were wed. We vowed our true love though a word wasn't said." Then we did our dances and we sang, "It's a long, long way to Tipperary, to the land of our dreams, where the nightingales," what?, I have forgotten the rest of the song. Miss Laura Manchester from Dundee played the piano for our songs. The piano belonged in the Episcopal Church reception room but Granddaddy sent three men to haul it down to the post office for the fund-raiser.

The white people were inside the post office but, except for the women serving cakes, the black people were on the porch. Granddaddy never let the black people be left out of anything because he helped them and he loved them and his father had been a teacher and a lawyer and a Greek scholar and had not come to Mississippi until after the Civil War. On Esperanza black people were appreciated and educated and treated with respect.

It's Granddaddy's fault I'm going to die, Larkin decided. I have thought of that before. I'm glad he's dead and doesn't know what he did to me. No, it's my own fault for getting Someral to come to the demonstration. That was the selfish act. I should have let him stay at Millsaps College. I shouldn't have gotten him involved in that. He was the only hope Delicios had. Maybe the only hope any of us had. I let him come. I got him to come. I egged him on to do it. So here he came, in his little crooked glasses and his skinny arms and legs and bookworm smile and he stood out in the crowd. He stood out anywhere he went. So maybe Jacob took him for a Yankee. I wish I could have asked him that before I shot him.

To twenty-one, that's how long Someral lived. To twenty-eight for me. To hell with it. I know death. I've seen it before. I saw Someral die. I saw Jacob die. I saw Granddaddy die.

Now they are going to kill us too. Steven first, then me, then Isaac and it's Granddaddy's fault and Big Momma's too for teaching us to respect all men and Momma and Daddy's for dying when I was five years old and leaving us to be raised by old people who read Greek at night and didn't believe in hating anyone.

Then why did Granddaddy teach me to shoot guns? Why did he take me out on Sunday afternoons to the clay pigeon field and pull the machine himself to fly the tablets and yell out, Here comes one, Larkin, get ready. Tell me why he did that if he didn't know one day I'd have to shoot Jacob Miley in the face and at short range too, so what was all the bother with the shooting range?

She looked at the watch they had let her have back that afternoon. It was still four o'clock. Not a minute had passed since the last time she looked at it.

Someral was studying anthropology, which was so new at Millsaps they didn't have a textbook. All they had was a young man from Harvard with a beard and a lot of copies of papers people were writing all over the world and some charts of where things were being dug up. "He goes to the NAACP like you do, Larkin," Someral had reported. "He doesn't bathe. He's a hippie. He said there's no call to use all the water for bathing when lots of people don't have good water to drink. He said the water in the Delta, in our well, isn't any good because of the DDT. Do you believe that?"

"And he wants you to dig in our Indian mounds?" They were sitting on the Millsaps campus, down by the bookstore where there was a bench and where Larkin came to meet him every Wednesday afternoon from the time he started there. She had graduated the year before and had a job as secretary to Charles Evers and had quit talking to anybody she knew. But she took care of Someral. She had made out all the papers to get him the scholarship and she went to see him every Wednesday and paid for anything the scholarship left out. She paid for it out of the money her granddaddy had left her and the money left from when her mother and daddy died. She had a lot of money in the Deposit Guaranty Bank but she never used it. She was ashamed of it because it had come from cotton and DDT. She just left it in the bank and lived on the money Charles paid her. If he didn't pay her she got some out of the bank and when Someral needed it she got it out too. This Wednesday stuck out in her mind because the head of the Anthropology Department walked by while she was sitting on the bench with Someral and nodded to them and she thought he looked as crazy as Someral had said he was. His beard was down to his chest and he was wearing corduroy pants on an April day. He was the head of the Anthropology Department and also the only professor in it.

"He wants to come down there with me, down to Esperanza, and look at it and decide if we should dig."

"Did you tell him there's no one there now? No one lives in the house. Did you tell him that?"

"He doesn't care. He wants to see Momma and Man and Big Jess and all of them. He wants to talk to Mr. Coon Wade and ask if they can dig in the mounds and then he has to write to Washington to the main place and get permission from the Indian tribes that were there."

"No one knows who made the mounds."

"Yes, they do. He told me about it. They know just which Indians were where. That's why he has to look at the mounds. You can come with us, Larkin. He'd like to know you. I told him about you."

"I've seen him. I've seen him at meetings. I didn't know that was Mr. Hirsh. I thought he taught science."

"It's him." Someral sat back, watching her. He didn't understand Larkin anymore. Ever since she went to work for Charles Evers she was changed. She was thinner and she pulled her hair back with a barrette and looked older. She was always looking around, like something was after her, even when she was just sitting with him on the bench or out somewhere getting something to eat. Even when they were in the colored part of town and safe as toast.

"You need anything? There's plenty of money, Someral. I want you to tell me what you need. Is your car working okay?"

"It's good. I don't need it much. I walk over here from the apartment and then I go to classes and the library. I have to write papers for Mr. Hirsh and all the classes. I think I'm doing well now, Larkin. I think I'm doing good work for all of them."

"Of course you are. You have a brilliant mind. You just got scared at first. Too many people we don't even know. I felt the same way the first year I was here. I don't trust any of them. People are nuts, Someral. I hate to tell you that but you'll find it out anyway. Bobby Kennedy's coming here next week. Did you know about it?"

"Mr. Hirsh knows him. They were buddies up north. Is he going to be the president, Larkin?"

"We hope so. Yes, he is going to be. If they don't shoot him first. I hate him coming to Mississippi. I was against it. I told Charles not to let him come."

"It wasn't up to Charles Evers. It was the university that invited him." Someral looked away from her. It was hard to look at Larkin if you disagreed about anything. Since she worked for Charles Evers she was worse than when she was little and everyone had spoiled her to death to make up for her momma and daddy dying. Now she was the worst she had ever been in her life. Someral didn't want to go to the NAACP and do all that stuff she was doing. He wanted to keep on going to his classes and get a college degree and right now he wanted to get back to his apartment to a little girl from down by Tupelo who was a nurse's aide at Saint Dominic's and had met him one night at a café and had come home and stayed ever since. Her name was Lily and she was nineteen years old and could stay up all night making love then get right up and put on her uniform and go on off to her job.

Someral was thinking about telling Larkin about Lily but he didn't. It was better if Larkin thought he never went to the meetings because he had to study.

"Let's go get some ice cream," she said. "I haven't eaten anything since yesterday."

"I better not," he said. "I need to get on home. It's sweet of you to come and see about me. I'm doing fine. I really am. You don't have to come every week."

"I want to." She took his hand and covered it with both of hers. It was cool. Charles's hands were cool too. Thick cool skin made for the tropics, made for heat. She held on to Someral. "You're all I have left now, Someral. I don't talk to Charlotte anymore. She tried to take all the money, all the rent money and everything Granddaddy left me. She had her husband file a suit to say I was crazy because I work for Charles."

"You were the smartest one in the class, the valedictorian." Someral laughed out loud, imagining prissy little Charlotte ever doing anything to Larkin. Imagine anyone ever doing anything to Larkin. It was not possible to imagine anyone cracking her iron will. "They didn't really file the suit, did they?"

"Yes, they did. At Christmas. I didn't want to tell you until it was all over. The judge threw it out. The federal court threw it out. Mr. Childs fixed it up for me. But it was so . . . it made me so mad I wanted to shoot her in the face. I would have too. If she had taken one penny of my money I'd just have gone over and shot her with a shotgun. Granddaddy pitied her. He told me right before he died, 'All I have for Charlotte is pity,' he said, because she didn't even come down to see him when he was sick. She came one time and didn't even spend the night."

"Well, you were there and Momma."

"And Miss Greenlee and everyone around and the Wades. There were plenty to take care of him. Someral, you are all that's left now. You're the one, the one we're counting on. Keep on doing well. It's so important. As important as what Charles is doing. Right up there with it."

"I'm trying.'" He wanted to get up and go home but he waited for her to initiate it.

"We could round up some ice cream and cake." She laughed and looked like herself at last.

"Not this afternoon. I better get on back to my place." She stood up then at last and let him go. He walked her to her car and stood watching as she pulled out of the parking place and drove out the winding drive to the gates on North State Street.

That was April I. On April 29 they had the demonstration about Jackson State and she called him up and told him to meet her at Charles's office and go along and carry a sign or not carry a sign. "I just think you ought to be there with us if you can," she had said. "I talked to Charles about it. He thinks so too. Later, when you're running for office or in practice, they might ask if you were there. It's not just another show, Someral. This is the big hit. All the television people from New York are in town. Two boys died on the campus last week. We know they were shot by rednecks. We just can't prove it and the police aren't doing anything. We have to march."

"I want to come. I read it in the paper. I was coming anyway. I want to bring a girl if she doesn't have to work. A nurse I know. Is that okay?"

"I don't know. I don't know if you should do that. Charles wants to meet you. He's pretty careful about who he lets around him. Especially when it gets hot like this week. He gets nervous. He doesn't like surprises. He wants to know who's in the room before he gets there. It's like Rome during Caligula's rule, Someral. It isn't easy. I can't just spring this on him. We're all pretty busy around here. Could she go with someone else and you meet her later?"

"It's okay. I'll come alone. What time?"

"Early. Be here by eight in the morning if you can. You know where the office is now?"

"On that street behind the Coliseum?"

"No, they moved it. I'll come get you. Be ready at seven-thirty. Saturday morning at seven-thirty. I'll be there. I'll just honk."

"Okay. Come on. I'll see you then."

He hung up the phone and lay down on his bed naked and thought about the class he had that morning about the new skulls in Africa. It was hot in the room. The curtains were still drawn. The bed smelled of Lily. He brought the pillow to his face and breathed it in and wondered if she would have a baby. She thought she was going to have one. He laid the pillow on his chest and began to feel his skull with his hands. He caressed his skull and then he fell asleep in a dream of heat and the sweet sweet smells of Lily's hair and skirts.

Larkin hung up her phone and tried to get back to addressing letters to people about the demonstration, begging for money to pay for the materials to make the signs. But she couldn't keep her mind on it. Someral's voice took her back to the safe, warm world of the past, to summers when the cotton was higher than her waist and the rains came at the right time and her grandfather got the Buick with the wide running boards and they danced at the post office to raise money for the Red Cross.

For the finale Larkin and Charlotte danced an Irish jig. Then they sang "Swing Low, Sweet Chariot," and then they got the gray blanket and carried it around the floor and all the men threw coins into it and her grandfather threw in a twenty-dollar bill which was a lot of money in 1952. They gathered up the money and took it to a table where Mrs. Alford was waiting with a box to count it. Then Larkin grabbed a piece of cake and went out on the porch and sat with the black people and Diddie was still clapping for her fifteen minutes after the songs were over and even Delicios was grinning from ear to ear and had been holding Someral up to the window to watch the show.

Jacob Miley was drunk when he deliberately ran his car into Someral after the demonstration. They were marching to make the city of Jackson build a bridge over the four-lane highway so the students at Jackson State wouldn't get run over on their way to school, also, to protest no one finding out who shot two students the week before. If Jacob hadn't been drunk, maybe he wouldn't have run over Someral. If he hadn't been drunk, he might have seen Larkin there and known she would recognize him. But he wasn't only drunk. He was in a blind rage over black people out on the streets carrying signs and the end of a system that had made his father a broke, struggling dentist in a small town in North Mississippi with a wife who was only five feet tall, which was why Jacob was so short no woman could take him seriously no matter what he did for her. He had been mad for years, and when he saw Someral standing on the side of the street in his little foreign-looking glasses and his nice blue jacket he just ran over him and knocked him into the post.

He didn't even recognize me, Larkin realized. He didn't remember my face. She had met him at a party in New Orleans a year before and afterward let him take her to Commander's Palace to eat dinner. They were drunk at the party and at dinner they got drunker. Jacob was working for a new member of the Mississippi House of Representatives. They were both in New Orleans for the convention of State Government Office Workers.

"We have to integrate the lower schools," she had told him, and he hadn't flinched at first. "There's no other way out. The feds will do it if we don't. Besides, we can't let black people live like they do. If we give them good schools it will work out. My grandfather had a school on the place where I was raised and everyone went on to have good jobs in other states. We have to build this together. We're here together, in this state, we have to make it good."

"Bullshit," Jacob said at last. "This is our state. It was built by white people. The drive and ambition and vision came from whites. We made it a cultured world of beauty and the blacks will ruin it if we let them. Get off your high horse, Larkin. You went to private schools all your life, didn't you?"

"Not always. When we were little we had a tutor and he taught the black kids too. He taught at the school. It was a good school, not some token thing. My uncle taught math and Granddaddy taught history and the tutors taught the rest. Everyone had to go until they were twelve. They had to be able to read and write and do numbers and the ones that wanted to could keep on going."

"But you weren't in the school with them. You were in the house with the tutor."

"So what? I didn't say it was ideal. I just say it shows what can be done when people are well meaning and work from ideals and work together. I used to teach in the school when I was older. We had two big fans and Charlotte and I would teach French and Spanish and bring the record player down and have Music Appreciation."

"That's why you're working for Charles Evers? You better come on back to your own people, Larkin. Before it's too late. You don't know what you're doing to yourself."

"Don't worry about me. I know who I am. I know what I'm supposed to do."

"Have another drink, for God's sake. Let's go down to Lafitte's Blacksmith Shop and get the bartender to make us something worth drinking."

They wandered around the Quarter for an hour and then ended up in a rented room in the Cornstalk Hotel and Jacob's body was surprisingly strong and powerful and the way he made love was interesting because it was so completely selfish. As selfish as the world is when the world is not changed by love. As selfish as salmon swimming upstream or trees crowding out their saplings in search of sun. The force that through the green fuse drives the flower. Larkin was always fascinated by that kind of elemental power or force or will. Liked to get close to it and watch it.

Afterward, Jacob washed his body at the sink and then dressed and offered to take her to her hotel. But she refused. She told him to leave. When he was gone she got up and walked around the room thinking about what she had done. Then she took a shower and put her clothes back on and wandered out into the French Quarter just at dawn and walked around wondering what had made her fuck a racist midget. I wish it had been a smarter day, she decided. A day when I didn't drink anything or learned something or taught someone to change their mind about being crazy.

So, when she saw Jacob's face in the window of the car that hit Someral, Larkin thought it was her fault. He was aiming at me, she decided. Someral was killed for standing near me.

It was after the march was over, when almost everyone

had gone home and the police were standing around on the Millsaps golf course looking the other way and she and Someral were standing out on Woodrow Wilson Drive not talking about anything and Jacob got his car out of the parking place and came driving down past the barricades and past the old Girl Scout Headquarters and saw Someral leaning on his sign and turned the wheel and hit him.

She saw the car and she leaped up on the sidewalk and she watched Someral bend and fall into the post and crumple like a rag doll onto the sparse, dandelion-covered grass. He was coming for me, she thought. What did I do to make him hate me?

Charlotte walked by the cell again holding on to the Episcopal bishop. She looked in at Larkin, who would not return her look.

"How dare you come to my house wearing those filthy clothes," Charlotte had said to her the last time they had spoken before the accident and the revenge. It was a Wednesday after she had met Someral on the bench at Millsaps. Since Charlotte lived in the neighborhood, Larkin had gone by to say hello to her nieces. Charlotte opened the door when she rang the bell. "I'm afraid to hug you, Larkin. God knows where you've been. Have you bathed? Your hair is dirty, did you know that? My God, I can't believe what you're doing with your life."

"I've been helping at Head Start all day. I'm not dirty. I'm just sweaty. The kids are teaching me to dance. Let me take a shower. Lend me a dress."

Charlotte moved back and Larkin walked into the immaculate yellow-and-white living room with its overstuffed sofas and too much of everything everywhere. She wanted to laugh and cry at the same time but instead she faced her sister. "No kidding. I'm in between apartments. I'm staying in a small place with a friend."

"You're living like white trash," Charlotte said. "You don't look right, Larkin. Well, come on. You can use the guest room. I'll get you a sundress. Do you want to wear a sundress?"

"A sundress would be great. And a drink. Make us a Bloody Mary, will you? While I bathe."

Charlotte came back with the sundress on a hanger. It was pale yellow piqué with white daisies and little spaghetti straps at the shoulder. She left and returned with the drinks. Larkin was out of the shower and drying herself with a pink towel. Charlotte sat on the bed looking at the pile of dirty clothes on the floor.

"They aren't full of lice," Larkin said. "I'll throw them in your washer if you're worried."

"Heddy will do them. Finish drying yourself." Charlotte went out into the hall and called the maid and asked her to get the clothes and wash them. Heddy slipped into the room and gathered them from the floor and left without a word. "She's a treasure," Charlotte said. "Floyd's mother gave her to me. Just gave her to me. Can you believe that? She wanted to be sure his shirts were ironed."

"Bobby Kennedy's coming Wednesday," Larkin began. She was standing naked before a framed mirror combing her hair. "I don't want him to come. I think it's too dangerous but Charles thinks it's okay."

"I don't want to hear about it," Charlotte said. "You're going to be killed, Larkin. Everyone talks about you. Annie heard about you at school."

"Good. I'm glad they're talking. That's what activism is about, Charlotte. To shake people up. To make people think."

"Let me get you some underwear. I forgot about underwear." Charlotte put her untouched Bloody Mary on the table and left the room and returned with a pile of underpants and bras. "I think these will fit. We always wore the same size, didn't we?"

"I may get fat." Larkin turned and faced her. "It's a political statement to be thin. Poor people can't afford the kind of food you need to eat to stay thin."

"The black people on Esperanza were thin. None of them were fat. Not a single one."

"And one year they got rickets and Uncle Bob and Granddaddy had to go to Greenville and bring back a boatload of oranges and canned tomatoes for them. It was not an idyll, Charlotte, no matter how much you want to make it one."

"How's Someral doing? Is he doing okay?"

"He's doing fine. He was scared at first but I think he's out of the woods now. He's got a good teacher, an anthropologist from Harvard they brought here to start a department. They want to go to Esperanza and dig in the mounds."

"No. No one can dig in the mounds. We promised Grandmother. She made me promise to protect them. The government won't let you anyway. They are a sacred burial place. No one from Millsaps can go there and touch them. Is that why you came over here, to tell me that?"

"No, I came over to take a shower and get a drink. And see my nieces when they get home from school."

"Are you going to stay?"

"Only until I see them. Don't worry, Charlotte. I won't hang around to pollute your life."

"I didn't say a word."

"You don't have to. We don't have to agree on things. And thanks for the drink. I needed it. I haven't had a thing to eat all day."

"Stay for dinner. Let me make you something. Is there anything you want?" Charlotte stood in the door of the room, so uptight, so anxious, so alarmed that it made Larkin's day just to watch her twitter.

"A sandwich will be nice. Anything that's easy."

Charlotte set off down the hall in her little canvas platform shoes, in her little silk dress from Francis Pepper, with the hips and belt just an inch too tight and a tiny little run in her hose in the back where she couldn't see it and go crazy.

Later, just at dark, when Larkin was leaving, when they were standing on Charlotte's wide concrete porch with the Greek urns full of azaleas, looking down the lawn to the other mansions and the fine sleek cars and the perfect flower beds and the absurdity and waste and pride, just as Larkin thought she was going to get away without any more discussions, Charlotte started again. "Why are you doing this? You are going to be killed. There are people wanting to kill people like you. You don't know how deep this goes, how mad people are."

"I was coming out of a church in Montgomery when a man tried to kill Charles with a knife. He stabbed Jonas Hill in the arm and lunged at me. He thought Jonas was Charles, that's how crazy they are. You don't need to tell me about that."

"Then why are you doing it? Why don't you care what happens to the rest of us?"

"You want to know why? You want the real answer?"

"Yes, I do."

"Because of the music. Because being with them is like music. Because the music is so damn good and when you're with them you hear it in a different way. This is the truth, Charlotte. You can believe me when I say this."

"I don't get it."

"You don't get much, Sister. Because you're dumb."

"How can you say that?"

"You know what else? They don't spend their lives on crappy anal-retentive chores they think up and then go hear some music for an hour to make up for it. They have music all day. Okay, maybe it's cultural, maybe it will end when we finish turning them into us, but anyway, there's no way you can understand this, is there?"

"So does Someral listen to music all day? While he's going to school?"

"No. Someral is white. Lots of things are already ruined for Someral. And Millsaps will ruin some more. But maybe it will be all right, now that he has this anthropology guy from Harvard. I was depressed when I saw him today but now I'm better."

"I am not dumb."

"I'm sorry I said that. Thanks for the shower, Sister, and the loan of the dress. I'll pick up the other clothes when I bring it back."

"You can keep it. I don't ever wear it." Charlotte drew herself up into a knot and Larkin left then, without kissing her goodbye, because she was sick to death of pretending things she didn't feel and had used up her store of that the hour before on her spoiled chubby nieces.

The governor of the state of Mississippi sat in his living room with his hands on his knees and listened to his crazy daughter,

Wilma Marie, talk and beg and plead. She had gone to camp with Larkin Flowers. Larkin had been nice to her when no one else at the camp liked her. Larkin was a heroine to Wilma Marie. She couldn't believe her daddy was going to let Larkin die.

When Wilma Marie quit talking the defeated candidate for governor, William Summer, started in. He took the Shakespearean tack and pled for mercy for mercy's sake. Then the representative from Issaquena County gave up talking and walked across the room and fell on his knees by Mr. Summer's side. The governor looked down at the fat sweet face of the representative and the lean solemn face of Mr. Summer. He looked at his daughter, then he got up and walked across the room and opened the door to the hallway and called in a guard. "Stay the execution," he said. "Call down there and get them on the phone."

His daughter began to weep. She got up from her chair and went to him and put her arms around him and her long unkempt hair flowed all over his suit jacket and she said, "I'll never have another drink as long as I live, Daddy. I promised you and I won't ever break my promise. You can count on this this time. You will never have to worry about it again."

He looked down at her troubled face and he wanted to believe that at least she believed it was true. It was his mother's face, re-created on the earth so that his suffering could never end.

"That's good, baby. I know it's true. I know you're going to make it this time."

Mr. Summer got up and stood and faced him. He had been the governor's Democratic opponent in two elections. He would be his opponent in the next election and probably until they both were dead. Still, they were friends and the governor trusted Mr. Summer to always tell the truth to him.

The representative got up and dusted off his pants. "I need to call the families," he said. "Where is a phone I can use?"

Larkin had decided to cry. She still hadn't let anyone in the cell but she had decided to cry, for Isaac and Steven and herself and her grandmother and granddaddy and Someral and Delicios and the river and the bayou and the bridge and the store and the burial ground at Greenfields and all the people who were lost and gone. She put her face down into her hands and cried slowly at first and then bitterly, bitterly. She cried for all the people of the earth, for the Mississippi Delta saturated with DDT and the fish in the bayous dead too and the bones of her ancestors rotting in their coffins where she would be rotting too.

The warden and her sister and the bishop came to the cell door to tell her the governor had called but she would not listen. "Get the hell out of here," she yelled at them. "Leave me alone. Can't you see I'm dying."

"He called," Charlotte kept saying. "He pardoned you. It's going to be all right, Larkin. No one's going to die."

"We're already dead," she said and stood up and looked her sister in the eye, as straight into her eye as an arrow. "Everyone's already dead. We've been dead since we were born."

"Let us in," the bishop said. "Please let us talk to you."

"Eat something," Charlotte said. "Just let us give you something you want to eat."

Miss Crystal Confronts the Past

IF YOU WANT to know why we had to go to North Carolina and spend the summer it is because of the inheritance. I am to blame too. My name is Traceleen Brown and I am old enough to know better but I got on the plane with Miss Crystal and went along. I have worked for Miss Crystal since she was thirty-two years old and I was thirty. I have worked for her since the day she married Mr. Manny and moved to New Orleans from Jackson, Mississippi, where her family lives. I have been with her through thick and thin. In return she and Mr. Manny have bought me a house and set me up a retirement income and given me more excitement than I need.

Now we are getting old and should retire from adventures but we cannot seem to learn. We can't even learn to stay away from Mr. Phelan, who is Miss Crystal's older brother and a big game hunter who has killed one each of every big, mean animal that roams the earth. Plus a lot of elephants and small pretty animals and he has the hides and heads to prove it. He used to have them. Now he has been forced to sell most of them due to the demands of his five ex-wives, especially the one down in Santa Fe, New Mexico, who tried to shoot him when he broke into her bedroom. That is another story.

I know it is mean to gossip and tell tales. I don't know what comes over me and makes me do it.

Still, somebody has to make a record. They write down everything about you when you go to a doctor's office. They write down how tall you are and how much you weigh. All I am writing down is the things that change our lives. The things that seem almost to happen of their own accord, as if a big mist falls over the land and puts ideas into our heads.

So we got on an American Airlines jet airplane and flew to Charlotte and were met at the airport by one of Crystal's cousins. "What's he doing?" Crystal asked. "What's going on over there?"

"They are playing cards for money," the cousin answered. "He has won the Dufy and the baby grand piano and the chandeliers. She has won his Cape buffalo and two zebra hides." The cousin started laughing this restrained North Carolina laugh. He is Crystal's first cousin and a close friend since childhood of both Crystal and Phelan. I guessed I trusted him. He seemed to honestly adore her and just because Phelan had taken him on safari many times when he was rich wouldn't make him want his own grandmother robbed blind.

His name is Robin Martin Taylor and Crystal took his arm and held it all the way to the baggage carousel.

"We're going to stay at Robin Martin's house," Crystal said to me. "He says there's tons of room and we'd be near to Grandmother's so we can reconnoiter without being in her power. It's not good to be in her power."

"Have you met her, Traceleen?" Robin Martin turned to me. "She's a force of nature." He warmed into his story as we waited for our bags. "We call her Miss Louise or Grandmother Louise. She went to Vassar and a year to the Sorbonne and knew Edna Millay and Elinor Wylie. Then she married our grandfather and had four children but she never took care of them a single day. Each child had its own nurse, which is why so many people in our family have trouble with relationships. Anyway, she was a liberated woman before there was a name for such a thing. She was the first society woman in Charlotte to openly support Planned Parenthood. She is so powerful it's unbelievable. Even crippled and sick she is a force of the first power. Well, you'll see. What else? She has a fabulous sense of humor and a seductive voice. She can talk you into anything. My grandfather adored her every minute of his life and she wouldn't even sleep with him after the babies came. You can stay there if you like, Crystal, but I'm telling you, they barely even dust. I'd be afraid to sleep there myself."

"She doesn't have help?"

"Anabelle is still with her but they only let a girl in to clean once a week. Miss Louise won't let her touch anything. She thinks something will be broken."

"Why are we worrying about her if she's so powerful?" I asked. "Can't she hold her own with Phelan?"

"He is her favorite," Crystal said. "He looks like her father, who was an adventurer too. She insists on perfect civilization from everyone else and then she goes and adores Phelan. She told me at her ninetieth birthday party that he was the only one who had the sense to have a lot of babies. Can you believe that? As if the fate of the women who have had them is completely unimportant."

"I thought you said she was so big on Planned Parenthood."

"She is, for everyone but Phelan. She thinks he's so superior he should be reproduced. If Grandmother and Phelan were young now they'd probably be cloning themselves. I mean, you have never seen ego until you see this pair."

"He supports the children," Robin Martin put in. "He has given them all the money he has ever made."

"Except the money he loses gambling, to say nothing of the fact that he has robbed my parents to support all those women and children." Crystal was getting mad. It is the thing that makes her maddest in the world. "Last year Mother discovered he hadn't paid their automobile insurance in seven months."

"They are all grown people." Robin Martin got this distressed look, like, oh, let's don't have controversy. "They put him in charge of their affairs. They must think he knows what he's doing."

"They give him anything he wants. They always have. They always will. Everything for Phelan. Nothing for me." I looked at her and knew it had been a mistake to come to North Carolina. Crystal looked like a different person from the happy, useful lady she is in New Orleans. Here she is thrown back into her powerless position in a family that favors males.

By the time we drove up the oak-lined driveway and went into Miss Louise's ancient house, she and Phelan had stopped playing cards and were playing chess. Phelan had ordered a huge chess set from New York City and they had it set up on a coffee table so Miss Louise could just ride her wheelchair up to the edge and move a piece. When we arrived they had just started on their third game of the day. Miss Louise was holding a glass of sherry. On a table near the chess set was a silver pot of strong black coffee.

"She's drinking sherry and coffee," Crystal noted later. "She's always lived on sugar and caffeine. She lived on pound cake and biscuits from the time Granddaddy died until George Manning came down from medical school and made her promise to eat some protein each day. I don't know if she still does, although she always keeps her promises. Coffee and sherry. That's just like Phelan. He is a complete and total sensate. He is a mess. I'm surprised there aren't cigars."

Miss Louise was surprised to see us. Of course she hugged Crystal and asked if she wanted some pieces of jewelry or a painting of the swamps near New Orleans but Crystal said no, she had just come down for a few days to pay her respects and see what was going on in Charlotte.

"I'm dying," Miss Louise said. "The same thing I've been doing for five years. It is taking a very long time, I will say that. It's taking longer than I thought it would."

"She isn't dying," Phelan put in. "She wouldn't dream of dying until I figure out a way to take her to New York to see the ballet. We're going in the fall, Sister. You should come and meet us. We'll stay at the Westbury and see all the young dancers Grandmother has been reading about in the *Times*." He went to her wheelchair and put his hands on her slim old shoulders. She beamed like a girl in love. She radiated.

Well, Phelan is the oldest grandson. It's a position of great and awesome power and the power runs both ways. The paternal grandmother and the oldest grandson have a river of power that runs between them like a torrent that never stops.

"How long are you going to be in town?" Robin Martin asked Phelan. Robin Martin is a pale shadow of Phelan in every way, thinner, softer, quieter, but there is something alike about them too, a self-assurance, a watchfulness.

"As long as Grandmother wants me here," Phelan answered. "This is how I'm spending this year." He squeezed her shoulders very softly and I could see Crystal's chance for an inheritance moving off like the ghost of Christmas past.

"Well," Robin Martin said, "have you been playing those tapes I brought you, Grandmother Louise? The ones of the tenors?"

"It doesn't work right anymore," she answered. "I can't get it to go up or down." She pointed in the direction of an antiquated set of stereo equipment. There was an old 33 rpm turntable, a tape player, and some huge old speakers stacked on top of each other underneath a table. There was a rickety wire table with 33 rpm records and shoe boxes filled with tapes. There was a small radio beside that on an antique glove box. It was the messiest arrangement I had ever seen in my life and we all walked over and began to try to figure out how to turn it on.

"Throw all this goddamn stuff away," Phelan said. "What the hell is all of this? I'm going out and get Grandmother some music and something to play it on. Come on, Sister, ride with me." He swept Crystal up and started out the door. "Keep Miss Louise company, Robin Martin. I'll be back in an hour." He turned at the door. "Throw all that goddamn stuff away, Robin Martin, while you're waiting. Just get it out of here. I'm going to need the space."

"You will not throw away my records," Miss Louise said. "Those were your grandfather's favorites that Dudley left here when he was in college. Don't throw anything of mine away, Robin Martin. Phelan, don't go off now. I've barely seen Crystal." She rose from her wheelchair and stood up as straight as a dancer with only her cane for support. "Where are you going?"

"You need some music," Phelan said. "I'm going to procure it."

"I do not need a thing," she answered. "I don't want anyone buying me a thing. I'm dying. I won't be here to listen to it."

"You are not dying." Phelan took a step toward her. Then another step. Then he kissed her on the face. "Stop saying that, Grandmother. I don't want to hear any more about it."

I was sitting on the sofa with my hands in my lap, not moving or saying a thing. I had never seen anything in my life like the electricity that went on between that old woman and her grandson.

"Where is he going?" she asked Robin Martin.

"I guess he's going to buy a CD player," Robin Martin answered. "Show me the new chess set, Miss Louise. I love the pieces. When did it arrive?"

"We'll have to get you something to drink." She turned to me. "Traceleen, would you go out into the kitchen and see if anyone is there. I never know if there's any help in this house or not. I'm paying someone a hundred dollars a week to be here but you'd never know it when I want something fixed."

"Who am I looking for?" I asked.

"A Watusi named Anabelle who says she works for me." Miss Louise laughed and Robin Martin laughed with her. It was some old joke I was not privy to. Also, I didn't like her thinking she could order me around just because I am on the Mannings' payroll but I decided just to do what she had asked.

"The kitchen's on the other side of the hall," Robin Martin said. "Would you like for me to go?"

"No." I left the room, glad to get a little private space in which to think.

Crystal told me later about the trip to get the CD player. First he stopped at a filling station and asked for the best electronic place and they told him to go to this place called Stereo One. Then they went there and Phelan found the only woman sales person and put some moves on her and gave her his phone number and then picked out a three-hundred-dollar CD player and speakers and paid for it with cash and walked out carrying the box.

Then they went to a record store and he found the youngest woman salesperson and did some moves on her and gave her his phone number and then bought a hundred dollars' worth of CDs of classical music and old dance music and then they came back to the house. This all was done very quickly. "My money," Crystal said. "Momma's money. Daddy's money. Money I'll never see. Money Manny and I will have to make up for when my parents are completely broke."

"Did you say anything?" I asked.

"What is there to say?" she answered. "He's the oldest son. He can do no wrong. He is forgiven before the deed. So I just rode along and watched. Well, I hope she likes the CD player. I even hope one of those tacky women calls him up and gives him a piece of ass. That's how he makes me feel, Traceleen. Like I'm watching a hurricane or a storm. Like there's no point in arguing."

I walked out of the old oak dining room and across the hall into the kitchen. The main floor of the house consists of large rooms off of a wide central hall. It was all very dark with the windows swathed in velvet drapes as old as God which have not been vacuumed in twenty years. The kitchen is behind the library, about as far away from where it is needed as a kitchen can possibly be. Beside the kitchen is a breakfast nook where Miss Louise takes most of her meals.

Anabelle was asleep in an old Stratolounger pulled up beside the refrigerator. The kitchen is a large room with a new white stove and a refrigerator big enough for a restaurant. There is a table in the middle of the room with pans hanging above it and a bowl of fruit that had seen better days attracting flies. The back door was open letting all the air conditioning out and there was Anabelle sound asleep in the Stratolounger. A fly swatter was in her hand and her hands were crossed across her chest like a pharaoh in his tomb. It was hard to tell her age while she slept but she couldn't have been a day under eighty. She was so tall her feet hung off the footrest of the chair and so light skinned I couldn't decide if she was white or black. I have tried to stop thinking in those terms, as my niece, Andria, calls them, but I was born in another age and have not finished adjusting to the one we live in now.

Anabelle's hair was swept back from her face in a bun and was as black as night. Whatever her age she was not letting it show in her hair. Also, she had these beautiful high cheek-bones and a wide nose. I was standing three feet away hoping not to wake her and watching her breathe through those wide nostrils when she spoke without opening her eyes. "I suppose she sent you in here to get something. Well, let her send her grandson for it. I'm taking my siesta. I told her I was not going to be getting anything for anybody until four o'clock in the afternoon and not to send anyone to wake me."

"I came to make tea for the company," I answered. "My name is Traceleen Brown and I have accompanied Miss Crystal Weiss here from New Orleans to see her grandmother. You don't need to get up. I can probably find what I need."

"Tea's in the canister on the counter. Tray's in the cabinet beneath. Tea set in the glass highboy in the dining room. Who needs tea? Who's here now?"

"Mrs. Weiss and her cousin Robin Martin and myself," I said. It was like having a séance or a palm reading. I was going to keep on being polite. That was all I knew for sure.

"Help me up," she said. "It's too late now. They've woken me from my sleep. I know better than to try to sleep where they can find me. Phelan's turned this place upside down. So much noise all the time. He's the noisiest boy who ever lived. Always was noisy. I used to hear him three blocks away when he'd come and stay in the summers."

"What's he doing here?" I asked. I am always gathering information. I think it's because I never had any children of my own and have to fill in the blank spaces but Andria says it's just in our bones, which is why she is a journalist.

"He is here to keep her from dying." Anabelle pushed down the footrest and let the Stratolounger bring her to a sitting position. She opened her eyes and looked at me. "He doesn't want her to die so he has come to stop it."

"We thought he was after her money." I took a chance on saying that.

"No. He has come to keep her here. I knew it when I saw him at the door. We had all decided it was time. She thought it was time. Then Robin Martin called him. He was off in Africa somewhere. Came home with some terrible itch he'd picked up on a boat and had to be treated every day for a week after he got here. He came right here and then they started the card games. Now it's that other thing. With the wooden dolls. It looks like voodoo to me and I told him so. Imagine having that in the living room of a proper house." She was upright now, getting on her feet. She towered over me. She was one of the tallest women I have ever seen of her age. She moved to the cabinets and got a copper pot and filled it with water and put it on the stove to heat. Then she continued.

"Don't mess with Miss Louise and Phelan. She wants him here. She doesn't like Crystal. We never did like Crystal, even when she was a little girl. Selfish little girl. Threw her clothes down on the floor. She'd wear three ironed dresses in an afternoon and throw them on the floor."

I moved back to the doorway. I was just watching all of this. I was not going to get in too deep and take a chance on drowning in this sea. This immense, old, sand-colored woman moved around her kitchen and I had time to examine how she dressed. She had on a uniform made of pale gray cotton but not like any uniform I had ever seen on a maid or nurse in New Orleans. It was hand made of some very fine cotton material and with it she was wearing long gray stockings and some soft flat leather shoes. She had ruby studs in her ears and on her hands were several rings with large yellow diamonds. She wore a man's watch with a leather watchband.

When the tea was ready she put it on a tray with three cups and saucers and linen napkins and silver spoons and a plate of English shortbread cookies she took out of a tin. She handed me the tray. Then she got back into the Stratolounger and pulled the lever and let the back down and the footrest up.

"You tell her I'm leaving at six," she said. "I am hired to

come from eight to four in the afternoon but I am staying until six today if she wants supper started. I will have to know soon or I'm going back to sleep." She closed her eyes. "Go on, before that tea gets cold."

I went back to the dining room processing all this knowledge. Perhaps he was here to keep Miss Louise alive. It made sense. She was something Phelan could not afford to lose, a woman who loved him no matter what he did. A woman who only asked that he love her in return, who did not question his passage through his life.

"She sent him to college," Crystal told me later. "She gave him a car and when he wrecked it she gave him another one. She has always liked him best. She never even pretended to like the rest of us as much, if at all. She liked Phelan from the start and she still likes him and I think I'll just get on back to New Orleans and forget about North Carolina."

"That couldn't be," I answered. "No one could play favorites like that. No one would be that mean."

"She's mean and he's mean, that's why they like each other."

Crystal and Phelan came back carrying the boxes with the pieces of the new equipment. Phelan and Robin Martin put it all together in the space in front of the old equipment and within an hour we were listening to Beethoven's Violin Concerto.

Robin Martin suggested drinks and got out a martini shaker. Crystal and I neither one drink alcohol but we got glasses of ice water and as soon as they started drinking they forgot we were sober.

"So how are Grandmother's finances?" Crystal asked,

when Miss Louise had gone up to her room to rest. "Tell me what's going on, Phelan. What is left to support her?"

"We've got Medicare paying for nurses and for Anabelle," he answered. "And she's got Granddaddy's Social Security check. There's a rent check from the place on the coast and I'm going to sell some lots she has downtown before I leave. Don't worry about it, Sister. I'm taking care of her."

"How is Medicare paying Anabelle?" She had sat up on the edge of the chair at that.

"I got it done. I got Home Health Services to hire Anabelle. Then they send her back to us and Medicare pays for it."

"Where are the nurses then?"

"Oh." Phelan laughed and looked at Robin Martin and they laughed together. "Don't worry about it, Sister. It's details. We're taking care of her. You just live your life."

At six o'clock we all pitched in and got dinner on the table in the dining room. Phelan went to Miss Louise's bedroom and got her up and wheeled her in to be at the head of the table. There was bread and lettuce and tomatoes and pickles and cold fried chicken and a plate of corn on the cob dripping with butter. Miss Louise drank a glass of vanilla Ensure and ate a little bread and a sliced peach. Phelan put a glass of wine before her and she winked at him and picked it up and drank it.

The phone started to ring. It was several of Miss Louise's grandchildren calling in from all around the globe. A grandson in Germany for the summer. A granddaughter in New York studying photography. I couldn't help but think what a rich country we have that can take a family in North Carolina and spread them out all over the world having adventures and learning things.

"I always hear from the grandchildren when I am eating," Miss Louise complained. "I never get to finish a meal."

"I wouldn't complain about that if I was you," I answered. "There are a lot of people your age who don't have so many people calling in to know how you are."

"My children don't call," she said. "Only my grandchildren. You'd think I was already dead for all my children care about me."

"That's not so, Grandmother," Crystal said. "Mother and Daddy came up here last spring."

"They came for one day and stayed at the hotel. They weren't any help to me." She turned and beamed at Phelan. As if to say, See who knows what to do. See who came to stay with me to ease my way into the afterlife. "Phelan is the one who got the money coming in from Medicare."

Crystal gives me a look and Phelan is on his feet to fill his grandmother's wineglass and change the subject.

After supper we all go in the living room to look at the new 35-inch Sony television set Phelan has had installed in front of the twin sofas that are exact replicas of ones at Monticello. He has bought a video of a film about the Muhammad Ali versus George Foreman fight which took place in Zaire where he has been many times and he is determined to make us all watch it. "I may take Grandmother to Africa," he declares. "Last week I almost had her talked into it. She's weakening. We'll go to London on the Concorde and rest up for a week, then go to Johannesburg."

"Don't be foolish, Phelan," she says flirtatiously. "I'm not going anyplace but to the grave." She was falling asleep and as soon as she was sleeping well we took her to her room and

Phelan laid her down on her bed and Robin Martin took Crystal and me home.

"What is this about Medicare money?" Crystal asked, as soon as we got in the car. "He isn't scamming the Medicare system, is he? I still don't see how he got them to pay Anabelle. That sounds very fishy to me."

"How could he scam Medicare?" Robin Martin said. "He's only been here six weeks. He's just gotten them to hire the help she already had. It's helping them. He's done everyone a good deed."

Scamming them was really very simple. He got some women who needed some excitement to think it was all right to steal from the government since the government steals from us every time they make a new tax. Then he got everyone in so much trouble they couldn't tell. Then he gave them all part of the money and kept the rest.

"He is the light of my life." Miss Louise was speaking. She and Crystal and myself were seated in her solarium having coffee from little blue-and-white china cups that were as fragile as the sunlight coming in the dust-covered windows onto the dust-covered plants. "I don't know what I would do without him. He came in the nick of time. I had given up completely."

"I would love to take an hour and clean these plants for you," I found myself saying. "I'm a green thumb if there ever was one. Crystal and I have a house full of plants I have nurtured. I clean them with a mixture of water and milk, using a very soft cloth. I think you would be happy with it." I smiled up into her soft old brown eyes. The same eyes Crystal has, also Phelan and every member of that family I have ever met, including Crystal Anne.

"Well, you are our guest. I couldn't let you clean the plants."

"We want to," Crystal said. "I'll help her. It won't take long. Let us do that for you, Grandmother. This is such a lovely room. It's a shame. Let us spruce it up for you when you take your nap this morning."

"I don't know," she said but she was weakening and an hour later Crystal and I had been to the store and were in there with Windex and bleach for the marble tiles and new rubber gloves and a bucket and mop and Hyponex and outside in the driveway were some healthy ferns in pots to add to the dying ones inside.

"It would be best if we could get someone to paint the wicker while we're at it," Crystal said. "But I'll be content to get these rotting cushions out of here and replace them with the ones in the trunk of that car Robin Martin lent us." He had given us the good car, a blue Oldsmobile, and driven himself to work in his old Camaro. He is a stock and bond salesman and should drive a better car than these but he has a weakness for gambling and that's where his money goes, not to mention both his marriages.

Crystal and I cheered up while we cleaned the solarium. Anabelle appeared in the doorway several times to sniff around but she didn't say much except that if we killed the ferns there would be hell to pay.

When we had done everything we could do (we didn't go outside and clean the outside of the windows because we didn't want to), we sat back to survey our work. I went in the kitchen and made us another pot of coffee without asking anyone's permission and then we just sat in the clean room and marveled at it. So that is why we were there when the nurse from Home Health Services came to the door and began to talk to Anabelle. She was about thirty-five years old and heavyset. She was wearing a pair of long white cotton pants and a red smock and as soon as we were introduced I noticed the big yellow diamond ring on her hand. It had Phelan's name all over it. Only Phelan Manning can find diamonds that big and that yellow and get women to wear them.

The nurse's name was Phoebe and she talked to Anabelle for five or ten minutes before she asked for Phelan. "He's still asleep," Anabelle said, although we had heard him getting up an hour before and then heard him go back upstairs. "He said to tell you he'd call this afternoon and let you know what was going on."

"Well, I guess I'll talk to him then." Phoebe smiled at Crystal and at me and left down the front steps and got into her car. As soon as she was gone Phelan came downstairs and admired our work in the solarium and asked if anyone wanted a glass of sherry.

"Be careful giving that stuff to Grandmother," Crystal began, but then she stopped herself. I could see her years of psychotherapy kicking in as she stood back and to the side of the situation and got a proper space. "We are leaving late this afternoon," she added. "I'm glad you're taking care of her, Phelan. Glad you're here when she needs you."

"I need her," Phelan said. "She's my grandmother. I want to be here with her. It's my pleasure." Anabelle was standing off to the side holding a set of papers Phoebe had left for him and he took them and went back upstairs.

"What are they doing?" Crystal asked, but she didn't need me to tell her. Phelan had been cheating different parts of the government since he was twenty years old and Crystal's father brought him into the family business to take over the income tax calculations. He had moved on from that to the stock market and international currencies. He had made fortunes several times and lost them. He had met the Mafia in Las Vegas and gone to their weddings. He had owned a gun factory in Texas and flown back and forth to Switzerland so many times that his seven children couldn't use up all the frequent flyer miles.

Running a little household Medicare scam and making his grandmother a hundred thousand dollars in nurses' fees was chicken feed for his criminal mind. He was doing it. Miss Louise knew about it and Anabelle was getting five percent.

Well of course we couldn't prove any of that and we were in danger of being accessories after the fact so Crystal and I got on a jet and came on home that evening. We arrived at the New Orleans airport at half past eleven and Mr. Manny was there to meet us. Crystal Anne was coming home from sailing camp the next day so we all drove home in silence and went to bed to get some sleep. I don't know what Crystal told him but I bet it wasn't half of what we knew. Mr. Manny is a lawyer. She didn't want him to be involved even by knowing what we knew.

In the fall Miss Louise died. She was walking across her bedroom with a cane. They had just had dinner. She had eaten a tuna fish sandwich and had a glass of wine. They had been watching Broadway musicals on the video player. They had watched *Camelot* and *My Fair Lady.* Then they had dinner and Anabelle had a short fight with her about where they had put the old Strasbourg tea service. Miss Louise wanted to give it to LeLe Arnold for a wedding present for her marriage to the rugby player she's been living with for five years. She thought

Anabelle had hidden it so she wouldn't have to polish it, but then Phelan found it in the linen closet and all was well. They parted friends.

Phelan rolled her to her room and got her into her bed and kissed her. Sometime about an hour later she stood up in her nightgown and started across the room toward the window that faces the backyard. Then she died. Either she died and fell or she fell and died. It couldn't have taken a minute, the doctor said. A massive stroke and hemorrhage, a swift and blessed end.

"Where did she think she was going?" everyone asked at the funeral. "She was moving away from the door."

"She was going to the window," Phelan said. "The same thing she did first thing every morning. She was an eternally curious person. She wanted to look out and see how the sun was doing. She told me she never took it for granted that it would return each morning." Then he started weeping. You have never seen a grown man take on like that over the death of a ninety-four-year-old woman.

He was in Europe by the time the agents started calling everyone and looking for the records of the round-the-clock nurses they thought they were sending to the house. They didn't get anything out of Anabelle, who wouldn't even answer their questions. Phoebe also clammed up. Crystal said she had no idea of any of it and finally they gave up and stopped calling us and asking her questions. "I have finally been drawn into a criminal conspiracy," she told me right before Christmas. "At last Phelan's insanity has managed to invade my life. I will be hating to open the mail for the rest of my life. How much do you think they stole, Traceleen?"

"Well, let's see. Ten dollars an hour at twenty-four hours a day is two hundred and forty dollars a day. Take that times seven days a week plus whatever they were paying Anabelle, minus Phoebe's cut, minus the French wine he gave her instead of the prescription drugs, plus the money they made for selling the prescription drugs."

"We don't know they sold the drugs."

"That's right. So forget the drugs and just concentrate on the nurses. Plus the computer he bought to create the nurses, plus whatever he paid the Mafia to do the rest of the paperwork. I don't know. It was a good living."

"I hope he saved part of it," she said finally. "I hope he has enough to live overseas for a while."

"I think you're imagining all this," Mr. Manny always says if we mention it. "All he was doing was taking care of his grandmother. Just because you didn't see the nurses doesn't mean they weren't there. That's a big house. They could have been asleep in the guest rooms." Then he would laugh this laugh that reminds me of the looks Phelan and Robin Martin gave each other. I will never understand the male psyche. They are running a different course than we women are, they are sailing different seas, they dance to different tunes. Even Mr. Manny, who has never done an illegal thing or told a lie or been unfaithful in his life lives vicariously when Phelan is around. Forgives him and watches him and gets some kind of kick out of his exploits no woman can ever understand. Amen.

A Sordid Tale, or,
Traceleen Continues Talking

I KNOW it's wrong to tell tales but someone has to keep a record. Some things just can't go unnoted, like Phelan Manning going over to Monroe, Louisiana, and getting Crystal's best friend from high school and taking her off to Las Vegas. They were traveling in Phelan's old station wagon, which is all he has left after five wives and dozens of African safaris. He has killed every large animal that roams the earth and he has the heads to prove it. Well, they say he is trying to sell some of them to a museum but we don't know that for sure.

The first thing we knew about the trip was one afternoon when Crystal's mother calls up from Jackson and says, "Oh, did you hear that Phelan is dating your old friend Canada Marks, from Monroe, Louisiana? They are in Las Vegas now."

Crystal hit the ceiling. She has spent her life trying to get her brother, Phelan, to stay out of her life and here he is doing an end run around her with her oldest friend.

I don't dislike Phelan myself although I disapprove of shooting elephants just for fun and even lions if they aren't doing anything to harm you. Phelan explained to me that the older lions are always killing the pups anyway and that the groups of lions, called prides, are better off if you shoot some of them but it still seems like a mean thing to do. Crystal never listens to him or believes a thing he says. All she wants from him is to be left alone.

Before we go any further I must caution you that my niece, Andria, who is a television anchorperson here in New Orleans, has made me promise not to call Miss Crystal and Mr. Manny that anymore but to call them Mr. and Mrs. Weiss or just by their first names. "Don't go writing any more of those crazy stories and casting yourself in the role of maid," she says to me. Well, I am the maid, or, more correctly, the house-keeper. To tell the truth, I come in four days a week and buy the groceries and tell the Handicapped Cleaning Service what to do with the vacuum and the dust rags and the mop. I am retired from active service since Crystal Anne is off at the Mississippi College for Women learning to be a kindergarten teacher.

Mr. Manny, I mean Manny, cannot do without me. "You have been here for the hard years," he always tells me. "Don't desert me now."

So it was Tuesday morning and Crystal and I were in the kitchen making a grocery list and watching *The Gossip Show* on the Entertainment Channel when the phone rings and it's Mrs. Manning giving us the news. As soon as she hears her mother's voice Crystal flips the phone to the speaker so I can hear the conversation. I am one of the few people who under-stand the complicated relationship Crystal has with her par-ents and the harm they do to her. Everyone else thinks they are saints, while I have seen the other side.

"Your father is very excited about Phelan and Canada getting together," Mrs. Manning goes on. "He thinks they should get married."

"What in the name of God is Phelan doing going to see Canada," Crystal screams into the phone. "You are all crazy, Mother. And Phelan is the craziest of all."

"I was just warning you," her mother said. "I think they're planning on coming there. I think he's bringing Canada to see you."

"Oh, no, he's not," Crystal says to me, when she has yelled at her mother some more and then hung up. "He is not going to involve me in this. He's broke, Traceleen, and he's going after Canada's money."

"How much money does she have?"

"A lot. She's a doctor's widow. Her husband died last year and she's been sad. I called her on her birthday last year and she was crying. When she answered the phone she was lying on the sofa crying her heart out."

So that was the situation as far as we knew it on the morning of Tuesday, June the ninth, Phelan and Canada in Las Vegas. Old Mr. Manning thinking he could pull off one last coup from his wheelchair in Jackson. Crystal and I doing the best we can with a pot of coffee and *The Gossip Show.*

Phelan and Canada were heading our way. They had taken a detour by the Grand Canyon and were crossing northern Texas as we finished up our list and got in the car to go to Langenstein's to shop for the week. Langenstein's is the most expensive grocery store in New Orleans but they have certain European foods Manny adores so occasionally we go there and squander money. We were back at the butcher section waiting our turn to order a smoked turkey when Crystal gets a brainstorm. "There's a chance he and Canada had something going in high school that I didn't know about," she says. "He was a football star and she was a cheerleader. They certainly never dated but what about all the times she slept over at our house? We don't know the past, Traceleen. All we have is this very selective memory that has been altered by hope and fear."

"It's probably not about the past," I answered. "You said she was lonely. You said she was crying on the sofa when you called. And Phelan's a handsome man. You may not like him but lots of women have fallen for him. He's probably lonely too, now that he doesn't have enough money to go on safari."

"Las Vegas," she says glumly. "He lost several fortunes in Las Vegas. He could bankrupt Canada. He could take her for everything she has."

He had not bankrupted her. No, instead he had helped her win ten thousand dollars at a roulette wheel and that is why they left when they did. "Let's leave while we're ahead," he told her. "Let's go to New Orleans and surprise my sister."

By the time Crystal and I were at the checkout counter they were driving through fields of bluebells on their way to the Louisiana-Texas border.

Manny came home at five and we gave him the news. I was still there as we had decided to make gumbo and it takes a while. Also, the Handicapped Service had been late and I had volunteered to stay and supervise the new dusting girl. Manny has this large collection of priceless photographs by the artist Ansel Adams, and you must be very careful with the way you clean the glass as glass cleaner can seep in around the edges and ruin the mats. I have taught three different handicapped persons to clean those photographs and I am getting tired of doing it. Andria says they're sending rookies to our house to get me to train them. Andria is extremely critical and suspicious since she became an anchorperson. "Be tolerant," I tell her. "Try to love and trust your fellow men and persons."

"Phelan will not get me involved in this," Crystal is saying. "If he thinks he can just show up in New Orleans with Canada and get me to forgive him for stealing all of Daddy's money he has another think coming. He raided the trust funds, Manny. Never forget that, as if anybody can."

"You aren't sure he did that," Manny answered.

"Am I not? Then where in the world did three hundred thousand dollars for the education of my children go? Did it just fly itself to Switzerland from the Hibernia Bank while I was asleep?"

"There's nothing we can do."

"I could sue him. I'm thinking of it."

I was stirring the gumbo, trying to decide if it was time to add the crabmeat. Crystal has been talking about those trust funds for five years. Before that she talked about the insurance policies he cashed in by forging her signature. Before that she says he stole her money for popcorn at the picture show but that was all in the distant past. I got out the crabmeat. I wanted to wait a few more minutes and cool the gumbo down before I put it in. You have to get it just right if you want it to stay moist and sweet.

The phone starts ringing. Mr. Manny walks across the

room and answers it. Crystal moves toward the stove to watch my cooking.

"Well, hello," Manny says. "Crystal said you might be coming to town. When will you get here? Come on over."

Crystal flies to the phone and takes it away from her husband. "Don't you come over here," she says. "Don't you bring Canada to my house. I won't be in on this, Phelan. What are you doing to her? What are you doing to my friend?"

"She wants to talk to you," he answers, and hands the telephone to Crystal's oldest and dearest childhood friend. I hear Crystal let out a long deep breath and then I'm proud of her because she doesn't start changing her tone and saying, Oh, sweetie, how nice to hear from you. She says, "What are you doing, Canada? How did you get hooked up with Phelan?"

After she hung up the phone she told us what was going on. "They're coming to New Orleans. I told Phelan to stay in the Quarter. I'm not having them here, Manny. I will not let that robber stay in my house. I don't care if Canada does get her feelings hurt. She will know why if she thinks about it."

Canada was not doing much thinking. She had been a widow for two years after many years of a passionate marriage. She was starved for love and being touched. Phelan showed up and took her arm and helped her into a car and after that she thought all his jokes were funny. He kept asking what she needed, what she wanted, and she kept saying, Whatever you want to do. That's what happens to us here on earth. There are certain things we need and we don't care what it costs to get them.

Canada and Phelan had both been getting more than their share of what they needed by the time they rang our doorbell at ten-fifteen the next morning. Phelan had decided to ignore Crystal's telling him to go stay in the French Quarter. He knew she couldn't be mean to Canada when she saw her face-to-face. Besides, no matter what happened next I still think Phelan was as much in love as Canada on the day they arrived at our house. I have never seen a man hanging on a woman and never taking his eyes off her like he was doing. Crystal says it was just the money. That Phelan loves money the way some people love God but I can't believe it was only that. Canada is a beautiful woman and sweet as she can be and funny. No one could look at her and only think of money.

"We won ten thousand dollars in Las Vegas," she was saying. "So we decided to come spend it in New Orleans."

"Have you found a hotel?" Crystal asked.

"Not yet," Canada answered. "First we wanted to come see you."

So of course they moved into the guest room and then we all made lunch. Leftover gumbo and cornbread and iced tea. It was like old times, before Crystal started hating everyone in her family.

"Phelan's going to take me to the zoo," Canada says and giggles. "He's taking me to see a sun bear."

"You've never shot a sun bear, have you, Phelan?" Crystal is still being mean.

"Never wanted to," he answers. "But I like to look at them. Go to the zoo with us, Sister. You look like you need a change."

So Crystal goes into her bedroom and puts on her new Solumbra pants and shirt that let you go out in the sun all day without sunscreen and then she pulls her hair back into a ponytail and off the three of them go to the zoo.

No one would believe what happened next. Not in a hundred years or five years or ever. I was almost finished for the day and was sitting at the kitchen desk paying some household bills when the phone rang and it's my niece, Andria. "Turn on the television set to my channel," she said. "Hurry up. You won't believe what you're going to see."

"Where are you?" I asked. "What's going on?"

"I'm on a mobile phone coming there. Don't ask questions. Turn the television on."

She hung up and I walked across the room and turned on the television to Channel 29. There was Andria, at the zoo, standing before the Monkey House with Phelan at her side. Next to him is an Asian woman with a small child in her arms.

"I just went after him," Phelan is saying. "I didn't think. You don't think when a small child falls in an alligator pond."

"How did you manage it?" Andria asks. "How did you get him out?"

"Damned if I know." Phelan lets out this big laugh and throws out his chest. The Asian woman moves nearer to him. The small child looks his way. In the background I imagine Crystal and Canada Marks.

"You could have lost an arm," Andria suggests.

"Oh, I doubt that." Phelan gives her one of his famous come-on looks. "Those old alligators are too fat to eat human flesh. I was more worried about the boy drowning in that dirty water. Hell, that place needs cleaning out." He holds up the sleeve of a ruined white safari shirt. It is wet and muddy. "You didn't think you were going swimming, did you, little buddy?"

He chucks the Asian kid under the chin and the boy puts his head down on his mother's shoulder.

Andria turned to the mother and began to ask her about her reactions. Was she scared? Did she see Phelan jump the fence? How did she think the boy fell?

The station cut to an advertisement for Ford trucks. I couldn't figure it out. How had Andria called me if she was interviewing people at the zoo? They must have put it on after it happened.

There was all sorts of noise at the front door and Crystal and Phelan and Canada Marks and Andria and one of Andria's assistants were coming into the kitchen. I started making coffee. Already I could see that things had changed. It was no longer Canada and Phelan hanging on to each other. It was Andria and Phelan showing off for each other. Andria has a long history of having to be the center of attention, which is why she has chosen anchorperson for her avocation. Also, we may have overdone it in telling her not to be afraid of white people. She is not above liking to make white women uncomfortable if she is in the mood, although she has always liked Crystal and been polite to her.

"We were the first team there," Andria said. "I couldn't believe it when I saw Crystal. He went into the alligator pond, Auntie Traceleen. Bona fide heroic act. People there said they couldn't believe it."

"I used to pole vault," Phelan said. "I ran hurdles but I'm damned if I know how I got over that fence. It wasn't me, girls. That was a higher power."

"When did all this happen?" I asked. "It seems like no time since you left here."

"As soon as we got to the zoo." Canada is talking now.

"We got our tickets and walked into the zoo and were going to the sun bear enclosure when we saw this woman standing by the alligator pond and the boy was with her and then he was up the fence and over. Phelan just bolted after him. I don't know how he climbed the fence either. Then he was holding on to a rail with one hand and he fished the boy out with the other and people were running from everywhere. We never did get to see the sun bear. We forgot about it."

Manny came in the door. Crystal had called him from the car phone and he had come home to join the excitement. "Open some champagne," he said. "Come on, Phelan. Let's go see what's in the cellar. This calls for a celebration."

ABC and CBS had it already because Channel 29 is an ABC affiliate but it was after we got the champagne upstairs that the newspapers and cable stations started calling. Phelan talked to them all. He gave interviews for several hours with Andria right beside him, coaching him. She was even in two of the interviews telling what the witnesses said.

Canada had retreated to the living room where she was talking to Crystal and acting like she hadn't noticed anything was going on. She was lapping up the champagne and Crystal even had a glass in her hand. "Should you be drinking that?" I asked. I have been to fifteen meetings of a group that keeps the close associates of alcoholics from doing things that help the alcoholic drink and I know what to look out for.

"It's ginger ale," she answered. "I'm making Canada comfortable. Don't worry. I won't drink, even if Phelan is a certified hero and I saw it. There are reasons for high testosterone levels and aggressive personalities, Traceleen. I must rethink some things. I was impressed. I don't mind saying that."

"You won't make her comfortable by encouraging her to drink too much champagne," I answered. "For all you know she has a problem with it too."

We had been talking in low voices. Canada was at the bookcases pretending to be looking at books. She turned to us. "I'd better call my house and see if there are any messages," she said. "If there's a second line somewhere. I guess Phelan's going to be talking to people all day."

"There's a children's phone," I said. "Follow me." So I took Canada to Crystal Anne's room and she called her house but there was no one there and no one had called her either. She was sitting on Crystal Anne's bed looking like she didn't know what to do next. Here she had been in the middle of a hot new love affair and now she was old hat and Phelan was upstairs with Andria being famous.

"I would slow down on that champagne if I was you," I suggested. "It is bad to drink too much when a situation is this exciting. Why don't you take you a long bath and put on a pretty dress. By the time you finish, all these media people might be finished with their interviews."

"Good idea," Canada said. She put her glass down on a table and straightened up her shoulders. I could see how she had been the homecoming queen and later the runner-up for Mrs. America representing the state of Louisiana. She had a style about her and beauty and pride. It was clear we had to save her from Phelan and if it took Andria learning a lesson at the same time then that was that.

"Phelan has had five wives," I added, looking her in the eye. "But I guess I don't need to tell you that. You knew him when he was young."

"I have been extremely lonely," she said. She stood up and

walked across the room and put her hand on my arm. "I have been acting like a fool, Traceleen. Thank God he brought me here. I was thinking of marrying him."

"Do not marry him," I answered. "No matter what you do."

Canada went into the guest room to bathe and change and I found Crystal and made a suggestion. "People are completely mad," I said. "Especially when they're needful. We must do nothing to add to the madness. Remember all the hours of our yoga, not to mention the meditation. Now is the time to call up those reserves. We must be objective and stay alert and help out here."

"He went right over the fence and jerked that kid out of the water. It is what men like Phelan are for, Traceleen. The gene pool knows what it's doing."

"We still should protect Canada, not to mention Andria. I'm ashamed of how she's acting. She will do anything to test my love. It's not the first time."

"All she's doing is helping with the interviews. It's her work."

"She's flirting with him as hard as she can flirt."

"He's sixty years old. She can't mean it."

"It's to embarrass Canada. It's that old black white mess you and I have disavowed. Not everyone has rooted it out of their hearts. It's part of that old evil."

"You're imagining that. She's just excited to be in on the story. Come on, let's go see what they're doing."

We found Andria packing up her things to leave. Phelan was watching her. "Mighty good to know you, little girl," he said and we saw Andria straighten up.

"What did you say?" she asked.

"I said it's mighty good to know you."

"Little girl. You called me a girl."

"Well, you are a girl, aren't you?"

"No, Mr. Manning. I am a woman, an anchorperson. I am not a girl. I don't know what a girl is." She moved to me and gave me a peck on the cheek. "See you later," she said to everyone and she was gone. Phelan looked like she'd slapped him in the face.

"What did I say?" he asked. "What was all that about?"

Crystal and I went into the kitchen and I got my things and left so I wasn't there for the next thing that happened. I was on the Saint Charles Avenue streetcar looking out the window and thinking about how crazy people are. Really crazy, open to suggestions, totally, completely mad. No, I told myself, they are also kind and wise and very, very smart. Think of the ruins of that bathhouse in Pompeii the year my church group went to see them. Think of all the things we make, songs and houses and mathematics and television stations. We are spotty in our madness and our goodness. Our lives are like clouds, moving, changing, coming apart. Or else our lives are just like riding on the streetcar, mostly just chugging along watching, then someone new gets on and we watch them for a while.

While I was thinking all this Canada was walking into the kitchen where Crystal was getting things out for supper. Phelan was behind her. "Phelan has asked me to marry him," Canada says. "And I have told him yes. We're taking a chance, Crystal, the hardest chance you can take with the most to lose and the most to gain."

This is one hour after she has told me she would never marry him. Remember that?

"I have loved her since I was a boy and she used to come

128

and stay with you," Phelan says. He puts his hand around her waist. "I have never really loved anyone else."

Forgetting his five wives, his four illegitimate and five legitimate children, his thousand mistresses and whores and so forth. Crystal said she couldn't open her mouth to speak. All she could do was pray time would undo some of the day's madness.

I came in at nine the next morning. The yard was full of television trucks from CNN. They were there to tape a live interview with Phelan. They were in the living room, having moved half the furniture and pushed the baby grand piano into the bookshelves and laid yellow cords all over the floor.

"Thank God you're here," Crystal said when she saw me. "More company's coming. Canada's son is flying in."

"Where will we put him?"

"In Crystal Anne's room. If he stays here. I think he's upset about the engagement."

"Engagement," I answered. "Stop right there. Let me put down my purse."

"Keep an open mind," she said. "I think Phelan's changed, Traceleen. I think he really is in love. He wants to make a home. He wants to settle down."

"And cats can swim," I answered. "It was only yesterday he was flirting with Andria. Have you forgotten that?"

"Canada's worried about her son getting here."

"I'm sure she's right to worry."

The son was coming to write a premarital agreement. It seems Canada has several million dollars and her son was not about to let that money get mixed up in a Louisiana community property law. The son is a lawyer from Denver. He is a tall good-looking man with black curly hair and a wide chest. He had on silver cowboy boots with a suit and he was in town on business. He and Phelan took an immediate dislike to each other. The son's name is Bob and no sooner did I get him settled in the living room with a cup of tea and some sweet rolls on a tray than the CNN station called up to say the interview was going to be on in ten minutes. Everyone moved into the den to watch the television except Bob Marks. He wasn't budging. He sat on the living room sofa eating the sweet rolls and looking like he would like to kill. In the den there was Phelan on television in a white safari shirt talking about alligators and how dumb they are. He was about to get off on a lecture about why big game hunting is good for the ecology when the announcer cut to an advertisement about denture cream.

We all went into the living room to join Bob. "I think you and Mother should put this off for a few months," Bob begins. "It's going to take some time to get the papers ready."

"I don't want to put it off," Canada tells him. "We want to get on the *Queen Elizabeth II* and go to Europe. We should be married before we leave."

"I can't get the papers by then," Bob says. "And I haven't told my girls. I have to have time to prepare them for it."

"They haven't written me in months," Canada replies. "They have their own lives. They didn't even thank me for their birthday checks."

"Well, we'd better leave you alone to sort this out," Crystal said and pulled me into the dining room and then the kitchen.

"We need to rent *Raise the Red Lantern* and make her watch it," I suggest. "I know she only said yes because he was flirting with Andria."

"Bob Marks will stop it," Crystal says. "He looks like a determined man to me."

"You can tell her Phelan's broke."

"I can't do that. I can't work against my own brother when he's a guest in my house, after he saved that child. I can't do that, Traceleen. I don't think I can."

"You can. I think you have to."

"Maybe I have to but I can't do it. I just don't think I can do it."

Phelan has decided everyone should go out to Commander's Palace for dinner. He is playing a close hand with Bob Marks. Not saying much. Letting Canada and her son row it out.

"He loves this," Crystal tells me. "He wanted to invite Andria but I wouldn't let him. I told him it had gone far enough."

"Tell him you're going to tell her he's broke." I was standing my ground, slicing onions for gazpacho as I talked.

"I will. Yes, I might."

Blood is thicker than water. Crystal couldn't undermine her brother while he was her guest so I saw that it was up to me. I went into the guest room and found Canada and told her as plain as I could what I knew. "He is completely broke and has sold all his property and doesn't have a job of any kind," I said. "He will expect you to support him. Are you aware of that?"

"I guessed it," she said. "I just wasn't going to say anything about it. I don't want to hurt his pride."

"I give up," I answered. "I am going home and straighten out my closets."

The Louisiana legislature saved the day. Two weeks before all this happened they had signed into law a bill that said from now on there would be two kinds of marriages in Louisiana and each couple must take their pick. One would be a regular marriage with the possibility of a no-fault divorce if it didn't work out. The other, new kind of marriage would be called a Covenant marriage. In it each person would turn over all their stuff and it would belong to both of them forever. Plus, if anybody wanted a divorce they could only have it for adultery, drunkenness, or abandonment. This Covenant marriage was not fooling around. If you chose it you were saying I am in this for the long haul no matter what happens or if you get broke or fat or one of us gets bored.

After Bob got the premarital agreements about money all worked out and signed they all began to have spats over the Covenant marriage deal. Phelan wanted one but now Canada was not so sure. Marrying Phelan for a lark with a good premarital agreement and a fifty-fifty chance at happiness was one thing. Signing up for better or worse with his track record was another thing entirely.

No sooner had Phelan and Canada and Bob come back from the marriage license bureau empty-handed since they couldn't decide what license to buy than the doorbell rang and Canada's granddaughters from Colorado were standing at the door looking like the sweetest two young girls you could ever want to meet. Their father had sent for them. He had also called all of Phelan's ex-wives and told them where he was and told them to start calling the house unless they wanted to have a sixth wife sharing Phelan's salary from now on. He had not told the wives who he was or that his mother had plenty of dough. He had led them to believe Phelan was chasing another waitress like most of them had been.

The phone began ringing. Two of the wives had better

things to do with their lives than dream they were ever going to collect any alimony or child support from Phelan but the other three were glad to lend a hand. They called their grown children and told them to call in and start asking for money for things. The girl in Denver called in and asked for a new mountain bike. The boy in Alabama called and asked for money for tuition. The twins in Houston called and said they'd been invited to go to Disney World if only they could buy their own airline tickets.

The whole time Canada is going around the house and introducing her granddaughters to all of us the phone is ringing with requests from Phelan's wives and children. Even Crystal started to think it was funny. "The dark side of testosterone," she whispered to me. "Well, at least he gives all of them everything he can make or borrow or steal."

I think Manny picked up the tab for the Disney World trip. By then I had gone back to thinking it was more madness than goodness and more complicated than evil and that we didn't have to worry about Canada and Phelan getting married on our watch as Manny calls it. He calls our lives our watches because he used to be in the U.S. Navy when he was young.

Canada packed up her clothes and went downtown to stay at the Royal Orleans with her granddaughters and her son. Phelan sat in the living room after they left, telling me and Crystal some lies about his business down in Texas where they manufacture guns for shooting elephants. He said it was making money steady and would soon be making money hand over fist now that the U.N. had relaxed its rules on elephant hunting.

Actually, his gun-making business has been closed for

two years but we didn't want to remind him of that. Not with Canada leaving and so forth, not to mention his untreated prostate cancer that he never mentions.

"I'll be heading on out this afternoon," he says at last. "If the kids are going to be at Disney World I might drive down there and ride some of the rides with them."

We let him go. I helped him carry all his bags out to his old station wagon and I stood on the sidewalk with Crystal as he said goodbye. I forget he is the biggest racist I have ever personally known when he looks up at you out of those sad brown eyes and keeps on lying to himself and being brave when the world he was given has turned completely upside down on him. He is what Crystal's parents made of him and he was brought up to live someplace that no longer exists in the world. He was brought up to ride horses and carry guns and look down on everybody and treat women like slaves, except for the time when he's reminding them of their fathers to get them in his power. It's a tangled skein.

So I felt sorry for him as he went driving off down Story Street on his way to Florida to pick up a little love from his children and ride some cheap tacky rides at Disney World.

"Disney World," Crystal said, fighting back her own sympathy and sorrow. "He needs Disney World about like a squirrel needs Dexedrine. Oh, to hell with it, Traceleen. Let's go clean up the house. I'm sick of houseguests. I want to lie down on my bed and think about my own problems, don't you?"

"I want to clean the house," I agreed. "Put on that Ninth Symphony we used to play when we'd clean up after parties. I get into the corners when I hear that music."

We marched back into our house and got out the twin Miele vacuum sweepers we bought when we thought Crystal had allergies. We got out a pile of dust cloths and a bucket full of furniture polish and window-cleaning aerosol cans and put on our double-lined plastic gloves and went to work.

Over at the zoo they were cleaning out the alligator pond and raising the fences around every dangerous animal. As Andria said later, we might be able to do without so much testosterone if we could get enough estrogen-driven vigilance in play.

Phyladda, or, The Mind/Body Problem

IT'S ALL in the mind was the watchword of the Phyladda Hospital on Lenox Street in south L.A. It was a one-story stucco building surrounded by a brick wall painted white. There was a parking lot for fifty automobiles, and two beautiful entrances, a back entrance with a wide double door painted red and a front entrance with a wide double door painted blue. Pots of geraniums framed the red door and pots of blue salvia framed the blue one. Inside was a long open room and a reception desk staffed by two pretty blond girls in long white uniforms. Their hair was always pulled back in neat ponytails. Their earrings were small pearls, one to an ear. They had soft voices and soft pink skin.

They handed out forms to be filled in and when they said it will only be a few minutes it was true. No matter what the problem the patient brought to the clinic it was addressed within ten minutes of entry through the doors. No one had to sit on a hard chair and stew in self-inflicted torment. No one had to be alone or afraid. They were taken back to a colorful examining room and greeted by one of the staff of seven.

The Phyladda called them the staff of seven because there were seven actors at work there twenty-four hours a day. They were handsome young men, in their thirties and forties, dressed in white coats and shirts and handsome ties. They had been chosen by Phyladda Hoyt herself after long interviews. They were all excellent listeners and had become well versed in the latest medical and scientific know-how on twenty subjects. Of course, if the patient was deemed to be actually sick, any of the seven was capable of getting them into an ambulance and to the hospital if necessary or to a real doctor's office in record time. This only happened once or twice a week but the real local doctors were so happy with Phyladda's services they were glad to be on call for any real illnesses that happened along.

In the meantime, in the day-to-day hard work at the Phyladda, the seven listened until their hearts almost burst with the burden of anxiety and fear that was unloaded onto them hour after hour, day after day, by housewives and lawyers and lonely men and women and even sometimes overweight or neglected children. Most of the patients, however, were women in their fifties and sixties.

Jodie Wainwright had started life in Harrisburg, Illinois. Only after he discovered he was gay did he leave and find his way to Los Angeles. He had a degree in theater arts from Southern Illinois University in Carbondale, where he had played Hamlet and Henry V and the Duke of Burgundy in *Lear.* Also, he had been a chorus boy in three musicals and had had several small parts in revivals of Albee. He was a gorgeous young man, as blond and blue-eyed and lithe and fine featured as anyone who ever showed up in L.A. looking for work. It was happening, he decided every morning. It was slow, but it was happening. He had also had a small role on a soap opera for a year and two walk-ons in movies. It was happening. His name was out there. He had an agent. It would happen soon.

In the meantime he made a living working four days a week at Phyladda. He went in at six in the morning, changed into his doctor gear, and was on call until six in the evening. By late afternoon he began to droop and really look like a doctor. In the mornings he was so trim and dapper and clean shaven it was hard to believe he had been doing anything more strenuous than reading newspapers while he drank coffee at sidewalk cafés. He was reading medical textbooks all the time when he wasn't at the clinic. He had got caught up in the details of the job. He had begun to think he was a natural-born diagnostician. There were reasons for his believing this. It was not just ego or wishful thinking. Other members of the staff believed it too. He had diagnosed AIDS in a forty-year-old society woman who seemed in perfect health. He had diagnosed it by listening so carefully and asking so many questions that she finally remembered a blood transfusion ten years previously. It was a very early diagnosis. As soon as he suspected it, he sent her to a clinic to have blood tests. Now she was on the cocktail and with luck would live another twenty years. She sent him flowers once a week for a month. She wasn't mad at him for finding out she was sick. She thought he was a hero.

Also, he had diagnosed a liver ailment that had been overlooked by two physicians. He had sent a marathon runner who thought she had allergies to a dentist to have a full mouth radiogram. She had infected molars that had been causing her to have a chronic sinus infection.

Jodie didn't know why he was able to ferret things out. He thought it was because he kept reading and reading and reading and thinking and thinking and thinking. He had to read and think because he had given up sex. Two scares with false positive HIV tests had revved up his small-town midwestern common sense. Until I find the right guy and want to get married and settle down it's over for me, he told his friends and they said okay and behind his back they said, Oh, right, give that a month and we'll see. It had been six months and he was still as celibate as a priest. He had forsaken sex for science.

Jodie was waiting in a blue-and-white examining room when Mrs. Gaithwright was ushered in by a nurse. She was a lady in her early sixties, medium height, slightly overweight but still fit looking. Her hair was pulled back in a chignon and she was wearing silk slacks and Birkenstocks.

"I know I don't have cancer," she began. "But it says you are supposed to report any change in your bowel habits and I have a change. Changes. I know what caused it. Everything that's happened has had a cause I can understand. Also, it's not so much a change as an exacerbation. I have always had trouble shitting. Long ago I had cesarean sections and afterward I got hemorrhoids from the painkillers they gave me. So since then I have always taken laxatives or Metamucil or whatever it took to keep me from having large, hard stools. Large, hard stools are the enemy of what I want, which is not to think about shitting one way or the other but to do it without pain every morning and then go on my way."

She took a deep breath. "This is so boring and embarrassing to talk about. I can't believe I have to tell this story again. I've told this story to three doctors: an internist, a proctologist, and a general practitioner. No one is helping me. The general practitioner sent me to you all. He said he thought the best place to go was Phyladda." She sat down and folded her hands. Jodie pulled up a chair and listened even harder. "My father died in the fall," she said. "I think this all began when that happened. He died of congestive heart failure. I watched him dying. His intestines shut down. So mine shut down too. I know that sounds stupid but I think that's what happened." She began to cry. Jodie reached over and put his hand on Mrs. Gaithwright's knee. They were not supposed to touch the patients but sometimes he did it anyway when he thought they needed touching.

"I live alone," she went on. "That's the problem too. I should get someone to live with me. I have a big house. It's stupid to live alone in a house with seven bedrooms."

"I want you to start eating oatmeal every morning," Jodie began. "With lots of sugar and butter or cream. I want you to drink a lot of the most expensive bottled water you can buy. Aside from that I want you to spend three days eating exactly what you want, what looks good to you, what tastes good. Then come back on Thursday and we'll do some tests. You're going to be fine, Mrs. Gaithwright. You don't have any serious problems. This is not serious or life-threatening. This is going to be just fine."

"It is? You really think so?"

"I can tell. I'm a diagnostician. I can smell cancer a mile away. I would know if you needed anything other than what I am prescribing. There is one more thing, however."

"What is that?"

"I want you to have a massage, tomorrow or the next day. Before you return on Thursday. Here is a list of people we recommend. Maurice might be nice for you. He's very gentle. Call him first, then Margaret, but any of them will do. Will you do this? Will you promise to get this done?"

"Whatever you recommend. I'm desperate. I can't live my life thinking about my bowel habits."

"I quite agree. Couldn't agree more." Jodie was sliding into his British accent, something he was always on guard against. It helped to dismiss the patient, however, and so he sometimes slipped into it against his own wishes.

Mrs. Gaithwright gathered up her things and went back into the reception room to pay her bill. She felt better, lighter, she had bestowed her anxiety on Jodie and was ready to head out for a brighter day.

"What's wrong?" Jodie asked. It was his second patient of the day, a Mrs. Bailey. She seemed bright and intelligent. She was wearing flowered harem pants and a hot pink shirt. She had on silver thong sandals and jewelry to match, several extremely large diamond rings, and long pink fingernails to match the shirt. She's trying, Jodie thought. It's always a good sign when you can tell they're really trying.

"I don't know where to begin," she said. "My husband left me. Went off God knows where. I have enough money, I guess, and I have a new job, but I keep thinking I'm hurting myself. If the slightest bit of hot water gets on my hands I think I've scalded myself. I think every freckle is a skin cancer. I guess I ought to quit reading magazines. I think I get these ideas from magazines. I read a lot of them. I'm the receptionist at the arts council building. You know, the museum by the post office. It's slow work this time of year. Maybe I'm just bored. I might be bored. You remember last year when we had the earthquake. The whole time that was going on I didn't think I hurt myself. I keep thinking about that. So do you think I'm losing my mind? Maybe I'm getting forgetful. Like why did I forget I had the hot water on when I stuck my hand under it this morning?" She held out a beautifully manicured hand.

"What did you do when it happened?"

"I held it under cold water for twenty minutes. Then I put aloe vera cream on it. It's a good thing Wimbledon is on. It gave me something to do while I waited to see if it was scalded. I used to play tennis all the time. I love Wimbledon but I never watch television in the morning. Never. I'm embarrassed to watch it at night as much as I do. Anyway, how does it look?"

"It looks perfect. You did the right thing. It isn't harmed." He took the hand. He stroked it. "I think you're having separation problems from your husband. I think you're distracted. There's nothing wrong with your brain. You sound very intelligent to me."

"So what do you think I should do? I mean, I'm really going to hurt myself if it keeps up this way. I ran into the back of a pickup truck the other day. It was lucky I was wearing my seat belt."

"Maybe you should stop wearing it. No, I'm joking. I want you to do something for me. I want you to take this list I'm going to give you and get a massage. I want you to get back in touch with your body. You're anxious about your body. It happens after a divorce."

"That's a good idea." She sat up straighter, looked him in the eye. "I love massages. Sure, I'll do that. You think that's going to help?" She crossed her legs, pulled in her stomach, started giggling. "I heard this was a good place to go," she said. "I heard this was the best doctor's office in town."

Jodie went into the attendants' lounge and got a Coca-Cola out of the refrigerator and drank it. Then he ate the biscuit he had picked up at Hardee's on his way to work. He had picked up three biscuits. Two for the ride to work and one for his ten o'clock break. Jodie was very methodical. He had become methodical to the tenth power since he gave up sex. He spread jelly on the biscuit, ate it, then went into the lavatory and brushed his teeth. He straightened his tie. He went back to work. He worked a long hard day and while he worked he kept thinking about his mother. Mrs. Bailey's harem pants had reminded him of her and the crazy clothes she used to make herself on her sewing machine. Harem pants and dresses with peplums and long full skirts with rickrack around the hems. I guess I was embarrassed by her enthusiasm, he decided. That was pitiful of me. I think I'll send her some flowers for a surprise.

That night he called to see how she was doing. "I'm okay," she said. "I'd be better if you'd come to see me. I'll pay for your airline ticket. I saw on television they were having a sale this week."

"I have frequent flyer points. You don't need to buy it. I've been meaning to come see you, Momma. It's just been so busy."

"I'm glad you're working in a hospital. I wish your father was alive to know. He'd be so proud." She was silent then and Jodie picked up the gambit and gave in.

"I'll come this weekend," he promised. "I'll come Friday and stay till Sunday." When he got off the phone he called the airline and used his last twenty thousand miles to purchase a ticket to Carbondale, which is the nearest airport to Harrisburg, Illinois.

His mother met him at the airport and drove him to his home. She drove and he concentrated on rolling his larger personality into a ball and storing it in a corner of his mind. He was her child and she did not want him to be gay or in any kind of danger. So he told her lies.

"I'll get a raise soon," he told her. "I'm going out with a nice nurse at work. I'm thinking about taking some biology classes in my spare time. I think I'll get a part in a movie pretty soon. If I do, I don't know what I'll do about Phyladda. The woman who started Phyladda has been nominated for a Nobel Prize in medicine. She probably won't win but you never can tell."

"You'll have to make a choice," his mother said. "I hope you choose to stay in medicine. You can't depend on movie people. I read all about them in *People* magazine. They end up having bad lives. And all those women look terrible. They're way too thin."

"I know." They had come to the house where he was born. It stood on its lot like a perfect living symbol of the Midwest. Every tree was trimmed, every leaf was raked, the striped awnings on the side windows had been cleaned for his arrival, inside would be a roast beef and a casserole of macaroni and cheese, the television would be on to CNN.

"I have some bad news," he lied as they got out of the car. "I have to leave tomorrow night instead of Sunday. They asked me to do extra work this weekend. There's been a flu epidemic. We're so understaffed."

"Oh, God, I hope you had a flu shot."

"We have everything. I could go to the tropics with my inoculations."

After dinner the long evening began. I can take a sleeping pill at ten, Jodie told himself. Or I can just go to bed and listen to my self-hypnosis tape. Tomorrow I'll catch the five o'clock flight back to L.A. It's less than twenty-four hours. I can take it.

His mother did the dishes and turned on the television set and Jodie wandered around the house looking for something to read. In a bedroom he found a shelf of books that had been in his paternal grandmother's house. His grandmother had been a high school English teacher and had belonged to book clubs. There, on the highest shelf, he found what later he would always believe had been the true reason for him going to visit his mother, two old books: *Magnificent Obsession*, by Lloyd C. Douglas. Beside it, *Doctor Hudson's Secret Journal*.

He pulled the books down from the shelf and went into the living room where his mother was watching a program called *The Coming Plagues*. He sat beside her reading. She turned the volume down low and watched rapt as victims died in jungle hospitals of dengue fever and Ebola and hemorrhagic fever and penicillin-resistant tuberculosis.

"Watching that stuff can make you sick," Jodie said at last. "Why don't you watch a movie instead?"

"I have to know what's going on," she answered. "There's no one to take care of me now that your father's gone."

"I think I'll go on to bed," he said. "I found these old books of Grandmother's." He held them out. "I loved these books when I was young. Could I take them home?"

"Of course. She'd want you to have them. What are they? Oh, those old books about the doctor who got rich doing good deeds."

"Secret deeds. He had to keep everything secret to get power from goodness. I used to try it when I was in junior high. I'd be nice to somebody no one liked or something like that and wait and see if I'd get a reward. Then, finally, I tried it with giving away money and something funny happened. Well, I can't talk about that. But I got my reward."

"Like what? What did you do? What did you get for it?"

"That's the thing. You can't tell even years later. If you tell, the power gets taken back."

"Well, that's pretty crazy. You can't tell something that happened in junior high? I don't remember anything special happening to you in junior high."

"That's because you were sick that year. Don't you remember? And you had to go to St. Louis to the hospital."

"Oh, well, I don't want to remember all of that. I put that out of my mind. I got well, that's the main thing. And I haven't had any trouble with that since."

"That's right. You got well." Jodie stood up and leaned over and kissed her on the forehead. He ran his hand across her thin shoulders and left it for a moment on her shoulder bone. Then he straightened up. "I'm going on to bed then, Momma. Call me if you need me."

She watched him leave the room. She was not fooled by the story about the nurse but she did sometimes think he couldn't *really* be gay. Maybe he was just gay in his head and didn't do anything about it. She turned up the volume on the television set. She gave her full attention to a ward full of patients dying of yellow fever in a hospital in Zaire.

Jodie got into bed and opened *Magnificent Obsession* and read until two in the morning. He was a fast reader and it was a short book. He was near the end when he turned to the last page and read it as he fell asleep.

On the plane home he read *Doctor Hudson's Secret Journal.* He had only hazy memories of the month his mother was in the hospital in St. Louis. But he knew he had taken sixty dollars out of his savings account and given it to a family of kids who needed clothes for school. He had skipped school one day and gone to the mother and given her the envelope with the money. Then he had sworn her to secrecy and told her to give the money to another needy person when she was back on her feet.

A week later his mother had come home cured. It had scared him to death. He told his father he threw the money away shooting craps in the schoolyard. He took the mild tongue-lashing he received and even sort of enjoyed it. His father was a mild man who never punished him physically and was secretly proud that Jodie had finally done something manly and bad.

Then Jodie put the whole thing out of his mind. If there had been some magic power, he didn't want to have anything else to do with it. It was too strange. Too far away from everything Harrisburg, Illinois, stood for. It was enough to have to hide his growing fascination with handsome men. He sure didn't want black magic added to his burden of secrecy.

He still felt funny about the books. When he got back to his borrowed apartment he put them on a high shelf in the unused guest room. He had given a twenty-dollar bill to a beggar at the newsstand where he stopped to buy a paper on his way home. That was enough of that craziness.

The next day he was glad to be back at work. He came in early and scrubbed up and put on his white coat and went to work.

His first patient was a woman who couldn't go to the mall because she was afraid she'd catch something from the recycled air. "I already can't go for walks because of Lyme disease," she said. "I don't step on anything green."

"Your shoes would protect you," Jodie suggested.

"They can climb up socks," she said. "Those little things get on the soles and move on up."

"I am going to send you to a psychiatrist," Jodie said. "I really think this is something you need to work out with an expert."

"There's nothing wrong with my mind," she said. "I just want to know what kind of gloves to wear and if there is a mask I can get that really filters out the germs."

It took Jodie thirty minutes to persuade the woman to make an appointment with the man whose name he gave her. After she left he became depressed thinking that she would not really go. "I don't like to be in doctors' offices," she said. "Too many germs. Too many people who are sick."

WASTE OF TIME, Jodie wrote on the bottom of the chart and decided it proved that giving twenty dollars to a beggar hadn't catapulted him back into Doctor Hudson's magic.

His next patient was named Suellen Smithe. She had a blood pressure problem. When she was at the health club working out, her blood pressure was ninety over seventy. When she was in a doctor's office it was one hundred and thirty over a hundred and ten. If a nurse would be patient and take the pressure over and over again it would finally drop into a normal range. Almost no nurses had the time or patience to do this, however, so Suellen had stopped going to doctors. It was too big a hassle to worry all week about whether she could control her blood pressure in a doctor's office. She treated her illnesses herself by going to the bookstore and reading all the two-hundred-dollar medical books on the shelves. Which was why she had allowed a simple cold to turn into a raging bacterial infection in her chest.

"Tell me what's wrong," Jodie said. He had honored her request not to have her blood pressure taken. They almost never took blood pressures at Phyladda anyway unless the patient requested it.

"This cold is keeping me awake all night. I coughed all night. I took some NyQuil but it didn't help. I think maybe I need some medicine. I don't know. I think I ought to get well. I've had it for three weeks. Three weeks is too long to have a cold, don't you think? Listen, I'm a distance runner. I'm a tennis player. I don't get sick. Nothing is ever wrong with me." She stopped talking and went into a paroxysm of coughing. She gasped for breath and coughed some more.

"Oh, my God," she kept saying. "I'm sorry. Oh, my God, what's wrong with me?"

"We're going to have to get you to a doctor," Jodie said. "Come with me." He pushed an emergency button on the wall and held out his hand.

"Aren't you a doctor?" She stopped coughing and stood up beside him.

"No, I'm a diagnostician. Come with me. We have a car and driver waiting. I'll go with you. We'll go to the emergency clinic. I think you need to get on antibiotics right away."

"What is this place?" she asked and then went into another spasm of coughing. "What (cough) is this if it's not an emergency clinic?" Cough, cough, cough. Deep throat and chest rattles.

"This is Phyladda," he answered gently. He took her hand. "We are a place of refuge. We diagnose. We sort things out. We can't treat or prescribe drugs. We listen. We help you decide what to do. I have some cough drops that might help until we get you something better." He fished in his pocket and brought out some Swedish cough drops. He held one out to her. She took it. She took off the wrapper and put it in her mouth.

"Then what's wrong with me?" she asked. "What do you think I have?"

"I think you have a bacterial infection. I think we had better get you to a doctor quickly."

"Well, they can't take my blood pressure. I'm a distance runner. My blood pressure is ninety over seventy. I don't want it written down on any records that it's any higher than that."

"Whatever you want," Jodie answered. He helped her down the hall and out the back door to the limousine and got in with her and they were driven to the Medi-Quick clinic down the street on Monroe Boulevard and he went into the clinic with her and waited while she was examined, given some antibiotics, and sent home to bed. "Let me drive you home," Jodie said. "You call later in the day and one of us will bring you your car. Is there anyone there? At your home, I mean."

"No, I live alone. My cat died last month and I haven't got a new one yet. Didn't have the heart."

"I thought so," Jodie answered and took her hand and held it in both of his own while the driver drove them to her pretty little stucco house on the corner of Hope and Ansley streets. Jodie got out and walked with her to the door and waited while she found her key. "Remember, you have to go to bed," he said. "Call us this afternoon and tell us how you're doing."

"I don't know how to thank you," she answered. "For all of this. Getting the prescription filled."

"Take another one when you get in the house," Jodie said. "Doctors always take two to start with. They just tell you one because they want to be careful. You really want to kick that infection fast since it's in your lungs. Don't be afraid, Suellen. We are a phone call away."

"I heard Phyladda was the best," Suellen said. "My friend who sent me there told me it was the only doctor's office she'd ever found that she wanted to go back to."

"We have good coffee." Jodie was embarrassed by her praise. "I buy it. I order it from Seattle."

Jodie got back into the limousine and was driven back to the clinic. It was a bright day. Jodie hated to admit it but he liked it when someone was really sick. As long as it wasn't something life-threatening. If someone was really sick there was always a chance they might get well. He sat back in the seat. He took a deep breath. He was proud of himself. He liked what he did for a living.

The afternoon was quiet. A woman brought in a six-year-old boy to see if he was fat. Jodie told her no, that the child was actually underweight for his age and needed more chocolate milk shakes and sandwiches. "You have to be so careful at that age," he told her. "Appearances are deceptive. Their growing cells are ravenous. They'll take calcium from the bones while they sleep. You might go on a diet yourself if you like. I can recommend a good nutritionist. I lost ten pounds with her last winter." He wrote down the name of a friend on a piece of paper and handed it to the woman. "You'll learn things that will also help your child. Meanwhile" — he leaned over and whispered in her ear so the boy couldn't hear — "don't say fat in front of him. It's a dangerous concept. Try not to think it either."

"Do you think I need to lose weight?" she asked.

"No. But if someone has to be on a diet, it would be better if it were you."

The woman left. It was not like Jodie to be unkind. It was highly unusual for him to be as mean as he had been to the woman. I better eat something myself, he decided. Low blood sugar will make you mean.

He went into the lounge and ate a turkey sandwich from the sandwich bar and then had a bowl of chocolate ice cream to make sure he would be nicer. He was just having the last spoonful when the call came from Medi-Quick wanting to know what battery of tests they wanted done on Suellen Smithe's blood. "Sorry, we lost the note," the technician said. "Don't know where I put it."

"The usual," Jodie answered. "Everything you can do. And an HIV profile. She wants it." Why did I do that? he asked himself after he hung up. What was that about? I wouldn't screw her if she was Marilyn Monroe. Would I? I don't think I would. Still, I always meant to try that route. Kinky? Well, it's a finite world.

He saw a couple of routine stroke-fear patients, examined them for forty minutes apiece, made them wait on a table with heating pads on their back and calves. He touched them, took their pulse, listened to their hearts, examined their facial muscles. "Nope," he concluded in both cases. "Can't find a thing. Healthy as a newborn colt. Healthy as can be. Wish I was as healthy as you are. I want you to go for a long walk this afternoon," he concluded. It was his appointed stroke-scare speech. "For at least an hour. And you have to take someone with you if you can find someone. If you get tired, stop and rest. If you tire easily, walk in the park where there are benches. Tomorrow, I want you to go to the Museum of Contemporary Art. This is an order. When you return next week I want museum passes and a report on the new galleries. There are two things you can have wrong with you. One is illness. The other is fear. Fear is the real killer. It evades all known drugs, all kindness, all cure. If you give in to it, it will kill you, so you are right to be afraid. Are you going to do what I tell you to do? Are you going to follow my instructions?"

The woman in room B said yes. The thirty-seven-year-old man in room D said he couldn't because he had to work.

"Then I can't help you." Jodie put his hands on his knees. Lifted his head, looked the man in the eye. "If you can't help yourself."

"My girlfriend works at that museum," the young man said. "My ex-girlfriend. I don't want to run into her. Isn't there anything else I can do?"

"Go to a CD store, buy three new CDs and play them all afternoon. Don't turn on the television set. Call a friend, anyone at all. Make them come listen to your music."

A nurse appeared in the door. "There's a call for you, Doctor Jodie," she said. "It's Suellen Smithe. She said you were waiting for her call."

Jodie left the clinic early and drove Suellen's Mazda Miata slowly and carefully to her stucco house. He parked in the driveway and walked up the flower-bordered path to the front door. Before he knocked she had opened the door. She was wearing a short violet-colored gown. She had on silver high-heeled bedroom slippers. She reached out her hand. She drew him in.

"I'm gay," he said. "After this I won't be able to be your doctor."

"We'll see about that," she answered. "I wouldn't kiss you anyway. Not today. I wouldn't want anyone to catch this cold."

He had forgotten about her cold due to the violet-colored gown. Jodie was a hypochondriac himself. All the young men on the service were hypochondriacs. The manager wouldn't hire any other kind. After all, how could they understand the torments of the patients if they hadn't been there themselves?

"I just stopped to bring the car," he said and held out the keys. "I don't want to catch the cold if I can help it. It looks bad at the clinic if we're sick. We don't want to project an image of anyone being sick."

"Comprendo," she said and backed off and held her keys lovingly in her hand. "No problemo. We have the rest of our lives. Call me next week then, or I'll call you." He was looking at her breasts. It was a revelation. They were very, very pretty. They hardly looked real, all soft and pink beneath the translucent material of the gown. Above the breasts a soft string of pearls hung down into the valley between them. Farther down a vulva, a vagina, a patch of light brown hair. Oh, my, he thought. This is so scary. God knows what you could catch from something like that.

"Better be going now," he said. "I'll call you when your blood work comes back. I'm sure it will all be fine. I'm sure that antibiotic will kick that infection in a few days."

She walked him to the door, keeping a respectful distance. Then she stood in the open doorway with the breeze blowing the gown as he got into the waiting limousine, which had followed him to Suellen's house.

"What a looker," the driver said. "You docs really make the contacts in that place, I guess."

"I'm gay," Jodie said. "What good would it do me?"

*   *   *

When Jodie got back to the clinic there was an emergency. A Right to Life group had mistaken them for an abortion clinic and was all over the yard trampling the grass. Three of the protesters were inside being calmed down by the nurses. "We thought this was the place," the leader said. "We got an S.O.S. If we aren't at the abortion clinic, where is the abortion clinic? We've got to get over there and our bus has left. We're late. We are going to be late."

"What's going on?" the nurse asked.

"A woman's aborting twins just because they're joined at the stomach," the leader said. "It's so important. Could some of you give us a ride?"

The nurse looked at Jodie for guidance. "This is Doctor Jodie," she said. "I'm sure he'll find a way to help you."

After Jodie called five yellow cabs and gave them the address of the California Bureau of Statistics building on Santa Clara Avenue, he went into the lounge to change. He was pensive. It had been a long day and he had been accosted by those breasts. The more he thought about it the more he wanted to suck on them. He had been breast-fed for two years by his mother and it was all coming back to him. The sling she carried him in. The long smooth power of her body when she held him.

"What's wrong, Jodie?" an attendant named Kevin asked. Kevin was new. He was half Indian and half British and had only come to the United States four years before. His accent was completely seductive. Also, he was slightly chubby. Chubby enough so there was a chance there were breasts beneath that white lab coat.

"I'm having a bad day," Jodie confessed. "I'm gay and

I got snared by a patient's breasts. It was very confusing. I'm going to a Chinese restaurant I know and watch the fountains."

"I'm free." Kevin surrendered and moved in. "How about some company and a talk."

Kevin had breasts. They weren't very big or well formed and of course there wasn't any milk but they were tan and had delightful little black hairs growing on them and Kevin was generous and let Jodie play with them to his heart's delight. They were out on the patio of Jodie's borrowed apartment. He was housesitting for a set designer for a month. Taking care of the dogs, keeping the robbers away.

They were on pallets beneath the stars. Not kissing, not fucking, not doing anything the slightest bit dangerous. Not even drinking. Just lying on the pallets talking about their work and breasts and what breasts meant and how symbolic they were and no wonder Jodie had been waylaid by Suellen's, which probably weren't even real.

"You could get some made," Kevin suggested and giggled a delightful, foreign giggle.

"No, no elective surgery. I'm against it totally."

"I don't mean attached to your body. Just to hold and look at. They wouldn't have to be on a mannequin. I mean, it depends on how good your imagination is. I could make you some. I'm a potter. I used to make things out of clay all day, then I got into acting, then into Phyladda. I'm proud of the work we're doing, so proud of the help we give to people. I've never been happier than I am working there."

Kevin rolled onto his back and began to count the stars. "Help me count them," he said sweetly. "Let's count all night.

We both have the day off tomorrow. We don't have to do a thing in the world but be happy."

"What a thought," Jodie said. "That's like this book I was reading about the Buddha. He said the purpose of life is to be happy. That's the very first line of the book. It's by a man who lives with the Dalai Lama. So they should know. I mean, the wise are with us if we look for them and if we listen. If not . . .

"Then we are like our patients," Jodie finished. "Scared to death from morning to night. Scared shitless in the daylight, in the United States, in the late twentieth century, in the only world there is."

"Don't think about it," Kevin said. "The darkness and the light. Take your pick. I pick stars. Sixty-seven, sixty-eight, sixty-nine."

"Seventy," Jodie continued. "Seventy-one, seventy-two, seventy-three, seventy-four, seventy-five, seventy-six, seventy-seven."

The stars kept on shining and they kept on counting until they fell asleep and didn't wake until it rained.

It was a good thing they got some sleep. Someone had come in the day before with a real stomach virus and half the attendants were down with it. At six a call came to Jodie's apartment asking him to come in on his day off. "We're trying to find Kevin Alter," the office manager said. "Do you have any idea where he is?"

"I'll try his friend," Jodie said. "I'll be in in half an hour. I'll have Kevin call if I can find him." He rolled over to the other half of the futon (they had come in during the night and unrolled the bed in the bedroom). "Do you want to go in with me? I don't want you out of my sight now that I've found you."

"Sure," Kevin said. "Twenty dollars an hour plus overtime. I can use the money." They got up and quickly dressed and were out the door. No doctors on E.R. were ever faster. They did go through the drive-up window at Hardee's, but it was on the way.

"What do you think will happen today?" Kevin asked. "I ask myself that every morning. What next in the world this morning."

"Unwrap that other biscuit for me, would you? It's the only fat I eat all day." Jodie stopped at a stop sign and smiled at his new friend. Kevin politely unwrapped the biscuit and held it out to him. Their coffee was sitting side by side in the holders underneath the radio–CD player. Steam rose from the cups. The sun was shining. They were young and beautiful and healthy. And they weren't afraid.

The first patient was a woman magazine editor who thought she was getting her electrolytes out of balance every time she drank a cup of coffee. Since her demanding job caused her to drink seven or eight cups of coffee every morning, there was nothing she could do but live in fear. "I've tried to quit," she said. "I can't get any work done if I don't drink it and I know it depletes my salt and potassium and sometimes gives me the runs, which really makes it worse, so what should I do?"

"What do you think you should do?" Jodie had decided to play the Socratic game with her. She was so nervous he thought it might calm her down.

"Well, I keep potassium tablets everywhere. I have a bottle

in the car and in the office and one in my purse and one in the emergency suitcase by the front closet. I'm afraid to take them because I heard you can have a stroke from too much of it. I don't know what to do."

"There is potassium in all food. All food contains it. Are you sure it's the potassium, not salt?"

"I don't know. How would I know? You're the one who is a doctor."

"Well, a diagnostician. It's not exactly the same thing."

"I've got to get this straightened out. I can't work thinking I'm going to start seeing white and silver lines before my eyes at any moment."

"That's what happens?"

"I will be reading along, then bingo, there are silver lines all over the page and I can't focus. Then I take one or two potassium tablets and lie down for an hour and it goes away."

Jodie wrote on his prescription pad for a few minutes. He pulled off the piece of paper and handed it to her. "I want you to go out this afternoon and buy this book," he said. "Then I want you to go two days without coffee. Then I want you to return on Thursday and tell me if you've seen any more white lines."

The woman read the piece of paper. She put it in the pocket of her jacket. "That's it?" she said. "That's all you can tell me?"

"You know what the problem is," Jodie answered. "The book will teach you lots of other things to put in your mouth to make you happy and make you energetic and make you work."

"It's just a book about food?"

"You need to get reacquainted with food. You've replaced food with caffeine. I see that all the time. It's easy to reverse.

Your body will be so happy to have some food to eat it will be dancing a jig. Try it for a few days. Trust me." He held his gorgeous wide shoulders back and held up his head and drew in his chin. It was a pose he had used a lot on the soap opera when he played a young lawyer who used women. It was the look the director had him use when he was moving in on new prey.

It worked. She smiled. She stood up.

"One more thing," Jodie said.

"What's that?"

"I want you to get a massage tomorrow. Here is a list of three people we think are very good. This is important. Will you do this for me?" He stood up beside her.

"I don't know if I have time."

"Make time."

"Well, all right. I mean, if you think that's what I should do."

"I'm sure you should." They shook hands. She smiled again. Fortunately her breasts weren't very big, so he was able to ignore them.

At eleven he met Kevin in the lounge and they decided to run out for a salad and pasta. They got into Jodie's car and pulled out of the parking lot just as Suellen's Miata came barreling around the flower gardens and pulled to a stop in a handicapped parking place.

"She saw me," Jodie said. "God, I'm glad I'm not there. She has a terrible cold. We're going to have to have an isolation room for people with contagious things. They didn't use to come in here with germs. That's only been happening in the last few months."

"How long have you been here?"

"A year last week."

"Who started this place? I answered an ad in the paper. I wasn't sure this was a good part of town but I was desperate for money so I applied. Then after I started I decided it was a great job. But the manager never told me very much. Just the standard attendant training and the vocal coach and the medical dictionary and the hand-washing thing. He said he was going to give me a history but they rushed me on in before I even finished the training course. After the rains last month and tremors, when everyone was so nervous."

"Okay, where to begin. Phyladda Hoyt got the idea from her aging parents. She was a registered nurse for many years before she started the clinic and she had seen enough to know there was a real need. Then her mother died of a stroke from worrying about what she would do if she had one. How she'd kill herself if she was helpless and all that. I'm not telling this very well. Maybe someday you'll get to hear Phyladda tell it herself. Anyway, there was quite a bit of money in the estate and Phyladda used it to start Phyladda in honor of her mother. Her mother was also named Phyladda. That's her portrait in the waiting room. The child with the long white dress and the flowers. It's Phyladda Hamilton Hoyt as a child.

"You see, a child doesn't think about its body. It's the parents' job to do that. A child just figures everything is going to work and if they get sick they don't think about it in the abstract like we do when we grow up. If it itches, they scratch and then go on about their business. What we are trying to do is get the patients back into some semblance of that childlike innocence and trust in their own bodies. Then the energy is freed up to heal instead of terrify. Well, it's been open for three years now and it's been a huge success. That's why you haven't met Phyladda. She's in Europe on a lecture tour, talking about Phyladda to foreign investors. If she gets what she wants, we'll open clinics everywhere. I'm an actor at heart. I don't want to give up the theater but sometimes I think about making this a career. It's seductive, knowing you can make a three-hundred-dollar-an-hour lawyer feel better by just telling him he isn't sick. 'There's nothing wrong with you' are the most powerful words in the world. Except for, well, 'You aren't going to die.'"

"God," Kevin said. They had come to the parking lot of the restaurant and Jodie had turned off the motor. "God, I'm so glad to be part of this."

Monday morning it was raining. That always boded well for Phyladda. The credit side of the ledgers went up and up, especially if it rained all day. People couldn't go for walks so they stayed in and thought about what might go wrong with them.

There were two, false, brown recluse spider bite alarms in twenty minutes between nine o'clock and ten. Jodie saw the first one and Kevin saw the second. "We could introduce them to each other," he suggested when he and Jodie met for a cup of coffee. "The guy I saw has made a science of studying them. He talks on the Internet with a biologist in Arkansas who's making an anti-serum. How old was the woman you treated?"

"About thirty-five. She had a friend who was bitten in Texas when she was young. The friend lost a piece of her nose. It's a valid fear but not in L.A. I try to concentrate on telling her we don't see much of it here."

"This guy thinks they come in on trucks with frozen chickens. He and this guy in Arkansas are writing an article about it."

"How old is he?"

"Forty. Good-looking man, short, strong, pretty face. He knows he's obsessed, but since he's writing the article he thinks it's worth the mental pain."

"When does he think he's bitten?"

"All the time. Whenever he has a small sensation on his skin. After he sees spiders of any kind or kills one. About ten minutes after he kills any spider or any small unidentified bug."

"How many does he kill?"

"Anything he sees that moves."

"God, that must take a lot of time."

"He's a lawyer. He works in an air-conditioned office. He only kills them at home or if he's out in the country. He's coping, as long as he can come in when he's scared. Before he found Phyladda he'd take Benadryl but then he couldn't work for hours and once he fell asleep at the wheel."

"I think you'd better send him to a psychiatrist. That sounds really bad. My woman was not much better. She's been to the emergency room three times thinking she was bitten. She's been here twice. One more bite and I'm getting her some help."

"Why do you think they believe they've been bitten?"

"Bonding issues. Something wrong with the mothering after birth, separation from the mother, it all begins in the early years, it begins at birth. Everything I'm reading tells me it begins so soon, before there is language, so it isn't easy to cure with language."

"How would you cure it?"

"With love, Kevin. That's what Phyladda is for. Listening and love, time and patience. I don't know. I may never get back to acting. I'm caught up in this now, especially with you here beside me. Working beside me. I think of you all day, so near and so in tune. Sorry, drink your coffee. I'm going mush mush." Jodie started giggling and Kevin pulled down his scrub suit and flaunted a breast. They started laughing so hard they couldn't contain it. They put their hands over their mouths and laughed until they coughed.

Cough, cough, cough. Jodie could hear Suellen coming down the hall. He said a mantra. He opened the window to the courtyard. He prepared himself.

"I'm reporting you guys to the government and the press," she said, as soon as the door was shut and she had Jodie to herself. "How dare you call this a clinic. This is nothing but a scam. You guys are scamming those poor bastards out there to death. Sixty dollars a visit, one hundred for a full history. What a deal. I'm calling this afternoon." Cough, cough, cough.

"How's the cold?" Jodie asked.

"It's better, thanks to real medicine and antibiotics."

"Are you having any intestinal problems with the medication?"

"Some. I'm eating yogurt."

"That should help. If it gets worse have them change the antibiotic. And beware yeast infection. I would use some Monistat prophylactically if I were you."

"Good idea. I meant to do that. So what have you been doing all morning, Doctor Jodie? I mean, what kind of crap have you been shoveling out in here?"

"A woman thinks she was bitten by a spider. I examined her arm and took her temperature and found out her sister was dying of breast cancer. I told an old lady she wasn't going to have a stroke this week. I drank a cup of coffee with my lover and shared some jokes with him. Are you feeling all right then, Suellen? Except for the cold, which we hope is going away?"

"Yeah, I'm all right. Except I haven't been laid in months and I wake up in the night and listen to my heart beat and think I'm having a heart attack and I don't want to take sleeping pills especially with this stuff in my chest. Oh, God, it's such a vale of tears." She sat down in a chair and bowed her head and began to cry. She cried and cried and cried. She cried a year's worth of tears.

Jodie sat very quietly and let her cry. Then he handed her a clean, ironed handkerchief and started writing on his notepad. "Sharon Dotson, Marrili Jenas, Tom Harrold, 555-5668, 555-4578, 555-7799."

"I want you to get a massage as soon as you're feeling better," he said. He very gently reached out and touched her knee, hoping the virus from the cold wasn't in the tears. "All of these people are good. They all work on the weekends. You are such a lovely woman, Suellen. Anyone would want to go to bed with you and someone will, very soon. I have a nose for these things. I know when something good's about to happen. I'm almost never wrong."

"Why are you being so nice to me?"

"I don't like to have sadness in the world. I don't want to have people hating me. I want to be loved and cherished. I'm an actor, for God's sake. I want applause. We're going to die when this is over, Suellen. We need to be nice while we wait."

She dried her tears. She sat up straight. She sighed and thought about it. "I won't call anybody," she said. "I don't know why I thought of that."

"Because it's raining maybe? We used to have fur. We don't like it when it rains."

She got up and took the piece of paper that he handed her. She started to hug him, then changed her mind, remembering her cold. She shook her head and left the room. He watched her walk down the hall, then got out the disinfectant and started cleaning the room. He turned on his pocket tape recorder and recorded the visit. "It's no rose garden," he began. "It's not always easy. Sometimes we are misunderstood. Sometimes we are hated. We do what we can. We climb up on that stage and we show them what we've got. We let them know we're coming. We project and project and project. It doesn't make us smaller. If we get tired, we'll rest and get back up there and try again. It's our job and sometimes we love it and sometimes we don't. We have to do it. The world cannot be left entirely in the hands of the rational because the world is not rational by any stretch of the imagination but kindness is rational in whatever form it takes. Amen, Doctor Jodie. To be continued."

II

It was Friday afternoon. Phyladda was crowded. Mrs. Gena Alstairs came in worried sick. She had swallowed a small hard object in the pasta and salmon she had carefully cooked for lunch in an attempt to stop her nervous stomach syndrome. By the time she got to the clinic she was feeling somewhat better about that. She wasn't certain it was broken glass anymore. Perhaps it was just a small hard thing in the pasta. Perhaps her intestines could deal with it. After all, animals swallowed other animals' bones and all and didn't die. Perhaps some of that ability was left in humans. She hoped so. The very sight of the red double doors opening onto the parking lot at the back of Phyladda made her begin to imagine her body as something that might perhaps be able to deal with a small hard object in the pasta. When she got out of the car and approached the doors and saw the fresh, lovely geraniums she raised her head and almost smiled. Kevin and Jodie had groomed the geraniums that morning, taking off every yellowed leaf or any reminder of decay.

"Before I even thought I'd swallowed broken glass I was worrying about this place on my forehead," she told Jodie, as soon as they were alone in the examining room. "I thought it was the first sign of AIDS, then I remembered the tests you made me get came back negative. So then I decided it was skin cancer but as you can see it has gone away. It was just because I kept rubbing it while looking at it. It's so pitiful. I'd rather kill myself than live at this level of hypochondria."

"What happened after you thought it was skin cancer?" Jodie asked.

"I took a bath to calm myself down and found a patch of red irritation on my ankle. I know it's only a place from where I was wearing socks with elastic but I thought, Oh, God, it's related to the cancer on my forehead. What will I do, Doctor? I can't go on like this."

"Did you call that masseur like I asked you to last week?"

"No. I meant to but I got caught up in getting ready for my grandchildren to come."

"Please call a masseur. I hate to say this, Mrs. Alstairs, but you need to be touched." He reached out and put his hand on her arm and kept it there.

"I'm not lonely," she said. "I'm going to have a houseful of company all summer."

"Good, well, let me see that place on your forehead." He caressed her arm as he examined her head. He gave her all the love he had to give. "There is nothing wrong with you," he said. "Please stop worrying. It will make you sick to worry at this rate. This isn't good for you."

"I know, I know," she answered. "As if I didn't know."

They sat in silence for a while. Then Jodie stood up and put his hands in his pockets. He turned to her.

"How much money do you have, Mrs. Alstairs?"

"I guess three million, counting everything, counting the houses I could sell. I should sell the place on the Baja. I never go there anymore because of skin cancer. It's no fun if you can't get a tan."

"I want you to find some people and make their lives better. Some of your family will do but it's better if it's a stranger. Someone who really needs you. Who needs something they can't get for themselves. All of this has to be a secret. Well, you can tell me if you need to tell someone but no one else. This is a secret power thing I read about in a book when I was young. Once or twice I tried it, and it made wonderful things happen. I don't know how to explain it. It makes you strong. Will you try this for me? We have to try something. You can't go on like you are."

"There are some children," she began. Then she began to smile. "Oh, I know just the ones."

"It must be a secret even after it's completed."

"I'll do it. I swear I will." She stood up and gathered her things. She was in a hurry to leave. She couldn't wait to get started. She had two illegitimate grandchildren in Missouri. They were living in a bad neighborhood in Kansas City. She had been wanting to buy them a house, but had kept herself from doing it. Now she would do it. She would do it that afternoon. No one need ever know. She had old friends in the real estate business there. It would be easy. She would get rid of a terrible weight of worrying about them getting mugged. She had only seen the children once, but she had seen photographs of them. A boy and a girl. She would buy them a home. She was able to and she would do it.

Mrs. Alstairs ran from the room and out the back doors of Phyladda. She had a mission and a purpose. She was a woman on her way to get something done.

"You're in a good mood," Kevin observed that evening. They were in Jodie's kitchen making mock duck from a recipe in the original edition of *The Joy of Cooking*. It was a complicated recipe with a marinade that had to be tasted over and over again to get it right. Kevin was grating cheese for grits while Jodie worked on the marinade.

"I should have been a research chemist," Jodie answered. "Cooking is simple chemistry. We should go back to school, Kevin. We may be missing our real callings." He added a small amount of garlic to the marinade, then a pinch of sugar, then stirred one last time and dropped in the chickens. He set a timer for twenty minutes and washed and dried his hands. "Let's go for a walk while that sits," he added. He reached over and plucked a mound of grated cheese from the top of Kevin's work and popped it in his mouth.

"All right," Kevin agreed, "but only if you tell me why you're in such a good mood."

"I don't know if I can. I'm doing something secret and the way it gets its power is by its secret nature. Still, I guess I can tell you if you swear not to let it go a person further. I mean, it could ruin the luck and the power."

"Da, da, da, da, da, da, da."

"I know it sounds nuts but it's this thing I know about for getting power in the world. I just remembered it recently. Come on, I'll tell you while we're walking."

The skies had cleared completely and were actually blue above the tile roofs of the houses on Jodie's street, not a trace of pollution in the air. Kevin and Jodie walked half a block before Jodie continued talking. "There is this old book of my grandmother's I first read when I was about twelve years old, about these doctors who got the idea in their heads that if they did good deeds and kept them secret it would give them miraculous powers to heal. This was long ago when there were no antibiotics and surgery was dangerous. There was an older doctor who tried it first and he left his journals to a younger doctor who found out how from them. The books are called *Magnificent Obsession* and *Doctor Hudson's Secret Journal.* I tried it a few times in junior high and strange things happened. Finally, I got what I wanted and it was so big it scared me so I put the whole thing out of my mind. You see, Doctor Hudson believed you had to be a really strong person to fool around with this energy, power, whatever you want to call it, and a skinny little boy in junior high sure wasn't ready for it."

"What happened? What did you do?"

"I can't tell. I can't ever tell or it might undo itself. This is deep stuff, Kevin. Not something to play around with lightly. You can't want selfish things for yourself. And of course you can't prove it's working. So this morning I was so frantic to help a patient get her mind off herself that I told her about it. She was so excited she ran out of the office. It's the power of a good idea, Kevin. That's all it really is, and yet, all day since then I've been filled with this elation, this feeling that good things are happening and I'm part of the conduit. Do you think I'm nuts?" Jodie stopped beneath a beautiful old madrone tree. He turned to Kevin and waited.

"I don't know. What kind of good deeds do you have to do?"

"Well, these books were written during the depression. The old doctor was mostly lending money to people and not collecting interest on it. No, he didn't get the money back at all. He told the people to give it to other people who were in need when they got the chance. It's pretty Zen really. Like knowing you are so rich you can share everything without fear. Anyway, that's why I'm in a good mood, since you ask."

"I want to do it," Kevin said. "I want to do it tonight."

"It has to be a secret," Jodie cautioned. "You can't even tell me. Also, you have to swear the person you help to secrecy. There won't be any power unless it's a complete secret."

"Good. All right. I see. I can do that."

"I'll know anyway." Jodie smiled. "I'll be able to tell by what's happening to you."

The dinner was divine. Mock duck and cheese grits and homemade bread and green salad and flan for dessert. When they finished eating Kevin helped clean up, then he disappeared until eleven-thirty. When he returned he was glowing with excitement. He had not known where to start. He had just gotten in his car and driven to a secret place and found a secret person in distress and begun his secret life.

As soon as Mrs. Alstairs got home she called the airlines and made a reservation to fly to Kansas City that evening. She made a reservation for a rental car and a hotel room. She called her real estate friend and told her what she wanted. She called her CPA and found out what she could do to help with taxes. I guess that doesn't matter, she decided. I mean, that won't ruin the secret, will it? She called the real estate person back and swore her to secrecy. Then she called her CPA back and swore her to secrecy. Then she decided she had done all she could in the secrecy department so she packed a suitcase and put it in the backseat of her automobile and lay down on her bed and began to dream of her little grandchildren in a clean, new house, in a neighborhood with good schools and parks and sidewalks. She fell asleep and slept for an hour.

When she woke she called the mother of the children and told her that she was coming to Kansas City to buy her a house. "I need the deduction for my taxes," she told the young woman. "You'll be doing me a favor."

"I don't know what to say," the young woman answered.

"Say you'll meet me after work tomorrow and look at whatever I've found."

"I pick up the children at five-thirty. I might be able to get off earlier and meet you. I don't know what to say, Mrs. Alstairs."

"Just say you'll help me find the house. And don't tell anyone about it. I want it to be a complete secret."

"Not even the children?"

Mrs. Alstairs thought about it. "Not even them," she said. "They're too young to wonder where a house came from."

"Whatever you say." The young woman who was the mother of the children hung up the phone and closed her eyes very tightly. She was the secretary to a bathroom and kitchen renovator. She dreamed for a moment of a shower that worked, a kitchen with a dishwasher. Why not, she decided. Why wouldn't a grandmother want the best for her grandchildren. A nice house in a nice neighborhood. It made wonderful, brilliant sense. It made the world seem full of possibility and light. She ran into her boss's office to tell him. Then she remembered it had to be a secret so she went back to her desk and worked on the billing records.

Mrs. Alstairs found the house in two hours. A three-bedroom cottage two blocks from an elementary school. It was painted blue with white trim. There was a fenced-in backyard with trees big enough for swings. There was a yellow-and-white kitchen with new appliances. It was brand new. A brand-new house in a neighborhood with bicycles and toys in the yards. A place where children could live and grow in peace. If they like it, she reminded herself. If not, we'll find another one. Her spirits soared. This had been there all along waiting for her to do. This wonderful adventure had been right before her eyes and she had been too afraid to see it.

"I don't know if we could be research chemists," Kevin was saying to Jodie. They were having a snack in the lounge at Phyladda. "I was thinking about that this morning. I'd rather be a psychiatrist, I think. You be a research chemist and I'll be a psychiatrist."

"Psychotherapist," Jodie corrected him. "The real ones call themselves psychotherapists."

"All right." Kevin handed him a sprout-and-lettuce sandwich with Tofu Rella and mustard and they sat down at the table and ate.

"What a day," Jodie said. "What a beautiful day."

"I'm feeling lucky," Kevin answered, hoping a tiny little hint wouldn't ruin the secret power. "I'm thinking about calling my brother-in-law and putting some money in the stock market. It's down another hundred points. I heard it on the radio driving in to work."

"Your brother-in-law?"

"He's a broker at Merrill Lynch. He's always after me to let him make me rich." They giggled and finished their sandwiches and then went back to work. At twelve-fifteen Kevin called his brother-in-law and put his savings account to work in stocks that his brother-in-law swore were at their all-time lows.

Then he forgot about it and went back to thinking about how he was going to quit smoking as soon as he and Jodie went on a vacation.

Which is why, four years later, the fifty-car parking lot at Phyladda is now one-third its original size and Kevin and Jodie are running a hugely successful stop smoking clinic in a beautiful modern building designed by Peter Waring of New Orleans and featuring a twenty-foot-long curved stone hot tub bordered by ferns and orchids where the patients can sit and soak the nicotine out of their bodies. The clinic stays open twenty-four hours a day and the patients can come in any time they are feeling weak and get massages or aromatherapy or have food delivered from seventeen different gourmet restaurants or take yoga or sit in zazen or choose from a three-page list of displacement activities while they wait to overcome their addictions.

Jodie has given up acting. Also, he has never fulfilled his secret ambitions to be a research chemist or a medical doctor but he no longer thinks he has missed his calling. The dropout rate at the Tax Shelter, which is what they jokingly named the smoking clinic, is fifteen percent. The cure rate after three years is ninety percent.

Jodie and Kevin are in the process of adopting a child, or, hopefully, several children. If that falls through they are considering joining the big brother program and spreading their maternal instincts out into the community.

"There's plenty of time to decide all that," Kevin always says.

"Not as much as you think there is," Jodie always answers.

"Plenty of work to do."

"Sick people lined up trying to get well."

"So they can make themselves sick again."

"Ours not to reason why."

"Ours not to judge, if we can help it."

Battle

ON KING'S WAY in Jackson, Mississippi, the battle was joined. Mrs. McPhee was going to have to send her husband of sixty-seven years to a nursing home that was only fifteen minutes away from her house and that was that. There was nothing else to do. He was killing her. He never slept. He woke her up every two hours every night to tell her things. He would rouse himself from his bed and struggle into his walker and go and find her. No matter where she found to sleep in the three-bedroom house he could find her. She was eighty-eight years old and the maid and the nurses left at ten every night and from then until the morning her life resembled the Lewis and Clark expedition. Finding a way to get him back to sleep. Putting him in bed and petting him. Assuring him that the black fireman who had bought the house next door was not going to come in with a gang and murder them in their beds. Playing his Books for the Blind tapes for him, although they had had to take away the Louis L'Amour tapes as they only made him crazier.

There was the matter of the gun. He had a loaded thirty-eight revolver in the apron pocket of his walker and he had thrown a fit when his children tried to take it away. He had pouted and complained for so many nights and become so paranoid that they had finally given it back to him, bullets and all. He had been armed since he was twelve years old. There was no way they could disarm him now. Mrs. McPhee and her sons put the bullets back in the gun and gave it to him and he returned it to the apron pocket of his walker.

Then there was the matter of Mrs. McPhee's children. Neither of her sons was ever in Jackson when she needed them, although their wives were sweet and helpful. One of the wives, a darling named SuSu, was even able to calm old Battle down when he became paranoid about the black people moving into the neighborhood. It was SuSu who thought up having the minister across the street come talk to him. The minister had black people living on either side of him. "They are very nice people," the minister told old Battle McPhee. "They are just trying to escape the ghettos and find a place to raise their children. None of them is going to hurt you. They are protection from the sort of black people you fear."

This calmed Mr. McPhee down and made him more determined than ever not to go to the nursing home. He had been willing to go to the nursing home when he thought his life was in danger from the black people moving into the neighborhood. Now that the minister had reassured him about that, he had decided to stay home until he died.

"I am living in the best black neighborhood in Jackson," he told his daughter when she called on the phone. "Did you hear about that?"

"I heard you were going to the nursing home where

Uncle Phillip went," she answered. "How do you feel about that?"

"Oh, I'm not going anymore," he said. "Now that the minister tells me we're in the hoi polloi."

"Oh, Daddy," she said. "You have to go to the nursing home for a few months while Mother gets rested. You have almost killed her keeping her awake. If you kill her, where will you be? She's the one who takes care of you. You have to let her get some rest."

"If only he would take the sleeping pills," her mother put in from the other phone. "If he'd take the sleeping pills he could stay home."

"I'm about to die," old Battle said in his most charming voice. "I want your mother with me when I get to the Pearly Gates."

"Shut up, Daddy. You are not going to die. That is not the issue here. The issue is Mother has to get some sleep. Take the sleeping pill tonight. Promise that you will. I take them all the time. They aren't going to hurt you. All they do is make you go to sleep. It's less dangerous to take an Ambien than an aspirin. If I were your age I'd take one every night."

"I'll promise anything," he said, and laughed his wicked, dangerous laugh.

Days were all right in the McPhee household on King's Way, a small boulevard in what had been the bright new part of Jackson when the McPhees' oldest granddaughter had bought the house for her first marriage. The McPhees' oldest great-grandson had been born there. It was a one-story brick house, on a hill, with a beautiful oak tree in the front yard and a landscaped backyard with rose gardens. The older McPhees had moved into it when the money began to shrink.

Everyone in the family had different ideas about why the money had shrunk. The McPhees' daughter, Ifigenia, blamed it on her brothers and had gone up north to live. She was mad at everyone for losing all the money. She was a perfectionist and couldn't tolerate anyone who was messy in any way. The brothers blamed it on each other. Old Battle McPhee blamed it on the government, which made so many crazy laws it was impossible to run a business. The grandchildren blamed it on bad luck and didn't really believe it was shrinking. If it was shrinking, they sure wanted to get one last house or car or a never-to-be-repaid loan out of their grandparents before it was completely gone. In the years that Mr. McPhee was a millionaire they had been able to get anything they wanted from him. They were in the habit of never having to get anything for themselves and it was a habit that was hard to break.

But the money shrinking was not the problem for Mr. and Mrs. McPhee in nineteen ninety-six, although more money would have made some of the problems less acute. The problem was that Mr. and Mrs. McPhee were eighty-eight years old and they had not expected that to happen. They had not expected to desire so much to walk across a room and out the door and get into a car and go and do exactly what they damn well pleased.

Instead they were stuck in this little three-bedroom house in a neighborhood that was turning black. In many ways the little house was turning into the plantations where both of them had been born and raised. There were black nurses and a black cleaning lady and Mr. and Mrs. McPhee spent their days helping the black people solve their problems in return for the black people feeding and cleaning up after them and, in Mr. McPhee's case, getting him dressed and bathed and bandaged. He had a bad foot that wouldn't heal. It was the first thing that had happened to either of them that medical science or their incredible bodies couldn't heal.

The black nurse who had been there the longest and become Mr. McPhee's right-hand man had plenty of troubles of her own. She had a daughter who was on a dialysis machine three afternoons a week. "Dialysis," the nurse, whose name was Phoebe, told Mr. McPhee. "It's a machine to clean her blood. We have to pay extra to have the filters changed on the machine. The filters cost a hundred dollars a week." Then Mr. McPhee would dip into his small store of dwindling money and pitch in to buy some filters.

Mr. McPhee had been allowed to drive until he was eighty-seven. He had a valid driver's license until he was eighty-two and his sons let him keep on driving for five years after that as long as he stuck to the streets near his house. They had put handicapped stickers in the front and back windows of the car and decided to take a chance on him not killing someone on his way to the bank or the library. Then he injured his right foot and the wound wouldn't close. Karma, the bright ones among his progeny whispered among themselves. That's the foot he used to kick us with. There were many bright ones. Bright, smart, powerful, ambitious, self-centered, spoiled, beautiful, cunning, and selfish. He had passed on his genes.

But the crucial problem was not the dwindling money or the selfishness of the gene pool. The problem was that Lila McPhee wasn't getting any sleep. Old Battle was sucking her dry. He was killing her. In the daytime he would charm the maids and nurses. At night he would whine and cry and pretend to be paranoid about the black people in the neighborhood or become paranoid by dint of his incredible imagination or whatever it took to get into her bed and make her pet him while he went to sleep.

"Sometimes I don't care if they both die," their daughter, Ifigenia, told her sisters-in-law. "Let them kill each other. It's their marriage, their insane relationship. They've been at it for sixty-seven years. I can't do anything about it."

In order to make sure that she didn't end up down in Jackson, Mississippi, in the middle of the melee over whether Mrs. McPhee put Mr. McPhee into a nursing home for three months while she rested up, Ifigenia bought airline tickets for her entire family to go to Italy for two weeks at the end of July. She made reservations for herself, her husband, and all three of her teenage sons. They would leave at seven in the evening on the twentieth of July. A vacation and an adventure.

Early in the morning of July thirteenth, old Battle McPhee was lying in bed thinking about his luck. He had had good luck, he decided, but made bad decisions. The bad decisions were going to lead to him being slaughtered in his bed by black people. Not to mention the effect the bad decisions were going to have on his arrival at the Pearly Gates. Old Saint Pete would be at his post. Old Battle would be approaching, hat in hand, all his power gone, his strong right hand, his strong legs, his good brain, most of his teeth and money, gone. "I did the best I could and you know I was the soul of charity. I fed the poor and clothed the sick and housed the homeless. I did my damnedest, Lord. But I made bad decisions. Miss Lila will be along to tell you a lot of stories about me, but they are not true. She was a hard woman to live with. I know I shouldn't have taken that little vacation from my vows but I am repentant and you know I have sorrowed over that."

"The devil take you," Saint Pete would say. "No one can enter here who does not have a heart that's pure."

Battle's mother was looking over the battlements of the Holy City. "Let my boy in here," she called down, and Saint Pete opened the Pearly Gates a crack, so Battle could speak to his mother. Still, he did not let him in. Down below, the devil waited with his fiery angels.

Battle struggled to get his good leg out of the bed and down onto the floor. He painfully pulled his body up into a sitting position and then sat for a moment listening to his heart beat. At any second it might stop. It would stop and he would be gone. I shouldn't have slept so long, he was thinking. I've got to get out of bed and get to work.

He pulled the walker over to the edge of the bed and began the struggle of pulling his body into a standing posture. His arms were still strong and well muscled. His arms were all he had left. He had pitched a hundred thousand baseballs with that right arm. He had caught a hundred thousand flies. He stopped for a moment and imagined himself on a summer afternoon in Sheffield, Alabama. Out on a vacant lot near the courthouse with his cousins and his friends. There are nine or ten of them divided into two teams. It grows darker. It's after supper and some of the grown men come out to play with them. The cicadas and crickets and tree frogs are as loud as a symphony. The women come and sit on the benches and gossip and watch the game. The black people are lounging on their benches by the livery stable. It is still light enough to see a fly ball. The ladies have on long-sleeved dresses for the mosquitoes. His daddy comes and stands by home plate and calls out to him. "Pitch him a curve, Battle. Strike him out and I'll let you drive the car." Battle winds up his arm, zeroes in on the catcher's mitt, throws a perfect curve ball that drops as it nears the plate.

"Now we're railroading," Battle says to himself and makes one last huge effort and pulls his body into a standing position behind his walker. Now he is ready to walk into Lila's room and wake her up and get her to help him go to the bathroom. It is the third time since midnight he has come into her room to wake her up.

At nine that morning Lila got her daughter on the phone in New York and issued an ultimatum. "You have to come and help me. I have to get him into a home for a few months. I have to be able to sleep. I get up in the morning and look in the mirror and don't know who I see."

"If he hadn't given William Battle and Joe all the money there'd be enough money to have nurses at night. It isn't my fault. I warned you and warned you. I have given up. I am not coming down there and spend my hard-earned money to make up for the money William Battle and Joe threw away in Las Vegas. That's that, Mother. I am not coming down there right now. We're taking the boys to Italy. It's been planned for months. If we change the tickets it will cost hundreds of dollars. Call the nursing home and tell them to come pick him up. Didn't you see *Streetcar Named Desire*? They come and pick them up."

"I deserve better treatment than this. I deserve your help. What have I ever done in my life but love and help you? I don't ask much, Ifigenia. I only need your help to get him into the home. Couldn't you come for one day? I'll pay for the airline ticket."

"You can barely pay your electric bill. I'll call you back tonight. Call the place and see if they won't come get him. Is he awake? Put him on the phone."

There was much clicking of receivers and whispered orders and finally Ifigenia heard her father's voice. My first love, she warned herself. The one who set the standards that have ruined my life. The alpha male. Beware, beware, beware. Snake charmer. Egomaniac, narcissist, king.

"Hey, Daddy," she said in her sweetest voice. "How's it going?"

"I'm going to die," he said in a pleasant, charming voice. "They're trying to put me in a nursing home."

"Mother has to get some sleep," she answered. "You're killing her, Daddy. She's eighty-eight years old. You have to let her sleep. You have to take the sleeping pills. If you'd take the sleeping pills you wouldn't have to go to the home. They aren't going to hurt you, Daddy. They are going to extend your life. I take them all the time. So do all my friends. I have taken hundreds of sleeping pills. You have to be brave and courageous enough to take the sleeping pills, Daddy. If you don't take them, she can't sleep. You are going to kill her keeping her awake."

"The thing that's killing me is that your brother didn't marry that nice girl from Illinois, your friend Cynthia. How did we let her get away?"

"Shut up, Daddy. That's not the issue. I don't want to hear about William Battle. I want to talk about you taking the sleeping pills so Momma can get some sleep."

"I don't want her to go away," he said in a childlike voice. "I need her with me when I get to the Pearly Gates."

"Daddy, you are not going to die but you are going to kill Mother if she doesn't get some sleep. Will you take one of the sleeping pills tonight? Will you promise me to do that?"

"All right. I'll take one tonight. Did you hear that, Lila? I promised Ifigenia I'd take the sleeping pill."

"I do not want to go," Ifigenia told her husband. "But there's nothing I can do. If one of them dies while I'm in Europe I won't be able to live with myself. We just have to put off the trip for a couple of weeks. I'm so sorry. There's just nothing else to do."

"You should go see about them. Go ahead."

Ifigenia's husband was glad to see her go. He was thinking about what would happen if he was old and infirm and she held his past against him instead of going to help. He thought it set a good precedent for Ifigenia to go on down to Jackson, Mississippi, and help her mother get her father to take the sleeping pills.

They were able to change the airline tickets without a penalty after their travel agent explained to TWA that Ifigenia's father was ill and she had to see about him before she left the country. "Bring a note from his doctor and mail it to me," the agent said when she called to tell Ifigenia and her husband the good news about the tickets. "Get something that says there's been a medical crisis."

"There is one," Ifigenia answered. "Me having to fly to Jackson is a medical crisis. It takes a year off my life to spend the night there."

Ifigenia left her sons with her husband and boarded the plane and flew to Jackson. Her older brother met her at the plane. He was accompanied by a woman he had brought home from San Antonio the week before. A tall blowsy-looking blonde who had been reading Anna Hand's books in William Battle's apartment and wanted to talk to Ifigenia about them.

"I don't talk about my cousin Anna," Ifigenia said. "Her death was the worst thing that ever happened to me. Just read the books and think your own thoughts."

"William Battle said you were a special friend of hers."

Ifigenia gave the blowsy creature a look that would have silenced the devil. "Get my bag, William Battle," she told her brother. "Let's get out of here."

Twenty minutes later they arrived at the McPhees' house and came in the kitchen door and moved past the registered nurse into the den and found big Battle sitting in a chair in a clean white shirt waiting for them. He was a gorgeous man. Eighty-eight years old and barely able to use his left leg and he was still gorgeous. It was as if age had made his skin and face and cheekbones translucent. If there were a Saint Peter and he was an aesthete, he would let Daddy in for sure, Ifigenia was thinking. Goddamn he's a handsome man. No wonder I love him.

She sat down beside him and looked at her watch. The last time she had been there it had taken him three and a half minutes to push one of her buttons. She wanted to see if he could break his record.

"That's William Battle's new lady friend," Battle whispered to his daughter. "She's not as good-looking as your friend Cynthia, but William Battle says she's related to the Bankheads. Well, we're mighty glad to have you here, Ifigenia. Your mother is very proud that you came." He was warming up. "I'm proud of you too," he said. "I never thought I would

be. You were the last one I ever thought would amount to anything, but there you are, with a nice husband and the boys
aren't bad, although that little one is mighty smarty."

"Got to put my bag away." Ifigenia got up and kissed her
father on the head and heaved a sigh and began to roll the
stone up the hill.

"Up, up, up the hill," Ifigenia sang to herself as she went
into the guest room that had a portrait of her when she was
sixteen hanging over the bed. "Up the hill down which my
self-esteem has rolled like a heavy ball." She lay down on the
bed and imagined her father taking one of the sleeping pills
and never waking up.

She reached over and picked up the old-fashioned white
phone and called her best friend in Jackson and asked if he
would meet her later at the park for a walk.

"Sure thing," he said. "Wait until it's cool. I'll meet you
there at eight and we'll walk for an hour."

Eight in the evening in July is still light in Jackson, Mississippi, but the intense heat of the day had started to dissipate
as Ifigenia got out of her mother's white Oldsmobile and
walked across the parking lot to meet her oldest friend. He
was her best friend and her astral twin, born on the same day
of the same year in the same state. He had been born in a five-
bed hospital in Smith County with his cousin for the doctor.
She had been born in Jackson at her grandmother's house
because her mother didn't want strangers to see her naked.

Her friend's name was Johnny Tuttle and he had become
a famous lawyer. He had gone to law school meaning to
become a federal judge. Then he had learned the real power
was in front of juries. The power and the money. He had

plenty of both now but he had not changed. He was still the tall gangly redheaded man Ifigenia had run around with at Millsaps College. They had met in the library when they were freshmen, both escaping college rush in the stacks of musty books. They had remained friends all these years, through his unhappy first marriage and happy later marriage, through the madness and death of many of their friends and the startling successes of others, through thick and thin. The sight of Johnny made Ifigenia a nicer person. She had never accomplished anything significant in her life but the fact that Johnny was still her friend meant that she was also special.

She took his arm and they began to walk down the circuitous paths of the Parham Bridges Memorial Park. "I don't know what to do for them," she began. "It does no good for me to come here. Neither of them takes my advice about anything. It's like I'm five years old trying to enter into one of their arguments. I guess Daddy would like to enlist me on his side against her. I don't know what goes on with them. Sometimes I think I don't understand men or women. I know I don't understand men like Daddy. They're working on some program that's far from me."

"Pride," Johnny said. "He can't be seen as someone who was kicked out of his own house."

"No, it's fear of death. He believed those old Presbyterian ministers who preached to him in his youth. He believes in the devil and he thinks he's going to be punished for something."

"I can't imagine your old man being afraid of anything. I think it's pride, Ifigenia. You don't know what a man will do for pride."

"If he'd take the sleeping pills she wouldn't send him away. Can you believe it? He's got a bottle of ten-milligram

Ambiens and he won't take them. If I had them I'd take one every night until they were gone."

"Give me a couple. I could use a night's sleep." They giggled in obeisance to their old pill-popping college days. They speeded up. They walked half a mile without speaking, then Ifigenia picked up the conversation in the middle of a thought.

"He does all this to get people to call up and come over. We know it and we still do it. It's not like they are ignored. They have servants in and out all day long. The grandchildren come by all the time. Hardly a day goes by that someone isn't over there. And they talk on the phone all day. They talk to their sisters and brothers constantly on the phone."

They passed the two-mile marker on the path and started down a tree-lined path to a creek. "Look at it this way," her friend suggested. "Think of the money you are getting back from the government in all that Medicare. That would make me feel better. I wish I knew someone who was benefiting from a government program, especially someone kin to me."

"We were on our way to Italy," Ifigenia said. "Not that those brats of mine would pay attention. Maybe now I won't have to take them. Maybe Jake and I can go alone. Oh, well, don't pay any attention to me. I don't mean to complain."

"Remember that summer we went to Italy with Professor Nelson? That was the best time I ever had in my life. I don't think I slept the whole time we were there. We didn't think of sleep as something to be desired back then." He stopped on a bridge over the creek and she stopped beside him, remembering the gaiety and fun they had shared when they were young.

"He had memorized the floor plans of the museums. He was so bossy. We were so mean to him. We didn't appreciate what he was doing for us."

"We were learning things whether we knew it or not. I had to work construction for two months to make the money for that trip. We were building the road from the tennis club to the airport. Jesus, it was hot."

"I just asked to go and they said yes. I didn't appreciate anything. No wonder my kids are such brats. Maybe it's the genes."

They left the bridge and kept on walking. They walked for four miles, up and down the small hills and the circuitous route, picking up the pace while the sun left Mississippi and the pink and blue clouds turned to gray and darker gray and the cicadas made their buzzing music in the trees.

I never had to want for a thing, Ifigenia was thinking. That old man made sure I had everything the world had to offer. And he kept me safe. I never feared a thing in the world. I knew he would protect me with his life, so I was free to be as stupid as I wanted to be, to stay a child forever. Then I married a rich man because I had a rich daddy and a rich education. I didn't have to be anybody or do anything. So how do I pay him back for that? I can't make him stop being eighty-eight years old.

"I would pay him back if I could," she said out loud. "I don't know how to help them, Johnny. It's so frustrating. Because there's nothing anyone can do. All he wants me for is to make me do things for old cousins of his in Natchez or people I don't know. He wants to use me like a tool and I won't be used."

"You can help him," Johnny answered. "You just haven't thought of the right thing yet. Take your mother somewhere so she can get some rest. Or make him take the pills. Slip him one in a drink. Outwit him."

"Oh, yeah. I'm really going to outwit that old man. If I gave him a pill without him knowing it he would kill me. He'd go completely crazy when he woke up. The last time he went to the hospital he almost tore the place up. He doesn't want to be in anybody's power, not even the power of a pharmaceutical company."

"I know. I've seen him in action. Well, call us if you need us." They had come to the parking lot and had stopped walking and were stretching their legs. The very last light had left the sky. It was dark.

Ifigenia hugged her wonderful, consoling, dearest friend and got into her car and drove away. I have been protected by wonderful men all my life, she decided. I am going to be grateful for that. I am not going to spend the rest of my life being the ungrateful wretch that I've become. I can change. I can be better than this. I know I can.

When Ifigenia got back to her parents' house she went into the den and sat near her father and really looked at him for the first time since she had been there. She looked at the beloved freckles on his hands and the wide clear brow and the rich thick hair that still grew on his head and his wide strong shoulders and still-strong arms. Everything about him was in perfect proportion to everything else. Eighty-eight years had not altered that.

He smiled at her and returned her affection. He told her a few jokes, laughing uproariously at the punch lines. "I'm going in the kitchen and see what your mother has to eat," he said at last. "Come eat supper with me." He began to struggle to move from his chair into his walker.

"Where is that wheelchair Medicare bought you?" she asked him. "I thought you got a wheelchair."

"It's in the living room," her mother answered. "Where it has always been. He won't touch it."

Ifigenia got up and went into the living room and looked at the wheelchair. It was sitting by a gold sofa. In between a gold sofa and a lamp table holding a Chinese vase that had been turned into a lamp. She unfolded the wheelchair, locked down the arms, and pulled it toward the center of the room. "Nice piece of equipment," she called back into the den. "You got the government to buy you this?"

"Sure did," her father called back. "They brought it right out."

"It's just equipment," she called. Her father had been a heavy equipment dealer. "It's no different than a horse or a car," she called out louder. "It's a tool and man is a tool user. I'm trying it. It's not about being an old man in a wheelchair, Daddy. It's about getting from the den to the kitchen table." She got into the wheelchair and rolled herself across the carpets and into the den. It was hard to make the wheels move on the thick rugs. "No wonder he won't use it," she announced when she got to the den. "The rugs are too thick. The wheels get bogged down in the carpets." She rolled across the den floor and into the back hall where the carpets were older and the going was easier. She rolled the wheelchair up and down the hall and then back into the den, then toward the kitchen. Her mother was standing by the fireplace. The nurse was sitting on the sofa by her father. "Goddamn," Ifigenia called out each time she passed them. "This is impossible. I don't know how he gets the walker across these goddamn rugs, much less a wheelchair. You ought to send him to a nursing home, Mother, if this is how you take care of him. He needs this wheelchair and there's nowhere to roll it."

Her father was paying attention. He was smiling. He loved it when people raised their voices and yelled out instructions to other people. "You'll have to take up these rugs," Ifigenia yelled. "It's nuts to have Karastan rugs on top of carpets anyway. It's unhealthy to have all this wool on the floor."

The black nurse began following Ifigenia around offering suggestions. She had worked at a nursing home once and knew all about wheelchair access. "Medicare will widen these doors," she offered. "They'll pay to get them done."

Ifigenia rolled past her father going at a good clip. She got out of the chair and rolled a rug out of the way into the kitchen.

"Let me see that thing," old Battle said. "Bring it over here."

Ifigenia rolled over to him and got out and helped him into the chair. "Your arms are all you have left but they're strong and fit," she said. "You have the arms of a young man. You'll be out on the sidewalk taking rides before too long. They have electric ones, you know. We'll get you one of those."

The nurse took hold of the left side of old Battle and helped get him settled in the chair. "Medicare will get him one," she said. "They'll send one right over. I've been telling him that but he wouldn't listen."

Battle shook the women off. He settled his hands on the wheels and began to roll. He rolled past the rolled-up rug and into the kitchen and up to the kitchen table. "Table's too high," he yelled back. "We'll have to get the table changed."

"I'll call Dinwiddie," Mrs. McPhee said. "He'll lower it, or cut the legs down." One thing about Mrs. McPhee. She knew when she was defeated. The two people in the family who could defeat her anytime they wanted to because they were ruthless about means were her daughter, Ifigenia, and her husband, Battle. Aligned against her they were an impenetrable wall. But it made her feel good to see Ifigenia and Battle on the same side for a moment. It almost never happened that their selfish desires coincided so perfectly.

Ifigenia was in high gear now. She was moving all the furniture in the house. She was completely messing up Mrs. McPhee's decor. She took two houseplants and put them in the garage. She rolled up the rose-and-yellow Karastan in the dining room and shoved it under the table. She made a list.

The nurse was supposed to leave at ten but it was almost eleven when she and Ifigenia finished making paths through the house and Ifigenia walked her to the door and handed her two twenty-dollar bills and thanked her for her help.

Ifigenia went back into the den. Old Battle was sitting by the fireplace in the wheelchair. He was nodding. He was almost asleep. "Come on, Daddy," Ifigenia said. "I'll roll you to your bed and give you a sleeping pill and take one myself and then we'll all get some sleep."

"Oh, God, that would be nice," Mrs. McPhee said. She watched as Ifigenia rolled her father into his room and helped him into his bed. The nurse had helped him undress and put on his pajamas earlier that evening. No matter how old he became or how much his legs wouldn't work, Mr. McPhee got up every morning and dressed in clean khaki pants and an ironed white cotton shirt. At night he put on ironed cotton pajamas with piping on the cuffs and down the button placket.

He didn't take the sleeping pill, of course. No matter what the minister told him he felt it was up to him to be on guard at night. But he did sleep very well and soundly for almost six hours. He had got to listen to plenty of yelling and to watch power being used and muscles being flexed and furniture being moved. That was more like it. That was something he could recognize as life.

II

Later, in November, Ifigenia began a journal.

"But he was going to die and maybe we all knew it and maybe we didn't know it. How could the strongest man we knew die? How could we have believed that? He believed it but I am not sure if he really believed in the Pearly Gates and all that bullshit. He kept saying he believed it and he gave all that money to the 700 Club and all the other right-wing preachers and he looked sincere when he went on about the God who made us. Still, I never knew him to think anyone was as smart as he was and I never knew him to think there was something he couldn't control so maybe he just pretended to believe it rather than believe in nothing. Maybe he just couldn't bear to think he would disappear, vanish, not be.

"I am going to forgive my brother William Battle for everything he's ever done to me because of what he did for Daddy in the last weeks of his life. He drove him to Sheffield, Alabama, to see his cousins. He put an eighty-eight-year-old man who could barely walk and was dying of congestive heart failure into an old Mercedes station wagon and drove him seven hundred miles, taking him in and out of the car to go to the bathroom and then setting him up in his cousin's river house overlooking bluffs and eagles and pine trees and stayed there with him for six days while he entertained his cousins. William Battle's oldest daughter came up from Memphis to stay with them. She brought her husband and her maid. They cooked meals. They poured drinks. They went with Daddy to see his mother's house and the school where he went to the first six grades. They sat beside him while his first cousins were wheeled in by their sons and daughters and while his younger brother, who was worse off than he was, was brought to visit practically on a stretcher. I will say this for my family. They can pull it off. They can imagine it and they can make it happen.

"I see them driving up the highway from Jackson, Mississippi, to Sheffield, Alabama, Daddy telling William Battle how much he has screwed up by drinking and gambling and fucking whores and not being faithful to his wives and William Battle telling Daddy so many lies it boggles the mind to think of them. William Battle will lie when he could tell the truth. Daddy has kept him in a double bind for so many years the main thing he knows how to do is to lie. Of course, Daddy never admitted that he knew William Battle was a liar. He couldn't tolerate such knowledge. He couldn't believe he could have a child who wasn't completely honest. 'I did the best I could, Saint Peter,' I can hear him saying. 'But I made mistakes. I made terrible mistakes.'

"'You can say that again,' Saint Peter answers. 'Loving the boys more than you did your daughter was your first mistake. She was your image, your most perfect creation, and you did not recognize what you had made.'

"'Oh, Saint Peter,' Daddy cries and now I begin to feel sorry for him and can't go on with the scene. Well, he's dead now, my first and truest love, my darling, crazy, funny, beautiful daddy, and that is that and I'm glad I wasn't along for the trip to Sheffield. I wouldn't have had a good time and I wouldn't have made him happy. I would have been complaining about something. I would have had a fight with William Battle and embarrassed Daddy in front of his cousins.

"My niece, William Battle's daughter, told me all about it anyway. On the last day they were there Daddy hauled himself all the way across the long room that overlooks the river. He pulled himself in his walker all the way from one end of the room to the other. He was going to his bedroom to go to bed but he had gone in the wrong direction. A man who had been known *to find anything* without a compass, who could tell by the sun and moss on a tree what was east and west and north and south.

" 'Where are you going, Granddaddy?' she asked, going to him and putting her arm on his shoulder.

" 'I'm going to my bedroom to go to sleep,' he answered.

" 'It's in the other direction. You're going to the wrong side of the house.'

" 'Oh, lordy, lordy,' he wailed, and it was the only time anyone ever heard him cry or complain. 'I'm an old, old man, Aurelia. I'm finished. I think I'm done.'

"Two weeks later it was true. William Battle drove him back to Jackson and they got to the house about dark. They went in and Daddy started to his room and fell and broke some ribs. It was the first time he had broken anything when he fell. When the ambulance came to get him, he told the young men that he thanked them but he didn't want to go to the hospital. They took him anyway. It was two days before he could get anyone to bring him home. By the time he talked two of his grand-sons into carrying him out of the hospital against medical advice he was wearing only a hospital sheet and a raincoat. The nurses had taken away his clothes because he kept getting dressed and trying to leave.

"Then he went home and then he died. Gone forever, dis-appeared from the face of the earth, dead and buried.

"My father is dead. Goddammit."

PART II

_____

The Triumph of Reason

WHAT TO DO while I wait for my fate to be decided. The fate is whether or not I get an abortion. It's taking four days to find out because the only doctor in northwest Arkansas who performs abortions is in Boston at a meeting of the Reproductive Rights Council. He has been talking to my father almost every day since I told them I was pregnant. How did I get pregnant? Well, it was because my father took us to France for two months, and we thought it was safe for me to walk around a little village so beautiful and old that romance rose up from the stones and took me.

His name was Moise and he wasn't even completely French since his mother was from England and had died the year before in a motorcycle accident. The French like to race everything. That's one thing I learned while I was there. And in the hot summer afternoons they make love and they think Americans are crazy to do anything else and they say it's also the reason we are fat. I was fat when we got to Montreuil but in a week I was not. I could see my rib cage. I could wear a loose blouse without a bra and still look good. The minute we arrived I stopped thinking food was an issue. It's so beautiful in France you won't believe it. You just want to be part of that beauty.

Data about me. I am sixteen years old. My name is Aurora Harris and I live in Fayetteville, Arkansas, where my father is the chairman of the Department of English at the university and my mother is a housewife who used to be a sculptor until my sister was born, when she gave it up and joined the middle class. I don't know if you have ever been around an artist who had to give it up for their family but I'll tell you, the family is the one who suffers. It's like my mother is some sort of cripple with a vital organ missing. Well, in France she had a studio behind the farmhouse we were renting and she seemed happier there. Marble had been delivered and she spent the first two weeks touching it and looking at it and having a pair of young men from the village turn it over and stand it on end and we didn't see much of her. I guess my sister, Jocelyn, did. Jocelyn is her middle name and she adopted it for our trip to France. She is the most rotten spoiled child who ever lived and can barely read so don't even ask about her.

With Mother out of the way and Daddy happy to sit in a hammock and read all day, I had France pretty much to myself from the word go. The first thing I did was fix up my room into an office and set up my computer so I could write poems and then I started going off on these long walks to explore the place. Montreuil is this beautiful hilltop town with lime-washed seventeenth-century houses that look like mirages in the morning sun. Roses grow in the oddest places, creeping around fences and bushes, running up the side of a building. I don't know. It smells so good and I was so glad to be away from Fayetteville, Arkansas, and the born-again Christian idiots I go to school with five days a week until I get to college. I could have gone to college this year but my parents wouldn't let me. They have dedicated their lives to making me a normal person, which is a losing battle since I am not one. I am a person who writes poems and does not believe in any form of God or gods and does not like to talk to fools. Imagine me in high school. Just imagine what that's doing to my spirit.

Moise was waiting at a bend in the road on the third day I went off walking by myself. Here's how he looked at seven in the morning. About five feet ten inches tall, very muscular, with long, light brown hair pulled back in a ponytail. Holding a mug of coffee and smoking a cigarette and leaning over to inspect a flower bed. He straightened up when he heard my footsteps and gave me this brilliant, unforgettable, perfect, flowering smile. He wasn't afraid of a thing in the world, that's what that smile said to me. He was ready for anything that happened, any event, any challenge, any girl coming down the road in a pair of khaki shorts and a white T-shirt that read "One Fish, Two Fish, Red Fish, Blue Fish." God, can you believe I was wearing that stupid T-shirt when I met him? You can believe I wasn't wearing it the next day.

He had on some sort of faded blue-and-white-checked shirt and a tie. I don't know what else.

All I said was hi or hello and then I walked on by, knowing right that minute that eating was over for me this summer. I was in love with him before he turned around and showed me his face. The psychotherapist I talk to when I get crazy says I was ripe to fall in love and there is nothing wrong or unusual with anything that happened next. He's for the abortion, I guess. He kept asking me what I wanted to do. What do you think I want to do? Do you think I want to be a pregnant junior in high school and ruin my life just because we quit using rubbers? No. The answer is definitely no and I am not going to change my mind. Doctor Masterson will be back on Friday. Friday afternoon I'm going in. It's over. It's done. It's decided.

Can you imagine how beautiful that baby might be? None of us are saying that but I know I'm not the only one who thought it. Jocelyn was in her room crying this morning. She can't take strife. She goes crazy if there's anything wrong in our lives. I don't know what she'll do when she grows up. She can't handle the bad parts. She can't even read a whole book because she has to skip the parts when anyone is sad or in trouble. I think it's sick the way my parents give in to these neuroses, but no one listens to me. This house has too many good minds and too many ideas. It's a wonder we don't kill each other. We are going to kill this fetus. That's done. That's for sure.

The second morning I was up at dawn and spent about an hour getting dressed to go for a walk. I decided to go totally American and put on black bike shorts and a white tank top. I let my hair just fly out behind me. It's pretty curly and has invited comparisons with Chelsea Clinton, whom I happen to know, by the way. Anyway, I didn't see any point in trying to look like I was French when I didn't even speak the language well enough to order breakfast.

I wore my dad's old watch and went on down the hill the same way I had gone the day before. I wasn't really expecting him to be there because I had forgotten that everyone likes excitement and the mysterious appearance of persons from another country. So he was standing by the flower beds in the same shirt and he was looking up the road as if he was waiting for me.

"Hello," I said. "Do you speak English?"

"A little bit," he answered and gave me another one of those indescribable smiles. The smile of someone who is so good-looking and sure of himself that he can just throw that sort of smile away on anyone who comes along. "Are you staying in the house on the cliff?"

"We rented it for the summer. My mom's father died and left us some money and we're spending it on France. We could never afford a villa like that. My father is an English professor. I'm sixteen. How old are you?" See, I had decided not to change my personality for this encounter. I always tell everything I know to anyone I meet. It's too much trouble to try to be quiet or mysterious. I'm never good at it. I don't even try. That's one thing the psychotherapist has taught me.

He laughed at all of that and put down his coffee cup and held out his hand to shake my hand. "I am Moise Vallery," he said. "I'm a student at the Sorbonne. But this summer I work at a resort hotel in Le Touquet. May I walk with you awhile? Which way are you going?"

So he walked to the village with me. He had on leather shoes and a shirt and tie and he strode along beside me and told me he was studying world literature and would like to meet my father.

Could I tell you how blue the skies were that morning? How green the fields and hills, how brilliant the clouds and flowers? Would you believe it if I told you I thought I had not been alive until that morning, that my whole life had been a preparation for this walk?

I told him about the poet in Fayetteville who had committed suicide because he was adopted and because his girlfriend talked his wife into divorcing him. I told him about the six-day wake we had at our house and how it was the day I got kissed for the first time and about how Dad hid all the poet's books for several years and finally last year I demanded to be able to read his poetry. I told him I adored Rilke. He agreed Rilke was the main man but he hadn't ever read the Stephen Mitchell translations and said he didn't want to if they had been made from a trot.

His main interest is in South American writers and magic realism. Can you see why I thought my life was lived to arrive at that moment? My father is an English professor. How else would I have been in a position to even talk to Moise?

He took me down a tree-shaded walk that leads along the ramparts of the town. A breeze stirred the leaves and made the shadows dance and my heart was dancing with them. This was it. What I had waited all my life to know. I don't know when we started holding hands. I guess when he told me about the people of Montreuil during the Second World War and how his relatives on the coast had helped save the stranded British and French sailors in a famous rescue. It was like they were with us as he talked, smiling down on the progeny of the Allies who had won the war.

I had made up my mind not to kiss him until I had seen him at least two more times but the decision was taken out of my hands. At nine o'clock by Dad's watch he said he had to go and catch a bus to Le Touquet or he would be late for work. He had left his car at his house and was riding a bus to work just so he could walk with me to town.

He walked me back to where I could see the road going

206

up the mountain to our houses and then he turned and kissed me on the mouth. In the sunlight, on the street, in the world no God made but that morning I would have believed in one. He kissed me the way lovers kiss and then he took my hands and said he would see me in the morning and would not go to work that day.

I said yes.

You have to know one thing about me. The poet who killed himself is not the only death I have suffered. My older brother died two years ago climbing on the bluffs above Beaver Lake. This is not something any of us can talk about. My mother spent the summer carving him in stone. That's what the marble was for. She made three almost-life-size sculptures in three months. They are all of Joe. There, I wrote his name.

Death is a reality to me. Not many sixteen-year-old girls in Fayetteville can say that. They didn't look down into a coffin and see a face they have seen every day of their lives. Joe was a master climber. My parents let him do it because they thought it was better than drugs. He was a student in the architecture school and worked at The Mountaineer on weekends and taught people how to rock climb in the studio on Dickson Street. Mother and Daddy don't think they did anything wrong by letting him climb. They think it was an accident. They *say* they think it was an accident. I don't know. I don't know when we'll get over this.

A month later my grandfather died in Kansas City and left Mom the money so we went to France and now I have this baby in my womb that would be born about on Joe's birthday, which is April 18, but it isn't going to be born because as soon as Doctor Masterson gets back we are going to stop it. I am a reasonable person. I cannot have a baby at this time. It would totally ruin my life and also my parents' and Jocelyn would probably love it so much it would be ruined. She has three cats already.

No, no, no, no, no. You see, I have a choice and the choice is no. If I could take it out and put it in a jar like in *Brave New World* and save it for ten years that might be okay, but the way it is, it would be my family and me taking care of it for the next twenty years when we aren't even sure how we are going to pay for college for Jocelyn and me. The money my mother inherited wasn't much. We spent half of it going to France.

This is like the four-day waiting period the born-agains want everyone to put up with. They want you to sit around and imagine the child you might have had if you agreed to give up your life for it. A child you didn't even want or plan or ask for. It just comes in like some parasite and makes its nest, which becomes a colony, which is more like a cancer than a blessing. So it would be cute. Who gives a damn?

The next day was Friday. I told my parents the night before I was going for a ten-mile walk and not to expect me back until afternoon (if I was gone when they got up). My father immediately got suspicious and offered to go with me but I threw a fit and said he didn't trust me and the usual bullshit and finally I won. Mother didn't want any trouble or for Jocelyn to hear any quarreling.

So I threw a bathing suit into a backpack and I was off at six-thirty and going down the hill to meet Moise.

Dad caught up with us about halfway to town. He was driving our rented Citroën and he stopped and walked over and I introduced Moise and we stood around talking about world literature. Dad shook Moise's hand and invited him to come to lunch at one. Moise said he'd be delighted and they stood there looking each other over and then Dad got back into the Citroën and drove away.

Erik Satie was what happened next. Moise took me to a restaurant owned by a friend of his father's. We had croissants and coffee and raspberries and fresh yogurt and Moise went behind the counter and put on a tape of Erik Satie played by a pianist they all knew and we ate croissants and drank coffee and listened to that music. He didn't even hold my hand. He just watched me eating and every now and then smiled at something I said or got very quiet when I told him about Joe. He didn't try to cheer me up or say he died doing what he wanted to do or at least he didn't have to get old or any of the things we had heard before. He knew I was talking about a life-changing experience from which my family was not going to recover although we would survive. We were surviving. I was always going to survive. I knew that about myself. I had seen myself survive two years of Fayetteville High School and now that I had met Moise I was thinking about getting into the Sorbonne and just going to school in Paris. There are French teachers at the university. I could start taking classes as soon as I got home.

"I would like to come to the United States and see where you live," Moise said. "Are the streets paved with dollar bills?" He laughed to let me know it was a joke but what I really knew was that we were in love. Capital L, o, v, e, like in books and songs. Like in fate and destiny and this is the real thing.

I didn't even bother to wonder if I would sleep with him. I'm not a virgin anyway. I mean I wasn't one. I had slept with two people. One at Governor's School. I slept with him twice. He was a brilliant guy from Little Rock. We didn't really fall in love but we keep writing to each other. The other person I slept with I just won't talk about. It was too stupid and my parents found out about it and haven't trusted me since. It didn't have anything to do with him anyway. It had to do with drinking beer and trying to be normal and popular.

So I wasn't thinking about if I would sleep with Moise. I was thinking how and when.

A vast pine forest surrounds Le Touquet Paris-Plage, which is the coastal town where Moise works. It was only planted about a hundred and fifty years ago. Inside the forest are beautiful villas. The air is so sweet, so clean and alive that you feel like you have been transported to some clearer, finer world.

It was in this forest that Moise took me for his bride. We said the marriage vows. I swear we did. Sitting in his Renault with the pines all around us we swore to be faithful and love each other until the end of time. I made up the words and wrote them down and we both said them. I don't think Moise had done it with many other girls either. He didn't know that much more about it than I did. Not what you hear about the French, is it? Or was he just pretending innocence to please me? That could be true. On the other hand it was me seducing him as much as him seducing me. The way I was thinking was it's either this gorgeous man or else it's going to be some basketball player in Fayetteville, Arkansas. Face it, I'm a healthy young woman with normal hormones racing through my blood. It was going to happen. I am not nun material, no matter how hard Alice Armene watches me. Alice Armene is my mother. I have been calling her Alice Armene since I was four years old. She doesn't think it's funny. My psychotherapist says it was my first successful rebellion. Anyway, she watches me like a hawk but it didn't do her any good in France. She was too busy mourning and making images of Joe out of Carrera marble to be on her usual guard, and besides she'd met Moise and she thought he was "lovely." Who knows? Maybe she wanted me to get laid.

"You didn't do a thing to prevent conception?" she kept asking me later. And all I could think of to say was, "Well, no." Just because I have a high IQ doesn't mean I have any common sense.

We said the vows and then we kissed once, very gently. Then we drove in complete silence to the guest house of a villa that belongs to Moise's uncle and we walked into the pristine still-ness of a room and lay down upon a bed and made love. Well, I won't regret it as long as I live but neither will I baby-sit a baby for the next twenty years to pay for it. Men are so lucky. They just walk away. We get pregnant. I know. I know. I should have had some birth control pills but how was I to get them? Think about it. It was not an option open to me.

We lay on the bed and looked up at the ceiling and out the windows at the pine trees and then Moise got up and opened all the French windows in the bedroom and we let the outside come in and join us. I will never smell a pine tree again in my life without thinking of that moment. So nature takes advantage of our needs and uses us to her purposes, but not me.

Doctor Masterson will be back Friday and I will go in and get this pregnancy ended, this possibility aborted. I have a life to live, a lot of things to do. I don't see me pushing a baby carriage like Etaline Silvers, whose daddy made her have her baby last year. She got pregnant on a one-night stand with a boy from Fort Smith and they made her have the baby and then he married her and beat her up and now he's out on probation and everyone's life is all screwed up. She lives a block from our house and the whole neighborhood was in on it. The women wanted her to get an abortion and the men thought she should have the baby. So her daddy won and everyone's screwed and the whole town knows the story so where does that leave the kid?

I am not weakening. I see no reason not to remember the day in the blue bedroom of the guest house in the forest and the smells and sights and love we had together. It was so very, very good and it's a good thing I have a scientific mind and am not, repeat, not slave material.

Moise is coming over here next summer. I will be seventeen by then and he'll be twenty. I have to write and tell him about this baby. If I don't tell him I can't write to him at all. I can't live with some lie. I have to get it out on the table and see if he hates me. But not yet. Not until it's over. Not until it's done.

September 18, 1996. I haven't written any more about the abortion incident because I had to process the information. It's the first cool day. It's six in the morning and in an hour and a half I'll get into my little Camaro Daddy bought me to make up for the trauma and I will drive down to Fayetteville High School and get to work fixing it so I can go to college. We are shooting for Vanderbilt or Princeton or maybe Tulane. My grandmother will pay for it but I think I'll get a scholarship. Anyway, that's where I am now. I could of course be sitting around waiting for a baby to be born. I could have given in to nature without a fight but that's not *my* nature. Two of my grandparents are descended from Highland Scots. We don't give up without a fight. Our family motto in Scotland was, loosely translated, nobody messes with us with impunity. This includes nature.

As for the fetus, I aborted it. I went to the doctor's office and was weighed and measured and lay down upon a table and we did it. I was pretty sore and sort of lightheaded for a few days. I couldn't believe it was over, that I'd been saved.

Dad bought me the Camaro the next day. Baby blue with off-white seat covers. It's a better car than Mother has. Well, her marble is being shipped home at severe cost so she can't complain. Alice Armene gets her share.

I had a few bad dreams. I dreamed the baby was holding my hand and trying to drag me into some sort of pit. I dreamed he was looking at me with this really mean face, like he could kill me. I am trying to figure out where that dream came from. I think it came from all the guilt and fear I felt when I was waiting to get the abortion. I mean, I was scared to death I was going to have to have that baby. Just petrified. I would have done anything to end that pregnancy. Taken any drug, stuck anything inside myself. If you haven't experienced this you can't understand what it's like.

Moise has not answered my letter. Dear Moise, it said. I was pregnant when I got home so I went down and had an abortion. Of course neither of us needs a child at this time in our lives. Et cetera. Just that ice cold. Do you think this is a trend? That I will go on being this self-protective to the exclusion of all other culturally dictated thoughts?

I'm working on this positive outlook. I live in the greatest country in the world in a time of great economic prosperity. I have a constant food supply and a heated and air-conditioned house. I can manipulate my parents if I need to and I'm on my way to get a great education at Vanderbilt or at least Tulane or Mississippi College for Women. I have medications for my skin if my skin breaks out. I have antibiotics for infections. I have a doctor who is brave enough to do abortions even though his office has been bombed and his life threatened.

I will turn each morning to the north and east and south and west and thank the universe for my species and my fortune. I am grateful for my life, and if I pray, it's to Athena, the goddess of reason.

Have a *Wonderful* Nice Walk

FROM THE breached files of Aurora Harris, age seventeen, born under the sign of Capricorn, destined for greatness or despair.

    Entry, Fayetteville, Arkansas. A typical nuclear family. July 6, 1997.

You won't believe what my little sister, Jocelyn, is doing. It is ninety-eight degrees in the shade and she is out on the street in front of our house painting a picture so that people who walk by will be cheered up by it. She has done this before and received so much praise and even a present left in the mailbox by a stranger that she has become like an insect that follows its habits no matter what. Last spring she made the first painting on the street. I should explain that we live on a road that goes around the top of a very small mountain and it is hardly ever traveled except for the cars of people who live here and people who drive up and park and go for walks in the early morning and late afternoon. One of the people who goes by at six every morning is a retired senator. Another is a famous painter. It is the painter who contributed the most to encouraging Jocelyn. A few days after Jocelyn's first painting appeared, a smaller painting of three flowers was on the sidewalk leading to our house. It was a perfect painting. Only the painter could have painted it. Beside the flowers it said, *Merci.*

That's all it takes to make Jocelyn believe the world is a wonderful place full of good people. The present that was left in the mailbox was a doll. I personally would not play with a doll a stranger left me but of course Jocelyn just added it to the dolls on her bed and hugged it every time she walked by.

Personally I am not too crazy about having a stupid sign painted on the street in front of my house but it's so hot this week I can't even bother to care. Have a *wonderful* nice walk it says in large letters with stars where the commas should be. Below that is a huge painting of a bug. I am not sure what it's supposed to be. It looks like a tick or a chigger but even Jocelyn isn't dumb enough to like them. It is more likely it is a ladybug since we had an epidemic of them in the spring. What happened was they were afraid the killer bees would come up here from Texas, so, without asking anyone's permission, the biology department at the university turned loose a lot of ladybug larvae. Ladybugs are supposed to eat killer bees, a wild assumption to begin with. Anyway, the ladybugs ate all the honey bees in the area, ruining a thriving Ozark business. Also, they proliferated past all expectations and our houses were filled with them all spring. In the mornings we would have to shovel them up around the doors and windows. I collected them on pieces of paper and carefully took them outside for the first week. The second and third weeks I just swept them up with a broom and threw them out the door. They aren't the beautiful, bright red ones you think of when you think of ladybugs. No, these are a darker, muddier-looking variety. We don't know if they are here to stay. We do not know if we are going to have our drapes and carpets covered with ladybugs every spring or if something will come along and start eating them. Next spring will tell that tale.

Meanwhile Jocelyn has painted one the size of a truck on the street in front of our house. At least it's only painted with colored chalk so it won't be there forever. However, it hasn't rained in two weeks and there isn't a cloud in the sky so if we have one of our famous midsummer droughts it will be there when Moise arrives from France. What will he think of that? Not to mention the general tackiness and waste of the United States? I don't care. He's coming to my home and he can take it or leave it.

I don't know if you remember, but Moise is the boy I met last summer in France and was impregnated by and then I had the abortion and he didn't write me back for six months after I wrote and told him I had killed his baby. When he did write to me he didn't mention it. I still haven't figured that out. Either he thinks it wasn't worth mentioning or else he just can't talk about it until we see each other. That abortion bothers me personally about as much as shoveling up those ladybugs. Sorry. I have a scientific mind.

July 28, 1997. Here's what got Moise about the United States. The fat people. The minute he got off the plane and walked through the airport he started noticing them. No, it might have been later when we took him to see the supermarket. Then he started complaining about the food. We ended up going to the farmer's market three times a week while he was here and letting him make soups. "I am starving to death in the midst of all these fat people," he kept saying. "Why are they so fat?"

"It's a class thing," my father explained. My father is trying to like Moise. He is working at it night and day. He is determined not to blame Moise for getting me pregnant since it is nature that is to blame, along with him taking us to France without putting me on the birth control patch before we left. He is determined not to blame other people for what happens in a finite and complicated world. That's one of the things he said to me when he got me in his office to talk before Moise arrived on the plane.

"The past is gone," he said to me. "We had a good time in France and you learned things I hope you won't forget. If you sleep with him while he's here I'll be deeply disappointed. You understand that, don't you?"

"It won't happen," I replied. "I'm not going to sleep with anyone, Dad. It wasn't the abortion that scared me. It was the AIDS test. That scared me to death, waiting for the results of that."

"I'm counting on you to display willpower." He sat up straight and looked me hard in the eye. "You have the strongest will of anyone I've ever known, except my mother. You are descended from a line of strong women. Your great-grandmother was married to the governor of Wisconsin. There were six Auroras before you. You are descended from women who lived into their nineties before antibiotics were found. No, don't turn away from me. I want you to know the genes you carry, the fortunate DNA. Don't throw it away on adolescent dreams. I want those grades to come up this year. I want you at Harvard or Tulane or the University of Chicago. Don't look away. This is the only talk we'll have all summer. Are you listening to me?"

"I'm going to pull them up. It's my main thing. Well, I'd better go help Mother. She's getting the room downstairs ready for him. He knows we aren't going to do anything. I wrote and told him twice. That's it. He's coming to see the United States. I'm not in love with him, Dad. Believe me on that."

I returned his look. I hate it when he starts all that genealogy stuff about our ancestors. But I can't help being a little interested in it. I mean, I really do have a strong will and I like to know my great-grandmothers had an education. I know what it means to be from generations of educated people. I appreciate it. I know how fortunate I am. He doesn't have to keep on telling me that. Also, I may be in denial about how much I want to go to a really great college like Harvard or Tulane. I know I have to pull up my grades, but you try taking social studies at Fayetteville High School and see if you can stay awake.

As soon as Moise got off the plane, I knew I didn't want to sleep with him again. He looked different in the United States. He looked a lot smaller. I've been hanging out with this guy who's the other editor of the literary magazine. He's six feet five inches tall and gangly and I've known him all my life. We went to first, second, third, and fourth grades together. Then he moved into the other district and I didn't see much of him until high school. His name's Ingersol Manning and he's deep into Mario Puzo and Michael Crichton. I can get him to read Rilke but his mind wanders. You see, Ingersol is not sad about anything although he should be. His mother died, about the worst thing that can happen to a human being. It is made better in Ingersol's case by the fact that his father is a saint and the closest thing to a mother that a father can learn to be. Well, that's another story.

His other family problem is a born-again grandmother who puts all this language on him about hell and damnation and Christ the Savior and really embarrassing stuff like that. She actually got some anti-abortion armbands and tried to make Ingersol wear one to school. He gave it to me for a joke because he knows about my abortion and agrees with me that reason rules and so what if you get rid of a six-week-old fetus.

You see, if I had loved myself I would have known I loved Ingersol from day one. In the first, second, and third grades I played with him every recess. But it took me two and a half years of high school to rediscover him. You know why? Because he is so much like me. Two wrongs make a right, I guess I was thinking like that. Why would I think that having an IQ of 140 is something wrong? Well, it's the tallest-poppy theory. The rest of them are always after us. They want us to be like them so they don't have to worry that we might be smarter than they are. All of this was explained to me by a psychiatrist I used to see. More about Ingersol and me as a couple later.

Ingersol went to the airport with me to pick up Moise and they hit it off right away. Of course, Ingersol can get along with anybody as long as they have a brain. We started playing chess every night Moise was here. My dad was on the chess team at Vanderbilt. He wouldn't play with us but he was coming in and watching. I guess that was the high point of his life as a father. Seeing his daughter with two young men who were sober and could play chess.

Even if I did get pregnant last summer by the short one and had to get an abortion. Sorry. I don't mean to harp on that.

"Basically," my father is continuing, "fat people are the lower, less-educated classes. They don't read well enough to be getting the information available about nutrition or else they were taught terrible eating habits and can't imagine breaking them. Whole families of people in the United States are fat. You will see them out to dinner together, propping each other up in their vices. Gluttony is a vice as it leads to ill health and mental problems, which leads to more gluttony, which leads to huge medical bills being picked up by the taxpayers. I resent having to pay for heart bypass operations for people who made themselves sick by eating. I resent taking care of alcoholics and won't leave my organs to science since I might be keeping alive an alcoholic who beats his wife."

Dad paused, waiting for a reaction, but Moise just leaned toward him with this intent expression on his face. The French are below the irony line, Dad told me in another context. He believes only southerners really understand irony. I usually take his opinions on such things. After all, he is the head of the Department of English. That stands for something, even in this pitiful little agrarian state.

"Mankind never stops thinking of ways to ruin his own life, foul his own nest, and yet we have built great buildings, painted, dreamed, made music, written books, tamed rivers," my father continued. "What do you think of our species, Moise? What's your take on the progress of Homo sapiens sapiens?"

Moise said he hadn't made up his mind yet about the species. "But your opinion," my father pressed. "Surely you think about it."

"I do not think about them as a whole," Moise answered. "I think of them in groups. Americans, English, Germans, the Spaniards, bicyclists, automobile manufacturers." He was still being very serious.

"That's good." My father sits back and gets this thinking, caring, intimidating look on his face that is probably the reason his students voted him the most challenging professor any of them had ever had. Also, it's the reason I will probably die too if he dies, which will definitely happen if he doesn't stop smoking. He has a deep sense of mortality and a fear of it but he won't even mention stopping smoking and his blood pressure is so high anyone else would already be dead. I guess someday I will understand how someone with his vices can lecture the world on not having them, not to mention keep me scared to death to do a thing I want to do. Well, except for last summer when I screwed Moise and got pregnant. See, I did what they told me not to do and what they told me would happen, happened. That's very powerful conditioning. I don't know if I'll ever recover. I may never be able to screw anyone again even after I get married and that will be okay because I already know I don't want any children. I will not grow up to be my mother no matter how much nature calls the shots. I will not have children. That is that. It's bad enough to have to baby-sit for a living.

But if I never get laid what will happen to all that libido? Well, so far I don't have any pimples and although you might say I am slightly chubby no one can say I am fat.

I wasn't even chubby while Moise was here. I followed him around and ate what he was eating. He eats these very small portions of food and he eats very slowly and he doesn't like to talk while he's doing it.

"I like to eat," Ingersol said. He was polishing off his second double cheeseburger. We were taking Moise out to McDonald's the week before he left to go back to France.

"But you are very tall," Moise said. "That's why you can eat such large meals and not be fat like all the people here." It was a bad day to be at McDonald's. It looked like every fat person in Fayetteville had decided to eat lunch together.

"Are they fat like this in other cities?" Moise continued. It was his favorite subject, especially since Ingersol had just beaten him at chess twice in a row.

"I haven't paid much attention." Ingersol was getting annoyed at Moise knocking the United States and harping on fat people.

I was getting tired of being in the middle of it. The summer was getting too long. So were the days.

"Let's go find out," I offered. "Let's go on a road trip. Moise needs to see more of the United States than just Washington County, Arkansas."

"Fantastic idea," Ingersol said. "We can take my car. I just had the oil changed. Where should we go?"

"I'll get the map." I ran out to the car and brought back a map of the south central United States. It only took a few minutes to choose a destination. New Orleans, of course. Where else would you take a Frenchman?

So the next thing you know Moise and Ingersol and I are going to New Orleans to visit my mother's aunt. She's this very wealthy lady who never had any children of her own. All she ever had was a husband who was a drunkard and one of the heirs to the Coca-Cola fortune. My mother visited there when she was a child and she had taken me several times when I was small. I could remember it but not very vividly. Mostly I remembered the beignets, which are these little fried doughnuts you get in the French Quarter.

"I don't know if I'll be a good guide," I said. "I wasn't old enough to drive when I was there and Aunt Betty is eighty-six years old. She won't be any help."

"I'll know what to do," Ingersol said. "My mother went

to Tulane. I've been down there with her. I know how to get around." He got this very Ingersol look about him, like he had given away more than he had meant to at that moment. To tell the truth, I know almost nothing about Ingersol's dead mother. This Tulane remark was one of the few autobiographical details he had ever given me. I looked at him with renewed respect for his ability to keep quiet about things that bother him.

You see, I have this theory about how we all live in two different worlds. The world of everyday consciousness, ruled by the cerebral cortex, which is the newest part of the brain, and the world of dreams and fears and secrets, which is the old part of the brain and the one that is really in control. It has to be. It's the part that smells and sees and reacts like a frightened, hairless animal, which is what we are. At night when we dream we sort out our fears and try to conquer them with images from the conscious world. The older and smarter and more in control we become, the more we can bring huge fields of data into play to control our dreams and fears. But the same old images keep cropping up. Water, water, everywhere. Because we were probably aquatic at some point in our evolution. Not to mention floating in the watery depths of the womb. We are like inlaid wood. The top all shiny and polished and perfected. Underneath, layers of wariness and trembling. Terror. And why wouldn't we be terrified, since we are definitely going to die?

My father says that is why we have children. To assuage our fears of death, but I have other plans for myself. I plan to feed my mind so much information and all the newest data from every science that I will overcome my fears of being mortal and just think, that's how it is and this is where I am and so what. Then I won't be afraid to face the darkness without bringing some more people in to face it.

I'm not sure why my parents agreed to let us drive to New Orleans but they did. I guess Mother was sick of having us around. All Dad did was give us some money and sit us down for the lecture. He had all of us in the room but it was Ingersol who was being addressed.

"You have to drive the speed limit. You have to promise not to drink. You have to protect her with your life." Ingersol looked him in the eye and promised. My father adores Ingersol. Ingersol was the first teenager ever allowed to drive me somewhere in a car.

So the deal was cut and the last week Moise was in the United States was spent driving six hundred miles from the central United States to the swamps of New Orleans. And being there. And coming back.

We left at dawn on a Monday. Ingersol arrived at our house at five-thirty and Moise and I threw our bags into the back of the old Nissan Pathfinder and Ingersol started driving. He had a thermos of coffee and some paper cups and a lunch his father had packed. He had a portable CD player and a box of CDs. He had a portable chess set. He was wearing the khaki shorts I helped him pick out at the Gap and one of the stupid baseball caps he still collects even though he is seventeen years old.

We drove up Highway 71, which is the most dangerous road in America. We drove across the new bypass that takes you down to Alma and points you east. We drove across the state of Arkansas and crossed the Mississippi River and drove through the cotton fields to Jackson, Mississippi, and down to Hattiesburg. We drove seventy-five most of the way and only stopped three times. Twice to go to the bathroom and once to get some coffee at a McDonald's in the Delta. We were on a road trip and a mission. I kept getting out the map and showing Moise where he was and he kept commenting on the size of everything and how much land there was.

We drove into New Orleans over the Bonnet Carré spillway and went straight to the French Quarter and walked around and had café au lait and beignets before we went to my aunt's. We had to kill some time so they wouldn't know how fast we had driven getting there.

It was eight o'clock at night when we drove down Saint Charles Avenue and turned onto Audubon Boulevard and came to a stop before my aunt's huge stone palace that looks more like a library than a house and is about as comfortable as one. She was standing on the porch with her cane and her nurse and a tall black man in a dark suit. "Where are we?" Ingersol laughed. "Is this a movie set?"

We went up the stairs and were greeted and questioned and told to call our mothers. Then we went inside and about three servants came out of different doors and took us up a flight of stairs to our rooms.

Then we had dinner with Aunt Betty. It was cold potato soup so good you could never forget it. Then some roast beef that was overdone and little fried potatoes and asparagus and carrots and flan and coffee for dessert. Aunt Betty was asleep most of the time so we talked to the servants and each other. Then she kissed us good night and was taken off to bed.

"Back to the French Quarter?" Ingersol asked.

"Why not?" I answered. "Let's go see what's happening."

*   *   *

Not much was happening down there. Mostly it looked like a lot of old people getting drunk and trying to act like they knew how to dance. Moise was really grossed out and Ingersol kept worrying about something happening to his car. In the end we just went back to the Café du Monde and had some more beignets and then walked up these concrete stairs to the top of the levee and watched barges going down the river. Then we went back to Aunt Betty's and went to bed and slept until ten the next morning.

We ate breakfast and talked to Aunt Betty and the black man, Al, who turned out to be a professor at some special school for gifted young musicians. He had been born in the house and had gone away when his mother died of sickle cell anemia. He doesn't have it, though. So when he came back to New Orleans to teach he went to pay a call on Aunt Betty and she asked him to live in the house and protect her. So they have this thing going that is sort of hard to understand. His mother was the maid but she was also this very close friend of Aunt Betty's because they both had a child die of pneumonia the same year. This was all a long time ago when people died suddenly of all sorts of things, especially down there with all those mosquitoes. It explains the cemeteries. The whole town of New Orleans is filled with these morbid cemeteries with the tombs on top instead of in the earth because when it floods the caskets would just get up and start floating and that grossed everybody out, not to mention being a health problem.

So Al invited us to go over to the musicians' high school with him and listen to the kids practice but we told him we had enough school in the winter and would just go on out and explore the town.

It is so hot in New Orleans in the summer that it takes a day or two to get adjusted to the heat and start moving. Like that morning. It was one o'clock before we even left the house and walked on down to Saint Charles Avenue to catch the streetcar and do some sightseeing.

We got on the streetcar in front of Tulane and rode on down to the Garden District. The live oak trees make a green canopy above the streetcar track and we were going by mansion after mansion and stopping on every corner to pick up passengers and let them off. Al had made us a map of how to get to the Lafayette Cemetery and the Garden District Book Shop.

The people getting on and off the streetcar were really good-looking people. Some were students from Tulane and some were housewives and some were black and some were white and one or two were oriental but they were all good-looking.

"Not as fat as in Fayetteville," Moise commented, and Ingersol gave me this look that said, Imagine, out of all this he still can't do anything but judge other people's bodies. It was at that moment, with the wind blowing his hair back from his face and his hand hanging out the window and his big blue eyes so sweet, that I realized Ingersol was the boy I loved. Even if I had known him since the first grade and there wasn't a single bit of mystery to stir the pot except not knowing how he felt about his mother being dead, it was Ingersol and no other. How could I have been so blind? We were the editors of the literary magazine, for Christ's sake. What does that tell you about who there is to talk to?

I got up from where I was sitting by Moise and went back to Ingersol and sat by him and put my hand on his knee.

"I love you, Ingersol," I said. "You are the best friend I ever had in my life."

I looked out the window of the streetcar and had this Zen moment, this total realization of where I was and what I was doing. How often does that happen? I actually knew how fortunate I was. I was on a streetcar in New Orleans, Louisiana, with two really good-looking boys. One a Frenchman and one who will probably be the governor of Arkansas or a senator or the next Bill Gates. Me, Aurora Harris, who was passed over in a cheerleader election so corrupt it puts nature to shame. Not natural selection, not the survival of the strongest or the fittest, but the election of the skinniest, the girls who suck up the most to the teachers and the ones who have been impoverishing their families the longest by taking dance and gymnastics classes. It was a system for which my parents were not prepared since they are intellectuals and had me studying Latin with old Mr. Sykes on the afternoons when I should have been in gymnastics classes if only I had known that was the secret to happiness at Donovan Junior High School. I used to hate my parents for not preparing me for cheerleader tryouts. Then I came to understand they didn't know what was coming. My little sister gets the classes. You can book that. She doesn't even want the kind of popularity being cheerleader assures but she is being hauled down to Kim Lee's dance studio three afternoons a week just in case she changes her mind.

I changed my mind that afternoon on the streetcar. Whatever chain of events, deep sadnesses, mistakes, or chance wonders had led me to be heading for the Lafayette Cemetery with my hand on Ingersol's knee and Moise in the seat in front was okay by me. I think I'm going to keep on being lucky now that it's started rolling. I think I'm in.

Ingersol started doing his head around like an Egyptian dancer, a sign he was getting nervous about my hand on his knee, so I slid it off and we started doing a riff on my dad's making us promise not to have a drink. We were going to keep our promise. We just thought it was funny that he drinks three martinis before supper every night, then has the gall to lecture us about alcohol.

"After we see the cemetery let's go back down to the French Quarter and get one last plate of those beignets," Ingersol said. "I woke up thinking about those things."

"Fine with me," I agreed. "I think I could live on them, to tell the truth." I didn't actually put my hand back on his knee but I moved it down his arm on its way to my jacket pocket.

Another thing about Ingersol you should know is that he is one of the few boys I have ever known who likes sugar as much as I do. He likes coffee Häagen-Dazs as much as anyone I have ever known. His paternal grandmother, not the born-again one but his father's mother who lives by the university, keeps coffee Häagen-Dazs in her freezer and anytime we go over there to clean her windows or rake up her maple leaves or any of the jobs I have helped him do when we want money for CDs, we finish up our work and then sit on the porch and eat all the ice cream in her freezer. She just sits in a swing and watches us eat it. She'd go down to the store and get some more if we'd let her. She worships Ingersol but she thinks she should teach him how to work before she gives him money so we clean a few windows or rake up half the leaves under a tree, then we eat her ice cream and get paid twenty or thirty dollars. Thinking it over I'm ashamed of how we never finish anything we start over there. The next time she wants us to work, I am going to do a better job.

I was looking out the window thinking about how much nicer I was going to start being to everyone in the world, starting with old Mrs. Manning, when Moise stood up and said, "This is it. Washington Avenue, that's where he said to get off."

We jumped off the streetcar and started across Saint Charles into the Garden District. Talk about mansions. This is like some sort of Disney World of mansions. But it's peaceful and it's beautiful and we walked along, Moise in front, Ingersol by me, crowding me off the sidewalk with his long arms but not meaning to, and then we crossed Prytania Street and there it was, the most ghoulish cemetery you could dream up in a million years, with graves stacked on graves in a wall. I mean that place is full of the skeletons of dead people. This was not my idea of excitement. I have enough problems with the idea of dying without going around acting like I think a lot of graves is a place to sightsee.

Moise loved it. It reminded him of France, he said, and we went on through the gates and began to walk around. Ingersol and I walked on alone back to the back of the cemetery because Moise was stopping and reading every inscription and even opened this little peephole to look inside and see a photograph of the dead person.

I started menstruating. Wouldn't you know it? Isn't that just the way things happen? I had felt this quirky little pain when we got off the streetcar and about the time we reached the back wall of the cemetery I felt my pants getting wet. I was wearing cut-off blue jeans. This was not something that could be stalled.

"I started menstruating," I said. I sat down on a tomb and looked up at Ingersol and knew this was a test of friendship and of love. "I'll be goddamned if I didn't just start."

"How do you know?" he asked, moving closer.

"How do I know? Because blood is getting on my underpants. I can feel it. Listen, you don't have a handkerchief or something, do you?"

"I think I do." He produced a clean folded white handkerchief out of his back pocket and handed it to me and I went behind a tomb and stuffed it in my underpants and then I walked back out.

"You are an angel," I said. "I'm lucky to get to live in a world with you. Okay, let's go over there to that restaurant across the street and see if they have a bathroom I can use. This handkerchief is great but it won't last all day."

"I'm sorry." He stood beside me in all his lanky wonderful tallness and kept his hands folded like he was at a funeral and watched me with those kind eyes. "Does it hurt?"

"No, it doesn't hurt. It is here to remind me that I am part of nature whether I like it or not. And I do not. Come on, that's a famous restaurant, I think. Maybe we'll just order something while we're there."

We collected Moise at a tomb and walked across the street and Ingersol found the maître d' and told him what had happened and a blond woman overheard it and took over and took the boys to a table and then led me to the ladies' room.

Which is how we got to have lunch at Commander's Palace, which is one of the best restaurants in the world. We had fried oysters and cream of asparagus soup and flounder amandine and Baked Alaska for dessert. We had coffee so strong I may never sleep again if I even think of it, and a French chef came out of the kitchen and greeted Moise and it turned out he was from Calais, which is practically Moise's backyard, and they talked about the tunnel under the English Channel and if they would ever want to ride on the train under the water.

The ladies' room at Commander's Palace is so beautiful and there were dispensers with free Tampax and everything I needed to get back to normal. I threw Ingersol's handkerchief away although I was tempted to keep it for a souvenir.

After lunch Moise begged to go back to the cemetery for a few minutes, so we went with him. He was writing down the names of people buried in the wall for something he wanted to write for his local paper when he got home. Ingersol and I wandered on back to the back again. We were both just stuffed with food and in a weird sort of mood. I lay down on top of a tomb and folded my hands like a mummy and then Ingersol lay down beside me and said we were the pharaoh and his wife waiting for a streak of light to whiz us up to heaven. Then I rolled over and hugged him. That is all this journal will have to say about that since my mother reads it anytime she wants to for which she will rot in hell or at least have to feel guilty every minute of her life. I will say this. It was very funny to feel the cold marble of our fate underneath my body and on top the soft moving breathing body of my best friend and maybe boyfriend if it comes to that. We didn't do a thing but hug each other and watch the leaves of the funny little flowered trees along the fence and the wall.

That's about it except for two more trips to the French Quarter, a tour of the Tulane campus and a trip with Al to see the New Orleans Museum of Art.

Then driving home with Moise asleep most of the way and Ingersol and me playing all our CDs until we were so sick of them we were ready to throw them away.

We got home on Sunday. On Tuesday Moise left to go back to France. I have never been so glad to see someone leave. As soon as I got him on the plane I went over to Ingersol's house to see if he wanted to play some chess.

"Let's lie down on my bed and pretend we're on a tomb in New Orleans," he said. "Just kidding."

"No, you're not," I answered. I got up on his bed and propped myself up on one arm and patted the pillow. "Get in. Let's neck or smooch or whatever stupid teenagers call the sexual drive and its manifestations." I was really glad I had on my new ribbed turtleneck and my paratrooper pants even if I was burning up in them. I was glad to be alive, to tell the truth.

"I like you more than any girl I've ever known." He was looking right at me. Not looming or hovering although he could at that height. He never gives you the feeling he is dangerous or too tall. He is just a presence and he lets himself be one. "If you want to you can keep my stupid high school fraternity pin at your house." He pulled it out of his pocket and handed it to me and I took it and stuck it in the pocket of my pants.

His hands were so warm on my back. Even through my shirt I could feel the warmth. Do you know that if a child isn't held by its mother right after it is born it will pay forever for the deprivation. In case my mother should be reading this journal which is marked PRIVATE, she might be feeling bad about how sick she was after I was born and I had to be in an incubator for three days being fed by machines and tubes. No wonder I like stereos and television sets. It's a wonder I could have gotten in all that trouble in France, much less be normal enough to have a boyfriend who happens to be the smartest kid in the entire Fayetteville school system.

If you think I'm going to be writing down anything private about Ingersol and me, you've got another think coming. Two people as shy as we are are lucky we can even think about putting our bodies within ten feet of a person of the opposite sex.

It is true that I am a very cold-blooded person about what's good for me. I know that going steady with Ingersol will solve a lot of problems for both of us. People at Fayetteville High School think there's something wrong with you if you don't have a steady boyfriend or girlfriend. It's their culture and what they believe. If I didn't have to go there I wouldn't have to pretend I don't think they are pitiful not to be able to conceive a larger world but I do go there. I have to go there for another year.

Everything I am thinking is divided like a coin with two sides. Half all sappy and feeling good and adoring passing for normal and the other half cold-blooded and knowing Ingersol is cold-blooded too and tired of people thinking he is weird because he is a genius. Being smart is good when you're very small or when you're grown but it's a minefield when you are in junior high or high school.

August 29, 1997. Update, Jocelyn. You should see what she painted on the street this morning. While I was sleeping, getting ready for the school year stretching out before me with

Ingersol's high school fraternity pin on the inside of my bra and about to be worn on the OUTSIDE any day now. Me, Aurora Harris, about to rejoin the middle class, not that Ingersol represents the middle class but he goes along with things, he likes to be happy, he likes to be liked, he is actually going to run for class president. I mean going steady with Ingersol is agreeing to be in on the deal and I guess I have to admit I got out of the deal because the deal wasn't being nice to me. I wasn't going to be part of any system that was putting me in second place. So here I am, in love with Ingersol. I'm getting more comfortable with it every day. Is this crazy or good? To be happy all the time and actually excited about school starting for a change?

She made this big curved sign that says, HAPPY FIRST WEEK OF SCHOOL. All around it were little symbols, lunch boxes, apples, rulers, a compass, a bar of music, and under that "School Days." I don't understand Jocelyn and I never will. She is completely happy just to be alive and have Mother and Daddy adore her every minute of her life. She will probably never leave home. She will live with my parents until they all die. Maybe she'll be a schoolteacher. She has the personality. I'm thinking of starting to like her. Even if the front of our house looks like some sort of garage sale for happiness. Ingersol adores her. He's crazy about her, to tell the truth, and wants to make a movie about her life. A documentary where we just follow her around and film all the crazy things she does like paint her room three colors of blue after a photograph she saw of this house in Sweden, or, if we could get up early enough one of the days when she goes out on the street and paints it with colored chalk.

The deal about abortion may not be as simple as I

thought it was. Mother and Daddy wanted to have me, they say, but they were "surprised" by Jocelyn. There's a philosophical argument that's been raging for hundreds of years about whether mind is a function of matter or the other way around. What if mind calls up matter as the Buddhist monks believe? Then if a life wanted to be manifest, it would override anyone's attempt to abort it, wouldn't it? Or is it all so unfinished that mind and matter slosh around in each other's workings and the balance is always shifting? Before the Big Bang there was perfection. Then it all split apart and it's still expanding. If I'd had that baby, where would Moise and I be? And I sure wouldn't have Ingersol. Just because he's a genius doesn't mean he would want to have a girlfriend with a baby. It would definitely hurt his chances to be class president at Fayetteville High School.

Well, that's the past and the past is a swamp where we wander at our peril.

Have a *wonderful* nice walk. Happy first week of school. Deeper in and farther out, as the mouse said when he jumped ship in *The Voyage of the Dawn Treader*, my and Ingersol's absolute favorite childhood book.

Witness to the Crucifixion

I WAS brushing my teeth when she started in again. "I want you to be in Paradise with me," she said, leaning her long blond hair so close to the sink it was hard not to get toothpaste on it. "I was praying for it when I woke up."

"Jocelyn," I screamed, foaming Crest going everywhere. "You are a little eleven-year-old Methodist in a small town in the Ozarks. You are not a television evangelist. Now get the hell out of this bathroom before I kill you." I turned and glowered at her. She is almost as tall as I am now. She is growing extremely fast for eleven. She has reached back into the gene pool and brought up some of Dad's old Scandinavian genes from when his ancestors lived in Wisconsin and fought the snow. Now we are in Fayetteville, Arkansas, fighting madness, low IQs, and Christians. Dad and I are fighting them. Mom and Jocelyn have joined up. They go to church about five times a week. Jocelyn is a Christian Scout and wears a blue vest with a flowered cross embroidered on the pocket and another on the back that she added just to be different.

"Don't you respect me?" she says. "If you curse me that means you don't respect me." This is one of the things they teach the scouts to say.

"No, I don't respect you. I don't even like you and if you don't get out of this bathroom I'm going to have to kill you. I'm giving you three. One, two . . ."

She moved back three paces and stood in the doorway looking sad and sadder. They teach her things to say but they don't teach her what to say *next* if the person she is working on doesn't respond with guilt or fear.

I pushed her out the door and shut it. I finished my teeth and started putting on my makeup. I had a meeting at eight o'clock with the other editors of the literary magazine. We were trying to find a way to pay for a field trip to SEFOR, a breeder reactor in Strickler, Arkansas, which is only twenty miles from the town where we live. A breeder reactor so hot a Geiger counter goes off as soon as you get within two hundred yards of the silo. It was built in the 1960s by a consortium of German and American utility companies to see how much uranium 235 and plutonium 239 they could squeeze into a building and not have it go critical, melt down, or, in other words, turn northwest Arkansas into Chernobyl. We were lucky. One melted down in Detroit, Michigan, first and after that the consortium cooled SEFOR down with liquid sodium, one of the most inflammable things in the world, talked the government into taking *most* of the uranium and plutonium up to Hanford, Washington, and then gave the reactor, the visitors' center for the reactor, and the six hundred acres of land around it to the University of Arkansas. The university took it. Can you believe that? And my dad teaches at the place.

*   *   *

"You didn't have to curse me," Jocelyn says when I sit down at the kitchen table to eat my scrambled eggs. For whose benefit, do you suppose?

"Aurora," my mother begins, getting her pitiful oh-how-can-this-happen-to-me-so-early-in-the-morning, why-is-my-life-this-way, where-did-I-go-wrong, why-am-I-here-in-this-terrible-family-when-I-meant-to-be-a-sculptor look on her face.

"I didn't curse her. I told her to get her goddamn hair out of the sink while I was brushing my teeth. It's okay with me if she wants to go to school with Crest on her ponytail but I bet old Jerry Hadler will want his friendship bracelet back if he sees it."

"Please don't turn this into an argument."

"Please tell her to stop pushing Jesus at me. She's out of control, Mother. You really ought to think of getting her some help."

"You're the one who killed your baby," Jocelyn said, so I got up and slapped her in the face with my napkin and went into my room and got my backpack and went out the side door and got into my car and drove off down Lighton Trail to school. I used to have a Camaro but it was wrecked when a truck ran into the side of it at the corner of Maple Street and University Avenue. Then my grandmother died and willed me her Toyota so I put the insurance money for the Camaro in my college fund and have been very happy driving Grandmother's baby blue car with leather seat covers. It's like having her around to get into her car every day. She adored me. She knew who I was. Sometimes I think she loved me more than anyone else ever will. The day before she died she got me in her bedroom and told me I was the only one in the family who had the genes. She didn't call it genes. She called it spunk. "I thought your daddy had it but then he married your mother and sank into stone," she said. "I love him. Don't get me wrong, but you're the one who has the strength to make something of yourself, Aurora. Thank God for you. I'm leaving you my car."

I never thought she'd die but she did. At eight o'clock the next morning, while putting on her makeup. She was living out in Cassandra Village where the rich people around here stash their parents while they wait to die. So, anyway, I don't want to talk about that. I want to talk about the goddamn abortion and get it off my mind.

I did not kill a baby. I aborted a six-week-old fetus that would have ruined my life. I'm not cut out to be a mother. Sixteen-year-old girls with high intelligence quotients have no business having babies they don't want. I guess I'm not as rabid about this as I used to be. All the goddamn anti-abortionists have planted doubts in my mind. They keep the balls in the air. They keep it on the table.

I stopped on my way to school to pick up my boyfriend (my new one, not the one who got me pregnant), Ingersol Manning the fourth, six feet five inches tall, completely sane in every way. What does he see in me? You aren't the first one to ask that question. He was walking to school because his Pathfinder is in the shop getting repaired. He worked all summer to make the money to have it fixed. Now it's taking two weeks and he's walking.

He climbed in the passenger side of the Toyota and wiggled around until there was room for his head. "What's going on?" he asked and handed me a strawberry toaster pastry.

"We have to do something about Jocelyn," I began. "She's

gone crazy down at the Methodist church. They've captured her, Ingersol. She's completely lost it over Jesus."

"It's the music," he answered. "Bach. She's an artist. The music gets them every time. It happened to me when I was thirteen. It was several months before I stopped having talks with the air."

"You were wonderful when you were thirteen."

"I was fat. I was shaped like a pear."

"I don't remember you fat."

"You wouldn't even play with me that year. One Saturday I came over and you wouldn't let me come in."

"No, I didn't."

"Yes, you did." He reached over and put his hand on top of mine to let me know he forgave me. He was right. There had been a couple of years when he was in the sixth and seventh grades when his jokes were too childish and disgusting for me. He had this friend, Charles Barton, who was on prednisone and would curse in strings of really gross, disgusting, bodily function words. Ingersol would egg him on to say them. Then he would die of laughter. I couldn't put up with that even if Charles Barton did have cancer. He lived, by the way. He is completely in remission and recovered so I don't have to feel guilty about thinking it was disgusting.

"We could get her to read Malthus or Darwin or Desmond Morris or Nietzsche. We could invite her over to my house and trick her into watching my new *Creation of the Universe* tape by Timothy Ferris." Ingersol was sticking to the subject, a great gift of his.

"Oh, yeah, as if she can read. This is all my mother's fault. She thinks the reason I'm not homecoming queen is because they quit going to church. She joined the church to get

Jocelyn a social life. Now Jocelyn's bought the program and from the way she's acting Mother's bought it too. So what am I supposed to do? Move out or fight?"

"First we think," he said. "Then we act. If it's social, I see why she's drawn to it. She's a social creature. She loves the world. All we can do is hope to plant some doubts in her mind."

We weren't getting any help from chance or luck. That very night our old brown Labrador retriever began to gasp for breath and fall down every other step. Dad put him in the back of the Explorer and took him to the vet and left him there. Jocelyn disappeared into her room. When I found her she was on her knees by her cedar chest, crying and praying. "What are you doing?" I asked.

"I'm asking Jesus to save Bill Bailey," she said through her tears. "I'm asking that he let him live until it's spring and he can run after the squirrels and bark at them. It's the wrong time for him to die, when it's cold outside and we couldn't even find a pretty place to bury him." She cried on and I didn't try to say anything to make her feel better. She was having a ball, kneeling on the floor like the virgin of the spring or Joan of Arc or someone. As if it was up to her to save a dog.

About twenty minutes later I went back in her room and let her have it. "If Bill Bailey lives it will be because an army of atheist scientists and biochemists have been going into their labs every day of their lives and believing in science instead of superstition and religion. It will be the techniques and drugs they developed that save his life, if it gets saved."

"And who made the scientists and biochemists?" she answered. "Who gave them the brains to find the drugs? God did. It's God's world and He made it all."

"So you like a God that would kill a poor old dog right at the beginning of winter? That's your hero?"

"You're the devil's advocate, Aurora. You're as evil as a black star." She ran from the room and found Mother and told her some blown-up version of what I'd said and I ended up having to go to Arsaga's coffee shop to get any studying done.

The next day Dad picked up Bill Bailey and brought him home. He had been pumped full of anticoagulants and antibiotics and put on a strict diet of low-fat dog food. He was going to live. Jocelyn gave thanks to God and asked Mother to donate her allowance for two weeks to the United Way.

"It's hopeless," I reported to Ingersol. "She has been programmed past all repair. 'And who made the scientists and biochemists?' she told me. 'God did.'"

"Maybe you should just ignore her," Ingersol suggested. "Just try not to notice her for a few years."

"That's easy for an only child to say. She's in my face with it. She prays over every bite of food. Three-paragraph prayers for cereal at breakfast."

"We must record this time in her life. Why didn't I think of that sooner!" The year before, we had won a home video award at the Walton Arts Center with a video we made of Jocelyn drawing one of her welcome signs on the street in front of the house. It was a life-size colored chalk picture of a maple tree in full autumn colors. Underneath the tree it said, *WELCOME TO THE FALL.*

Ingersol had interviewed her while I held the camera. He had gotten her to say some amazing things about why she painted the street and if it bothered her when the rain washed it off and how long it took her and things like that. She was so cute that year. I have to admit she really is a pretty little girl. "Why do you think you paint the street?" he asked her. It was the end of the video.

"Because it looks so pretty when it's done and people like it and it makes them feel better to see a painted tree." She stood up with the brown chalk stick in her hand and beamed into the camera, so sure of herself and of her world.

We had won second place but still it was a triumph. We had been wondering if we'd enter the contest again. Now here it was, right before our eyes, Jocelyn's conversion to the Methodist church.

"If we get it right," Ingersol said, "this could be the one we send to the competition at the Museum of Modern Art. They love stuff from the South. This will fit right in with their preconceived notions about what goes on out here. If she will let us interview her."

"If she will? She wants a podium more than she wants God. Besides, she loves you. She'll do anything for you."

"I love her," he answered. "I think she's the cutest little girl who ever lived. Oh, God, I hope she doesn't lose her faith before we get it on film."

"Don't worry. Jesus spared Bill Bailey due to her intercessions. This has months to run."

We waited until an afternoon when Mother was gone. Then Ingersol brought over the video camera and Jocelyn put on her Christian Scout uniform and sat on the piano bench and I filmed while Ingersol asked the questions. We got some good stuff but nothing noteworthy. I think she has become suspicious of our motives. Also, she kept making us run it back so she could see what she looked like on the monitor. We wanted her to wear the hat but she wouldn't because she said it squashed down her hair.

We wasted two hours and a lot of film. The next Saturday we tried again in Walker Park with her sitting in one of the swings. Still, nothing good enough for the Walton Arts Center contest, much less the Museum of Modern Art.

Then we had a stroke of luck. A girl in the scouts got the flu and the Monday-night meeting had to be moved to our house. It would have been Jocelyn's turn sooner or later anyway, but the way it turned out there was only a day's notice. All day Sunday she was in fury trying to get our house cleaned up enough for her new friends at the church to see. I called Ingersol as soon as it began and he came over and filmed the whole thing. He filmed her cleaning up the bathrooms with a towel tied around her head. He filmed her vacuuming the living room rug and behind the sofas.

He filmed her pushing poor old Bill Bailey out into the garage and yelling at him not to come in. He filmed her throwing her cats out the back door. He filmed her yelling at me to clean up my room. He filmed Mother coming in the door carrying sacks of groceries. He filmed the blueberry muffins being baked and Dad sweeping the sidewalks and the carport and trimming the hedges. *ALL IN THE NAME OF JESUS*, we called it. We got some great audio bits. We got the best one at five the next afternoon.

"Get out of the way," she yelled at me. "I've got to get this table set. Get your books out of here."

"Can't I do my homework first? It's only five o'clock."

"They're coming at seven. These are rich girls, Aurora. They live in rich houses. I have to get this place fixed up. And get rid of that dog. Every time I put him out he comes back in. I don't want that old sick dog lying around the living room."

"Could I help?" I volunteered, knowing Ingersol was getting every bit of it on tape and she was so stupid she had forgotten he was there.

"Put the bikes away. Go shut the garage so they won't have to look at Mother's old car. Then go get dressed. Put on some nice clothes for a change and some makeup. Please get dressed, Aurora. Don't embarrass me to death." She stood with her hands on her hips. Poor little Christian martyr, little social climber, little artist trying to make the world a more attractive place.

She was about to cry. Ingersol caught it all. Afterward both he and I helped her as much as we could and then we left while she got dressed and only came back and filmed the part of the meeting where they do the prayers and the pledge of allegiance. I have to admit they looked adorable all lined up in their uniforms and sashes with their hats on their heads.

Needless to say this video is going to make our reputations when it's edited and finished. I know I should feel guilty about taking advantage of Jocelyn and using her pitiful little life as material for our work, but I don't really have any choice in the matter. If she does these things in my presence, she had better watch out. I'm a creative person on my way to fulfill my destiny in the world. The Jocelyns of the world are here for me to plunder.

Besides, what do you think the chances are of her being at the Museum of Modern Art next year when they give out the prizes? Zero. My mother is a classicist. She doesn't even like modern art.

*   *   *

Let's say she was there, sitting in the audience watching herself on the big screen. Would she recognize her obsession and begin to doubt it? I doubt it. She'd be thinking about the opening scenes when she was sitting on the piano bench looking like a child movie star and reeling out the party line about love and service to the world. There is one thing I must admit, and Ingersol admits it too. Christianity is a force for good in the world in many ways. It is a civilizing force in the midst of chaos. Not everyone is able to look out over the chasm of space and time and say, that's it, that's how it is, maybe it's even beautiful. Some people have to have the Pope or the Methodist church. They can't all worship Freeman Dyson and Timothy Ferris like Ingersol and I do. We are studying like crazy. We can't wait to get to Princeton or Harvard or Stanford or wherever those guys are teaching. We are going to be happy just walking around a town where great minds live. Meanwhile, we are doing the best we can with Fayetteville. More later.

Aurora Harris

Ocean Springs

IT WAS November. The north wind had blown the water from the beaches, and the casinos across the bay rose up like bad memories to remind us of greed and craziness. Not that anyone in Ocean Springs needed to be reminded of craziness in the fall of nineteen ninety-seven. We had spent September and October fighting off a plan to build a waste treatment plant in the marshes beside the Pascagoula River. Don't even think about that. Think about good things. Think about the herons that nest along the shore. The sea gulls and rooks and crazy little terns that sing to us when we go walking in the morning, a song made of crackles and the beating of wings and hunger. Think about the wonder of flight and the improbable, yes, divine creation all around us and for God's sake don't think one rape wreaks a fall or defines a culture. Even if it was Miss Anastasia Provine. Even if it was the sweetest lady who ever lived.

Was the rapist black or white? She won't tell. I want to tell you something about this little town of five thousand souls down here on the Mississippi coast, across the sound from the casinos in Biloxi, where the French first landed three hundred years ago this winter, where they first set foot in what would later be called the Louisiana Purchase. In the first place it belies the cynics who think a southern town can't have good relations between black people and white people and all the shades of people in between, from albinos to darkest Africans. A long time ago the city fathers of Ocean Springs decided not to accept the government's offer of public housing. Because of that, the black people of Ocean Springs are the same black people who have always lived here. They are handsome and tall and very proud. The poet Al Young is from Ocean Springs, although he never comes back to visit. The mystical painter Walter Anderson lived here all his life and left his legacy everywhere. Everyone paints. Ten-dollar sets of watercolors fly off the shelves of the expensive toy store on Washington Avenue. Back to the rape.

Miss Anastasia lives in a white house set back from the beach. When she was young she was the president of Mississippi College for Women. After she retired she came home and moved into her mother's house and began to do good deeds. Good deeds she has done include tutoring bright children in Latin and French, overseeing the school lunch program for four years, including eating lunch at the public schools in town at least four times a week. Teaching children not to complain or put their elbows on the table. Walking everywhere she goes unless it's raining. Setting an example of superior behavior twenty-four hours a day and lending books to anyone who likes to read.

After he banged her head against the wall and forced her to undress, the rapist relented and fled her bedroom. Why did he do that? Because she began to chant a Buddhist chant she had learned in her youth from a devotee of the Dalai Lama. *Om, mani, padme, hum,* she chanted over and over and he lost his erection and fled the house. She put her clothes back on before she called the police, which is probably why the police dogs lost the trail at the railroad bridge.

Rape is a capital offense. You could be put to death for raping an eighty-year-old woman at nine o'clock on a Thursday night. She was in her bedroom trying to stay awake to watch *ER.* "I didn't know you watched *ER,*" I said when she told me that. "I would have come over and watched it with you."

"They have it on too late," she answered. "But I have to watch it. One of the writers went to MCW. I knew her mother. I'm fascinated by television. If I were younger I would write about it. No one since McLuhan has really tried to plumb the phenomenon of watching television. Of course we didn't question the printing press, did we? We just made and read the books."

"Are you all right?" I kept asking. "Is there anything we can do for you?"

"Come over on Sunday afternoon," she said. "We are going to plant daffodils on the front lawn." Her house is on a rise of land beside a small harbor. There is a wide front lawn with two live oak trees that shade the way to the beach. On Sunday afternoon the members of her Latin club were gathering to plant hundreds of flowers in honor of her escape from the madman. We have all decided he is mad. The police want to know why neither of her dogs went to her defense, but one of them is fourteen years old and the other one is blind. The police have also spread a rumor that her back door was unlocked and many who know her secretly believe it's true. The rumor has slowed down the affixing of dead bolt locks to every door in town. For several days after the rape locksmith trucks from Biloxi, Gulfport, Pass Christian, and Pascagoula were descending like a cloud of locusts adding dead bolts to doors that already had perfectly good locks on them. I had a vision that for years to come I would be noticing the double locks on bedroom doors and think of them as a communal art form, a monument to the night that madness entered the home of Miss Anastasia Provine and made us think we were not safe.

"Except we are safe," she insisted, when I told her that. We were on our knees digging holes for the daffodils. She had spread out a piece of canvas and we were kneeling on it, trying not to get the Mary Copelands mixed up with the King Alfreds. "We are safe because our ancestors have striven to create a civilization where the weak and strong serve each other. The young men who came out when I called were so wonderful. The young woman who took the phone call sits up all night to guard us while we sleep. The people at the hospital also. We must have an appreciation day for everyone who is awake all night and on duty. When the daffodils bloom I will take baskets of them to the people who came to my rescue." She sat back on her knees. How does an eighty-year-old woman kneel on the ground without pain? By walking seven miles a day, rain or shine, along the shore, her hair tied back with colored ribbons, her feet encased in the latest model Nike running shoes, her arms swinging, an example being set.

There is a long red mark along the side of her face and the white of her left eye is blood red because he tried to choke her and her arm is bandaged. Aside from that she seems just like herself. This worries me. I think she is in denial. I think we had better get someone to come and live in the house.

I dug down into the earth. I heaved a long sigh. I turned and looked her in the eye and was quiet. Miss Anastasia is not a lady to whom you give advice, even if you are the principal of Ocean Springs Middle School, which is my hard-won post.

"I was thinking I should come and give a lecture on preparedness to the young women in your school," she said. "Do you agree that should be done?"

"It would be marvelous. I can't think of anything that would be more helpful. Anytime you feel like doing it. Just let me know." I looked down across the lawn to the beach and the clear bright air above the water. The barrier islands that guard the coast were very clear in the distance, their tall pine trees like sentinels. It has only been a year since we fought off a plan to build a bridge out to the nearest island. The developers wanted to cut down the trees that keep the sand in place and put up a hotel and a casino. We are not the only town fighting for our life against insanity and corruption. We do not have petrochemical plants spewing toxins into the air like they do on the Louisiana coast. We have pollution of the spirit. The slot machine addicts wet the seats rather than leave their machines long enough to go to the bathroom. Forget I told you that. It was told to me by the parent of a student at my school. She was working in the all-night restaurant at the Grand. I got her a job at the school cafeteria so she can be home at night with her children. We do what we can.

"He told me he was going to kill me." Miss Anastasia got up from her kneeling position and pulled her tall body into its most commanding posture. I stood up beside her. The great live oak tree behind her was not more powerful or imposing, and I tried to imagine a madman encountering this vision. "And I said, 'No, it is not me you wish to kill. I am only a symbol of someone who has been cruel to you. Let me give you

253

money. Let me give you food and drink. Tell me what is troubling you.' So I got up from my chair and that is when he grabbed me and banged my head against the wall and began to choke me. Then he released me and told me to disrobe. I said, 'Oh, please, let me put on my robe and slippers. I get cold so easily. Surely it is not me you hate. I have done nothing to engender your hate. Please think this over before you go any further.' That is when he threw me down upon the bed and the dogs began to whimper and I saw the photograph of the Buddha Celine brought to me from San Francisco last year and I began the chant I used to console myself when my mother died. *Om, mani, padme, hum,* I began to chant and he raised up from the bed and fled the room. It was a miracle, Louise. I was saved by a miracle. By Celine going to San Francisco to meet with the Save the Oceans people and by their taking her to the museum to see the jade Buddha and by her kindness in wanting me to have a photograph of it and all the web of being in which we live." She looked off toward Deer Island, and I rededicated myself to fighting evil wherever I find it and especially when it only seems like simple ignorance, which is all a teacher does, which is what we are here for, our mission.

"He thought you were some sort of witch," I answered. "He thought it was voodoo. There you were, in that bedroom full of artifacts from the religions of the world, and he thought he had wandered into a voodoo den. Will they catch him, do you think?"

"He may harm another person first." She hung her head. "I will regret all my life that I stopped to put on my robe before I called the police. I was cold, Louise. When I was a child my mother would warm my clothes before she dressed me on winter mornings. Well, it's that memory I will focus on.

Not this evil I have told you. Bury the evil with the daffodils. Come, let us go and see about the others." We walked over to where the Episcopal bishop was planting a circle of Semper Avantis beside the driveway. The director of SCAN, the society for the prevention of cruelty to children, was beside him. It would impress you if you knew who was on that lawn planting flowers. When they bloom in the spring we will have obliterated the footsteps of the madman. We have taken back the ground beside the harbor in Ocean Springs.

He was caught by a series of events that are as bizarre as the crime itself, as strange as the chemistry that will turn the bulbs we buried into flowers, as miraculous as the flight of herons, as dark and troubling as the misplaced hope that causes a human being to urinate on himself or herself while playing a slot machine.

A young man Miss Anastasia helped get into Harvard University several years ago was home for Christmas and out walking on our beach at dawn. He noticed that the dog who prowls around the yacht club was tied to a post by the pier. This is not normal. For years that dog has stood by the driveway waiting to follow joggers down the beach. No one has ever seen him tied to the pier and besides the tide was coming in and the rope that held him wasn't long enough for him to reach the pier if he needed to go there. So this small, neat-bodied young man named Howard who used to play a trumpet in the marching band slowed his pace and went to investigate. There, beneath the yacht club in the hammock, was a dark-coated figure asleep beside an empty vodka bottle. The young man untied the dog, walked quietly back to the road, and pulled out his cellular phone and called the police.

They found a list of names and addresses on the man. My name was at the top of the list. I will be thinking of this for years to come. Is it because my photograph was in the newspaper several times this fall when we fought the waste treatment plant? He told the police he found the names in the newspaper and the addresses in the phone book. He said he did not know why he had written them down and put the paper in his pocket.

I still cannot tell you if he was black or white. Miss Anastasia is adamant about that. She says the only relevant information is whether he was wanted or loved. She says children who are not wanted or loved grow up to be mean. She says Planned Parenthood is the long view and the short view is wariness and locked doors.

She identified him at ten o'clock the morning after Howard called the police. She picked him out from photographs and in an old-fashioned lineup. Then she asked if she could be allowed to talk to him.

"You don't want to do that," the chief of police told her. "You might prejudice our case. Let us prosecute him first."

"What would you want to talk to him about?" I asked. I was there with her. I had driven her to the police station for her appointment.

"We might learn something that would be useful," she answered. "The work of the world is never done, Louise. How often have we talked of that?"

The bad thing about Miss Anastasia is that there is no arguing with her. How do you argue with someone who has decided to view her rape as a learning experience and her rapist as someone she should counsel? On the other hand I am not a yes person. I don't pretend to go along with a lot of left-wing hogwash and blame-the-victim thinking.

"I have to learn his history to put my mind at rest," she continued. "I have to know the series of events that led him to me."

"He had a list and I was on it. That's all I need to know. I want him in jail. The way the men are talking the safest place for him is jail."

"We must be privy to his records," she insisted. "Who do we know who can get that information for us?"

My niece's sister-in-law works at the police station. She copied the files that afternoon. Then my niece brought them to me and I took them over to Miss Anastasia's house and she opened a bottle of sherry and poured us each a glass and we read the files.

It was completely depressing. He was born in south Florida and is thirty-nine years old. There are four arrests for public drunkenness and two for possession of marijuana. He worked at one of the casinos as a bellboy for a while. Now we have him on our hands in the Ocean Springs jail.

"Why would he suddenly go from being a drunk to becoming a burglar and a rapist?" Miss Anastasia asked. "This doesn't make sense, Louise. I've been reading transcripts all my life. So have you. When does a person go from one modus operandi to another with no apparent cause? There's something wrong here."

"Gambling," I said. "He was working at a casino, then he was fired. He must have been gambling."

"Not necessarily. He could have been fired for drinking, but you have a point. Could a person become addicted to gambling on top of alcohol? If so, he could have wanted money to go back to the casino. I offered him money, however, and he still wanted me to disrobe." She drank her sherry. I poured us both another glass. "I need to understand what happened," she added.

"Well, you aren't going to ask him and that is that."

"I know someone who could. Isobel Madison is in New Orleans. She's a renowned psychoanalyst. If she would talk to him we might sort this out. Perhaps there's a treatment center where he could be sent for rehabilitation. I'll talk to Judge Arnold tomorrow and see what he says."

"And who will pay Isobel for driving to Ocean Springs to talk to a drunken rapist? She treats the richest people in New Orleans. She isn't going to come over here to do charity work."

"She would come if I asked her to." Miss Anastasia sat back in her wicker chair and drank her sherry. Her mind raced off to a world where a great psychiatrist would come to Ocean Springs and rehabilitate the poor lost creature who had banged her head against the wall and tried to rape and kill her. I stayed quiet. I drank my second glass of sherry and poured us both a third.

"Am I getting carried away?" she asked. "Yes, of course I am."

"My name was on that list. I don't want to put ugly dead bolt locks on every door in my house and wear a bracelet that calls nine-one-one and go up to Woolmarket and buy a German shepherd." The police had been trying to get Miss Anastasia to get another dog. They want to give her one of the black German shepherds the Hargrave family raises for them at Woolmarket.

"It might be better to get German shepherds than to have a man in Parchman Prison because I sent him there."

"That's it," I said. "You've gone too far. You are not doing anything to that man. He did this to himself and I'm not listening to any more soul-searching. I am going for a walk. Put down that sherry and come along with me. It will be sundown soon. Let's go and watch it happen."

She put the glass on top of the copied files and we got up and left the house and started down across the lawn. We were almost to the road when we remembered to go back and lock the front door. Then we set off again. Let me describe her walking to you. She has on Nike shoes, a long skirt with a silk petticoat underneath, a dark green sweater buttoned up the front, a wool cloche she bought in Belgium thirty years ago. It is a lighter green than the sweater and comes down over one ear. Her soft white hair sticks out around the edges of the hat. She strides along the path beside the beach. Her arms swing, the wind moves in to meet her, the skies open out before her, the waves move in along our gentle, sandy shore. She moves as if she knows where she is going and who she is. Progress is being made, her walking seems to say. Much has been accomplished. Much remains.

Of course I adore her so I read a lot into her slightest whim. Which is why I have to be on guard against being caught up in her academic, ultra-liberal slant on things. She ran a small college for privileged girls. I run an integrated, understaffed, underfunded middle school. I love my job, but it is much closer to reality than the manicured lawns of Mississippi College for Women.

"I will come and lecture to your young women this week, Louise," she was saying as we walked. "I'll tell them to lock their doors. I'm not sure my back door was locked. I have to admit that."

"If it hadn't been your house, it might have been mine," I answered. "I have a gun, you know, and I wouldn't have been afraid to use it. I might have shot him in the face."

"More reason to call Isobel and see if she can get him

into a rehabilitation program. You would have been sorry you shot him. You'd have to live with that forever."

"I would not be sorry. I'd be glad." We picked up the pace and walked around the beached sailboats by the Washington Avenue entrance to the sound and out onto a spit of land where dozens of sea gulls were resting on the wet sand. The tide was so low the beach went out halfway to Deer Island. A blue crane came in and made a landing. He turned and looked us over.

In the distance a fake pirate ship was being hauled from Mobile Bay to a new mooring at Biloxi, where it is slated to become the fifty-first casino on the coast. We watched its progress. We watched until the drawbridge opened and it passed through. Then we moved around the sea gulls and the heron and kept on walking.

She will call Isobel Madison and Isobel will come over, I decided. Then Judge Arnold and Isobel will pull strings and the wretched man will be sent to a rehabilitation program instead of prison. Then he will get out and come back to Ocean Springs and break into my house and my pair of black German shepherds will tear him limb from limb while I shoot him.

"I told you so," I practiced underneath my breath, but she heard me.

"What did you say?" she asked.

"I said I'm going up to Woolmarket on Saturday and look at those dogs. I want one whether you do or not."

"Don't be foolish, Louise," she answered. "Of course we aren't going up to Woolmarket and get some vicious dogs."

"I'm getting one," I answered. "I might get two."

Be careful what you say in jest or fear or anger. Two days later we were up in Woolmarket looking at the dogs. A young police officer had driven us there in a police car. There was a litter of five puppies the chief of police wanted us to see. They were three months old. The mother was a beauty. We petted the father and watched him go through his paces. He had been a Seeing Eye dog but his owner died and he had been retired to the breeding program. I thought he was the smartest dog I had ever seen and I told Miss Anastasia so. She was already holding a puppy in each arm.

Which is how three-fifths of a litter of black German shepherds bred to be working dogs are now living the life of leisure on the coast. Two are at her house and one is at mine. I named mine Cincinnatus after the Roman hero and she named hers Rafaela and George. She says it's pretentious to name dogs after historical figures and I say it's pretentious to name them the first thing that pops into your head.

Miss Anastasia's presentation to the young women at the middle school went well. It was a cold day and she wore the long dark green velvet cape lined with fur which she has had since 1946. She talked to the girls about being aware and protecting themselves and the sacred beauty of the human body and also its resilience and power to forget and heal.

She fielded questions, including one from an animal-rights activist about the cape. "I would not buy it now," she answered. "Neither do I see any need to throw it away."

"Have you forgiven this guy then?" a girl asked. "Or do you secretly want to hit him or do something bad to him?"

"I *want* you girls to work very hard at math and raise the overall math scores in Mississippi," she answered. "I *think* about the man who harmed me and try to figure out what society can do to lower the number of desperate people who live among us. Filling the world with jails is a primitive solution to our problems and doesn't seem to be solving them."

"That's enough questions for now," I broke in. "You are all going to be late for third-period classes. Miss Anastasia will be eating lunch with us in the cafeteria. You may talk to her there, later, if you wish."

The lovely girls of the Ocean Springs Middle School broke into applause. Miss Anastasia stood beside me while they filed out of the auditorium and into the hall.

"What if they really raised the math scores?" I asked. "What if they actually did that?"

"It could happen," she answered. "If the winter is long and it rains a lot and the parents turn off the television sets."

The wretch in the jail was set free. The police were forced to let him go for lack of evidence. Fingerprints in Miss Anastasia's bedroom did not match his fingerprints. Footprints did not match his shoes. There was nothing but her identification, and that is not enough for the law. The local newspaper put the story on the front page. *SUSPECTED RAPIST FREED, NO EVIDENCE*, the headline read. We all expected Miss Anastasia to be embarrassed by this but I think she was relieved. I was the one who got scared and made my daughter sleep at my house for two nights after they let him go. After all, this dog is not grown yet and I don't really want to use my gun.

In spring five hundred daffodils bloomed on the lawn of Miss Anastasia's house. Also, math scores on the standardized tests at the middle school went up seven points for the year, but, of course, we cannot prove Miss Anastasia did that.

PART III

ABSTRACT AND BRIEF
CHRONICLES OF
THE TIMES

Excitement at Drake Field

YES. My name is Phyllis McElroy and I am the one who captured the Greek fugitive at the Fayetteville airport. I'm not the one he threatened. He was threatening my fellow worker, Dale, but I'm the one who called the police. "Nine-one-one, there is a man at the American Airlines counter at the Fayetteville airport threatening us with a gun."

"What airport?" she asks.

"Drake Field," I answer. Can you believe that? The operator asked me what airport. This is a town of sixty thousand people, give or take the students and not counting all the new people moving here to escape real estate taxes.

Dale had come in about five that morning to work the early flights and was in a bad mood anyway. I'd come in at seven. I've only been working the counter for four months. Talk about a crummy job. Listen, this Greek fugitive is not the first person to threaten us. Mostly they threaten us with writing the management and so forth when we let them check in and then the planes don't take off due to weather. It is a

265

crummy way to treat customers, but what can I do? I'm going to be a photographer or a dancer if I ever get out of school and pay off my school loans and get a house and a life. For now, the check-in counter at American Airlines.

So Dale is just standing there, checking people in as fast as he can when anybody with a brain could look out the windows and see that the ceiling is too low for these little planes to take off. Saab Turbo Props, that's what American Eagle flies out of Fayetteville. Northwest and Delta and TWA have counters too. Listen, this is a very busy airport for a college town of sixty thousand people. The world offices of Wal-Mart are twenty miles away at Bentonville and this is where the salesmen land. There are a thousand of them a week, all dressed in black and slick-looking clothes, with their shoes shined, carrying heavy briefcases and looking worn. The Waltons and their cronies are building a new airport twenty miles from here, thank God. Who needs airplanes full of salesmen flying over their houses at night? We'll be glad to get rid of them and hopefully I won't need this crazy job by then.

Back to this fugitive. He was here as an interpreter for a Russian poultry buyer. The poultry buyer was trying to buy chickens from Tyson Foods, our other big industry. The fugitive was mixed up in the Iran-Contra scandal and was convicted ten years ago of trying to smuggle missiles out of the United States. Then they let him out of prison while an appeal was going through and he disappeared. Can you believe it? I called the police and now he's been sent to Atlanta with federal marshals. This poor buyer guy from Russia didn't know what to think. The police came running into the waiting room and grabbed up his interpreter and took him along for questioning. I mean, this guy had lived in Communist Russia and he was at least sixty years old. I suppose he thought his number was up. I'm the one who went over and told the police the buyer hadn't done anything. It was only the Greek guy who threatened us.

There was an archaeologist from the university in the airport who spoke a little Russian. He came over and tried to calm down the Russian and then they called the Tyson corporate headquarters and they sent someone out to rescue him and get him on his flight to Russia. He missed the one he was scheduled on but they got him on one later in the day. I mean, the Russian wasn't in on it. He was just in town to calm the waters about a Russian poultry deal that had gone sour. The Tyson folks are having a hard time with their foreign sales because in many countries the refrigeration isn't dependable enough for storing chickens.

One of the policemen is a guy who's on my boyfriend's basketball team. Everyone in Fayetteville plays basketball or watches it. It's how we make it through the winters, and this winter has been especially bad. These are the Ozark mountains and you put snow and hills together and you've got some people in a bad mood. Plus, last week it was so cold again, right at the beginning of March, when there should have been some relief.

Plus, I think my boyfriend's running around on me with my best friend. I'm not sure and I can't prove it but he takes her out when I have to work at night. There ought to be someone you can trust but there's probably not, except your family and that's another can of worms. You can trust them to suck off of you when you are healthy and making money. You can trust them to think you're always supposed to lend them your car.

If he's running around with her, what am I supposed to do? Kill them or kill myself or be surprised? Listen, I took this drama course last year and every play we read was about something that happens every day in Fayetteville. So what else is new? When I had to write a paper for it, that was my theme.

In other words, if this is going steady, I'm a woodpecker. One of the cops that came out to the airport, his name is Hadley Townsend, puts his arm around my waist and asks me if I'm coming to the basketball game that night at the youth center.

"I guess so," I answer.

"How are you and Dan getting along?" he says. "If you ever break up with him, you know who to call. You sure do look great in that uniform. I like that little skirt."

"Are you here to collect this fugitive, or not?" I answered, or something like that. Of course, I didn't know he was a fugitive yet. To tell the truth, he looked like a drug runner to me. All haggard and mean and half crazy. We get all kinds here at the counter.

"I hope you come," Hadley said and gave me another squeeze.

Well, it was Friday so as soon as I got off work I went home and did my Computer II homework and then got all dolled up and went down to the youth center to watch the guys play ball. There was a new moon in the sky and a pretty little planet right above it. Venus, I bet it was. I had astronomy last semester and I made an A in it. Venus will be lucky for me, I decided. I don't care if I have two guys showing off for me at a basketball game. Let's see if Dan, my boyfriend, picks up on me and Hadley making a connection. He deserves it, the bastard, not to mention I will probably have my name and maybe my photograph in the morning paper.

By the time I got to the youth center, the story of the capture of the fugitive had been on the five o'clock and the six o'clock news. My boyfriend, Dan, was jealous. Nothing like that ever happens to him. He's in drywall construction. All he's doing all day is fighting his allergies and lifting things. When his back goes out that will be the end and he knows it. He's only twenty-five. "Stop drinking beer and go back to school," I tell him when he bitches.

Anyway, he was a really good athlete in high school and he can shoot and he was really hot Friday night. We beat the McElroy Bank about sixty-two to twelve. I'm a McElroy but not the ones that used to own the bank. The Waltons own it now like they do half the stuff in town. We never did own it so it's nothing to me. My dad was a carpenter until he drank himself to death.

Back to Dan and me and Sergeant Hadley Townsend trying to show off for me. After the game we all went down to George's to hear the Cate Brothers play.

"So what happened?" everyone is asking me. "He really had a gun?"

"No, he didn't have a gun. I just thought he had a gun. He told Dale he was going to kill him if the plane didn't take off, so I called nine-one-one."

"We got there in six and a half minutes," Hadley puts in. "I was way out by the university when I got the call. We had two squad cars there in less than seven minutes."

"I saw the cars going there," a girl kept saying. "I was on my way to the beauty parlor when I saw the police cars with their sirens on."

"So are you going home with me or not?" Dan whispered in my ear and I said yes, and the rest is secret. I will say this: If it takes a fugitive showing up in town to make Dan Fairly get that interested in me, I'd like to have one come by every day.

About two in the morning he asked me to marry him. I told him I'd think about it.

"I'll think about it," I said. "If I decide I want some kids, I will."

"I want them," he said. "I want us to have a baby."

"You always think that when we're making love," I answered. "But you don't know how much it costs to keep them. People with kids don't have a thing but kids. They get trapped by them. I've seen it all around me. I don't know if I want to be in that trap. I don't even know if I want to stay in Fayetteville."

I don't know why I was so philosophical when I had just had a proposal of marriage from the best-looking guy I had ever dated. As I say, it's been a long winter and I've been reading too many books.

Maybe it was because Hadley had put his arm around my waist and told me to call him. Maybe it was because I read this book about how men have only one purpose and that is to have as many children as they can by a lot of women and get their DNA passed down. According to this book, the only reason they even try to be faithful to us is so they can protect the children.

Maybe we are only on the earth to breed. That might be it. But I'm only twenty-two. I don't have to believe that yet. I don't have to marry the first guy who asks me and stick my feet in the concrete and watch it harden. I want to try out for a dance class next semester. I want to set up a studio for my photography and make something happen. I want to get on one of the Saab Turbo Props and go somewhere.

"We'll have three or four boys and maybe a girl," Dan was saying as he went to sleep. "Hell, I'll have a basketball team. I'll build them a full-size court in the backyard. It's easy to do. All you have to do is pour concrete."

"Go to sleep," I told him. "I haven't even said I'll marry you yet." And I might not.

A Lady with Pearls

WE WERE on our way to the Vermeer exhibition when I realized I didn't love Duval anymore. We were on the plane, high
up above the state of Mississippi, when I knew our love was
through. All those years, children, friends, houses, all gone
down the drain. He was a boring, depressed man and I was
still young at heart and happy to be here, on the planet earth,
in the year of our Lord nineteen hundred and ninety-six.

"What do you have to be unhappy about?" I told him.
"Here we are, on our way to see an exhibition that thousands
of people worked for years to create. On our way to look into
the heart of genius. We have a Carey limousine coming to
meet us at the airport. The snow has melted. You are a rich
man in reasonably good health. If you don't know what you
are about to see, that's okay with me. When you see the paintings you will know. I wish I hadn't brought you with me. You
are ruining my dream come true." I sat back in the seat. We
were on our way to see twenty-six of the thirty-one extant
paintings of one of my favorite painters. I had to appreciate

that. Even if I did have this depressed sixty-two-year-old man by my side.

"I think we are going to lose Allen," he said. "He's lost, Callilly. We have to admit he's lost."

"He is not lost. He's living on a sailboat in the Virgin Islands. He has an adventure every day. He toils not. Neither does he spin. How can you feel sorry for him? He doesn't have children. Why should he care?"

"He's thirty five years old. It's too late now. He'll never have a home. Never marry. It breaks my heart. I'm sorry I can't get excited about your paintings but I can't think of anything but Allen."

Our son, Allen, had showed up the day before. We live in Pass Christian, on the beach, in a house that was Duval's summer home when he was a child. At one time his family owned two newspapers and half the land in the Delta. Now the fortune has dwindled to a small pile of money in the bank. Duval's sister drank up a lot of it. His brother gambled away the rest. Then they died. There is nothing left of the family but us. Duval is a good and sober man. He is a lay reader in the Episcopal church and he talks to stockbrokers on the phone and does good deeds.

"Okay," I said. "Our kids didn't turn out well. It's not our fault. We are still on our way to see the Vermeer exhibition in Washington, D.C., even if Allen is staying in our house and will probably have a party and ruin the carpets while we're gone. I told you not to let him have the house but you did it anyway. Brighten up. Are you hungry? You didn't eat a bite this morning."

"Sally lives in an apartment with a cat. Allen lives on a boat. No one achieves a thing. I can't take it anymore, Callilly. What are we doing on this airplane?"

"Okay. That's it." I got up and went to the back of the airplane and sat alone near the bored stewardesses. I got out a book I was trying to read. *The Best Poems of 1994.* It was bleak. There were elegies, laments, sadness. I think I'll go to Mexico, I decided. I'll go feed the children on the streets.

I put down the book and took a magazine from a rack beside the stewardesses' station. It was *Mademoiselle*, the January issue. *Are You Having Orgasms?* the cover asked. No, I answered. I guess I forgot about that. I turned to the article. I read it. I got up and went back to my seat by Duval and sat down beside him and put my hand on his dick. "What are you doing, Callilly?" he asked. "What's this about?"

On the limousine ride into town I stroked his arm and leg. This is my life and I'm taking charge of it, I decided. As soon as we got to the Four Seasons Hotel, I took off my blouse and brassiere and followed Duval around until I got him into the bed. It was four in the afternoon. We made love like there was no tomorrow. We made love like we hadn't made love in months, maybe years. It was nasty and bad and fabulously fulfilling. Afterward, we fell asleep. We ordered dinner in our room. We drank wine and ate filet mignon and had dessert. Then we watched a movie on television and then we fooled around some more and then we went back to sleep.

"We are already under the spell of Jan Vermeer," I told him that night. "He had ten children and died young. Tomorrow we are going to view the record he left behind. I'm already starting to want to paint. As soon as we get home I'm going to paint."

The skies are very beautiful over the beaches of the Mississippi Sound, which runs into the Gulf of Mexico. Every

moment they change. All day long the sky and sea make paintings of such intensity and wonder a mortal human cannot
hope to capture a millionth of that beauty. That *should* free us
to paint but it has always made me afraid and shy. After this, I
won't be afraid, I decided. What do I have to lose, at age sixty-
two?

When we woke in the morning Duval called Allen to see if
he had destroyed our house yet. "Don't call him," I warned.
"Don't spoil this happiness. Get back in bed. Let me make
love to you again."

He called him anyway. It was eight in the morning in
Pass Christian and Allen was up and dressed and on his way
out to try to find a small house to buy. "I want a place to come
to so I won't always have to stay with you," he told Duval. "I'll
fix it up and rent it when I'm not here."

"How will you pay for it?" Allen asked.

"I have some money. I've been working in the islands.
You never listen when I tell you that."

"Don't start thinking Allen is going to be all right," I told
him at breakfast. "One sober morning does not a break-
through make."

"I can hope," he answered. "Without hope, we're really
lost."

The paintings were divine, that's all there is to that. *The Geographer* is the image that killed Duval. He couldn't stop looking at
it. "These paintings prove how depressed women were in the
past," I told him. "Of all the portraits, only the geographer
looks really happy, really engaged. Of course the women look
satisfied, with their satin dresses and their maids and their
pearls. But only the geographer looks like he's in charge of

what he's doing. Maybe we underestimate Allen. Maybe we just don't understand what he's doing. He's a geographer, Duval. He has sailed across the Atlantic Ocean. Why do we keep thinking he's a failure?"

"He doesn't have a home. He doesn't have a family. What will become of him when he's my age?"

"He has us. We'll probably never die. And he's buying a house. This very morning he's out looking for a house."

"He'll want me to co-sign the note."

"So what? The house we live in was given to us. Left to us in a will. Where would we be if we hadn't inherited money? Allen's okay. I've decided to believe he's okay."

"He's drinking. He'll never settle down as long as he drinks. No one in our family can drink. He will die like my sister and my father."

"Duval." I pulled him over to a corner of the gallery and reached under his coat and put my hand on his dick.

"Oh, God," he said. "Not that again."

We returned to the exhibition the next day. It was still terribly crowded but this time we knew what to do to make our way into the center of the circles around the paintings. I was concentrating on looking at the musical instruments and Duval was caught up in the idea of camera obscura. I think we both forgot about Allen until after lunch.

"Let's go home and see him and help him out," Duval said. "I've had enough of Washington, D.C. I want to go home and talk to my son."

"Nothing will come of it. You'll just end up getting mad. He'll stomp out like he always does."

"Maybe not. Maybe I'll sit down with him and get him

to show me on the map where he's sailed. Hell, maybe I'll go back to the islands with him for a week. We have to keep on trying, Callilly. Have to keep on believing something good will come of something that we did."

He hung his head. I could see the trip sliding away, all the good I had achieved going back to sadness.

"Okay," I said. "Let's go pack up. Let's go home and see about our child."

And so we did. It was, you might say, as T. S. Eliot did, referring to the journey of the Magi, satisfactory. Allen was getting better. He was growing up. He might live and thrive and flourish. We might get to have some pleasure from him and not end up going to his funeral. I guess that's hope. If it isn't, I guess I can always paint or take a walk.

Excitement in Audubon Park

(Some events that took place after the Frenchman almost broke up our friendship and before we took up tennis)

AFTER THE FRENCHMAN fell through, Abby and I decided to give up on men for a while and concentrate on our bodies. We bought some new running shoes and started meeting every morning at Exposition Boulevard to run in the park. All the professional runners were out that time of day. Just because we were giving up on men didn't mean we were going to stop flirting with them. I had this yellow silk scarf I kept tying around my waist or head or neck. It was my signature for running. White shorts and shirt and this yellow scarf tied in a different place every day.

A federal judge we admired who had been forced to slow his pace due to age was letting us run with him for the first two weeks. The editor of the newspaper was his usual running buddy and he got jealous when the judge let us come along. He called us "the housewives" behind our backs.

"Are the housewives coming today?" the judge said he'd

asked. "Are we going to have to listen to their nonsense? I tell you, Fred, you are going to have to choose between me and them."

It really made Abby mad when she heard he'd said that and we decided to pay him back by getting this very incredibly gorgeous swimmer we knew to start riding over on her bicycle and joining us. She was so beautiful that any man who saw her forgot everything else he knew as long as she was within sight. I mean, she was so beautiful it was dangerous. Her name was May Garth and she was a dancer with three children, who had moved to New Orleans to try to revive her career. No one can return to ballet when they are twenty-eight years old, but May Garth was giving it a try. Abby and I had met her at a dance class we were taking over on Maple Street just to give us something to do in the afternoons, when it was too hot to run or go shopping.

So Abby asked May Garth to come over to the park on her bicycle and see if the judge would choose the newspaper editor over us for running companions after that. I mean, she's not just another beautiful girl. She's like Candice Bergen or Ingrid Bergman and athletic. Not a runner though. She saves her feet for dancing.

The next afternoon at dance class we cornered May Garth and told her what we'd planned. She was at the bar, stretching her already perfect legs, extending. Her arms alone are enough to make any human being fall into an attitude of worship.

"This editor is the most stuck-up man running in the park," Abby was explaining. "He wants to keep the judge all to himself so he can bore him to death with world affairs at seven in the morning. I know that's early for you with the children, but we'll pay for a baby-sitter. Just one morning ought to do it."

"I live right on the park." She stretched farther down the bar. I pulled my stomach in. I extended my arms. My body turned into flight just from watching her. "So I could run over for a second on my bike, I suppose. My neighbor is right there and my oldest is ten years old."

"You couldn't have a ten-year-old child." I meant it.

"I was eighteen and in love. Well, I'm glad I have her. Even if it did interrupt my dancing."

"Then you'll come?"

"Tomorrow morning. Be watching for me." We giggled. We were transported. Something was going to happen in New Orleans. We weren't going to be bored to death forever. "I like judges and newspaper editors," May Garth added. "They have such interesting minds."

The next morning at seven o'clock I met Abby at Exposition Boulevard and we ran toward Magazine to meet the judge, who always ran around the other way from his home on Saint Charles Avenue. The editor was with him, looking serious and talking nonstop as they ran. I guess he was trying to get in as much world news as possible before we joined them. He hadn't been the editor of the paper for very long and was still feeling his way into New Orleans. He still believed he could turn the *Times-Picayune* into the *New York Times*, a common failing of journalists when they first come to the South.

"Hello," he said, and barely nodded. We slowed our pace and turned and began to run along beside the judge. "I don't care who is president," he was saying. "The issue is who is on the Supreme Court. Douglas can't last much longer. Neither can Black. There will be at least three appointments in the next four years. It's critical, Judge. You know that's the issue."

"You're looking mighty pretty this morning, Rhoda," the judge said. "I see you have the scarf around your head again."

"It keeps my hair out of my eyes."

"I saw your wife at Langenstein's yesterday," Abby put in. "She said she's so glad we're running with you. I just love her so much. The work she's doing at Loyola is exciting."

"We're having a panel at the paper next month with some people from Washington I want you to meet," the editor said loudly. "I'd give anything if you'd sit in on the panel. If you have time, of course."

I saw May Garth coming around the curve on the bike. She was wearing a bright pink shirt and little pale yellow shorts and pink socks and tennis shoes. Her long hair was pulled back in a ponytail. She drew near and we smiled and waved and kept on running.

Fortunately, the road around the park was originally designed for cars so there was plenty of room for the four of us running abreast and May Garth's bicycle beside us.

"This is our friend, May Garth," I panted. "She's coming to meet us. The judge, May Garth, and Mr. Porter. He's the new editor of the paper."

"I brought the radio in case you want to listen to some music while you run," she said. She had a small portable radio hooked onto the handlebars of the bike. A black station was playing the Neville Brothers. It was a delicious sweet sound and I watched as the editor almost fainted at what had happened to him. He had started out the day to have a long serious run in the park in the company of an illustrious federal judge and now he was surrounded by women and ponytails and music pouring out of a radio ruining the peace of the morning.

I guess it must have been about then that my scarf came off and drifted across the road onto a patch of fallen Spanish moss. I didn't notice it was gone. I was having too much fun watching the men admire May Garth. It was really a wonderful thing to watch the effect she had on men. It was like a light had gone on in the world; it made you believe in Helen of Troy. It didn't even make me jealous. No one can be jealous of perfection. It was enough just to be her friend and be glad that she existed.

She rode along beside us for fifteen minutes. "Where are you from, May Garth?" the judge asked. "Are you from New Orleans?"

"I'm from the Arkansas delta," she said. "I was raised in the little town of Magee."

"I know it well," he answered. "My wife's from Little Rock. I've driven through Magee a thousand times going to see her family."

"There's more to Magee than you see from the road." She giggled and gave him a dazzling smile. The editor had retreated into a world of his own. He was running along looking straight ahead. At the flower clock he bade us goodbye and turned to go back toward his house on Henry Clay, but I knew he was just going to cut on over to the streetcar tracks and finish his five miles alone.

"I have to be leaving too," May Garth told us. "My ten-year-old is watching the little ones but I never leave her for more than half an hour with them. I live a block from here," she told the judge. "You don't think it's bad to leave them for thirty minutes on Sunday morning when they're sound asleep, do you? My neighbor is on the lookout. I live in a duplex."

"It sounds all right to me." He returned her smile. All this time May Garth was pedaling and we were running at a nice pace. "But you'd better get on back. Bring them with you next time."

I collapsed at that. I could barely keep on running for wanting to die of laughter. Wait until the newspaper editor came out one morning and found out we'd added three children to the crew. I reached for Abby's arm. She was running along beside me. Only Abby could appreciate this moment.

So who do you think finds my scarf and to whom does he return it? I forgot to mention that the newspaper editor was young, even if he wasn't much fun. Also, he was in the process of getting a divorce. Abby and I didn't know about the divorce or we might have been more compassionate to begin with. After all, having a woman leave you right in the middle of a big career move can make a man seem gloomy, not to mention antisocial and morose.

Anyway, the newspaper editor, his name was Farrell Porter, had run along the trolley tracks to State Street, then doubled back into the park to finish his run alone. He had stopped at the corner of State and Camp to talk to an employee, then come back into the park just at the point where my scarf had fallen. He probably tried not to see it, but, of course, once he did he was too well raised not to pick it up and take responsibility for getting it back to me. One problem, he didn't remember it was mine. He thought it belonged to May Garth. Everything about her is so shiny I guess he just gave her credit for every bright color of the morning. Although I must add, I had been wearing the scarf for weeks. Surely he noticed it even if he was gloomy and depressed.

While Farrell was doubling back, May Garth had gone

home and collected her children and brought them out to play on the swings at the front of the park. She had the small one strapped to her back and the middle one on her lap. She was swinging in one swing while her ten-year-old was swinging opposite her in another. When their swings would meet at the bottom they would laugh and smile and the babies on her lap and on her back would laugh too.

This is the scene that Farrell met when he came running up and saw her. One of the most beautiful women in the world, in old clothes, with children all around her. A cross between a Madonna and Helen of Troy. Brought to him by the housewives, it's true, but blessed by an illustrious federal judge. The presiding justice of the Fifth Circuit Court of Appeals. Not that it would have mattered if he had met her in the middle of a hurricane or a war. Because Farrell Porter fell in love and began forgetting how to act.

He dragged the yellow scarf out of his pocket as if it were a time bomb. He held it out before him. "Is this your scarf?" he asked. "I found it by the side of the road, back that way."

"No," she said. "It belongs to Rhoda. Wait a minute, let me get rid of some babies." She stopped the swing and put the beautiful little girl she was holding on her feet by Farrell. She unhooked the backpack and took out the little boy and set him down beside the little girl. "Eloise and James," she said. "This is Mr. Porter. And this is my oldest daughter, Jeanne. Say hello, children."

"Hello," Eloise said. "Would you like to swing with us?"

"Take a child," May Garth said. "These are fabulous swings. The best ones I've ever found in a park." Of course, she was accustomed to men falling in love with her and knew how to behave and put them at their ease. She picked up James and handed him to Farrell. "Go on. Swing him. He likes to swing with people. He'll hold on."

Of course Farrell did it. Took the little boy on his lap and began to swing with him.

It was at exactly that moment that the judge and his wife, Elaine, came riding by on their new Schwinn bikes. The judge's weekend routine in good weather was to run four miles, then go back and get Elaine and ride bikes with her. Later, they had brunch on the terrace and then got in bed for a while. I'm not supposed to know the last part but Elaine confided in me during the judge's funeral out of her distress.

So the judge came riding up just in time to see the newspaper editor sitting in the swing surrounded by the riches we had shown him. "He looked like a fish out of water, floundering on a pier, but he was holding on and I didn't stop and rub it in." It was the next morning and the judge was running along beside us and telling us about it. "You notice he didn't come out this morning." The judge was as delighted as we were.

"He asked her out to dinner," Abby told him. "We've already heard that part."

"And is she going to go?"

"She said she might." We started giggling, running about a twelve-minute mile in the rising heat, with the fog lifting out of the low parts of the park and still hanging on in the lagoon. With the live oak trees listening to every word we said and the big world and all its trials and lawsuits waiting. The judge ran along beside us and giggled like a girl.

"Can't ever know what will happen," he decreed. "Did you girls run her in on purpose?"

"Housewives, my aunt Betsy," Abby muttered. "We'll show him housewives. How I hate that word! I'm not married to any house, well, I'm not." We picked up the pace. We ran faster. We went up to about a ten-minute mile. I wasn't going to say a word about the five-hundred-thousand-dollar mansion on State Street that Abby and her husband slave over and serve like worker ants. Who was I to talk with the three-hundred-thousand-dollar house over on Henry Clay, for which I hire servants and decorate and worry over twenty-four hours a day. Thank God for the park. At least we don't have to stay in those houses *all the time.*

Free Pull

AH, THE LIFE of the casino. Gambling tables filled with
handsome people. Ladies in long dresses. Gentlemen in tuxe-
dos. Sharp-eyed dealers dealing out the cards. Peons playing
the slot machines. Slots, as they are called in the trade. If you
believe that, I will sell you the bridge between Ocean Springs
and Biloxi, Mississippi, and you can join the rest of the citi-
zens of the United States in their pursuit of unearned riches.
It has never appealed to me, since I am a Scot where money is
concerned. I don't believe in luck. I don't believe in God and I
don't believe I am going to win the one-million-dollar jackpot
at the Isle of Capri Casino no matter how many times I take
my allergy-racked head into the upstairs room of the casino
and pull the handle on the Free Pull machine. Talk about a
metaphor. It sounds like a come-on from a hooker on Bour-
bon Street. Yes, it's me, Rhoda Katherine Manning, and I am
back at my typewriter after a long vacation spent trying to live
a normal life and act like a sixty-year-old woman who has
learned something from experience. I have learned one thing

this year. The reason I kept on wanting to have lovers when all I ever got for my trouble was bladder infections and large bills for cosmetics from Neiman-Marcus was the estrogen my gynecologist had been plying me with for seven years. Seven years. It sounds like a spell I was under. Since I stopped taking it I feel like a spell has been lifted. I can be friends with men now. Thank you. Wake up. Reality check.

So what was I doing at the Isle of Capri Casino in Biloxi, Mississippi, paying ninety dollars a day for a room with a view of the parking lot? I was trying to escape the ragweed pollen which was covering the Ozark mountains like a mushroom cloud. Once again I had jumped on an airplane carrying a bag filled with antihistamines and decongestants and nose sprays and I was running from the stuff that makes me sick. Only this time I had a plan. I was going to buy a second home. I was going to dip into my hard-earned savings and find a place on the ocean where I could walk and ride bikes and spend the last twenty years of my life doing something more interesting than keeping lists of the medicines I was taking.

Why doesn't the government of the United States eradicate ragweed? Where are my fellow sufferers? Why haven't we banded together to demand our rights?

Back to the Free Pull machine. I tried not to do it. For four days I managed to walk past the signs luring me into the casino. I snubbed the casino. I was only staying in the casino hotel because it was near the place where I was looking for a house to buy and because it was brand new and there wouldn't be dust mites in the carpet or the mattress or the drapes of the room where I was sleeping.

Every time I got my rented car out of the parking lot the attendant handed me a ticket giving me a Free Pull. Every time

I paid for breakfast in the dining room I got a ticket for a Free Pull. Every time I went down the escalator I ran into the Free Pull sign. $1,000,000 Cash, Free Pull Every Two Hours. Be a Winner. Get Your Isle of Capri Gold Card NOW.

I know there is no Free Pull. I am smarter than the ugly tourists getting off the buses from Georgia and Alabama and Texas and Tennessee. The denizens of the Isle of Capri are not the glamorous gambling creatures of the silver screen. They are overweight middle-aged men and women wearing sad and worried looks on their faces. Abandon hope, all ye who enter here, it should say on the doors for that is the expression these people wear. Like children with their hands caught in an empty cookie jar. Like robots programmed to self-destruct. Like people who want to go on and get something unpleasant over with.

For four days I walked past these people with a superior look on my face. I sneered at their money belts and Bermuda shorts and tacky T-shirts. I sneered at the plastic cups of quarters they clutched like beggars seeking alms. One morning at the pool I saw a young girl sitting in a chair holding hers like a baby. It contained two hundred dollars she had won the night before and she was trying to decide how much of it to keep and how much to stick back into the slot machines. "Does twenty percent sound right to you?" she asked me.

"Sounds perfect," I answered, too contemptuous to argue with her. "Go on down there and get it over with, why don't you."

"I will," she said. She put out her cigarette and marched bravely to the elevators.

I got out of the pool and got into the hot tub to think it over. I did not know death had undone so many, I decided, thinking of the refuse I had been watching get off the buses and come filing in the doors. Ugly couples, ugly women my own age, ugly old men with rounded shoulders, ugly white people, ugly black people, gamblers, smokers, idiots, filing into the casino to be took.

It is a test, I told myself. As long as I never pull the Free Pull machine, I am free. If I pull it, then I am programmed too and might as well go on and start reading my horoscope in the papers.

I thought I was safe. I had a Realtor coming every morning to show me condominiums on the beach. Later in the day I would swim forty laps and then walk around the little town of Ocean Springs waiting to see if I started sneezing. There might be new things here that I was allergic to but I was ready to take a chance. As long as I bought something with good resale value I could afford to lose a few thousand dollars trying to find a place to live that didn't make me sick every single spring and fall for the rest of my life.

The fifth day I found it. A cozy little white condominium on a gentle man-made beach. Fifteen hundred square feet of white wood floors and windows and light. Too small and insignificant to attract robbers. A place where I could wake up in the mornings and walk along the water's edge and dream and sing and breathe without Seldane.

One catch. It cost one hundred and fifty thousand dollars and the most I could afford was eighty. I could not have it because I could not afford it and that was that. "Too expensive," I told the Realtor. "Take me back to the hotel. I'm depressed."

"There is a smaller one by the bridge to Biloxi."

"No. This is what I want and I can't afford it. I'll try again tomorrow. I'm giving up for the day."

✵   ✵   ✵

She took me back to the hotel and I went up to my room and turned on the television set and watched the hurricane knock out the island of St. Martin in the Greater Antilles. I called room service and ordered a club sandwich and a chocolate milk shake. I decided I would appreciate the day I had in my hands. I decided I would not under any circumstances think I was poor or in need. I am a reasonably successful freelance writer with a home in a place that makes me sick and at least I could afford to leave for a week when it got really bad. It was okay not to be able to buy a one-hundred-and-fifty-thousand-dollar second home. It was fine to live in an imperfect world.

Most of the people in the world are either starving or being shot at. Most of the people who have ever lived on the earth never even got to be sixty, much less had all their teeth and enough sense not to gamble in casinos.

The tray came. The club sandwich was soggy and the milk shake was so-so but the steak fries were magnificent. I ate them with ketchup and began to feel better about the world. I ate the turkey and lettuce out of the club sandwich. I counted my blessings. I resolved to be happy whether I wanted to be or not. I moved the flower vase on the tray and picked up the Free Pull ticket and stuck it in the pocket of my blouse. Who was I fooling? I asked myself. I was dying to see the Free Pull machine and as soon as I drank the chocolate milk shake I was going down and give it a pull. Now was as good a time as any to descend into the maelstrom. Since when was I too good to gamble?

I dressed for action. I put on my faded star pants. I put on a red silk blouse. I put on lipstick and earrings. I wanted to look like a cheap tart and I tried my best to do it. I put water on my hair and slicked it down behind my ears.

I walked out of the room and down the stairs and into the casino and up to the desk and filled out a form with my real address and phone number on it and was issued my Isle of Capri gold card and walked back to the Free Pull machine and stood in line for my Free Pull. When that was over I went to the cashier and bought a hundred dollars' worth of quarters and sat down in front of a slot machine. I started playing. I put quarters in that machine as fast as I could feed it. I had only one objective. To get rid of those quarters as fast as I could get rid of them. To stuff them into the machine. I was annoyed when twice I got a few quarters back. I didn't want to be slowed down in my attempt to throw away a hundred dollars. I wanted to get it over with.

As soon as I was finished giving the hundred dollars to the machine I was planning on packing up and flying home. I had had it with the Mississippi Gulf Coast. I was through.

I tried a new tack. Stick the quarter in the machine and don't even look to see what happened. I was doing this when the noise began. Quarters started pouring out of the machine. They poured out and out and out and out and out. People stopped and came and watched me. I was transfixed. I had no idea what three jokers meant. "She won five thousand dollars," someone said. "She hit the Joker Pot."

"I don't know what this means," I said. "Is this going to change my life?"

"Would you like some help?" A uniformed man appeared at my side. He was beaming from ear to ear. A big jackpot this early in the evening cheers up everyone at a casino. Especially if the winner is a little old lady in star pants who looks like she should be behind the desk at a library.

"Do I have to pick them up?" I asked. I suppose I should

stop here and explain that the quarters are not real quarters anymore. They are slugs the size of quarters printed with the name of the casino. They stand for quarters in the same way that quarters stand for twenty-five cents. They are as real as quarters in every way and make more noise when they fall into the steel tray at the bottom of the slot machine.

"I'll help," the attendant said. "The tray won't hold them all." He produced a large black plastic bag and held it under the tray and began to scoop the quarters into the bag. He filled a plastic cup with some of them and handed it to me. I stepped back, holding the cup in one hand and my pocketbook in the other. The machine was still spewing out quarters. "Dante wrote this," I said out loud, hoping to meet a face that thought that was funny, but the faces around me had changed now. They had grown sadder, smaller. I reached into the cup and took out a handful of coins and handed them to people near me. "Play with these," I said. "These are lucky coins. They will bring you luck but only if you save your winnings." A few people took the coins I offered. They smiled and moved away. The others kept on watching.

When the machine finally stopped I followed the attendant to the cashier and watched as they counted out the coins. I had five thousand and ninety-one dollars when it was over. I gave the attendant five dollars for his help, stuffed the package of money into my expandable Donna Karan microfiber pocketbook, and walked outside into the fresh air. I sat down beside a pool decorated with pink dolphins and tried not to be giddy. I was a lucky woman, that was evident. Not in the slot machine business only but in the world in general. Lucky to live in the United States after the invention of penicillin, lucky that my children were alive, lucky to have an immune system so good that it hits the jackpot every time a flower blooms. Lucky and crazy and old. I could borrow money to buy the condo that I wanted. I could fix it up and rent it when I was gone. I could find a cheaper one and restore it. I could do anything I wanted to in the only world there is. I looked down at my watch. In twenty minutes I could go back in and have another Free Pull.

I threw a dime into the pool by the dolphin and made a wish for world peace. Then I went back into the hotel and called the Realtor and told her to come and save me.

Down at the Dollhouse

WHEN MRS. WOODS-LANDRY left the house that morning she had no idea she was going to die. She was eighty-nine years old and still driving and she intended to keep on driving. Not that anyone had said she should stop driving. She was eighty-nine years old in fine health and without a crooked bone, which is more than could be said for most of the patrons of the Dollhouse, in Woodland Hills Shopping Center. The Dollhouse had been fixing the hair and nails and toenails of the ladies of Jackson, Mississippi, for forty years and Joseph, the proprietor, was certainly not going to stop now just because it was forty years since he was the hot new hairdresser from the Delta and the darling of the Junior League. He had been fixing their hair for forty years and he was going to keep on fixing their hair no matter how old they became.

"I can't believe you drive all the way over to Woodland Hills by yourself," Mrs. Woods-Landry's daughter said to her when she came to visit. "I can't believe you get out on the highway."

"Well, I'm certainly not going to be taken." Mrs. Woods-Landry put on the face that she reserved for her daughter. There was no one else in the world for whom Mrs. Woods-Landry had to be mean. But her daughter, Donna, was mean and the only way to protect yourself in her presence was to be mean. "Why say such a mean thing, Donna? No one ever questions my driving to get my hair done."

"I just think you should get a driver if you're going to get out on the highway."

"I'm doing everything I can. When I can't go in anymore, Joseph will come to me. He has promised me on his honor. We share a birthday, as you might remember."

"We could get someone to drive you."

"No, I'll go under my own steam or not at all. I've seen too many people die in there."

"Someone died at the Dollhouse? My God, what a way to go."

"Donna! Not like that. I mean, come in more and more weakened and unable to walk. I don't want to be remembered like that."

That had been several weeks before. Mrs. Woods-Landry had a good sense of humor. After Donna left and went back to her home in Kansas, Mrs. Woods-Landry mused upon it. Would one die under the dryer? That would be ignominious. While getting a manicure? The hand would loosen, drop, the girl would gasp, the body would fall. What a mess that would be. Or would it be in Joseph's chair, with the hair all in place, every hair combed and styled until it was perfect?

On the last day, Mrs. Woods-Landry got into her Oldsmobile and backed carefully out of her driveway. Not that there were any children in the neighborhood anymore, but still, a dog or bird or squirrel might be there, not to mention trying to miss the mailbox.

She drove down the tree-lined street and out onto Meadowbrook and down and across it to the highway and up the ramp and drove carefully along at fifty miles an hour in the slow lane and turned off and went up a ramp and over and arrived at Woodland Hills with ten minutes to spare. She got out of the car and locked the door and walked past the drugstore and the antiques store and into the door of the Dollhouse. There were ladies in every chair. Ladies she had played bridge with, ladies she had known in altar guild, in the Junior League, ladies she had gone to All Saint's with when she was young, ladies she had known in the Delta, in Cleveland and Greenville and Clarksdale and Rosedale and Itta Bena. Ladies who had sat by her in classes at the University of Mississippi. There was not a lady in the Dollhouse who had ever had a bad word to say about Mrs. Woods-Landry or who could think of a bad thing to say about her under oath. She was a good person, in thought, word, and deed. For eighty-nine years she had walked the ground of the state of Mississippi and done no harm to a soul. She liked gay people and she liked women Episcopal ministers and she was not a racist and had never been. Her grandparents had been pioneers from the state of Pennsylvania and come to Mississippi after the Civil War and taught their children to love their fellowmen.

Mrs. Woods-Landry walked past the chairs and back to the hair-washing stands and a black girl washed her hair and received three dollars in return and then Joseph put her in his chair and began to do her hair.

"What do you hear from Donna?" he asked. He liked

Mrs. Woods-Landry's mean daughter, Donna, and thought she was funny.

"Not much. She gets into moods where she won't call us."

"Is she still mad at your husband from the last time she was here?"

"They have always argued. I can't remember a time when they weren't yelling at each other." Mrs. Woods-Landry laughed, then she started giggling and Joseph giggled too.

"I want to swoop this front up a little bit," he said. "I want this just a little higher over here."

"All right, as long as I can comb it out if I don't like it."

"She always combs it out," he announced to whoever was listening. "She thinks I don't know that."

"Darling girl." A lady got up from one of the dryers and walked over to Mrs. Woods-Landry's chair and took her hand. "It's Rebecca Garth from Rosedale. You remember me."

"My darling one." Mrs. Woods-Landry squeezed the hand that was in her own. "She was my little sister at Oxford, Joseph. This darling girl."

"I had to come up for some tests," Rebecca said. "I have them all tomorrow. Keep your fingers crossed."

Mrs. Woods-Landry crossed the fingers on both hands. A young girl came up behind them and was introduced. She was Rebecca's granddaughter. "I'm going to the drugstore to get Grandmother a sandwich," she said. "Please let me bring you one. She's so glad to see you."

"Of course," Mrs. Woods-Landry said. The girl smiled as if in answer to a prayer and later, when she returned from the drugstore with the sack, she came over to Mrs. Woods-Landry and whispered in her ear. "Grandmother is very sick. It's very bad. We are worried to death about her. So good of you to stay and eat with us. Come on back to the tables when you finish." Joseph stood with his comb poised. Mrs. Woods-Landry sat up very straight and let him finish her hair-do. It looked wonderful. It was the best comb-out she had had in months.

"Thank you, angel," she said to him and put ten dollars underneath the rollers. "Well, let's go and see about Rebecca." She went back to the manicure room where there was a long table the clients and hairdressers used when they ordered food in or got sandwiches from the drugstore. No one was seated except her old friend Rebecca and the granddaughter.

"I'm sure I'll pass all the tests with flying colors," Rebecca said and handed Mrs. Woods-Landry a lovely little toasted tuna fish sandwich cut into fourths. Mrs. Woods-Landry ate the sandwich. They gossiped and recalled old times and held hands.

"I have to go on home when I finish this," Mrs. Woods-Landry said. "James needs me. He is practically blind now but still nice. I'm lucky to have him."

"I lost Carlton, but you know that."

"I know you did, my darling angel. I'm so glad I got to see you. Be sure and call tomorrow afternoon and tell me about the tests. I'll be praying for you, thinking about you. Don't forget to call." She looked deep into her friend's eyes, refusing to add her to the names of the dead. Maybe prayer will work, she decided. There are always miracles. They happen every day. She leaned down and kissed the darling woman who had been her darling girl a million years before in another world.

"How did we get so old?" Rebecca asked. "How did this happen to us?"

"How did we get to live so long and have Joseph do our hair?" Mrs. Woods-Landry answered. "How was I lucky enough to have you running into my room every morning in your bloomers and silk stockings. It's not over, Rebecca, just because we have to keep having tests made. Don't be afraid. I'm right across town and I'll be waiting for your call." As she talked she remembered a dorm room at Ole Miss and Rebecca coming in to borrow thread to mend her stockings and the birds outside in the oak trees singing their morning songs and coffee waiting in the cafeteria when drinking coffee was dangerous and sophisticated and the in thing to do. It seemed as if a long yellow ribbon of light led from the present to that past and farther back and back and back.

"You have been a light unto us all," Rebecca said. "I don't mind going in. We have to patch and mend and take what we have. At least we're all in it together."

Mrs. Woods-Landry gave her the secret Chi Omega handshake and they started laughing and had to bow their heads to keep from choking with delight. "We are not going to die," Mrs. Woods-Landry whispered in her friend's ear when they had stopped laughing. "We aren't going to get off that easy, I fear."

Rebecca touched her cheek against Mrs. Woods-Landry's cheek. "Precious Celia," she said. "You have always been the queen of joy."

"Let me walk you to your car," the granddaughter said, as Mrs. Woods-Landry began to move away.

"Nonsense. I'm fine. I can still get around, thank the Lord for that. Next year will be soon enough for being helped."

"I'll be here to do it. You can call me any time." The granddaughter stood to the side and watched the beautiful old woman begin her progress through the salon to the door.

Mrs. Woods-Landry knew she was being watched and so of course she held her shoulders back and walked with majesty. She walked past the chairs of women whom she liked and knew. Goodbye, she said to every one. How nice to see you. What a pleasure to see you today.

She walked out into the parking lot and unlocked her car. She got into the driver's seat and resisted the impulse to pull down the sun visor and look at her hair in the mirror. Instead, she picked up a little zippered purse that was lying on the passenger's seat. It contained all the fingernail scissors she had collected the night before from around the house. She was planning on taking it to the Singer Sewing Center to have the scissors sharpened. She studied it. It was very old and stained, but her granddaughter had given it to her many years before and she treasured it. She studied the small faded paisley design. Such a darling granddaughter. Such a treasure, going out and choosing this for her at such a tender age. How old had she been then? Seventy perhaps, and Little Margaret had been five or six. Mrs. Woods-Landry held the small purse in her hand. Then she laid her head down on the steering wheel and fell asleep. The sun was very hot and sweet coming in the windows of the car. It warmed her head and shoulders and her hands. It sank down into her hair. She could smell the hair spray Joseph had sprayed on her hair. The sun was like a great caress, a dawning prayer, a benediction and a blessing. I must remember to pray for Rebecca, Mrs. Woods-Landry almost had time to think.

She did not wake up.

The Southwest Experimental Fast Oxide Reactor

THIS IS REALLY about how Kelly got a new boyfriend but it is also about why you should register to vote and vote in every election even if you don't know which one is the worst liar and scoundrel and thief. If you don't vote, somebody else will. If you don't have a say in what happens, you might wake up one day and find an experimental fast breeder reactor going up in your backyard and it's too late to stop it. I live in a town where thirty years ago when the whole town was dirt broke and scratching for a living the politicians who run things came in here and let a bunch of electric power companies and the West German government build a breeder reactor and use it to test whether it would blow up. This is exactly one mile from the Fall Creek cemetery where two of my father's uncles who were shot down in the Second World War are buried beside their parents and grandparents. I don't hate Germans or anybody else. Some of my ancestors are Germans. I'm just saying that in 1964, when the Second World War was hardly over, they let the West German government come into Strickler,

Arkansas, and build a reactor to see if the Doppler effect would cool it down if it got too hot. It contained plutonium oxide. One-thousandth of a gram of plutonium oxide will kill a human being within hours. One-millionth of a gram will cause cancer in a few years. This is not speculation. These are facts. The other thing about plutonium oxide is that it is a very active sort of powder. It moves around in a sprightly dance. It clings to things. Inside our reactor it was mixed with uranium. At one time at least half a ton of plutonium oxide was inside a building right here in Strickler, Arkansas.

The reason I'm so interested in this right now is that I ended up on the roof of the reactor for two and a half hours. And then I went inside. I was on the roof for two hours and ten minutes and inside for fifteen minutes. I keep thinking about that plutonium oxide and wondering if some of it might still have been there. I keep thinking of all the places it could have found to hide, the bark of trees, the tar on the roof, the dust on the walls, the shelves, the glove boxes in the wall.

This happened in December. My boyfriend, Euland Redfern, and my cousin Kelly Nobles and myself were sitting around one Saturday morning freezing to death because it was twenty degrees outside and Daddy still won't turn the heat pump up above sixty-five and Momma said she thought we ought to go out to Evane's Hardware Store and buy some insulation for the doors.

"Come on," Euland said. "We've been sitting around all morning. Let's go get something done." Kelly got up off the couch and giggled and started putting on her hiking boots. I was already on my feet. I don't watch TV. I hate it. I think it's ruined everybody's minds.

"I want to go up to Devil's Den and hike over to the old reactor," Kelly said. "You promised you'd go walking with me if I came over."

"We will," I answered. "As soon as we go to the store and get this stuff for Momma."

We all live in Strickler, which is near West Fork, which is just south of Fayetteville. All our families have lived there for ages. I guess my daddy would have moved to West Fork to be near the schools but then G.E. came in and built the reactor and that made work for all the contractors in town. Daddy paved the roads from town to the site. He made eighty thousand dollars that year, which is what built us the new house and dug the well and put money in the savings account. His brother sold the concrete for the silo. His older brother is the principal of the West Fork High School, which got the new gym paid for by the taxes G.E. paid. Now the university has to pay them.

Nobody in West Fork or Strickler is mad about SEFOR even if it is just sitting there and Uncle Rafe says the concrete is okay but the metal is probably starting to deteriorate. Plus the liquid sodium they used to cool it will catch fire in water and they ought to get the government to come in and take it apart and get it out of here.

"It would make a really good tornado shelter if they just kept the outside," Momma always says. She hates to waste anything. That's the way she was raised.

So as soon as Euland and Kelly and I got the insulation we went straight to Devil's Den and decided to hike to the reactor and back. We are all babying Kelly because her boyfriend quit liking her. He's going out with a girl in Fayetteville who works at the university. I never did think he was good enough for her to begin with but I see why she liked him. He is a really good-looking man, and sexy. He looks a lot like Alan Jackson, who is Kelly's favorite singer. Sort of a cross between Alan Jackson and Don Johnson. There was no way he was going to stay with Kelly after she gained all that weight last year. I told her to go on a diet but she wouldn't do it. She is so stubborn it's unbelievable, just like all the Nobleses.

Now she has decided to walk six miles a day until some of the weight comes off. I'm not going to be the one to tell her it won't do any good if she doesn't stop sitting in front of the television set eating snacks.

Devil's Den is our park. People come from all over northwest Arkansas to walk around it and be in nature. It has a waterfall and nature trails and is a good place to go if you're feeling sad or just want to remember you are on the earth. Euland and I have made love all over the place there, in tents, at night and in the daytime, and once in the car outside the visitors' center on a Christmas afternoon. It is never hard to get Euland and me to go to Devil's Den. We have such good memories of it.

"One thing about going to Devil's Den in the winter is you don't have to worry about chiggers," I said. We were in Euland's truck with the package of insulation on the floor.

"Are you sure we can get from the trails to the reactor site?" Euland said. "I think we'd have to cross Lee Creek to do that. I'm not in the mood to spend all day tramping around somebody's pasture."

"You just have to cross Fall Creek and it's dry as a bone

right now. Then we're on university land. They don't care if someone walks over there to look at SEFOR. It isn't even fenced in until you get to the building."

"Why are you so interested in SEFOR all of a sudden?" Euland asked. "It's been there all our lives."

"Because there was an article in the paper so I looked it up one day when I had some time on my hands." Kelly works at the Fayetteville Public Library. She's been there a year, the longest she has ever stayed at a job. "These guys that built it were using it to do experiments to see if it would blow up. They thought they could start it up and cool it down but they weren't sure. For three years, when all of us were babies, they were right over there mixing uranium and plutonium together and seeing if they could cool down the nuclear reaction fast enough to keep it from exploding." She leaned toward us and there was this look on her face I have never seen before, like maybe she had actually forgotten for a minute about her boyfriend and buying makeup at the Wal-Mart and watching television and charging things to her charge card. "They were releasing this plume of heat into the air above our pastures where our cattle feed and inside of it was God knows what. That's what that long pipe sticking up is for. That's where the steam came out. When they build a reactor now that pipe has to be six hundred feet above the ground. The one at SEFOR was a hundred feet. So why do you think they built this little experimental breeder reactor in the middle of nowhere in a pasture outside of Strickler, Arkansas? Because our politicians let them. Governor Faubus let them and Senator Fulbright let them, too, the senator who has everything in Fayetteville named for himself. I've been thinking about calling up *60 Minutes* or *20/20* and telling them to come down and do an investigative report on it."

"Just because you broke up with your boyfriend doesn't mean you have to call up *60 Minutes* and get them down here poking around in Strickler and causing a lot of trouble for everyone," I said.

"They shouldn't leave that thing sitting there that near to our houses," she said. "The companies that built it should come and take it down and take it away from here."

"Well, hell, let's go take a look at it and see how it's doing," Euland put in. "I would have gone to see it a lot of times but you can't climb the fence in front without messing with the Penningtons' dogs. I don't like those dogs. I got bit once by a dog and that's enough for me." He pulled me over close to him and put his hand around my waist right under my breasts. We were standing outside the visitors' center where we made love that Christmas day. I started getting really horny and I knew he was too. I wished Kelly wasn't there with us but she was. I guessed that meant it was just going to be that much better when we got home that night. Euland likes to be horny. He likes to go around all day thinking about screwing me that night. Not me. I like to do it the minute I think of it. I am spoiled from getting laid by him any time I wanted to since we were juniors in high school and he was All State in football and basketball and track. He was the best and I picked him out and I have kept him. Well, I know how to keep him, but that's another story.

Euland runs his daddy's heating and air-conditioning business and I teach at West Fork High School and, yes, we are going to get married but not until we can buy a house. We are happy just like we are and we don't need anybody telling us to have kids when we haven't even paid off our student loans. It's the nineties and we're living our own lives.

He got out of the truck and came around and opened

the door for us. He has the loveliest manners of any man you could want to meet. Also, he's got those shoulders and those long straight legs and if I start thinking about it I'll never get this finished.

We started off down the path beside the waterfall. It was so cold and dry we had to really watch our step. It was the coldest day we had had all of December. "What a day for a walk," I began, but Kelly interrupted me. Part of her being stubborn is she never lets you finish what you are saying. No wonder she never keeps a boyfriend.

"I'm walking every day if it's over forty degrees," she declared. "I'm not going to stay fat. Fat is death and I'm going to walk it off."

"What did you bring to eat?" Euland asks. She was wearing her backpack. We knew she had food in it.

"Some graham crackers and low-fat cookies," she answered. "Well, are you guys ready?"

"Let's go to the reactor," Euland said. "You've got me interested now."

We hiked past the waterfall and down to the bottom of the trail and started back up toward the east. There wasn't a leaf left on a tree but there were bundles of bright orange pine needles on the path and beautiful hawthorn berries here and there. Hawthorn berries are the most beautiful color of red in the world. No Christmas decoration has ever been as nice as stark winter woods with hawthorn berries under a gray sky. There was also red holly and barberries and dark green mistletoe in the high branches of the oak trees. Everything you see is sexual if you start thinking about it. Everything is seed and reproduction and sperm and egg. Thank God for birth control pills. Well, it would have been too cold to make love even if Kelly wasn't with us so I stopped thinking about screwing Euland and concentrated on pulling my fingers back into the palms of my hands inside my gloves. I knew something was going to happen. I knew this was going to be a day that mattered and it wasn't just because I was cold and horny that I felt that way. There's Welsh blood in all the Nobleses. We know things we can't prove we know.

We hadn't been walking half an hour when we saw a man coming down the other way. He was wearing a black leather jacket and some sort of thick light brown pants and his hair was jet black and curly. He wasn't wearing a hat. I love a man who can stand the cold without a hat. If I see a man in a hat I think he's old, no matter what his age.

We stopped at a wide place in the path and let him walk down to us. He was smiling this lovely wide smile like we were just what he was hoping to find in the woods. When he got about three feet away he stopped. "Hello, there," he said. "I was wondering if I had this place to myself. It's so quiet you can hear a leaf drop." He smiled the gorgeous smile again and I could see Kelly changing gears. She pulled her old AMOCO hat with the earflaps off her head and shook out her long red hair. She has the best hair you've ever seen in your life. Brilliant golden red and so curly it is like a bouquet of flowers. She never cuts it. It hangs down halfway to her waist. Fat or thin, Kelly can get a lot of mileage out of that hair. So then she unbuttons the top button of her jacket.

"I walk any day it's above forty degrees," she said, throwing her hair down on her chest.

"Then you shouldn't be out today." He laughed and pulled back his sleeve and showed us a watch with a digital dial that gave you the temperature. The watch said thirty-two. We all laughed and he took out a package of cigarettes and offered them to us and Euland and I took one and we lit them and then we all stood there smoking.

"What are you doing out on a day like this?" Kelly answered.

"I'm the new professor in the botany department," he said. "I've only been in town a week. I'm lonely. Everybody's married so they sent me out to see the woods. It's very interesting. I'm from Massachusetts. This is all new to me." He waved his hand around at the flora and fauna and I thought, I may have given up on Jesus but that doesn't mean I don't believe in providence.

"You want to see something interesting you should go with us," I said. "There's an abandoned breeder reactor a mile from here. We live near it. We're walking over there because you can't get in the front. You want to come along?"

"A breeder reactor?"

"An experimental breeder reactor that was the only one of its kind in the world. We're going over to check it out." I loved the expression on his face. I love it when people think Strickler is the end of the earth and then find out it's not.

"I'm the one who thought up going," Kelly says. "No one pays any attention to it anymore but I'm interested in it. I just broke my engagement and I decided I'd better wake up and find out what's happening in the world." She had completely moved in. She isn't all that fat and even if she was you couldn't tell it underneath all the basic black ski clothes she was wearing.

"I'm Ed Douglas," he said. "I'd love to tag along."

So we set off back down the path with Kelly and Ed in the rear and Kelly telling him everything she'd been learning about SEFOR and Ed turning out to be a really good listener, something every Nobles finds seductive to the tenth power since we all talk too much.

"They built it right beside Fall Creek," Kelly is telling him. "Which runs into Lee Creek which is a category five white water river. Not to mention Fall Creek is where the people in my family teach their children to swim. All three of us learned to swim there, Chandler, Euland, and me. All our grandparents are from Strickler. And our parents too. Anyway, they built that nuclear reactor right beside our creek without asking anyone if they could do it. I think we can still sue them. I'm looking into it."

I didn't look behind me. I didn't want to turn into a pillar of salt and I didn't want to start giggling. I just held on to Euland's arm whenever there was a place where we could walk side by side. It was beginning to look like we might not be stuck with Kelly all weekend after all.

It wasn't as easy getting from the park to the pasture that leads up to SEFOR as we thought it was going to be. The path through the little woods was covered with honeysuckle vines. Euland and Ed had to get out pocketknives and cut vines every ten or twenty feet. I guess we would have given up if Ed hadn't come along but Ed was showing off for Kelly and Euland was showing off for Ed so they kept on hacking down the vines. It wasn't that far. I could see the pasture and the top of SEFOR through the trees. All this time Kelly is having the time of her life saying all the stuff she's been reading in the library and making copies of in her spare time. "The heat produced by the nuclear reactions was transferred to liquid sodium metal, then transferred to more sodium, then the steam came out of the pipe to float around on top of our pastures and houses and creek. Can you see why I got interested in this?"

"Well, of course," Ed answered. "It's one thing to think

about nuclear power in the abstract. It's another thing to have it in your backyard."

"So one of these breeder reactors blew up in Detroit, Michigan. Well, they don't call it blowing up. They call it melting down."

"A disaster either way."

"You got it." She was letting him get a word in here and there, but not many. "Anyway," she goes on. "After that happened in Detroit they shut this one down and gave it to the university. Our uncle sold them the concrete. He says it's probably okay but that the metal might be starting to deteriorate."

"I can imagine it might."

"Anyway, I keep reading everything I can find but there's not much information. The university should sue the power companies that built it to make them take it down but they won't because SWEPCO, our local power company, was part of it and they contribute money to the university. There are other connections about that but I haven't finished finding them all out."

Kelly was casting herself in the role of some investigative reporter with secrets to keep. One thing about all the television she watches, she can find lots of outlets for her dramatic side.

We finished hacking through the vines and came to the rickety wire fence that separates the park from SEFOR. Euland climbed over it and held it while I climbed over and then Kelly and then Ed. Just as we got to the other side and were straightening up our clothes, the sun came out for the first time all day. It was so beautiful, this big patch of sunny sky in between the banks of clouds. It cast beautiful shadows all over the yellow pastures. It made the world look beautiful and interesting and gay. I moved over to Euland's side and started thinking maybe we ought to go on and get married in the spring. We could rent a house for a year or two before we buy one. Kelly was unbuttoning her jacket another button as if she isn't the most cold-blooded person in the world.

"It's just half a mile from here," Euland said. "Let's hike."

"This isn't the only time nuclear power came to Arkansas," Kelly was telling Ed. "I guess you know about the Titan II missiles in Damascus, don't you?"

"Damascus?"

"Damascus, Arkansas. It's a town down west of Little Rock. We had this representative named Wilbur Mills and he got so crazy from drinking and screwing whores that he let the government put eighteen Titan II missiles in the ground in Arkansas. He volunteered the state for all sixty of them but Kansas and Arizona wanted some so we only got eighteen."

"You are centrally located." Ed was laughing at everything she said, like she wasn't discussing the fate of the world. She still had her hat off. She gets terrible ear infections. I was hoping her hair would keep them warm.

"You got that," Euland put in. "We could guard the United States from east, west, south, and north."

"People aren't educated," Ed puts in. "If they were, they wouldn't let politicians get away with these things."

We stopped for a moment in a low protected place beside a man-made dam. We huddled together and Kelly finally put on her hat, turning it around so the AMOCO sign was in the back and her curly bangs fell down across her forehead. Before us was a long sloping pasture leading up to the reactor in the distance, the Southwest Experimental Fast Oxide Reactor, a concrete silo sixty feet below the ground and fifty feet above the ground with a smokestack rising another fifty feet. There was a power line running from the silo to the road and a chain-link fence with a gate. Above that the gray-blue skies of December in the Ozarks.

"So anyway," Kelly is saying. "They came down and dug these holes in the ground and put in the missiles, each one containing the most explosive devices ever aimed at an enemy in the history of the world. Right there, in Damascus, they put the one that melted down, blew up, whatever you want to call it. Two people were killed." She was losing her audience. We were freezing. Ed pulled out his watch and the temperature dial said thirty. "Let's walk while we talk," he suggested. "Let's get on up there."

We started hiking really fast in the direction of the silo, but the conversation was started now and no one could let it alone.

"I worked with this guy who was a soldier stationed in Little Rock when the Titans were down there," Euland said. "It was his job to drive one of the trucks that took the war-heads back and forth to Fort Chaffee to be checked and cleaned up. There were two men driving each warhead. He said one night the brakes went out on the truck, that was before cellular phones, and they had to keep pouring water on the brakes every twenty miles to make it to the base. He runs Jackson's Air in Fayetteville now. He's a smart guy."

"Your tax dollars at work," Kelly puts in. Not that she pays anything compared to me. You ought to see what they take out of a single teacher's salary.

We were halfway up the pasture when we saw the dogs. I'm always worried in a pasture that I might meet a bull but it never occurs to me to worry about dogs. Everyone around here keeps their dogs tied up. If they didn't their dogs would be dead. So when I saw the dogs in the distance I didn't get worried at first. Euland was the one who stopped. Euland's been bitten.

"Are those dogs going to be okay?" Ed asked. He took hold of Kelly's arm. I guess it was the first time they touched each other.

"I don't like loose dogs," Euland answered. "I don't trust them. Hell, I wish I had a gun." We were within sight of the fence surrounding the reactor. There was a gate on it but it didn't look like it was padlocked. Euland picked up a dead branch from the ground. It broke in two in his hand. "Let's go," he said. "Run for the fence."

I guess it was a quarter mile. Too far to outrun dogs but we did what we were told. The dogs kept trotting in our direction. They didn't bark. They just kept trotting with a big yellow dog in the lead.

"Stay in front of me," Euland yelled. He had the ends of the stick in his hands. I'll say one thing about boys from Strickler. They aren't afraid of the devil when the time comes. I'll say something for my cousin Kelly, too. She can sprint. We were on basketball teams together and you could count on her to get a basketball down the court. So Ed didn't have to wait on any girls from Strickler. We beat him to the gate. All three of us from Strickler were probably thinking about the dog pack last summer that killed a child near Hogeye. There are wolves and foxes in this part of the country and all sorts of wild creatures.

We got to the chain-link fence just as the dogs stopped trotting and started running. Euland threw himself against the gate and it opened. I don't know what we would have done if the caretaker hadn't left it open. He said later it was open because someone from the university was supposed to come by on Sunday and double-check the radiation badges in the containment vessel. Whether that was true or not, he had neglected to put the lock on and Euland pushed it and it opened. About the time we got inside these three dogs as big as mastiffs got to the fence and started throwing themselves against it.

"Do you have that cellular phone?" I asked Kelly.

"No, the battery was down. It's at home on the charger."

The dogs kept throwing themselves at the fence and at first I was sorry I'd made Euland stop carrying a gun in the truck but then I decided he wouldn't have had it out here anyway. "I'll be goddamned," he said. "Well, Ed, I guess you didn't plan on this much excitement. You think we could have scared them off if we hadn't gotten in the fence?"

"I'm glad we didn't have to try. I think they're feral. Will they go away, do you think?"

"I wouldn't trust it."

"Is there a caretaker to this place? Surely someone watches it."

"Just Mrs. Pennington. She lives in the old visitors' center. It's her dog that keeps you from getting in the front gate. I'll be damned. I don't know how we're going to get out. Well, I guess we can look around and find something to use for weapons. An iron rod would do."

"They check it every Saturday," Kelly put in. "That was in the newspaper article. A man from the university comes out every Saturday and sees about the radiation. Do you think he's been here yet?"

"Maybe that's why the gate was open." Ed turned and looked at the building behind us. The dome-shaped containment vessel and the flat-roofed building that adjoins it. It looked like a fallen rusting spaceship stuck in the ground, not really evil, just a pile of concrete and metal and bad ideas, abandoned and forlorn. The ladder going up the side of the dome was cut off twenty feet above the ground but there was still a ladder to the flat-roofed part. Ed buttoned his jacket up around his neck and walked over to the ladder. "I'm going up," he said. "Let's see if we can get inside. There might be an alarm we can set off or a phone." As soon as he was on the roof Euland started up after him. I looked at Kelly. "Let's go," I said. "I don't want to be left out."

I started up. As soon as I was almost to the top she got on and started climbing too. I was getting off the ladder when I heard it start to slip. "Jump," I screamed down at her. "It's loose. It's falling." She ignored me and kept on climbing, half her body on the ladder and half on the brick wall. Two years ago when she was going with a rock climber she put in a lot of hours on that fake rock wall in Fayetteville behind the brewery and I guess it wasn't all wasted time because she made it onto the roof. By the time she came over both Ed and Euland were holding on to her arms.

We stood in a circle. We looked at each other. It was cold as hell. It was Saturday afternoon. The ladder was on the ground. No one on earth knew where we were. Not to mention that the University of Arkansas Razorbacks basketball team was playing Louisville in the Bud Walton Arena and anyone in northwest Arkansas who wasn't at the game was watching it on television.

"They'll find our cars," Ed said.

"There's a forecast for snow," Euland answered. "We better all just hope that doesn't happen."

"I hate dogs with all my heart." Kelly walked to the edge

of the roof to look at them. They were still hanging around the gate. "I hate the whole idea of dogs and keeping them penned up and putting collars on them and if you let them go they get wild and try to kill you."

"Well, I wish I had my dog," Euland said. He has a Doberman. "I'd love to turn him loose to kill those hounds."

Ed had walked over to a black shed on the back of the roof and was inspecting the door. He took out his pocketknife and began to undo the screws on the side of the door. He didn't curse or act like he was mad or anything. He just stood there taking the screws out of the door with the flat blade of a Swiss army knife. I guessed that if we didn't catch pneumonia this was going to be the day Kelly finally found what she'd been looking for all her life. A ticket to a bigger world.

"I'll be goddamned. I'll just be goddamned," Euland said about six times. Kelly was just standing off to one side like she didn't have a care in the world. She had fixed the main thing wrong with her world by finding an unmarried professor out in the woods and getting herself marooned with him on top of a breeder reactor, so why should she care if we starved to death or caught pneumonia before someone missed us and came to help?

"Can you lend me a hand here?" Ed called out and Euland went to him and began to help with the screws.

"There might be an alarm we can set off." Ed took a different blade out of his knife and began to wiggle it around along the sides of the lock. I pulled a scarf out of my pocket and asked him if he wanted to put it on his head but he said no. It must have been about twenty-five degrees by then. The patch of sun we had seen earlier had entirely disappeared. There was nothing to be seen in four directions but the roof of Euland's mother's house on the hill near the cemetery and the old visitors' center looking deserted and the two-lane blacktop road no one could hear us from and snow clouds coming in from the west.

No alarm went off but the lock did begin to come loose around the door and Euland got really excited and started calling the hogs. "Sooieee, pig," he yelled out. "Go hogs." He was pulling on the lock while Ed cut around it.

All I could think about was my thin gloves and how it would be just my luck to get frostbite and lose a finger just when I had almost finished learning how to play Erik Satie's *Second Gymnopédie.* I was learning it to play for Euland's mother's sixtieth birthday party.

"It's coming," Euland yelled. "Sooie, pig, here it goes." There was this crashing, breaking sound and a big chunk of lock and wooden door was twisted and torn out of its place and then Ed and Euland kicked the rest down.

"A hollow-core door," Ed said. "This is the craziest thing I've ever seen in my life. Well, let's go in. There may be a phone that works."

"What do you think is down there?" Euland asked.

"Well, surely not the radioactive core." Ed stood with his hands on his hips. "If it's been decommissioned that's gone. In any case that would surely have been underground."

Only it wasn't underground. Later, when Kelly was poking around the files in the university library, one of the things she found was a letter from a nuclear engineer to the Atomic Energy Commission. It was dated 1972, the year SEFOR was decommissioned. It said one of the problems with SEFOR was that they had no idea whether they would be able to cool down the nuclear reactions they were starting and they should have built it underground just in case. The nuclear engineer is named Richard E. Webb. We wanted to write him a letter but Kelly can't find an address for him anywhere although she has used up about six hours of Fayetteville Public Library computer time in the search. When last heard of he was in West Germany working for some organization called the Greens. The part of the letter I liked most was the very end. He told them, "As officers of the federal government, who are bound to support the Constitution, the AEC and the Joint Committee on Atomic Energy should recommend that Congress submit an amendment proposition to the states so that the people can make a value judgment of whether a civilian nuclear program is both necessary and safe, *as is their right.*"

Also, he says twice they should only build something like SEFOR *deeply underground* in case something to do with safety had been overlooked.

The something that was overlooked was me sleeping a mile down the creek. The something that was overlooked was Euland's parents' house up on the hill and Kelly and her brothers right down the road.

"I would think this was the lab area," Ed was saying. "I don't know much about nuclear reactors but I've seen plans. There had to be a lab and they wouldn't want it near the core. I visited Los Alamos once when I was a graduate student."

"Let me go in first," Euland said. "I know about equipment. I'll be able to tell if there's anything that might be contaminated. Let me find the lights."

"Imagine this being out here in the middle of nowhere."

Ed buttoned the top of his leather jacket and turned to look at Kelly and me where we were huddled together watching them.

"Strickler isn't nowhere," Kelly told him. "It's where we live. I learned to swim in that creek. That one right over there. The one you can see from here."

"I'm going in," Euland said. Ed held open the broken door and Euland disappeared into the hole. "It's a ladder," he called back. "There's a ladder going down."

"I'm right behind you," Ed called back. "You stay here, girls. Don't come in until we find some lights."

We've found out something else since that afternoon. The half ton of plutonium oxide that was in the core doesn't take up much room. Stacked all together it wasn't much bigger than, say, eight six-packs in a pile. For some reason I find that comforting when I start worrying about the dust that was everywhere when Kelly and I finally went down the ladder and were inside.

"Come on down," Ed called up. "We found a light but it's not much. Watch your step. There's a steel ladder with fourteen rungs. Count them."

Kelly went down first and I followed her. The light was only one bulb in a ceiling fixture. And it wasn't a laboratory or a nuclear core. It was an abandoned office with desks and three chairs and a stack of wire baskets pushed against a wall. A set of stairs led down to the space below.

The lower level was a laboratory with beakers and stacks of equipment and sealed containers marked GENERAL ELEC-TRIC. There was a steel door locked and padlocked. DECON-TAMINATION CHAMBER, it said. DO NOT ENTER.

In the laboratory Ed had found two lights that worked. It was much brighter than the upstairs part. We stood in a group looking around. There were glove boxes in the corner. That gave us a chill. If there's a glove box in a laboratory it means something was inside it that no one should touch.

We stood there for a minute not saying a word. Then Euland walked over to a table and picked up a telephone and held it to his ear. "It works," he said. "I've got a signal."

"Call the West Fork police," I suggested. "It's 555-8777. Jo Lynn works there on the weekends."

Euland dialed the phone and our cousin Jo Lynn Nobles answered and then she put him through to Dakota Jackson, who used to go out with Kelly in high school. "Get out of that building," Dakota said to Euland. "Get back up on the roof. I've been there when they tested those badges. Don't stay in there any longer than you have to."

"Dakota said get out of the building," Euland said. "Go on. You girls go first. They're coming as fast as they can. They've got to get the fire truck for the ladder."

Kelly was already running up the stairs with Ed behind her, but I refused to run. I just walked back up the stairs and across the office and up the ladder.

It was snowing a soft light snow when we reached the roof. A darling misty snow that filled the air with mystery and a hundred shades of white. The soft yellow hills and evergreen trees were disappearing into white. Above us the sky was turning every color of pink and gray and violet. Then the black leafless trees. The dogs had disappeared. "Well, at least you got to see the prettiest part of the country," I said to Ed. "This is our home. I guess we can't help it if we think it's gorgeous."

"It's beautiful country," he answered. "This is the first time I've felt at home since I got off the plane a week ago. That's a joke, isn't it? Feeling at home on top of a decommissioned nuclear reactor. Not many people would understand that, I guess."

"We understand," Kelly said. "Why do you think we all still live out here? Why do you think I haven't moved to town? I'm a librarian at the Fayetteville Public Library. I have to drive fourteen miles every morning to get to work."

It gets dark at five o'clock in December in the Ozarks. It was pitch-black dark by the time we saw the four-wheel-drive vehicles coming down 265 in our direction. It was another twenty minutes before they got the jammed front gate open and drove in and put up the ladder from the fire truck and took us down one by one.

"I'm going to kill those goddamn loose dogs," Euland kept saying to anyone who would listen. "I'm coming back tomorrow and hunt those bastards down."

"We'll trap them," Dakota agreed. "It's part of that pack that attacked that kid last month. I'm glad you flushed them. You aren't the only one with those dogs on a list."

Kelly and I rode as far as Devil's Den in the deputy's truck. The men rode in the police car and made out the reports. "I'm going to ask him to stay and have dinner with us," Kelly said. "You think we can take him to that sushi place we went to last month? Or should we just stay home and cook something for him?"

"Let's just go to El Chico's like we always do," I answered. "Don't go changing your personality just because he's a professor. Besides, Euland hates Japanese food. He's had all he needs today."

They took us to our cars at Devil's Den and Kelly rode with Ed to show him how to get to Momma's house and we all went in and saw Momma and Daddy and told the story and then Kelly and I put on some fresh makeup and the four of us went in Ed's car to get some supper. We'd decided to just stay in West Fork and go to the White Tiger Haven and get a hamburger and a beer. We played the jukebox and talked about nuclear energy and the global warming meeting in Japan and told Ed all about Fayetteville and what there is to do there. We tried to teach him to call the hogs, but he wasn't ready for that yet. They had beaten Louisville 87 to 65, by the way, after our embarrassing loss to them the year before.

Then Ed took Euland and me home and he and Kelly went off and spent the night at his apartment although I had begged her in the ladies' room not to do it.

I had had an epiphany up on the roof of SEFOR. As soon as we were alone I told Euland I wanted to get married in April for my birthday.

"I don't know," he said. "I don't know if we should rush it, Chandler. Everything's all right like it is, isn't it?"

"No, it's not. We've been going together since the dawn of time. It's time to get married. We're a laughingstock for not getting married. I'm sick of it."

"I can't believe you'd start this tonight. After all that happened to us today."

"I'm starting it. So just get used to that."

The next day I threw away my birth control pills. I knew he'd never leave me or let me go but I wanted some insurance.

Postscript: Euland and I got married on April 28, 1998, out in my mother's backyard by the wisteria arbor, which is where

McArthur Wilson and I used to play doctor together. He was at the wedding with his wife, Cynthia, and their two little girls. He runs a television station in Fayetteville. He's gone pretty far in the world.

No, I wasn't pregnant or pretending to be but I'm still off the pill. Nothing's happened yet but we're not worried. No one in the Nobles or Cathaway or Redfern or Tuttle families has ever had any trouble having babies if they wanted them. I kind of want it to happen and then again I don't.

I wore Momma's wedding dress with new lace all around the sleeves and hem. It's been in a box for thirty-six years. It had not turned yellow thanks to Mrs. Agnew's having sealed it up so well when she ran the cleaners down on Main Street.

What else? Nothing has happened about SEFOR. Not a single thing has been done and Kelly is still thinking about calling *20/20* but she hasn't done it yet because she doesn't want to make trouble for the university while she's dating a professor. She thinks Ed's going to marry her but Euland and I think the odds are about fifty-fifty. Of course, Kelly *will* get pregnant if she needs to. She is the most ruthless of my cousins, plus the most stubborn. She has lost eleven pounds. She doesn't look like some starving model yet but she is definitely back in the game and holding cards.

Well, that's all from Strickler for the moment. It's October again. Time to start getting ready for the winter. Euland's so busy this time of year I hardly see him. Everybody wants to get their heat pump checked before it snows. We like to keep things working around here.

"*Wasn't that the ending?*"

"*You call that an ending? With practically everyone still on their feet? My goodness, gracious no. Over your dead body. There's a design at work in all art. Surely you know that. The ends must play themselves out to an aesthetic, moral and logical conclusion.*"

"*What's that in this case?*"

"*It never varies. We aim for the point where everyone who is marked for death, dies.*"

"*Marked?*"

"*Generally speaking, things have gone about as far as they can possibly go, when things have got about as bad as they can reasonably get.*"

"*Who decides?*"

"*Decides? It is written. We are tragedians. You see, we follow directions. There is no choice involved. The bad end unhappily. The good end unluckily. That is what tragedy means. Next.*"

TOM STOPPARD

ALSO BY ELLEN GILCHRIST

The Courts of Love   *Stories*

"Some of the most indelibly etched characters in contemporary fiction. . . . This is the first book I've read in years that I found myself consciously not wanting to finish, wanting it to last forever. . . . Ellen Gilchrist should be declared a national treasure."
— *Washington Post Book World*

Net of Jewels   *A novel*

"Gilchrist refracts life through a prism of precious gems, a net of jewels. Her fiction is always a kind of prose poem, a dance of seven veils. . . . *Net of Jewels* dazzles and pulsates." — *Los Angeles Times*

Rhoda   *A Life in Stories*

"Rhoda's feisty, sexy, and devastatingly acute sensibilities make her one of the most engaging and surprisingly lovable characters in modern fiction" — Robert Olen Butler

Sarah Conley   *A novel*

"Touching and intelligent. . . . The love affair of Sarah Conley is hopeful and precarious — like life itself." — *Chicago Tribune*

Victory Over Japan   *Stories*

"Gilchrist's writing is funny, wise, and wonderful. There are plenty of small, goofy victories for us to cheer at in this book. That's the good news for all of us who wish these stories could go on and on." — *USA Today*